MURDER AT ASTRON BAY

Rowland and Margot Davis

PublishAmerica
Baltimore

ISBN: 1-60836-714-2
PUBLISHED BY PUBLISHAMERICA, LLLP
www.publishamerica.com
Baltimore

Printed in the United States of America

To Helga Barisits, our sharpest and most devoted reader and critic. We wish you could have seen our book with its dedication to you.

Table of Contents

Prologue
Bloody Flashbacks

"Well! They deserved a fairy-tale wedding, don't you think?" My wife Sophie was on cloud ten, replaying her walk down an aisle at the Astron Bay Resort in Crete behind a procession of Greek children strewing rose petals from side to side.

Our plane had reached cruising altitude, high and beyond the smog of Athens. I had my eyes on the drink cart, watching the slim, green-eyed stewardess with her lush head of red hair approaching down the aisle. I wondered whether she was Irish. I'm a redhead too—one reason they call me "Red"—but I'm slim like Orson Welles in his middle years. Sophie says if I don't lose some belly fat soon, we're going to have to start booking three seats across for the two of us. She exaggerates. I may look bulky, but that's mainly because I'm six feet tall. I suppose my paunch *has* gained on me in the last year, and the wedding didn't help. I can still taste the roast lamb, grilled zucchini, salad with tomatoes, cucumbers and feta, and the braided Greek Easter bread. Nobody celebrates weddings or Easter like the Greeks, and when you combine the two, it's an Olympic feast.

I was going to order a martini from Irish Rose when the drink cart got to me, but as it moved toward us, it happened again. A haunting image flitted through my mind like a bat. But it wasn't the sight of a man falling from the parapet of an ancient palace. In my dreams, I am that man, falling, falling, waking with a sleep-start, sweating. No, the sight of the stewardess approaching reminded me of the bride walking toward me down the grassy aisle two days ago at the wedding. Sophie in a mint green gown came first, the afternoon sun lighting her golden curls and the white lilies in her bouquet. Then the bride walked carefully behind her, a short transparent veil covering her hair and face. As she neared the groom standing next to me, she lifted her eyes to me, and through the veil I saw them glisten. Picturing that look triggered a flashback to a moment eight months earlier—when she walked toward me down the gangplank of a yacht in the harbor of Ágios Nikólaos. She was a hostage walking toward freedom, who breathed her thanks to me as I passed her. The two moments could not have differed more, but her gratitude suffused them both.

"Red. What do you want? Martini?" I looked up as Irish Rose handed a Bloody Mary to Sophie to pass to the man sitting on the other side of her. I didn't need to see the clear plastic cup passed in front me, looking as if it was filled with blood. I declined the martini, a rare decision. My therapist warned me that alcohol exacerbates post-traumatic stress. I'd hoped that memories of the dying man would just fade naturally as I slipped further into middle age. But how do you muffle a murder in your mind? Murder is vivid. A man lay on his back, his eyes bulging. He moved his head from side to side and clutched at his throat as though he was strangling himself. Blood leaked between his knuckles. His mouth trickled red, and blood spattered his white shirt and gray jacket. I knelt next to him, my right hand extended. Another gargle escaped him. I reached forward toward him, but his eyes bulged terribly, as though he feared I might choke him. A ghastly grimace revealed his gleaming teeth, tinged with red. I smelled blood. My knees were soaked.

My shrink's advice is not to repress the bad memories, but to remember them in their entire context, as belonging to many other events that befell us in Crete last August. For once, I follow her advice. I order a ginger ale, lean back in my seat, close my eyes. With my free hand, I reach my hand into my pocket, and feel for my worry beads, my lapis lazuli *komboloi*. Who would have thought they'd be the most useful souvenir we brought back from Crete? I sip my drink and pass the beads between my fingers, recounting to myself the days and nights of our intimate brush with murder at Astron Bay.

Chapter 1
An Aegean Paradise

It began in August of 2005. I'd had enough of ruins in Athens by the end of our first day. The Greeks, instead of hauling off the broken marble and rebuilding their city, leave it lying around, clean it up, and charge foreigners a bundle to gawk at it. Sophie was in heaven. She would have trotted around gawking for a month. She's a sharp-eyed vulture for culture, studying up on Greek art, making checklists, and dragging me around the city, brooking no argument. But the smog and traffic were worse than L.A., and she was finally glad we'd be spending the second half of our vacation in Crete. Crete would be an island, still a little wild and undeveloped—a perfect place to unwind. So off we went to Heraklion on Olympic Airlines, where despite the short, low hop, Sophie struggled, courtesy bag in hand, to keep down the octopus she ate the night before.

We landed, got our rental car, and sped east and south to the Astron Bay Resort. On the way down, we saw only small dusty towns and great views of the sea. I already felt more at home. As usual, Sophie already knew more about Crete than I would ever want to know. Sophie's a volunteer librarian at the high school. Before we go on vacation, she buys books, books, books, and after we come back, she donates them to the library. If she were a salaried teacher, we could take a tax deduction for these trips. This trip to Crete was inspired by James Joyce's *A Portrait of the Artist as a Young Man*. Wasn't the guy Irish? Go figure.

"Did you know that Daedalus built a hollow cow for the queen so she could get in and copulate with Poseidon's sacred bull?" Not my idea of romance. Sophie should try something more modern, like Jane Austen. I kept my eyes on the road, and soon new ideas for a drug synthesis edged into my mind. I'd rather not think about my job as a pharmaceutical chemist when I'm on vacation, but it beats the hell out of a mad queen mating with a bull.

"Hey!" I said, "we're here!" We couldn't see the hotel from the road, which ran along a high bluff. Only a discreet sign announced the Astron Bay Resort. Another marker, close to the ground, pointed us down a driveway to the hotel entrance at the uppermost, sixth floor of a broad, white building that sprawled down the steep slope to the ocean.

We found the resort much more elegant than we expected for the price. It was mid-afternoon, and the lobby was almost deserted. An attractive blonde in a trim linen suit and without luggage waited at the desk. A young clerk emerged from the back room as we entered, summoned by the little domed bell on the counter. The blonde asked for the fitness center schedule. Very nice, I thought. Very nice. Stays here, speaks American English. Especially nice, since we didn't expect many other Americans. Sophie works at broadening our horizons, to have new *cultural experiences*, maybe pick up a little French and German. So she booked the Astron Bay Resort, which catered mainly to Europeans. I had expected a bunch of fat old-country folks, so seeing an American cover girl was an agreeable surprise. Mind you, I'm only a looker. Like Jimmy Carter, I feel adultery belongs in the eyes and the mind and not in the bed. I watched Blondie, spa schedule in hand, glide over to the elevator, her hips moving gracefully in her beige linen skirt. Sophie nudged me to move up to the desk.

The clerk—Heidi, according to her nametag—also had blonde hair, with bangs in front and the rest pulled back in a long braid. She gave us the usual forms to fill out with our passport information, got a credit card imprint, and gave us card keys. Modern and convenient, not like the old days when we'd have gotten a big heavy ball with an iron key on it that couldn't be duplicated. In retrospect, an old-fashioned key like that might have saved everyone a lot of grief on this particular visit. Heidi pointed down the hall, telling us how to get to our room, on the same floor as the lobby. Finally, she handed Sophie a small printed card with an olive wreath border.

An official with a thick head of gray hair and a gray moustache with upturned ends emerged from a door next to the reception desk. He beamed as he approached us. "Welcome, welcome, please, to Astron Bay," he intoned, reaching out to shake our hands. He looked over sixty, but his eyes sparkled behind his spectacles. "I am Spiro Santas, your manager, and I am here to make your visit memorable." An understatement, as it turned out. He spoke his formal English with a charming Greek accent. "Ah, good, good. I see you have your invitation." The only Spiro I knew was the Veep that blew it in the Nixon administration, but they can't all be bad.

Sophie looked down at the card in her hand. "Oh, wonderful!" she squealed. I looked over and saw a graceful script that announced:

Tuesday, 6 August 2005
Madame Delphinos invites you to a social hour in the Midas Lounge
16:00 hours

"The lounge is around the corner," Santas Claus said. "We offer complimentary wine and appetizers. This is our way of bringing our guests together to meet and make friends during their stay." Just what I needed to ruin a martini. Sophie cooed her enthusiasm, and we shook hands again with the manager before we let him get back to his office.

I turned to Heidi. "Ah, excuse me. Could I have one of those fitness center schedules?" Heidi handed me the leaflet as Sophie looked at me, disbelieving. I picked up our small totes. Sophie considers me the poster boy for sedentary corpulence, another exaggeration. "Hey, Soph, it wouldn't kill me to get in shape, would it?" And it wouldn't kill me to have a look at Blondie in a leotard, either.

We re-parked the Renault, got our luggage, and went to our room well down the hall from the lobby. We knew it would be special, situated high over the ocean. Sophie cheered as we opened the door and stepped into the cool interior: white plaster walls, blue and green painted furniture, rattan chairs. A bench with pillows in a small seating area by the French doors to the terrace. Earth-colored tile floors—a dream come true. Stepping out onto the long private terrace, we looked out into the blue, early afternoon sky above the water.

The hotel was built into the steep hill, facing a bit north of east. Its six stories covered the bluff from the road above down to the Olympic swimming pool under palm trees to our left. From our height, we could see mosaic dolphins frolicking on its tile bottom. Down a slope to the right lay an outdoor seating area with a stage. Beyond that, a lawn stretched from the hill to the sandy beach of the cove.

All the rooms had private terraces like ours, projecting from the slanted face of the building. Bounded by low walls facing the sea, and high walls on the sides, they assured privacy. Mirabello Bay lay beyond the cove, and the cobalt ocean spread beneath a cloudless sky, reaching a sharp horizon in the distance.

I squinted as I looked out on the scene. "I could park here for a year."

"Sure you could, Red," Sophie replied, "and in two weeks you wouldn't be able to get up if you pig out like you did in the Plaka." Ah, the Plaka…taramosalata, souvlaki with homemade pita, tzatziki—the redeeming experience of Athens. I'm rotten with foreign languages, but I'm a polyglut when it comes to foreign food.

We unpacked, and Sophie called California while I relaxed on the terrace.

"Hi Meredith! I hope I didn't wake you! We just arrived in Crete from Athens! It's *lovely*! How are the kids?" The kids, as she calls them, are two black-and-tan dachshunds.

She paused as she listened to our daughter's reply. "Oh Meredith," Sophie said, "I hate it when he does that. But even if he starts chewing Dad's slippers again, keep Ezra on the kibble or he'll get fat." Sophie gave me a glance as if my genes contributed to Ezra's weight problem. If I did, what would that make *her*? Sophie named the doxies after Ezra Pound and Gertrude Stein the year she was on a modern literature kick. They follow her around like ducklings.

Once Sophie was sure Ezra and Gerty were okay and got the latest on our grandson Archie in San Francisco, we went down to the Midas Lounge. The long, airy Lounge was well lit from its arched eastern windows. Pale blue couches and stuffed chairs faced the windows.

"Darn," Sophie said, seeing the social hour well underway. People sat about the room in small groups with glasses of wine, chatting in a mix of European languages. German, Scandinavian, Russian, from the sound of it. And Austrian. We have an Austrian governor and an Austrian chef in California, and I've seen enough of Ahnold and Wolfgang on TV to recognize an Austrian accent when I hear one. The cigarette smoke hung a little thick, great to breathe once again. At one end of the room, a wide alcove held a quiet bar, unattended, but with free wine, glasses, cheese, crackers, and olives set out for the social hour. We helped ourselves to the fare and walked back into the lounge area carrying our wine and little plates. I cocked my ear for the sound of English.

I heard a high, *awfully* nasal British accent and turned to see a skinny woman, part of a trio of guests. "Dreadfully warm, yes," she said, "but cooler tomorrow, I should hope." The woman's bright little eyes jumped furtively behind her steel-rimmed glasses as she spoke to the couple beside her. Fair reddish hair in a bun, no eyebrows that I could make out. Dressed in a rust print dress, she looked about forty. Thin, stately, civilized, and a little manic, by the sound of her voice.

Sophie followed my eyes and nudged me. "Let's see if we can join those folks." I would've been happier by ourselves but there were no free tables and at least these folks spoke English. Bony Steelrims went silent and peered at us as we neared the table. Her companions were a man and—glory be!—the blonde we'd seen at the front desk. She'd changed her linen suit and looked even better in a silk blouse and slacks.

"Hello," Sophie said, "I wonder if we could join you. We just arrived."

The man looked up. "We'll need to be taking off soon." Not exactly a welcome, and surprising since most people instantly warm to Sophie's freckled heartland looks and cheery manner. As we settled ourselves, he gave us the once-over, like a creature with its eyes out of the water, waiting for prey. He brushed some ash from his thin cigar off his foulard. A foulard, for Pete's sake! Who wears foulards these days? French or British, I would have thought, except for his southwestern American twang. Not bad looking, despite his heavy-lidded bug-eyes and a carefully tended baldness.

"Name's Redfield," I said. "Rowan and Sophie. People call me Red." I held out my hand, and he took it slowly with his long fingers. I was pleased he didn't have claws.

"Tanner," he said. "Lyle. My wife—Danielle." So Blondie was Danielle—and married to Lyle the crocodile. She looked at us carefully from dark-blue, knowing eyes and nodded. I found her even more beautiful from the front than from the back, with her diagonal sweep of straight blonde hair from forehead to neckline. Her smile was cool, and she looked as enigmatic as a cat.

Steelrims chimed in. "How d'you do. Gwendolyn Frawley here. Delighted." I shook her hand with its maze of veins and passed it on to Sophie.

"Hi, Gwendolyn, how are you? You must be English." Sophie doesn't hesitate to tell people what they are. "So are you all vacationing together?"

"Oh, dear, no," the woman said and smiled at her friends, "I just made the acquaintance of these good people a few days ago when I arrived." I stole a glance at Danielle. Very easy on the eyes. I tried to picture her on a massage table, covered lightly by a towel.

"See, these socials are good for something, Red." Sophie gave my arm a good-natured poke. "But I'm sorry we missed meeting Madame Delphinos."

"*Madame* never appears at these affairs," Gwendolyn sniffed. "She prefers to remain an invisible hostess."

"Yes," Danielle volunteered in a low voice. "*Madame* was the black sheep of the Delphinos family. Well born, but ruined her reputation in a bohemian life in Paris in the thirties. No stranger to the tabloids of the time, and you know the French." I didn't, actually, but I let it pass.

"Celebrities, movie actors, lovers of both sexes." Gwen whispered this as she looked at us over her spectacles. "An exciting figure in some circles, but in time Old Money wouldn't let her pass their marble doorsills. Yet even a woman with an exotic past must retire gracefully. She took refuge in a last marriage to an urbane man from a shipping family of more than modest wealth. She and her last husband bought this resort about thirty years ago."

Danielle gestured vaguely toward the windows. "The unlucky man died soon after they arrived. In a speedboat accident one night, crashing at the beach—right down there at the cove." She smiled wryly. "Ironic, for a shipping magnate."

"How sad!" Sophie's heart is a marshmallow.

"Indeed, tragic for Madame," Gwen concurred.

Lyle blew a perfect smoke-ring into the air. "Maybe it didn't happen the way everyone thinks," he drawled.

"What do you mean?" Gwen frowned

Lyle leaned forward. "It might not have been an accident." He looked up to see if he got our attention. "Think about it. Madame landed herself a fine place to retire. We live in Las Vegas, where women lose rich husbands all the time, not always by divorce. Never can tell." Lyle's eyes were half closed, as though to ward off argument. I warmed to him briefly, an unsentimental fellow realist. Why shouldn't a giddy flapper go for it after she was past her prime? Killing off a husband sounded a bit extreme, but as Lyle said, you can never tell.

"Surely you don't subscribe to this wicked theory?" Gwendolyn shot a severe look at the croc, who merely shifted his eyes knowingly under their slits.

I saw Sophie rub her freckled nose with her forefinger, the sort of signal you recognize only after twenty-four years of marriage. She smelled conflict and Sophie hates its eruption in public. She's a peace-maker by nature and has perfected her own intervention—changing the subject. The U.N. should put her on the payroll.

"Well!" Sophie said, "with or without *Madame*, I'm sure we can find our way around by ourselves."

Gwen took a dainty sip of wine. "I know Spiro will be most helpful to you. He is endlessly obliging. Madame trusts him like a son to maintain the *éclat* of Astron Bay." Whatever the hell that is.

Lyle stubbed his Danish cigar out in a marble ashtray. "How do you know the bastard *isn't* her son?" He broke into an insinuating grin, leering at us though his heavy lids. Rude dude. Gwen and Sophie looked stony and following the direction of their eyes, I saw why. Spiro, evidently chatting up guests at the table behind us, had turned around. I thought I saw a moustache tip twitch and wondered if he had caught the slur.

"But how lovely that Madame continues to host these afternoon affairs after all these years." Gwen's voice was raised by a decibel, clearly for Spiro's benefit. "They recreate the spirit of the *salons* of her youth, a place where guests can mingle and form a cultured *comm-yu-nity.*"

Spiro was gone, heading to another part of the lounge, and the Tanners exchanged significant glances.

"I put no credence in such slanders, don't you know." Gwendolyn's whisper sounded displeased, but didn't she just dish gossip like a trouper a few minutes ago?

Danielle abruptly uncurled from the couch and stood up. "We have to be going." Lyle stood too and stretched a lazy arm in its blazer. There was no handshake forthcoming. If Sophie and I had any wish to be in this little *comm-yu-nity*, Lyle plainly didn't.

"Well," said Sophie, "I hope we'll see you again." What could she have been thinking? Only Danielle could make me want to see Lyle again.

The Tanners gone, Sophie turned to Gwendolyn. "So, what brings you to Crete?"

"I am actually here on a bit of a busman's holiday." Gwen blushed and smiled at us crookedly. "You might call me a certified antiquities expert, although I dislike calling myself an expert. Sounds rather vain, don't you think?"

"What exactly is it you do?" I wanted her to get on with it. The bartender had arrived and a possible martini was beckoning.

"I date and authenticate artifacts. I once worked for the British Museum, but now I consult with individuals and dealers in the UK and sometimes in America."

"How exciting!" Sophie leaned forward to nip her last olive.

Gwen gave a gratified nod. "Right now the Greek government has been making test digs a bit south of here. I'm on hand informally to look over what they find." Boring. I could feel my brain drifting toward those drug syntheses again.

"Well, isn't that wonderful!" Sophie almost clapped her hands in excitement. "Could we see these new excavations of yours, Gwendolyn? We have a car." There, I thought, goes a day at the pool.

"Oh, dear, no." She looked a tad startled at Sophie's presumption. "I'm afraid the area is closed to visitors, and hardly of interest if it were open. They're simply trying to determine whether serious excavation is advisable." She frowned and lowered her voice. "A German firm is surveying to develop an airport on that land, land that may contain treasures of Minoan culture. Isn't that beastly?"

Had we been smart, we would have asked Gwendolyn Frawley to tell us more about this whole issue, but at that point archeology was no more than culture fodder for Sophie and a looming interference in my lazy days at the swimming pool for me. So we blew our chance.

"Well, we should probably start with Ágios Nikólaos anyway. Maybe with some shopping tomorrow." Sophie is always pragmatic. "We need gifts for the family back home. It's the nearest city, isn't it? On a pretty bay? Lots of shops?"

"Oh yes, indeed. Agnik is lovely. It has a beautiful view over Mirabello Bay. You'll find much to your taste, I think, especially near the waterfront. And a *splendid* museum."

Guests were rising and moving about. Gwen drained her glass and rose like a stork from its nest. We noticed that she was much taller than she appeared when seated, with an extra boost from spiky high heels.

"We'll see you again soon," she said. The royal *we*. Gwendolyn's heels clicked on the marble floor as she went off.

Her prediction turned out to be a grotesque understatement. We would see much more of Gwendolyn Frawley and the Tanners, among others, than we bargained for. Madame's social hour would both exceed and violate its best intentions. Before the end of our two-week vacation, Madame's little 'community' would be twisted by lies, betrayal, sabotage, and ransom, all in a fog of bizarre events and glimmering suspicions. And in the midst of it all, I would stumble onto the scene of murder at Astron Bay.

Chapter 2
Madame Delphinos

We slept in a bit and arose to a cloudless day. Breakfast in the restaurant offered a splendid buffet, an opportunity for the overeating I need to maintain my bulk in comfort. Cereals, fruits, cheeses, and muffins; caviar, lox and smoked fish; pancakes, waffles, and omelets made to order. Even baklava and what turned out to be a fabulous Greek walnut cake. I don't mind looking like a glutton when I come back from a buffet table, unlike Sophie who makes a half dozen trips for tiny little portions. Jeez, it's a breakfast, for heaven's sake—not a cocktail party. Though combining the two would be most agreeable.

After breakfast we explored the hotel complex to see what might satisfy my constitutional indolence and Sophie's curiosity about the place. The grounds were elegant, with olive trees dotting expansive lawns and long concrete balustrades on the ocean side. Urns held spiky green foliage and trailing flowers. Astron Bay: a resort you might imagine in a Victorian novel. A tennis court was tucked discreetly behind some flowering shrubs, and Sophie was glad to see a yoga class in progress on the lawn. We went back a stretch beyond the pool to check out the north corner of the hotel. As we reached it, a white toy poodle bounded toward us from a solid iron gate, slightly ajar, set in a stucco enclosure on the side of the building. A cracked voice called from within, "Basket, Basket," and something else in another language.

"Basket?" I said, "what the hell is that?" Sophie has pheromones for instant rapport with dogs and so gathered the wagging pup in her arms and let it lick her face. Gerty and Ezra would have been miffed, but at least the little mutt's smell wouldn't last till we got home. We approached the gate and saw an old woman in a sparkling lilac dress, loaded with silver bangles and necklaces. She struggled from a cushioned chaise with a lorgnette in one hand and a silver-handled cane in the other. As she saw us, she called "Oh, Basket, *mon cher*." So this was the name of the creature. Sophie put the pup on the ground, and it bounced back toward the woman, who wobbled to her feet with the help of her cane.

"Oh, thank you so much. Do please come in and close the gate," she said in English tinged with French. "Spiro must have left it open by accident. What luck you were there to capture my naughty Basket!" She must've recognized me as an American by my Anaheim Angels tee shirt, my flip-flops, and my slouch. We stepped in and closed the gate, though the lady seemed deaf to the clang. She shuffled up to us slowly, peered at us through her lorgnette, and smiled a crinkled smile. She was well coiffed, her white hair almost as bright in the sun as the white face of the building. She must have been well into her eighties, but her gray eyes were lively.

"I am Madame Delphinos," she announced. Whoa! Our mysterious hostess! I stuck out my hand before realizing she had no hand free for a shake. "I see so little of my guests. Please come in for a *petit* visit. I shall have Zoë bring us *tisane* in the drawing room." She turned around, simply expecting us to follow, and headed toward a white wrought-iron table surrounded by chairs. After she put down her lorgnette and lowered herself into a chair, she took a small bell from the pocket of her dress and tinkled it. The naughty Basket hopped on the comfortable chaise, curled up, and went to sleep.

So this was what remained of the legendary Madame. Drawing room, for heaven's sake, a real Continental. I saw Sophie admiring the beautiful walled garden with its roses and jasmine and heliotropes. What the hell was *tisane* and what the hell were we doing here? I wanted to get on with our day, but the old woman's invitation was so gracious we couldn't refuse. And I was frankly curious, given the conversation in the Midas Lounge the night before. Sophie gestured to me with a shrug and so we joined the *grande dame* at her table. In a moment a young woman in a black maid's uniform and a white frilled apron emerged from the French doors and departed after a few words of instruction.

"I *do* hope you are enjoying Astron Bay." Madame put down her lorgnette and again gave us a smile that creased her face. "I once greeted arriving guests in person, but now I am hardly able to get about. The doctor says that my heart is not strong. So I welcome my visitors in spirit—perhaps even *as* a spirit, some say." The gray eyes twinkled and she winked. "My guests can let their imaginations play. A little mystery inspires the atmosphere."

Indeed, the Frawley woman had made Madame an enigmatic figure while that Tanner dude had made her a sinister one. I looked carefully at her, my curiosity aroused by this odd, frail lady, trying to imagine her conjuring the death of a rich husband and matching her to the garish reputation of her youth. Some myths are true, but she didn't look very dangerous to me.

"Well," Sophie said, "we've just arrived, and your hotel is *wonderful*. We were in Athens for a week but Red got fed up with so many antiquities and ruins, and wants to just…" I put my hand on her knee to slow her down and steer her away from reciting my shortcomings. Not undeserved, mind you. Fortunately, Zoë appeared at the door to say our *tisane* was ready in the salon. Sheesh. What country were we in, again? Madame rose from her chair, this time with Zoë's help, and led us inside.

The room, bright with morning sun filtered through sheer curtains over the windows, looked like a Parisian bordello. Okay, I've never been to a bordello, in Paris or anyplace else. But the room was pretty ornate, with brocade wallpaper and long mirrors in gilt frames beside the tall windows, and golden sconces on the walls. The old lady's dashing reputation seemed less farfetched now that I'd seen her royal chambers.

Looking around the room, I felt that Madame's youth must have been more interesting than most people's entire lives. On the walls, against the heavy rose wallpaper, we saw framed and signed photos of the smart set of the '20s and '30s. Chaplin, Swanson, Gable—even Garbo. There were photos of other people—the young, dark-haired Hemingway and probably other writers I didn't recognize. Sophie exclaimed and pointed to a picture over the fireplace mantle that I did recognize: the famous photo of Alice B. Toklas and Gertrude Stein walking toward the camera, led by a stately standard poodle.

"Basket!" Sophie cried. "You named your puppy after Gertrude Stein's favorite dog!" Mystery solved. At least now I knew who the hell Basket was.

Madame, now seated with Basket in a comfortable chenille chair, waved us over to a velvet sofa across the coffee table from her, where we sat down. "Indeed I did," she replied and looked dreamily into space for a moment. "I knew all three of them! Such an interesting couple, very devoted." This seemed to have an obscure significance to her. "I spent a wonderful decade in Paris. I miss it very much. But do have some tea."

Steam still came out of the spout of the china pot of tea, tisane, whatever, lit by the morning sun. I felt like an oaf in my baseball tee shirt and shorts, picking up a tiny cup with little roses on it in my paw. The tea tasted unpleasantly of herbs, but I politely faked little sips. Once Sophie told her of our dogs, Madame launched into anecdotes about the *real* Gerty and Ezra. My wife had found a soulmate. Madame had been very young during her heyday in the Paris salons of the '30s, but young as she was, she seems to have had a wild old time.

"Ah, but just before the war it all came crashing down, my dear." She patted Sophie's hand across the table and again looked wistfully into the distance in a senior reverie.

"It must have been a terrible political scene." I was trying to work my way into the conversation.

"Yes, yes, of course." Madame now patted Basket and focused back on us. "But my own tragedy was, *au fond, une histoire d'amour.*"

A shiver of delight rippled through the shoulders of Sophie's top, and her eyes opened wide. "*You fell in love.*" She said this to Madame with an air of hushed expectation.

"*Oui, chérie,*" Madame went on, "with a rich Greek man ten years older than I. We met at the casino in Monte Carlo when I vacationed there in 1939. He swept me off my feet. Gavras was tall, a shock of black hair and a flashing smile of perfect white teeth. And I still hear his laugh, full of *joie de vivre*. He was mad about me, showered me with jewels and perfumes. And when I returned to Paris, he followed me, sending lilac bouquets to my apartment every day. I was helpless, helpless. He came into my life, into my dreams, into my heart. A grand passion that became the talk of Paris."

"How romantic!" Sophie's dimples deepened in profound satisfaction. A grand passion? From what we'd been told the evening before, she was a revolving door of amours. "How thrilling it must have been for you!" Sophie seemed to forget it was a tragedy she was hearing. I wasn't surprised when Madame's smile collapsed, and she looked at Sophie and closed her eyes as if reliving a secret woe.

"I was intoxicated and wrote to my parents telling them that I wanted to marry Erasmo Gavras. My father telephoned the concierge after he read the letter. She woke me to speak to him. He *roared* at me and said, 'You ask that Gavras about his gambling, his wife and children! If you ever see him again, I will kill him with my own hands!'" Madame's voice had risen a full octave. Sophie's a sucker for love stories, and this one was a doozie.

"So…what happened?" I wanted to bring this show back to earth.

"An impossible situation." Madame's voice now quavered. "I confronted Gavras with Papa's information, and he cursed and said he would keep me forever. I would live in luxury, surrounded by beautiful things, have anything I wanted. But I was destroyed by his deceit. I would not share him, and said I would never see him again. I went on to Zurich and joined my parents for the rest of the war."

"And your gambler?" I asked. Madame enjoyed her role like a diva at the end of Act Two. Sophie drags me to operas, so I know a diva when I hear one.

"He took his wife and three—*three!*—children to the United States and did not return to Europe again until well after the war. I saw him again only once, at the wedding of Grace Kelly and Grimaldi in Monte Carlo. I was married then, my husband had been invited, and Gavras was there, without his wife but with two beautiful daughters. It was awkward, electric, *et très triste.*"

"You have lived a full life, Madame Delphinos." Sophie was giving the woman her heartfelt best. To me it was tabloid fodder. Madame could've made a bundle selling the juicy story to a Continental scandal sheet specializing in mud and crud. She sure as hell didn't keep any secrets.

"Have you thought of writing a memoir?" My question was logical, I thought, given Madame's self-absorption.

Madame frowned, surprised. "You have heard of my memoir?" she asked sharply.

"No, no," I insisted and shook my head for emphasis. "I just thought you could bring a great and bygone era back to life." Good save, I hoped. The last thing I wanted was to blunder onto the tricky shoals of the unlucky last husband's demise.

Sophie must have had the same thought. "Madame, I hope you found happiness in your later life?" My clever wife steered carefully around the memoir and headed straight for the waterfall.

Madame looked at Sophie and again crinkled her gray eyes. "Ah yes, Pierro saved me from the loneliness of an aging divorcée. After my second marriage, I lived in emptiness until Pierro brought me back to life." She pointed to a framed photo on an inlaid table against the wall. "But tragedy followed again! I lost him in that dreadful boating accident." She waved behind her vaguely toward the bay, and said this as though we knew all about it. "We had only five years together, so happy at our age, and then he was gone." She stopped to pull a handkerchief from her pocket and dab her eye. If this was all an act, it was a boffo performance.

"I think of our joy every day," she went on. "We had bought Astron Bay, and this resort became my passion after his death. Twenty years of addition, renovation, and management. All in his memory. With Spiro's help, of course. Such a sweet boy. He is my godson, you know—the son of a dear family friend. Spiro, Astron Bay, and my Basket are all I have left."

A helluva lot more than most biddies that age, I thought to myself. When you think of nursing homes with wheelchairs lined up like grocery carts, Astron Bay was a geriatric paradise.

Now that the issue of Pierro's 'accident' was behind us, Sophie felt safe to return to the earlier topic. "Well, this was all a long time ago, Madame, but, that shouldn't stop you from remembering and writing your memoir. It sounds so interesting—I know my book club would be just *fascinated*."

"You are very kind, Mrs…"

"It's Sophie, Sophie Redfield. And this is my husband, Red. You should call us Sophie and Red." Nice to be finally introduced after two cups of herb tea and a soap opera.

"Yes, my dear Sophie, thank you. I feel lucky to have lived in the world, always alive in the present moment. But, yes, I must now set my story down before it is lost forever. It is a race with time and death, and indeed, my book is almost done." Then she again slipped into tragic mode. "Yet it may never see the light of day."

"My goodness, why ever not?" Sophie was genuinely surprised. So was I, given that the lady showed no compunction about telling her tale to perfect strangers.

"The Gavras family will not allow me to tell Erasmo's story. They say it stains the family honor. *Honor*, they say, can you imagine? He became a well-known financier, close to those dreadful colonels after Constantine left the country. 'But it is all true,' I tell the family, 'I have Erasmo's letters to prove it.' But Erasmo's grandson threatens to stop the publisher, to sue me for libel or slander."

"You'd think he'd be a little more enlightened about old family history in this day and age." I thought I'd be supportive. "What harm could it do anymore?"

"Nikos accuses me of exploiting his grandfather's memory for money, but of course that is not why I tell my story. As you say…" She turned to me, groping for my name.

"Red," I said.

"Red, yes, as you say, I wish to tell of the days when passions were strong, the rules of our fathers were broken, and we tasted freedom for the first time! We paid our tragic price for a *grandeur* of the spirit!"

Wow. End of Act Three. Now the bouquets!

Just then, little Basket popped up on the chaise and gave a few sharp barks just as we heard a knock at the door, and Spiro came in with hardly a word from Madame. The curled tips of Spiro's moustache quivered when he saw us. He looked ready to reprove us for intruding on Madame until she held up her hand and told him how we had retrieved the wayward Basket from the grounds. His face melted as he smiled at us.

This was the perfect opportunity to extricate ourselves. We got up and took our leave, with Sophie leaning down as she took Madame's hand in both of hers.

"Thank you for the lovely *tisane*, and the lovely visit." Sophie dimpled again as she beamed at the old lady. "Please don't get up, Madame, I'm sure Spiro will see us out."

Spiro, attentive as a courtier, smiled again and ushered us back through the French doors and pretty walled garden to the iron gate where we had come in. When we reached it, Spiro bowed graciously, and under his voice said, "Thank you for listening to Madame. She is often lonely, and enjoys a chance to talk. It is good for her to have a visitor from time to time."

"Oh, it was a great pleasure to hear the wonderful story of Madame's youth, even if it is a story of great heartbreak and sorrow." Sophie was still entranced by the romantic foofaraw. "I only hope she can publish her memoir so the story of her life lives on after she is gone!"

Spiro's brow furrowed, his face became red, and his moustache trembled like an aspen leaf. "That scoundrel Gavras will do anything to stop her. He will break her heart once more like his grandfather did." His voice growled out the bitter words. "And mine. He has already made terrible threats, and no one knows where he will stop." He stopped abruptly, evidently shocked by his own indiscretion in blurting such things to strangers.

Whoa. I did not want the Redfields entrained in any Greek family feud, and I'd had about enough melodrama on my first morning in Crete. "Hey, I'm sure everything will work out for the best, and it was a great pleasure to meet the old lady—um, *Madame*." Time to split. Spiro regained his composure and returned to his host mode. He bowed graciously and gestured to the exit.

As we opened the clangy iron gate, the little poodle came bounding up to us again. "Basket," Sophie said sternly as we closed the gate, "you've had enough of an adventure this morning."

So, I felt, had we.

Chapter 3
Wally and the Masterbilker

"So what do you think of our wrinkled hostess?" I waited until we were out of earshot of Madame and Spiro before speaking. "Grendel, or Gwendolyn, or whatever her name was last night, made her sound like a relic, but the old lady's actually a pretty live wire."

"I just loved her," Sophie said. "And I'm irked at the Tanners for bringing up such an ugly rumor about her. Madame was devastated when she lost Pierro and it's cruel to suggest she had anything to do with his accident." This explains why Sophie never buys tabloids. She hates it when people speak ill of the living.

We came round to the pool area, whose waters glittered with sunlight and the splash of guests and children in the pool. Other folks lay on chaises on the tile borders, towels over their bodies against the sun. Some were fat and red. I should talk.

I shrugged. "Whatever that story, I admire what she and Spiro have done for the place." I looked over the balustrade toward Mirabello Bay. "But she herself admits she has other P.R. problems. I wonder what she says about the gambler in her memoir that makes his grandson so mad."

"Well, honor is everything in this part of the world, Red. Remember *Zorba the Greek?* They killed that poor woman because she fell in love with Alan Bates." When they call stories like that tear-jerkers, they must be thinking of Sophie. She keeps a box of Kleenex next to the television.

"I don't, but I'm sure that's a thing of the past." Time to change the subject and take a dip in the pool before lunch. Sophie agreed but only to a short swim. She took my wrist and looked at my watch. "We have a little time, but I don't want to start too late for Agnik." Sophie spends thirty minutes with the British stork and she's talking 'Agnik.'

It was after noon when we set off in our tinny Renault for Agnik. I wonder what the Greeks call it. Ágios Nikólaos means Saint Nicholas, I had read. Santa's Village on Crete. It was thirty minutes away to the north, the largest city around. Greek traffic has its own logic, but we managed to reach a public parking lot in the town center near the big lake, actually an inlet from the ocean through a little waterway. We were ready for the day, wearing shorts and sunglasses, carrying cameras and guidebooks in our tote bags, and looking like the ugly Americans we were. To be fair, Sophie wears colored outfits with beading and appliqués, and actually looks pretty cute for her age.

Tourist shops and restaurants abounded as we walked along a boardwalk starting at the outer end of the inlet, heading across town toward the main harbor. Sophie bought gauzy scarves, straw slippers, and little mugs sporting dolphins from the outdoor displays. Tourist ceramics always wind up in the back of our kitchen cabinets, demoted after a few years to the garage sale. She also bought me a stupid baseball cap with a blue-stitched "Kriti" above the visor. Punishment for forgetting to apply sunscreen. I sunburn easily, but at least the sunburn disguises the glow from my nightly martini.

Finally, she picked up a string of smooth blue beads with a blue tassel at the clasp. "These are *komboloi*," Sophie explained to me as she held them up to catch the light. "Greek worry beads, for Meredith." Our daughter is a law school student with no worries about her grades. But she frets constantly over corporate corruption, the state of the environment, and especially the pharmaceutical industry, her pop's much reviled employer. I approved Sophie's purchase. Anything to help Meredith chill out.

At the main harbor, boat slips were lined up on short docks and a large moored yacht caught Sophie's eye. Under Greek letters on the stern, the name *Ikaros* appeared in Roman letters. I woke up to the fact that this was the Greek guy, *Icarus*.

"Wasn't that the dude that built the labyrinth somewhere around here?" I asked.

"No, silly, that was Daedalus. Like the boy in James Joyce's *Portrait of the Artist as a Young Man*. Icarus was the son of Daedalus, and Daedalus gave his son wings made of feathers and wax to fly away from Crete."

I wouldn't go that far to get out of here. For me a plane to Athens, Paris, and on to L.A. would do the job just fine in a couple of weeks. "Where did he land?"

"In the Aegean, where he drowned," Sophie said. "He got too close to the sun, and the wax in his wings melted."

That's the trouble with Greek myths. They have lousy endings.

Back on the tree-lined street leading away from the waterfront, we stopped at a classy place whose window held a tasteful display of jewelry, ceramics with ancient designs, silver items, and things that looked like antiquities—not tchotchkes but high-end stuff. A silver bowl caught my eye. Not too bulky and only a little pricey, 80 euros—a hundred bucks or so, but I told Sophie I could haggle. "Just like *The Golden Bowl*," she giggled.

I looked up at the sign: *Gavras Greek Arts*. "Gavras," I said, looking at Sophie approaching the door, "sounds familiar. Where…?"

"It was the name of Madame's husband or something," Sophie said. "No…I think it was the gambler. But it could be a common name, like Smith or Jones. Wasn't there a filmmaker named Gavras?"

"Let's go on in." Much as I dislike family feuds, I was intrigued.

The shop door's bell tinkled as we entered the bright, square room with vases, bowls, goblets, urns, and clay figures on several display tables. More wares stood on shelves that lined the walls, most of them mirrored to highlight the objects and make the room appear larger. A man stood behind a glass case full of jewelry in front of a curtained, arched opening to the back of the shop.

He stepped out from behind the counter as we entered. "Good morning, may I help you?" He was of medium height and athletic, sporting a trim moustache and black hair carefully parted in the middle. Handsome dude, with thick black hair and gleaming white teeth—just like Madame's former lover boy as she described him. Could this actually be the grandson after all? He spoke what sounded like New York English with a light Greek accent.

"Yes. I wonder if we might have a look at that bowl in the window."

"Certainly." He got it from the window case and put it in my hands. It was about four inches tall, a round vessel mounted on a round base by a short stem. A simple design went around the top, just under the rim.

Sophie peered at its gleaming surface. "It's lovely."

Quiet, Sophie, I thought. I wanted to bargain. Nice workmanship. I turned the bowl over. The under side of the base had a short segment of a Greek key design stamped into it. "So," I said to the man, "what's this?"

"A hallmark, showing it's silver. The bowl is based on an ancient Hellenic design, but without the small handles on each side."

"Is it old?"

"No, it's modern, only about thirty years old."

"How much?"

"It's eighty euros. But before you decide on it, I have four others in various shapes made to go with this one, either for display or use at the table. If you like them, perhaps we can discuss a discount for the set."

This was a bit fast for me, but I didn't have to buy anything, much less five whole bowls.

He turned to the back and called, "Elena." A woman dressed in black stepped out from behind the curtained arch. She looked a bit older than the man, with black eyebrows, beautiful, sad black eyes, and longish black hair gathered into a loop in back with a tortoise-shell comb. He spoke to her briefly in Greek. She went back, returning with four more bowls, which she set on the counter.

That's a bevy of bowls, I thought. Really nice, but what the hell would you do with them? Fill them with mustard, relish, ketchup, and mayo for burgers? Chopped onion?

The shopkeeper handed me a small business card, "My name is Nikos Gavras," he said. "This is my sister Elena." I looked closely at him. Nikos Gavras. It must be him. I looked at Sophie. Her expression was not entirely happy and I guessed she was thinking the same thing. She looked disinclined to patronize Madame's nemesis.

"We're from California. Name's Redfield. This is my wife, Sophie. You speak like an American."

"I'm flattered." He smiled. There they were—the perfect white teeth under his sleek moustache. "I attended college at NYU and worked hard on my English. It has paid off in this business, where I deal extensively with U.S. and U.K. import firms. Are you here on holiday?"

I didn't want to get too familiar before we made a deal. "Yes," I said briefly. "We're staying at Astron Bay for a couple of weeks." He looked away for a moment, unsmiling, but only for a moment, barely ruffled.

The other four bowls made a curious, varied set. Similarly stemmed, their upper parts differed. One was fluted, another flared, the third round and straight-sided, and the last four-sided. "Well, we'll think about the bowls. We've just begun to shop, and were just walking around when we looked in your window. Just for comparison, what are we looking at in terms of price?"

Nikos looked at the row of bowls on the table. "These as a set would be over five hundred in the U.S., but here I can give them to you for four hundred."

"Dollars?"

"I'm sorry, euros."

"They're just lovely," said Sophie, in spite of herself. She might be leery of the shopkeeper, but she admired his arty wares. I gave her a sidelong look, hoping to curb her enthusiasm.

Nikos flashed a perfect smile. "You appreciate their beauty," he said. "That is a rarer gift than you think. Many people buy things to impress others, but you appreciate these for what they are, for their grace and form."

I had to hand it to him—the dude had Sophie's number. In the meantime, I was getting confused trying to convert dollars to euros and back and figuring out just how much money we were talking about.

The shop door opened with a tinkle, and a short, stocky fellow came in. Saved by the bell, I thought. He was dressed in khaki shorts and a plaid shirt, with a big canvas shoulder bag slung across his chest.

Seeing the shopkeeper busy, he approached the sister. "G'day, ma'am. I was here before, and I'm back again," he said, "back to see the kylix I looked at the day before yestiddy. The lovely lady, Nia, I think her name was, put it aside for me. Name's Pinnock, Wally Pinnock." He had a stage Irish accent flavored with Crocodile Dundee 'Strine.' His shorts and sandals revealed legs as hairy as a hobbit's. He was built like a fireplug but had a sprightly air and a round face—the kind of guy some women find improbably adorable. Sophie instantly beamed a bright smile in his direction.

Elena looked at him, and said something in Greek to Nikos. He answered her and she went in back, returning with a curious wide, shallow goblet on a stem, ceramic, with small handles on each side. It was painted black but looked surprisingly cracked and chipped. Elena asked, "This is it?"

"The very one, Miss," Pinocchio said, holding it up and admiring it. "'Bonny piece of work,' me Da would say. Now if we can confirm the price the young lass quoted me, I can be taking meself and this little beauty off."

Elena spoke again to Nikos, who excused himself and went over to them. It appeared that Nikos named the goblet at ninety euros, while the Aussie said he was quoted seventy. After an exchange that sounded a little stiff, Nikos agreed to the lower price, though, it appeared, only with Elena's intervention. Nikos flashed a forced smile at the fellow as the deal was closed.

The extra time allowed me to keep Sophie in line, but I was distracted by the talk and didn't figure out my next move. Nikos returned to us as the Aussie left.

"Tell you what," I told him, "I'll give you 200 for the set right now. They look great, but I don't think we can go higher." I hoped he would think I was talking dollars, but what the hell.

Nikos shook his head, looked at the bowls, then steadily at me. "I understand your feelings, but I really can't go that low. It would be well below cost—giving them away. But if you're serious, you can have them for three fifty." Progress, I thought. The first of many moves. Soon, as Sophie watched, Nikos and I were acting out our parts. He was steady, I was slow and cool. I tried to talk dollars to his euros. Finally, I made my last, best offer: three hundred dollars.

He frowned and sighed. Looking at Sophie, he said, "I value putting them into the hands of someone that appreciates beauty." He then flashed Sophie a warm smile. "You can have them for three hundred."

"Done, thank you." I tried not to gloat.

"Do you have American currency or traveler's checks? We prefer not to take credit cards." I liked the bowls, I *loved* the bowls. Sophie beamed.

"Yes, I'd prefer traveler's checks in any case." I felt like dancing. Was I good or was I great? A five hundred euro set for three hundred bucks! And Christmas presents for five sets of relatives in one swell foop! Inwardly, I smirked like a weasel but put on a hangdog smile.

Elena began wrapping the bowls and putting them in boxes. I pulled out my traveler's checks and signed them.

As Nikos made out the receipt, he said, "If you like, I can make the receipt for a hundred and fifty. It will help you on your customs allowance."

"That would be great," Sophie interjected quickly. It took me a few seconds to get it. This way she could spend like a princess without going over our customs quota. I wanted to reproach her about cheating the government, but I wasn't exactly clean with my overtime haggling. Mum was the better part of ethics here.

Nikos handed me the low-ball receipt and Elena handed me a bag with the boxes. We shook hands and exchanged hearty wishes for a great vacation, good health, and long and happy lives.

We stepped out of the shop. I felt great, almost skipping with gratification.

"Nikos Gavras!" Sophie hissed. "The one blocking Madame's memoir! That's him!"

"I know," I said, "I remembered the name in the shop. But I didn't mind haggling with him. He's not our problem."

Sophie frowned. "Well, you're right. He was a lot nicer than Madame made him out to be. I guess there's two sides to every story."

I gave her shoulder a quick squeeze with my free hand. "Let's get a drink to celebrate." We found a nice restaurant overlooking the boat slips nearby, and settled down under the umbrella of an outdoor table.

After ordering my martini, I smiled at Sophie. "They think they're good at haggling, but I could give them lessons. Can you believe we brought him down from four hundred euros?"

"'Scuse me, mates." A jolly voice behind us. "If you worked Nikos Gavras down in price, you've bested the masterbilker." I twisted around and looked at the table behind us. It was the hobbit from the shop, just unwrapping his goblet to have another peek at it.

"Wally Pinnock here, hope you don't mind the intrusion. I saw you in the store and couldn't help overhearing.

"Not at all—nice to meet you. My name's Redfield. Red, and my wife Sophie." We shook hands awkwardly between tables.

"Wish I could do the argy-bargy like you Yanks. This here set me back a pretty penny. Even so, took the sister to keep the bloody bloke honest. But grand workmanship! Lovely, 'tis."

"What is it?" Sophie asked.

"A kylix—an ancient Greek drinking goblet. Let me show ye a little surprise." He got up, came around to our table, and tipped the goblet so we could see the inside of the bowl. On the inside black surface, there were two naked figures doing something pretty heterosexual.

"My goodness," Sophie said, "I didn't know the ancients made things like—that."

"They used these kylixes at their *symposia*. That's what they called their drinkin' bashies in the old days. The figures on the bottom were a little reward for chuggin' yer wine." He cackled softly.

"Is it an antique?" I asked.

"'Fraid not. 'Tis a handsome likeness, though, and I should know, bein' a potter meself. Nothing shonky about Gavras's replicas and I'd love to match them, I would. But me techniques have a way to go 'fore I can conjure a grand piece like this." He smiled happily, turning the goblet in his hands.

Outgoing fellow, good heart, and surprising sensitivity. Our drinks arrived, and I figured Sophie might enjoy some arty talk with him, so I invited Wally to join us. He accepted gladly. "Just let me collect me swag." Retrieving his canvas shoulder bag and glass of ale, he moved himself and his kylix to our table.

After our drinks arrived, we asked him more about his business.

"I'm collecting a sampler of these little crocks for me shop in Canberra," he told us. "I heard of Gavras in London a few years ago from a dealer bloke there. Been comin' back here like a bee to honey ever since. London blokes get dandy replicas from him to sell in posh hotels in the city, even export to America. Would love to suss how they make 'em. All I can mangle out is reproductions."

"I'm sorry, what's the difference?" Sophie asked, "between replicas and reproductions, I mean?"

"It's just me way of speaking. Replicas look like real artifacts, cracks and chips and all, made to look like museum pieces." Wally took a draught from his oversized glass of ale. "Big trade in the little buggers, not exactly the sunny side of the business. Especially now the government's whackin' down on lurks in exports. But reproductions look brand new, like they come hot out of a Minoan kiln. New copies of old pots. Agnik must have some crack craftsmen for both kinds of work, but I've never had the fortune to catch 'em at it."

"Maybe we should have bought a Greek replica instead of our silver bowls," Sophie said doubtfully. "I didn't realize they'd be so special."

"Gavras's silver thingos look smashing too," Wally said. "I'd fancy havin' a squint at them if they're no trouble to unwrap."

Bless his little heart for inviting a show-and-tell. Give me a chance to show off my argy-bargy—is that what he called haggling? Sophie lifted several boxes from the bag and got the bowls out, setting them on the table between our drinks in front of us.

I took the round bowl and held it up as Sophie unwrapped the others. "We saw this one in the window, and Nikos brought out the others afterward. He offered us a discount on the set. I acted like we weren't really interested and pretty soon he came crashing down on the price." I turned to Sophie, "Was I brilliant, Soph, or what?"

Sophie beamed in satisfaction. "You can see hallmarks on the bottom," I went on. I held up the round bowl and showed him the key imprint.

Wally inverted the fluted bowl he had picked up. "I don't see the mark on this one."

"Really? Let me have a look." I took the bowl. It seemed a little less substantial than when I handled it in the shop. Indeed, there was no hallmark. In fact, none but the first bowl had a hallmark, and that one felt a tad heavier than the others. An ugly feeling coagulated in my stomach.

Wally looked up sadly and shook his head. "I'm as sorry as I am serious, mate, but I'm afraid these four be plate." He set the four extras apart from the first one. "'Bite the guinea 'fore you trade,' me Da says. That keeps the game fair dinkum." Seeing Sophie crestfallen, he added quickly, "But yer wee bowls look aces, even so, and I'd enjoy them greatly neverth'less."

"Damn him! Damn that creep!" I yelled, "That...that...masterbilker...is that what you called him?" Of course, I wanted to call him a son of a bitch, but Sophie put a muzzle on my potty-mouth when our grandson Archie was born. "I'm going back there and get our money back."

Sophie tugged my arm. "Red, sit down and take it easy. It's not going to work, not when you're like this." I sat back down, realizing she was probably right. She's kept me from losing my teeth in disputes with soccer coaches and neighbors more than once.

"I'd say let it go, mate." Wally looked out ruefully from under a bushy brow. "Tuition, ye'd best call it. Gavras's deals are done when they're done. No money back, no exchanges. I paid that tuition meself a while back."

"We have a receipt," I blustered.

"O lord, Red." Sophie looked stricken. "That phony receipt he gave us! It's made out for only a hundred fifty bucks."

I felt apoplectic. "Shit! That...effing...operator!"

"Sounds like Gavras all right, mate. Sugars his deals like a cookie maker. I'd wager he never said these babies be silver, either."

"Damn, damn him!"

"Red. It's only money. Calm down and sip your martini. Don't let this ruin our first day in Crete."

My face felt red, but she was right. Much as I wanted to grab our stupid bowls and head back to the shop, the frigging receipt made it useless, and I noticed Sophie rubbing her nose. She would be more upset by an ugly fight than by losing a couple hundred bucks. So I gritted my teeth and kept quiet while she and Wally carefully shifted the subject back to archeology and artifacts, pottery and places to visit, and all we might do during our two weeks in Crete. Wally knew the island well and had such great suggestions that we exchanged cards and phone numbers so we might get together before we left.

When Wally learned we were staying at the Astron Bay Resort, he whistled. His bright blue eyes glinted. "Nikos Gavras has been spittin' the dummy with the owner of yer hotel, don't ye know. Been all over the papers a few weeks ago. Downright cranky over some memoir or book the old granny at Astron Bay was about to zoom into orbit."

"I know." Sophie frowned. "Madame Delphinos told us all about it just this morning. I wonder why he was so nice to us, knowing we were staying at her resort?"

"It's 'cause you charmed him with your appreciation of fine art, Pumpkin," I said. The endearment was my thanks to Sophie for not reproaching or embarrassing me for my foolish haggling. With that, we headed back to Astron Bay. But I sunk back into the grumps on the way.

Chapter 4
Basket, Lost and Found

After leaving the restaurant, we walked back through the tree-lined streets to the car. I was fuming to myself, but kept my lid on for Sophie's sake. "Can you believe that son of a bitch pulled that scam on us? I'd still like to go back to the shop and punch the creep in the nose." At least yell at him, or intimidate him with my bulk.

"I know how disappointed you are, sweetie, but don't let it get to you." Sophie worries about my blood pressure. Suddenly she brightened. "You know, we could let Gwendolyn Frawley look at those bowls. She can tell us whether or not they're plated."

"We already know they are."

"All we have is Wally's word. We just met him. How do we know if he's really competent to judge the quality of silver? Or if he doesn't have some old grudge against Nikos?" Sophie's desire to think the best of everyone sometimes runs into conflict: Nikos and Wally couldn't both be good guys in this situation. And dragging the Frawley woman in would just complicate things further, and not in my favor, as far as I could see.

"I'd just as soon not be embarrassed twice." Even slobs like me have their dignity.

"Well, I'm going to ask." Sophie set her jaw. "We need the best information we can get before deciding what to do."

We drove back, hoping to get to the Midas Lounge early for free wine and a free silver appraisal from Steelrims for Sophie. As we passed through a dusty little village sporting only a restaurant and a few businesses, a furry white critter darted into the road in front of us. I slammed on the brakes with a loud crunch that drove the creature back to the shoulder. We would have been rear-ended if there'd been a car behind us. With our car stopped we saw on the side of the road, looking baffled and shaken, a white toy poodle.

35

"Basket!" Sophie opened the door and jumped out. She leaned down. The dog wagged his pom-pom tail and leapt into her arms. One of these days she's going to get herself bitten and die of rabies. Only Sophie would assume that there was only one poodle in all of Crete.

I pulled the car further over onto the shoulder and got out. "What the hell do you think you're doing, Soph!" I yelled. "That stray could've bitten you!"

Sophie's eyes widened in outrage. "This is *not* a stray." I recognized her tone. "This is *Basket*. Madame's dog."

"It could be *anyone's* dog. Madame isn't the only person with a toy poodle in Crete. Put it down, Sophie, and let's get out of here." Sometimes I wish I could get Sophie to be more rational.

"Look!" Sophie turned the small dog toward me and lifted one of its ears. Embedded in its curly fur was a glitzy rhinestone collar.

"So?" I said. "Does it have a tag?"

Sophie ran her finger around the collar and shook her head. "No. But this is Madame's dog. I picked it up yesterday. You didn't. And I can tell."

Sophie was right. It was Basket. "What the hell is it doing out here in the middle of nowhere? We must be six miles from Astron Bay! That stupid mutt probably gets out all the time, like it did this morning. But there's no way Twinkletoes could've run all this way from home." At least *I'm* logical, even if events are not.

Sophie gave me a *look*, and with a flourish got back into the car. A minute later I was tooling down the road toward Astron Bay with a miffed wife and a dazed dog in the passenger seat. No point talking. The mystery couldn't be resolved until we got back to the hotel. My theory was that if it was Madame's dog, one of the staff had probably taken it along to the little town, and it got away.

We walked into the hotel lobby, Sophie with the dog in her arms and me laden with several bags and Sophie's tote. Heidi at the desk took one look at us and yelled "Basket! Basket! Oh, thank heavens you've found him!" Sophie shot me a triumphant look and broke into a dimpled smile.

Heidi dashed around the corner of the counter and gathered the little mutt in her arms. "Where was he, where did you find him? Mr. Santas is still out looking for him in the hills across the road." She was breathless with relief and looked as though she was going to burst into tears.

"He ran right in front of our car on the road about six miles from here, back in a little village south of Ágios Nikólaos." I couldn't be more specific.

"It has a pizzeria on the right side of the road." Sophie remembers these things.

Heidi shook her head. "Impossible. The only pizzeria on the road is only two kilometers south of the city. Basket could not run that far away. He never leaves the resort grounds, even when he gets out of the garden."

"Could one of the staff have taken him along for a ride?" I asked.

"No, no." She shook her head. "Zoë helped Madame get settled on her drawing room sofa for her afternoon rest. She always checks the iron gate to be sure it is closed, but we do not bar it during the day so the gardeners can come into the garden When Zoë left, Madame and Basket were both sleeping on the divan. She even locked the door of the suite to the hallway. But when Zoë came back from consulting with the chef, Basket was gone! The gate was closed, and Basket was gone!" Her chin trembled and her eyes filled up again. She was only a young employee, but she clearly took her responsibilities as Spiro's second-in-command seriously.

"How awful!" Sophie cried. "Madame must be devastated!"

"Oh, we did not tell Madame." Heidi emphatically shook her head. "Zoë told her that Basket's nose seemed hot, so we asked Ernesto to take him to the veterinarian. Thank heavens we can give her little dog back to her."

Go and do it already, I thought, looking at my watch. Cocktail hour was underway and I had to pee. "All's well that ends well." I said this with great cheer and picked up our totes to make it clear we needed to split. After even more effusive thanks, Heidi ran off to the elevator with the baffled Basket in her arms, and we hurried to our room.

"So how on earth did he get out?" Sophie made it pretty clear that she wanted an explanation. She's pretty strict when it comes to dog safety.

"Who cares," I said as I fumbled with my key card to open our door. "It's cocktail hour, and I need a drink." Never mind that I'd already enjoyed an early martini in Agnik.

After dropping off our stuff in our room, Sophie took the parcel with the bowls and we headed to the Lounge. There we saw the Frawley woman and the Tanners enjoying themselves on a sofa in front of one of the arched picture windows. Sophie strode straight over to them and asked if we could join them.

"Please," Danielle said, looking up from under her hair and gesturing to some armchairs by the sofa. Cool as always. Lyle, next to her on the couch, nodded, his eyes looking sleepy. He held his thin cigar with studied elegance.

No foulard this time, but a stylish turtleneck. His wardrobe was straight out of Noel Coward.

"We're glad we found you here," Sophie said after we returned with our wine and little cheese plates from the bar. "We've had quite a full day and we need to talk to you about it." Sophie can be disconcertingly direct. By dispensing with small talk, she preempted any moves on my part to derail her appraisal mission.

"How's that?" Lyle slid his eyes over toward her.

"Well, we went to Ágios Nikólaos—Agnik, I guess you call it—and Red sees this silver bowl in the window of a shop. It's a place called *Gavras Greek Arts*. We go in and look at it, and the man offers us…"

Danielle put a well-manicured hand on Sophie's arm. "Did you say Gavras? Is that the name of the shop you visited?"

"Yes, *Gavras Greek Arts*. The man was the owner, Nikos Gavras. More on that later, because that's a whole other story. But to go on, Gavras offers Red four more bowls to make a nice set, but he's asking four hundred bucks. Or was it euros? Anyway, we really liked them, and when it was all over, Red bargained him way down on the price."

"Sounds like you made out like a bandit," Lyle drawled in his lazy way.

"'Fraid not," I said. I wanted to get this over with. "The bandit was Gavras, we think. We met a guy afterward who says four of the bowls are silver-plated. The creep sold them to us as solid silver!"

Sophie had pulled the bowls out of their boxes and set them on the coffee table in front of the sofa. "We wanted to ask if you think they're genuine or plated?"

Everyone leaned forward as they each picked up a bowl. "This is the real one—we think." Sophie pointed to the round bowl.

Gwendolyn, who held it, turned it upside down, looking for identifying marks. "This looks genuine. It has a hallmark." She took each of the others, and did the same thing. She also hefted them and held them against the light.

"Oh my dear," she said to Sophie when she had finished, "I'm dreadfully sorry to say so, but yes, I'm afraid these four are plate. Work in a museum alerts one to these things." Seeing Sophie crestfallen, she added quickly, "But they are really *lovely*, especially as a set. They may tarnish more easily, and you mustn't abrade them when you clean them. But they really *are* awfully nice." Her consolation worked no better than Wally's.

Lyle looked smug and asked the question I most feared. "So how much did you get taken for?" The snake speaks.

Sophie, honest as always, blurted out, "Not that much. We got the whole set for three hundred dollars."

"Gracious," Gwendolyn said. "That is a bit dear. Such things generally cost twenty euros or less each. At least you have one real silver one here, the one with the hallmark."

"That *creep*," I said under my breath. Then a little louder, "That miserable *creep*." I was again steaming inside like an untended espresso maker.

I felt Danielle's cool fingers on my arm. "Red, I have to tell you something. I do business with Gavras as buyer for the Parthenon and other hotels in Las Vegas. Nikos is certainly shrewd, but I've never found him to be dishonest. I'm sure this is a mistake, and if you go back he'll make an adjustment."

"Not according to the Australian guy we met later. He deals with him and calls him a shady operator."

"Surely it might be worth a try?" Gwendolyn said, looking at the Tanners. "You have a receipt, don't you?"

I held my breath. Sophie bit her lip and winced, not sure what to day. "Yes, but he made it lower to increase our customs allowance. And we agreed." She blushed.

"Who's we, Tinkerbell?" I might have been the idiot who let Nikos screw me, but Sophie was the one who jumped on the phony receipt. Not the Redfields' finest hour: stupidity married to cupidity.

Lyle shook his head in mock sympathy. "Hoisted by your own petard, fella." Harsh Shakespeare—just what I needed to hear.

"That sonofabitch!" I said, loud enough to turn a few heads at nearby tables. Sophie was rubbing her nose with her forefinger and looking at me with alarm.

Lyle smirked "He got you by the short and curly, man." He looked sidelong and took a drag from his skinny cigar.

"I could kill the bastard!" I fumed, leaving it unclear which bastard I meant.

Sophie stepped in. "Red, take it easy and be careful with your language." She looked at me seriously. "Danielle and Gwendolyn are right. Maybe we should go back and speak with Nikos. What have we got to lose?"

"Sophie, don't be naïve." I said this more sharply than I intended. "We won't get anywhere with him. Pinocchio called him the masterbilker! And Santas says Gavras has been making threats to Madame Delphinos!"

"Red. Let it go." Sophie leaned forward to collect and repack the bowls.

Danielle looked straight at me with her indigo eyes. "What on earth does Nikos have to do with Madame?"

"He's blocked publication of her memoirs in some sort of family feud. She and Nikos's grandfather were an item way back."

"What memoir? And how do you know all this?" Danielle's look was uncharacteristically intense.

"You won't believe it," Sophie said, seizing the moment. "But we actually met Madame!"

"You jest," Gwendolyn said. "Even while we were speaking of her last night, I wondered if she was really still alive! How on earth did you manage to see her?"

"We did more than see her." Sophie said. "We actually got to visit her *salon* and have *tisane* with her. And she told us all these stories about her past." Sophie was now eager to be sharing her scoop, seemingly relieved that the bowl business was behind us.

"Do tell," Gwendolyn requested, "What is she like?"

"Slow down, Soph," I said, eager to foster the change of subject. "Why don't you start at the beginning with that little mutt. Brisket? Is that his name?" I knew it was Basket but this was payback for Sophie's silent treatment in the car.

Sophie snapped "Basket" and gave me a look. "But that's still another story I'll get to. Oh, but Madame is such a *dear* woman," she went on. "She's very old, and a little unsteady. But she's beautifully turned out in glamorous clothes and jewelry. And her mind is still totally sharp. She's full of stories of her eventful life with all its raptures and tragedies." Sophie would have been good on stage with Madame.

"Fascinating." Danielle raised a cool eyebrow for effect—the one not hidden by the sweep of blonde hair. "What does she say about those scandals in Paris that we've heard rumors about?"

Sophie had hooked her audience. Even Lyle was listening. "Well, the way Madame tells it she was swept off her feet by an older man who was leading a double life and who broke her heart. So it's not a scandal at all but an—an—an *histoire d'amour*," Sophie blurted out, finally able to use her bit of French.

"Oh, do tell! I simply adore a love story!" Gwendolyn was all ears.

"Well, when Madame was still very young, she met this romantic Greek man at the casino in Monte Carlo—a *gambler* you know—and he courted her with passion. But she learned he was already married with three children. He couldn't marry her, you see, but he wanted to make her his mistress. He promised her jewels and luxury but she just couldn't do it. So she left him—but it broke her heart!"

"It sounds like a sordid love triangle to me." Danielle said this coldly. "They might have called it a *grand passion* in those days, but an affair is an affair."

Sophie positively scowled at Danielle. "Madame has been the victim of scurrilous rumors." Her freckles and cheeks glowed with indignation. "She followed her feelings and her principles in her first great love. And she adored her third husband—Pierro—the one who died in that tragic boating accident." I could practically see the daggers shooting from her eyes at the scurrilous Tanners—warning them to lay off their widow-maker theory of Madame.

"That's why it's so important for her to tell this story in her memoir," Sophie concluded.

She looked up in startled surprise. Spiro Santas was standing next to her, bowing not once, but several times, and beaming. He carried an open bottle of champagne in an ice bucket.

"You have saved the day, my dears," he said warmly, putting bottle and bucket down. "I just concluded my search in despair, to find you have rescued us all."

Sophie responded with gratified spirit. "Oh, Mr. Santas, we were so glad to have found little Basket. It was its own reward, since Madame was so kind to us this morning." As the others looked on, speechless, Spiro departed to summon champagne flutes for the party.

"What on earth?" Danielle looked from Spiro's departing back to Sophie. "It looks like you've had more adventure than you've told us. What on earth happened?"

"Basket is Madame's little toy poodle." Sophie flicked a look at me, demanding credit for turning us into Spiro's heroes. "We met him this morning when we had tea with Madame. And when we were just coming out of Agnik, it ran right in front of our car on the road! Thank goodness Red slammed on the brakes in time." Sophie may ask for credit, but she also gives it when it's due.

"But how could you know it was Madame's dog?"

A joyful laugh escaped Sophie. "I just know dogs. It's a gift, I guess. Red couldn't believe it was Basket, could you Red? We picked it up and brought it back here and gave it to Heidi at the desk to return to Madame. And Madame never knew he was gone."

Spiro had returned to the table with a tray of glasses and dispersed them to the group.

"But we still have no idea how it got out there. It wasn't the staff, Heidi says."

We looked at Spiro, who was carefully pouring champagne, for an explanation. But he clouded over like a changeable summer day.

"Someone took him from the hotel and let him loose out there," he blustered, gesturing in the direction of the bay, and nearly spilling the bubbly.

"But that makes no sense a-tall," Gwendolyn Frawley piped up. "Why would anyone want to kidnap Madame's pet? That makes no sense a-tall."

Spiro set down the last glass in front of Lyle, and looked at Sophie and me with an intense glare. "It was that Gavras, I am certain of it. That man will stop at nothing to destroy Madame's happiness." The dude doesn't have much self-control, I thought. Here he goes again, like he did this morning, shooting his mouth off about Gavras to perfect strangers. No wonder Nikos is threatening to sue the lot of them for slander and libel.

Sophie, rubbing her nose, looked at Spiro with a frown and asked, "When did Madame take her siesta?"

"One o'clock, I think. Maybe two at the latest."

Sophie shook her head. "Mr. Santas, we met Nikos Gavras in his shop around that time. He couldn't have driven between Agnik and Astron Bay between the time Madame started her nap and when we saw him." She thought for a moment. "Or between the time we left his shop and the time we found Basket on the road." That's my Sophie—brilliantly logical with illogical people, a strategy that has backfired on her more than once.

"You *know* Gavras?" Spiro sputtered, his eyes wide open under his spectacles.

"We just happened to see a silver bowl we liked in a shop window, and it turned out to be *Gavras Greek Arts.* " I was temporizing a bit, of course. No point splashing gasoline on the flames. "We didn't know this would be *your* Nikos Gavras, and anyway, all we did was buy a set of silver bowls from him."

But Spiro continued to look apoplectic and then, to everyone's surprise, the cool Danielle piped up. "Mr. Santas," she said in her calm, purring voice,

"Nikos Gavras is a long-time supplier of my business. I can assure you he is a thoroughly professional…"

She didn't get to finish her sentence because Spiro, apparently buying neither Nikos's alibi nor Danielle's forthcoming testimonial, turned on his heels and left the table. With his formal courtesy, only extreme emotion could have caused him to do that, we knew. What on earth did he think—that we had deliberately sought out Nikos to provide him with an alibi? Or had conspired with the Tanners to cover for him? But, in a way, Spiro could be right. Nikos could've bribed some worker at the resort to kidnap the mutt. No, it was ridiculous. Nikos might be a scammer, but he didn't look like a petty fool. What could he gain with a stupid stunt like that?

The celebratory toast to Madame and the toy poodle, and to us as animal rescue heroes, was aborted, and a day that had begun so pleasantly—our first full day in Crete—ended in glum confusion and consternation. Much later we would understand that the strangely intertwined events of that day, hearing Madame's story, visiting Gavras's shop, and the rescue of little Basket, had involved an unlucky coincidence or two, to be sure. But they were underwritten by a series of precise and intentional machinations that would enmesh us in murder at Astron Bay.

Chapter 5
A Turkish Family

I awoke the next morning with a pounding headache, moss on my teeth, and a furry tongue. I was badly hung over from the wine and retsina Sophie and I had polished off the night before, following an argument about our strange dinner with Lyle and Danielle. Strange because it was sly Lyle who invited us for a meal, ostensibly to rescue the evening from Spiro's champagne fiasco. Sophie accepted for us both, thinking Gwen would be joining us. But Gwen begged off, and there we were. After the afternoon martini followed by champers and wine, I was feeling a bit of a buzz, and who was I to pass up some time with Danielle? After more booze in the form of retsina in the room, I faulted Sophie for spilling our guts to strangers about getting scammed by Nikos. And for falling for the fake receipt ploy. Sophie in turn berated me for taking the bait on the bowls in the first place, and for drooling over Danielle, as she put it. "I did not *drool* over Danielle," I retorted. Sophie then brought up my cruel demand that she leave li'l ol' Basket by the side of the road.

I love my martini and all the libations Bacchus has poured over the earth, but on mornings like this I see my father's alcoholism rear its ugly head. Bad, sad hangovers are too stiff a price to pay for pouring the grape on moods like ours the night before. Most mornings Sophie and I wake up with our arms and legs entangled, the warm residue of twenty-four years of marriage and two kids. We may be getting on, with me a bit flabby, but we still get it on. Not today. We were back-to-back on opposite sides of the bed when we opened our eyes.

It was only our second morning in Crete, and I was already sick of the place. Sophie got up, put on a robe and made us coffee. I took mine, and in my own robe, followed her out onto the terrace into a cloudy morning. An early fog hung over the bay, an apt reflection of my disposition. I had spent the whole day before doing what other people wanted me to do, and my one accomplishment, getting us a bargain on those silver bowls, had dissipated in outright shame. But nothing would work today if I didn't break some ice with Sophie. I know better than to let things fester, even if I have to swallow hard to make amends.

"Sorry." I looked at her unsmiling profile across my coffee mug. "I was unfair last night. It was me I was mad at."

"Same here."

I raised my eyebrow. "What does that mean?"

"It means I was mad at you too."

"Then how about a truce? It's over. I feel bad. Don't pile it on."

"I'm sorry I ever accepted the Tanner's invitation. It's a wonder Lyle didn't punch you out the way you cozied up to his fox of a wife."

I hadn't realized I'd been so obvious. "I'm only a window shopper, Soph, you know that. And the way I felt last night I was glad for the company. I was just showing a little appreciation for her attempt to cheer me up, that's all."

That was pretty much all, and I hoped Sophie would see it that way. We both looked out to sea, under the clouds, lighter now. Finally, I asked, "What did you make of the dinner conversation? Every time we asked the Tanners about themselves and their Vegas business, they turned the topic back to our problem with Nikos. Ticked me off. Still does."

Sophie thought for a moment. "You're right—they did keep coming back to the Gavras shop. Maybe they just wanted to convince us that Nikos really *was* reliable and that his way of doing business is conventional here in this part of the world."

I still didn't buy it, if that was the Tanners' argument, but I was relieved that Sophie was moving past our fight and accepting my truce.

"Well anyway, it was nice that they encouraged you to go to the museum with Gwen." Sophie brightened at the reminder. "Yes, I was glad they suggested it would be a useful orientation for sightseeing. It would be great for you to go too."

I wasn't quite ready to go that far. "I need a while to cool off and start vacationing."

"I know, sweetie. I've got a proposition for you. I'll go back to Agnik this morning to see what I can do with Gavras. Maybe I can make something work with him. At least I can let him know we're onto him." She flashed me one of those dimpled smiles that always signal redemption for me. "You go to the pool and relax and clear your head. And tomorrow or the next day you can be free again when Gwendolyn and I go to the museum."

I could've kissed her. In fact, I did, leaning over to plant one right on her cheek.

"Deal," I told her "Just don't get into any discussions with Nikos about Madame. There's something weird about that whole feud thing, and I don't want us to get mixed up in it."

"I'll be careful, but you be careful too. If the sun comes out, use sunblock or you'll burn like a baby."

By the time Sophie went off, it was a little after noon, and my head had pretty much shrunk to its normal size. The early clouds had given way to a gorgeous sun, so I changed into trunks, put on my Kriti cap and flip-flops, and headed down to the pool with a towel, my crossword book, and *Twilight in the Ruins* tucked under my arm. I may not want to visit ruins, but I don't mind reading about them in novels as long as there's plenty of necrophilia, smuggling, and vampire bats in and around the tombs. Most of the reclining chairs in the shade were taken, but a few were still available in the open on the other side of the pool. No matter—it was cool with a slight breeze, and my cap would protect me from sunburn. I settled my bulk into a comfortable chaise. I noticed the Tanners looking for recliners on the other side of the pool. When Lyle sat down, the chaise tipped and he fell on his butt. Danielle laughed and helped him up and then took off her sarong to reveal a marvelous bikini. Okay, I marveled at what surrounded the bikini. Life was good.

Big decision: sleep or read? I lay back trying to decide and went to sleep. After a time, I awoke to the sound of people arguing in German next to me. A man and a woman were trying to convince someone of something. Opening my eyes, I saw a thick, hairy middle-aged man, his plump gray-haired wife, and a teenager I took to be their son. The boy was a handsome Mediterranean type of about seventeen, and not at all happy. The three were sitting on lawn chairs around a small table next to me. The mother, brandishing a huge bottle of sunblock, was clearly urging the kid to put some on. Reminded me of Sophie. No wonder the kid was miserable. When the mother moved toward him to put the stuff on him herself, he recoiled like a snake and jumped up, mortified. His father said something to his wife, and the kid sprinted off to the edge of the glittering pool.

Kids. Thank god ours were grown and out of the house—except when we went on vacation and Meredith took care of the pups. But teenagers are no picnic. Colin was a pain in the butt at that age. I still can't figure out how our sweet freckled boy with a lisp and a paper-route turned overnight into a six-foot jerk who treated his father like shit. But marriage and a kid of his own straightened him out. Made me old before my time, but it was worth it, even if it means I now sleep with a grandmother.

The father noticed me watching his son and said, "*Ach, mein Sohn ist sehr un…*"

I spread my hands above my chest. "I'm sorry, *Ich*… um…" Two years of college German and I couldn't even say I didn't understand in German. *Verstehe?* Whatever. "I don't understand German. English?"

The man smiled apologetically. "Yes, of course," he said, in an accent that didn't sound at all German. He didn't look German either; his dark hair and complexion looked Greek. "My son is not happy here," he went on in English. "He think Greece would be teenage paradise and look what he has. *Elderhostel*, he calls this place. Now Hegel beg us to go to Cyclades. But I am here on business and cannot leave."

"Hegel?" I asked the man, "is that his name? Do you come from Germany?"

"Turkey, we are Turkish," the man said, "but we have lived long time in Germany. Ever since we are married." He smiled fondly at the plump woman across from him. Her baggy bathing outfit looked like a gray flour sack, and she was slathering sunblock on her arms. "I admire German culture," he went on, "Goethe and especially Hegel the philosopher. So we name our son Hegel." He shook his head sadly. "But he does not like it. He make his friends call him Keanu—some American movie star, I think."

I really didn't need insight into the conflicts of Turkish family life, but once people open up to you, you can't just say 'Well, good luck with the little punk—I gotta get back to my book.' The best thing was to change the subject.

"So what business brings you here?" I asked.

"I am engineer with Bohnen-Essen, a German contracting firm. We now make estimates and plans for airport to build in Pachia Ammos south of here. We hope to begin soon, but there are big problems…"

"Sorry to hear that." I meant it but not the way it sounded. I added, "Actually, I'm surprised they need another airport so near to Heraklion. Is that why you're running into problems?" As far as I was concerned, underdevelopment was this island's main asset. Last thing it needed was more tourists piling in and clogging the roads with tinny rental cars.

"Yes. It is small airport, not big. But some people in government think there is ancient palace underground where we plan runway. This make people angry at my firm. So now bad things happen—what you call?—sabotage. Tires on trucks are cut and equipment damaged. Now we have to put fence around our machines, trucks."

Sheesh. For a place that looked like paradise, there sure was a lot of bad karma going down. Sabotage? Haven't they heard of letters to the editor? "Why would people think you're building on a palace site?" I personally didn't give a fig, but the nature of the conflict eluded me.

The Turk seemed happy to talk while the wife was getting her towels and flip-flops and bathing cap together. "For last fifty years people say that Minoan town called Gournia must have palace near it. Thousands years ago Gournia was busy farming area. Such area must have government. Ancient tablets—like map—show palace near there So people look for palace by ocean at Pachia Ammos. For months my firm make drillings and other tests for Antiquities Department to look for palace, but so far we find nothing. So we now search palace in other places."

I remembered Gwendolyn Frawley talking about test drillings and exploratory excavations, and that she was a consultant. I wished Sophie were here to be part of this conversation. Road kill for a culture vulture like her.

The man's wife now had her stuff in her arms to go to the pool and began to look impatient.

He went on quickly. "If we find nothing, we build. If we find antiquities, we stop. Bohnen-Essen will lose contract and much money if project cannot go on. But Greeks could lose treasure big as Knossos if we cover over archeological site. Is painful—what you call?—dilemma. But I understand feelings of people here. Ancient city of Troy is still big archeological place in my country, in Turkey. And we still find things right under ground."

Pretty forgiving for a guy who's been having his tires slashed and his work place sabotaged. "Well, I hope it all turns out for the best."

I wished him well, but I was getting a bit bored. To my immense relief, Sophie emerged from the poolside exit by the gift shop. A most welcome sight. Compared to the plump Turkish woman with the thick eyebrows and dreary duds, Sophie looked like a teenager. Not a bit like a grandma. I stood and waved to her impulsively and told Turko, "There she is, my wife, Sophie!"

My new pal picked up his towel, motioned to his wife, and said, "Forgive me please, but we go swimming. Maybe we talk more later."

Sophie reached us, and as if to cancel his curtness, the man stuck out his hand to me and said, "My name is Latif. Gabor Latif, and my wife Samira." She smiled for the first time under her beetled eyebrows and gave a friendly nod. It occurred to me that she probably didn't speak much English. I shook his hand.

"I'm Red Redfield," I said, "and my wife here is Sophie. I'll tell her about your business predicament. It's very interesting." After last minute nods and smiles, the couple headed poolside, the Turk going first, his wife waddling behind.

Sophie pulled up a chair from the Latifs' table and flopped down, dropping her tote bag with its appliquéd seashells next to her. "Oh, arggh, Red, you were right," she said.

"Didn't go so good, then, did it?"

"Awful." She retrieved a bottle of water from her tote and began a long account of her visit. She went in and a shopgirl, Nia, was there. She said Nikos was out for a while, so she fetched Elena from the back room. Elena wasn't happy when she saw the bowls and heard about 'the problem,' as Sophie called it. She was very polite about it and kind of embarrassed but said Nikos had a policy of no returns.

"That's about what I'd expect her to say," I said. "Did you tell her about old Gwen Frawley's opinion?"

"I did. I told her that a woman at our resort who works for museums told us that four of the bowls were silver-plated. We felt sure a mistake had been made and that the shop would make some sort of adjustment."

Sophie took off her sunglasses and ran her hand over her forehead, dewy with sweat, before putting them back on again. "Elena asked if it was a young blonde woman and I said, no, it was a British antiquities expert. I think maybe she's met Danielle but not Gwen."

"From what you say, the sister seems a little uncomfortable in that shop, doesn't she?" I said. "She got our pal Wally his original price rather than Nikos's sly little mark-up. I wonder if she and Nikos are on the same page."

Sophie took another sip of her mineral water. "I don't think Elena knows much about the business, even though she works there. She told me she and Nikos inherited the shop from their folks, but Nikos ran it while she worked for her husband in Athens in a shop in the Plaka. Her husband died a little over a year ago, and she then came to Crete so she wouldn't be alone. She actually lives upstairs over *Gavras Greek Arts*."

"She told you all that?"

"Well, Nia had left and there was no one in the shop and it was awkward not to say anything while we waited for Nikos to turn up. Maybe she also wanted to explain why she couldn't help me on her own. I got the idea that her husband was pretty controlling and strict about a woman's place. He used her as a clerk out front, but never gave her any training in the business end. Sounds like Nikos is doing the same thing."

Why did this seem like a day when I was going to hear about Mediterranean domestic life whether I wanted to or not? "So when did Nikos show up?"

Sophie took her sunglasses off again since the sun had shifted and we were now in the shadow of the hotel, and went on with her story. It seemed Nikos came back just as Sophie was about to leave, and was surprisingly smooth and friendly when he first saw her. When she told him the bowls weren't silver, he picks up the first bowl and shows her the hallmark to prove her wrong. Then she says the others aren't silver, and he said he never said they were. They were just made to match the real silver one. I had pretty much predicted something like that in the morning.

"Did you ask for your money back?"

"I did. I told him that we would never have paid as much for them if we'd known. But he said no dice, or words to that effect. I was so mad that I told him I was going to warn tourists at Astron Bay Resort not to come to his shop if they were going to get cheated.'"

"Good for you, Pumpkin. He needed to hear that."

"Well, not so good. It made him surprisingly angry. His eyes blazed and he practically yelled at me. 'Did Spiro Santas send you? Did that walrus tell you to come here and make trouble in my shop?'"

That creep. I knew I should have gone with her. "What did you say?"

"Well, I started to tell him that Spiro had nothing to do with anything when the phone rang in back, and Nikos went to answer it. Elena just looked stricken and there was nothing for us to say. So I couldn't help overhear Nikos on the phone. He was speaking in English and making some sort of appointment, and I could swear it was at Astron Bay. He repeated a room number and everything. Isn't that weird?"

"You didn't hear him say a name or anything?"

"No. I was sure it wasn't Spiro because if it was, he would've been yelling at him too. And he was speaking in English. So I wondered whether he was arranging a meeting with Danielle."

"Seems possible. Why not, if she does business with him as a sales rep?"

"But at the hotel? Doesn't it seem weird to you that they'd do business here at the resort rather than at the shop?"

"You're not implying something—uh—romantic, are you?" Sophie's mind goes in odd places in times of uncertainty. I'd feel worse about Danielle with a bottom-feeder like Nikos than with slick Lyle.

"Oh Red. She'd have to be pretty stupid to arrange a tryst at her own hotel, with her husband around. Now that you put it like that, I don't think it could've been Danielle." She frowned and thought for a moment. "Maybe it was Madame and Spiro after all, but with Heidi or someone phoning to make the appointment for them. To argue about the memoir or something."

"Sophie, maybe you just heard wrong and it wasn't Astron Bay at all. Or if it was Astron Bay, there must be dozens of people here who might use English to speak to a Greek. Don't let it bug you. Finish your story. What happened after Nikos got off the phone?"

"Nothing. He still looked upset but he just repeated that there would be no refund and then returned to the back. So I just told Elena that I'd enjoyed talking to her and left. I can't believe she's his sister."

The afternoon had exhausted Sophie, and she took a last sip of her mineral water. Her mention of Nikos having dealings with someone at Astron Bay brought up Spiro's stupid accusation the night before—that Gavras was behind the kidnapping of Basket. I hated having my pleasant day perturbed by this whole feud thing again. I looked out over the pool scene and saw a determined Hegel step confidently toward the outer end of the high diving board on the other side of the pool. He jumped, sprang on the board, did a graceful somersault, and knifed into the water headfirst with hardly a splash. Awesome, as the kids say. I remembered seeing Keanu Reeves in a movie called *Speed*. Keanu—maybe not such a bad pseudonym for the boy. Beats Hegel. The little punk then walked, dripping and unsmiling, past his father, who grinned broadly and clapped his hands softly at Hegel's perfect dive.

I turned back to Sophie. "You done good, Pumpkin, even if you didn't get our money back." I felt grateful to her and still a bit guilty. She had endured an afternoon of aggravation while I got to see Danielle in a bikini and Lyle fall on his ass, enjoy a little snooze, and meet a guy whose project might give our friend Steelbuns headaches. Not a bad afternoon, all told. All I needed to top it off was for someone to tell Gwendolyn how the Turks and the Germans planned to hustle the Greeks and pave over their ruins forever. I didn't have to wait long, although there was a dark detour along the way.

Chapter 6
The Silver Bowl

Even though Sophie's errand to get satisfaction on the bowls had failed, putting the business clearly behind us ushered in a kind of honeymoon. Without much discussion, we made a series of moves that afternoon that put us back on the happy track. To dry out a bit, we skipped cocktails at the Midas Lounge, and instead took a late afternoon dip in the nearly deserted pool. The leaping mosaic dolphins on the bottom inspired a similar frolic on the surface. Then, by getting to the dining room early, we found a booth in a quiet corner where we enjoyed an intimate dinner for two. A little port for a closer during a congenial hour under the stars on our terrace pretty much erased the aggravation of the last two days. We fell into bed, had some bracing intimacies, and went to sleep in each other's arms. We awoke to a fine Friday morning. At breakfast we agreed that ruins, museums, and all the other stuff tourists are supposed to enjoy could wait a day or two. Why come to a place like this if you're going to go off in a car and never see it? Sophie deferred the museum trip with Gwendolyn, and—hallelujah—absolved me from joining her in a yoga class. And so I got to enjoy another morning at the pool—interrupted only by a gyro sandwich lunch at the cabaña on the beach.

"Red, you're drooling again." Sophie was standing over me as I opened my eyes against the sun. "It's two-thirty and you look like a boiled tomato. You've got to cover up." She sat down beside me on the chaise as I put away *Twilight in the Ruins* and struggled into my tee-shirt.

"How was yoga?" I winced at the scraping of the cotton against my sunburn.

"Well, yoga was wonderful. We began with a little moment of meditation, before we went on to our asanas—that's what our Hatha yoga postures are called. It was so relaxing, taking deep cleansing breaths, and doing a rooster pose, and a lotus forward bend, and a great sage asana…"

Sophie began bending and contorting her arms and I hoped she wouldn't get up and embarrass us by doing any of the more graphic poses here by the pool. From what little I've seen of Indian statuary, the stuff looks like porn ballet.

"I've got good news and I've got bad news," she said, taking a sip of my bottled water.

"Oh, oh."

She patted my arm reassuringly. "After I was done with yoga, I went to the lobby and asked Spiro if he thought Madame would mind if I took Basket out for a walk."

"Sophie, I swear, you just don't get it. We're on vacation so you can get *away* from walking dogs for a few weeks. Madame's got Zoë and Spiro to do that kind of chore for her, not to mention an entire resort staff." If I don't keep an eye on Sophie, she'll start bussing tables and making people's beds.

"Anyway, Spiro took me down to Madame, who was in her drawing room on the velvet sofa, with little Basket snoozing beside her. She had her lorgnette out and was looking at old photo albums and letters and things spread out on the coffee table."

"I thought she said she was finished with her memoir."

"Well, that's the interesting thing. When I asked her just that question, she suddenly acted very mysterious and said that she was getting ready for a really important visitor tomorrow. I was dying to find out who it was, but when she saw that I looked curious, she apologized and said the visit was something she had to keep private. But she looked very pleased about it."

"Good. That means we can skip the old *tisane* with her and her mutt for a while."

Sophie shook her head in exasperation. "You're not getting it, Red. Remember that phone call Nikos got from Astron Bay yesterday? The one I overheard? Well, I began wondering, with all those albums and stuff, whether Madame was getting ready for a visit from Nikos."

"Sophie, it could be anybody," I said. "Yesterday Nikos was her arch enemy. Things like that don't change overnight." When Sophie gets impatient waiting for the future to arrive, she just makes it up. That way she can enjoy it twice. "Anyway, why would she keep that a secret from you?"

"Well, think about it. She doesn't want a lawsuit and so she'd want to negotiate with Nikos. But she's too feeble to meet him at the shop, so she invites him to come here to Astron Bay."

Sophie glowed as though the deal was done, and Madame's memoir would be on Amazon.com before we got home. Somehow, she forgot that Nikos had been a perfect turd who wouldn't give anybody a break—least of all a 90 year-old woman who was about to expose his grandpa as a sleaze-ball. Or that Spiro, convinced Nikos was behind Basket's kidnapping, would never let the guy set foot in the place. But after her yoga class, Sophie was at peace. Her tank top said "If you dream it, you can be become it." No way I was going to prick her balloon.

"Oh, one more cool thing," she said. "Madame let me look through the photo album she had out and there was one amazing photo that I just couldn't believe. Guess what it was?" How the heck was I supposed to do that? I took a quick sip of her water, and cut to the chase. "I give up. What?"

Sophie took her sunglasses off for emphasis: "It was Madame with Elizabeth Taylor and Nicky Hilton at their wedding in 1950. All three of them looked fabulous. Elizabeth Taylor was only eighteen, and breathtaking! And Madame, even though she was a bit older, looked stunning!" That *was* pretty impressive. Madame sure made the rounds of the rich and famous in her day.

"Wonder if old Hilton gave her tips about the hotel business," I said. "That could explain how this place runs so well!"

"Elizabeth Taylor," Sophie said dreamily, still thinking about that young wedding photo. She clearly forgot that there would be a lot more marriages under *that* bridge during the next fifty years. Sophie must have been reading my mind, because she suddenly looked at me and said defensively, "You've got to say one thing for Liz: she wasn't afraid of commitment. That's more than you can say about those hussies in Hollywood nowadays."

"So what's the bad news?" I asked. Sophie might have wandered into romance nirvana, but I wanted her to finish her story so I could get back to my afternoon.

She winced. "I ran into Gwen on the way to the pool and she wants to join us at the barbecue tonight."

Astron Bay offers this shindig down by the beach every Friday. They close the restaurant that night, so there's no other option for dinner except gyros in their coffee shop or a drive back to Agnik. I wouldn't have minded the barbecue, but they threatened traditional Greek dancing and music! Having seen this crap at the infamous Olympia Restaurant in my own hometown, I knew what we were in for. As a crowning burden, at the end of the evening there would be disco dancing for the young and—I kid you not—"the young at heart." Young at fart, more likely.

My frown must have told Sophie that I was looking for an escape hatch. "Don't be such a curmudgeon, Red," she said sternly. "It'll be nice for Gwen to have company. And you'll love it." Like I love baby showers and white sales. I'd rather get my navel pierced.

We were the first customers at the Midas Lounge bar at 5:00 sharp. Sitting with Sophie on an adjoining stool, I was deep into my mart when The Frawley joined us. Old Gwen wasn't in the best of spirits. The antiquities department hadn't called her in for consultation yet, and she was telling Sophie that she worried that some shady negotiations were going on between the authorities and the firm working on the planned airport. I pricked my ears up at that, remembering the Turk and his dumpy wife down at the pool yesterday. After our cocktails, the three of us went down to the beach area, passing a stage set up with microphones and amps before arriving at the lawn beyond the terrace. There the hotel staff had set up a group of canopies that arched over tables set with blue-and-white checked tablecloths and piles of white embroidered napkins wrapped around eating utensils. In the area behind the tents, staff in white chef's hats tended tables topped with warming pans. A row of smoking grills was set against the rock face of the hill behind them. Sophie watched my eyes light up and shook her head. "Oink, oink," she mumbled in my ear, low so Gwen couldn't hear.

We grabbed a table near the cabaña, where we could look out over the blue water and ordered some wine and mineral water. A short wooden dock jutted into the cove down the beach to our left. A rowboat pulled up and five young people in colorful Greek costumes got out and headed past us toward the stage. Before the wine arrived, Sophie also spotted the Tanners coming down the path toward the canopies. They were talking to a burly fellow wearing white pants, a blue shirt and a Greek fisherman's hat over his white hair. He looked like a local, a real old man of the sea.

Sophie waved and yelled at them before I could stop her. "Lyle, Danielle, how are you? Would you like to join us?"

It took them a moment to look over and wave to us. Well, what the hell. If the forgiving Sophie didn't mind having the gorgeous Danielle around me, I wasn't going to complain. After a minute Danielle came over to our table, while Lyle stayed behind and continued to talk to the guy with the silver hair. We repeated our invitation, but Danielle graciously accepted for herself alone. Lyle was apparently a bit under the weather, and preferred to spend the evening in their room. Perfect, as far as I was concerned. I was frankly a little apprehensive about seeing Lyle after our dinner the other night. If Sophie noticed me panting over Danielle, maybe Lyle did too. Last thing I needed was a tense barbecue. But luck was with me. In a moment Lyle waved and started up the walk to the building, while the fisherman fellow headed on down to the beach with a rolling walk and over to the dock. An old salt, picturesque as the scene demanded.

"Well, it's wonderful to see you again," Sophie said to Danielle as she seated herself next to Gwen. Like I say, Sophie's fair. She might blame me for flirting with Danielle, but as far as she was concerned that wasn't Danielle's fault.

"Yes," said Danielle quietly, peering around with her cat's eyes. She hesitated a moment, then said, "We just talked to a captain about chartering an overnight cruise to Rhodes. That seems a little much, but he also makes day trips to other nearby islands. I think that's what we'll do. I just hope Lyle feels better and is up to a trip tomorrow. It's his first time here and I'd like to show him a little more of the area."

The wine and mineral water arrived, and I poured glasses for everyone, although a short one for me. I had to behave myself tonight. I picked up the conversation from the earlier dinner by asking Danielle some more about her and Lyle's work in Las Vegas.

"What sort of stuff do you buy?" I said, "I mean other than the Greek stuff?"

"Not much else for the Parthenon, whose shops I represent now," Danielle answered, "They prefer to project a classical Roman and Greek motif. It's a high-end clientele, so I make regular trips to Athens and Rome to get quality reproductions and professional replicas if I can find them. Not the sort of thing that can be made by machine."

Gwendolyn leaned forward to pour herself a little more wine, having already chugged off her first glass. "Indeed" she said. "In my business, we see everything from plastic and Hong-Kong 'knock-offs,' as people call them, to beautiful craftsmanship. The faithfulness of some reproductions of ancient art is quite astonishing. Like museum pieces. But, distressingly, the real thing turns up as well. Shocking, the state of the trade these days."

"Meaning?" I asked.

"The expropriation of artifacts for profit," she explained.

"Like the Elgin marbles," I said, and felt a quick kick from Sophie under the table. Sophie's not especially political, but she knows by my tone when I'm trying to get a rise out of someone.

Old Gwen diplomatically ignored the provocation. "Traffic in artifacts is a serious problem, even though the Greeks do their best to deter it. Museums and collectors then encounter pieces whose origin and authenticity are in doubt—'unknown provenance,' as we call it. My work involves the inspection and authentication of such materials."

"Do you use thermoluminescence?" I asked. I wanted to show off a little. People never ask chemists anything about their work because they don't know what to ask. But we know lots of cool stuff, some of it even relevant to real life. I may not know my rhyton from my kylix, but I do know what happens to the electrons in ceramics when you heat them up. I've read about the dating method where they give off light from the background radiation they absorb over time.

Gwen peered at me with her steelrims in surprise—as though she were seeing me for the first time.

"Indeed, I do," she said, nodding until her spectacles bobbed. "I've retained access to my old laboratory in Oxford with its state of the art luminescence equipment. And I've been able to arrange use of the portable gamma spectrometer belonging to the Antiquities Department here." She looked at me sharply again from behind her specs. Good to get a little respect out of old Snoots.

"Why can't you just assume that anything you find in the ground is authentic," Sophie asked.

"Oh, my dear, there is *such* duplicity in this field. Sotheby's recently detected forgeries of ancient Chinese pots that had tiny bits of clay from genuine antiquities inserted into them to fool the luminescence tests. Marvelously clever and inventive, these forgers."

The waiter arrived and put hummus and pita bread on the table. Danielle dipped a slice of pita into the dip and said carefully to Gwen, "That sounds a bit paranoid to me."

Gwendolyn visibly bristled at this. "Some people find it easier to wear blinders when it comes to shady dealings in the art world than to confront the truth." She said this with a sniff that sounded almost accusatory. "And, of course, people's ethical standards may vary."

I noticed Sophie starting to rub her nose, and figured we'd best head for the barbecue before a cat-fight broke out. When I suggested it, Sophie flashed me a grateful smile. "Great idea, Red. But it's getting a little chilly. Would you be a sweetie and get me my turquoise sweater from the room?"

"You're welcome to borrow mine," Danielle said quickly, and started to peel hers from her tanned shoulders. "Oh, no, Danielle, many thanks, but I couldn't. You'll clearly need it yourself."

So I got up to do Sophie a good turn—a reward for her tolerance in inviting Danielle to join us, and for being nice to Danielle.

I walked up to the rear entrance of the hotel by the pool and went to the ground-floor elevator. Sophie always urges me to take the stairs for the exercise, but I was in a hurry to get back to the barbecue. The varied meats and sauces had roused powerful juices in my stomach, and I was hungry as a lion. I keyed myself into our room, and after failing to see the sweater in the hall closet, I went to the green-painted armoire with the TV and drawers for the clothes we didn't have to hang. When I opened Sophie's drawer, I was surprised to see things a bit disarranged. It wasn't like Sophie, but I figured she'd dressed in a hurry, having decided—women are like this—to change clothes after she was dressed perfectly the first time. "Seeking redress for a past mistake," she calls it. And there was her light turquoise sweater. I took it and was ready to head back down, but wanted to relieve myself while I had the chance. I'd already had some drinks and I know my capacity.

As I turned toward the bathroom I registered that the bathroom light was on. Now that was a little weird. After years of yelling at our kids to turn them off, we've developed a family reflex and never leave a room with a light on. I could've sworn we turned everything off when we went down to meet Gwen in the Lounge. No big deal, since we weren't paying for electricity. I walked in, heading for the john, and was stopped dead cold by the sight of one of our silver *bowls* on the counter by the sink. It was round, making it our one and only silver one. What the *hell* was that thing doing there? Did Sophie decide to use it for something? Maybe for rinsing her teeth after she brushed them? A frigging eighty dollar dribble cup! I couldn't believe it! For someone who's generally sharp as a tack, Sophie can make some hare-brained moves.

We were going to have to have some words about this. But first I was going to put the damn thing away so it wouldn't get tarnished sitting around in the damp bathroom. I picked it up and stopped with the bowl in mid-air. What the hell? It had fluid in it! *Yuck!* On reflex, I dumped it into the sink. It was dark red and viscous. *Blood! Gack!* I couldn't believe my eyes. I retracted my hand and the bowl from over the sink as if it was a snake and lost my grip on it. The bowl dropped to the floor. *Blech!* I jumped away from it as it fell. It bounced with a clatter on the tile, and came to rest by the baseboard. My head was spinning, and my double mart and the wine in my system nearly made me pass out. Scared shitless, I spun around in terror, expecting to find someone with a knife lunging at me from the room. But there was no one, and the patio door was closed. I remembered I had checked the closet for Sophie's sweater, and the clearance under the bed was too low for a person to hide.

I made myself focus on what was before me. I was a scientist, I told myself, if not the best in the trade. Okay. Breathe. So one of our bowls was out of its box, on the bathroom counter, and full of blood or something. Was it really blood? I took a tissue from the box on the counter and forced myself to pick up the bowl. I sniffed the inside. Chemists can tell a lot from odors, like good cooks. Esters, hydrocarbons, mercaptans, all have their signature smells. But what the hell does *blood* smell like? I sniffed again. The sensation in my nose belonged to the kitchen. More like soy sauce and, if I would bet on it, *ketchup*.

Was I relieved? No. The bathroom light had been on. I remembered the mussed clothing in Sophie's drawer. Someone had been in the room. *What the hell was going on? Who got in and pulled this stunt, and how and why?*

C'mon Red, I said in a whisper, take it a step at a time. Okay. We'd been gone from the room about an hour, maybe even more. Someone got in. How could that happen? I tried to calm myself down by thinking of the means, not the meaning. How did he—*he?*—get in? The staff has master keys. Did the maid come in to turn down the bed? Had never happened yet, and if it did, surely she'd leave a freakin' *mint* instead of an ugly surprise in one of our silver bowls. Nope, that made no sense, but left me with something even more unimaginable. Namely, that since we left for the bar and the barbecue, the door was opened, someone looked and found one of our damn bowls, filled it with a grotesque slop, left it for us to find, and snuck out.

Jeez! I asked myself for the first time: what did they *take?* That's chiefly why people break into hotel rooms, isn't it? Frantically, I began to go through our stuff. But our camera, all our gear, all our stuff was still in the room. Looking for Sophie's jewelry, I remembered she'd locked it in the safe enclosed in her night table. Sophie's trusting but sensible. The safe was unopened. When I checked the armoire drawers I found the bottom one full of our recent purchases, including the four aluminum-foil bowls in their box, abandoned by their big brother with the hallmark.

My heart was pounding. I was improbably wishing it *was* burglary. Burglary's a common-sense sort of crime that's in no way personal. But this was *blood*! Not real, maybe, but meant to look like blood. I walked back to the mess in the bathroom and had a moment's urge to taste the red goop just to make sure it was benign. If it was blood, whose? Animal or human? I felt my gorge rise. HIV. What did *we* do to deserve this?

"Nikos!" I said this out loud. He knew we had the bowls and he'd know which one was silver. He's after Madame, now he's after us! He took the dog to threaten her, and now he tries to get to us. But why us? What the hell did *we* have to do with Madame? Spiro said he'd made threats. Terrifying resort guests with blood was a threat all right! Or was it revenge? Just because Sophie wanted her money back? Sophie was stupid to threaten to spread the word about his rip-off shop. Was that what got to him? I remembered Spiro quivering with fury at Nikos and felt the same sensation. Get a grip, Red. Nikos couldn't have taken the dog, *didn't* take the dog, remember? We were with him at the time.

They were waiting for me down at the barbecue, and I felt panic. What should I be doing? Calling the police? What? Call the desk, ask for the police, say someone got in and left slop in one of our bowls? I could picture Spiro on the phone. Yes, Mr. Redfield, right away. What did you say was in the bowl? What bowl was that? I'm sure there is some explanation. I'll send someone up.

"Spiro!" He knows we bought silver bowls from Nikos! Didn't I tell him so myself, to convince him Nikos couldn't have kidnapped the dog? Did Spiro set all this up to implicate Nikos? Did Spiro spirit little Basket off to Agnik too? He wouldn't do that to Madame, surely? But then he never told Madame the pooch was missing. And the animal could've been run over. What a crappy trick to pull on us, using Nikos's bowl to scare us—especially after we rescued the stupid mutt.

C'mon, Red. Get a grip. This was all too far-fetched. What the hell do I do? Going to the police was out. You never know how to approach police in a foreign country, never know how they'll take a weird, stupid story like this one. Except for a few drops and residue, the slop in the bowl had gone down the sink. The management was out too. Even though Spiro was the hotel manager, he was a sleeping volcano when it came to Nikos. My mind began whirring again—Nikos! Spiro! Spiro! Nikos! Was I on vacation or was I a fly in someone's ointment? Or someone's web? What would Sophie say or do?

I breathed deeply and let my mind go completely blank. Finally a pathologic calm stole over me, a passivity I often experience in times of unshared stress or fear. I took a mass of tissues from the box in the bathroom and began cleaning up, the floor, the counter, the sink, till all traces of the glop were gone. I rinsed out the accursed bowl thoroughly and dried it. I flushed the Kleenex down the toilet. I noticed the bowl had been dented on the rim when it fell. I put it back in the box in its wrapper in the drawer. I smoothed out the clothes in the drawers and restored our belongings to order. I picked up Sophie's turquoise sweater, turned out the light in the bathroom, and after testing the patio door, left, making sure the entrance door was firmly locked.

I started down the stairs, slowly, to regain my composure and have a story to tell the folks at the barbecue about my long absence. It had already been twenty minutes or so, and I didn't want to meet Sophie coming out of the elevator. After a few steps down, I realized I had forgotten to pee. As I went back into our room I had another panic attack, expecting to see the bathroom light back on and one of our tinfoil bowls now filled with real blood.

Chapter 7
Dancing the Syrtaki

By the time I reached our group, I was still breathing hard. As I approached, I saw that the three women had been joined by the three Latifs, Gabor, Samira (was that her name?) and that Hegel kid. I was just as glad, since they would distract the girls from my long absence. I also saw they had gotten their food and were already eating. My appetite was totally gone.

"Hey, Red, let me have my sweater. I'm freezing. Where have you been?" I was unaware I was even holding the sweater. I passed it to Sophie, not even helping her put it on.

"I'm okay," I told her, touching my paunch. "Just a touch of indigestion. I'm okay now." I hoped this would take care of my long absence *and* my anomalous lack of appetite, in case Sophie noticed it after I got my food.

"Red, look who's joined us. Gabor and Samira, and their son Hegel. They couldn't find seats when they came in, and we had plenty of room."

She smiled at them gladly, and they looked happy to be included. Next to them Gwen and Danielle were munching away and not saying much. Ordinarily, I would have wondered how the Latifs and Gwendolyn were going to get along once they realized they were on opposite sides of that airport issue. But these "normal" concerns had little resonance in what had become, for me, a parallel universe. Astron Bay Resort had become two worlds for me. One was full of feuding, intrigue, and threats with unknown people kidnapping dogs and perpetrating pranks to scare the crap out of guests. The other was an Aegean luxury resort in a gorgeous setting on the water, with terrific food and cultured people who should be having the time of their lives. Only one of these worlds could be real, and I desperately wanted the benign one here at the barbecue table. I decided to treat my recent shock like a hallucination, a flash from a Hitchcock movie rather than an actual event. I was only partly successful.

"Sweetie, don't just stand there. Get some food." Sophie's voice broke through my fog and I mechanically lumbered over to the buffet. A heady, smoky aroma drifted over from the grills and I saw the table spread with wonderful meats, including things that Sophie, the animal lover, won't let me have at home. Veal and rabbit in addition to pork, sausage, and fried cod with garlic sauce. On an ordinary night, I would have been in heaven. But tonight the sliced meats were leaking juices and blood and I felt I would be sick. But I would have to eat something or at least pretend to. I picked up a piece of chicken and a little rice and salad and returned and sat down by Sophie.

"Are you sure you're all right, Red?" Sophie stared incredulously at my meager plate. "I sure hope you're not coming down with what Lyle has." She looked at Danielle quizzically, but other than giving me a sympathetic look, Danielle offered no details. I hate keeping secrets, and the thought of what I would have to tell Sophie once we got back to our room was making me even more sick than the barbecue sauce dripping off the ribs and kabobs and chunks of sausage everyone was eating.

The radio silence at the table, and the sight of me picking at my food, finally got to Sophie. "I can't wait to see Gournia," she said, jump-starting conversation again. "But what I'm really dying to see is Knossos. That's where the famous bull-vaulting fresco is, isn't it?"

Gwendolyn, who had been glum and fidgeting in her chair, brightened with interest. "Yes, indeed, the fresco is there, but they don't believe the courtyard at Knossos was used for bull-vaulting." She took a sip of wine, cleared her throat and intoned, *"a dancing floor like that which once in the wide space of Knossos / Daedalus built for Ariadne of the lovely tresses."*

We looked at her in surprise. "From *The Iliad*, Book VIII.," she said, reddening a little.

"So, is bull vaulting anything like a rodeo?" I felt I had to say something since I was barely touching my chicken.

"It was a religious ceremony, in which men leaped over the backs of running bulls," Gwendolyn explained.

"Oh dear." Sophie would worry about both species.

"Indeed," Gwendolyn agreed, "tragic for both man and beast. The men were frequently trampled, and the bulls were always sacrificed."

"Cool," Hegel said—the first time anyone at the table heard him speak.

Danielle turned to Sophie. "I wouldn't get too excited about Knossos. The reason it looks so wonderful is because a British fellow reconstructed much of it. Most of what you see isn't the actual palace. It's just a replica."

"So how do you know what's real around here? At least in California you know when you're in a theme park and when you're not." I started to pour myself some wine but it was red and made my gorge rise again. Sophie's eyes bulged in disbelief when she saw me pour mineral water instead.

"I take exception to your characterization of Sir Arthur Evans, the man who restored Knossos, *if* that's the man you've just slandered." Steelbuns, in high dudgeon, glared at Danielle. "Evans put his entire fortune into the excavations. Without them we would not have a fraction of what we see today."

Gabor Latif spoke up. "This Evans, he employ half Greek and half Turkish workers—to make peace among the people here." The group looked at him, a little puzzled. "We are Turkish," he explained. "To me, this Evans have forward vision."

This softened Gwen, but not Danielle, who stood up. "I hope you'll excuse me. I really need to go and look after Lyle. I'm going to take a plate up to him in case he gets hungry later on. I hope he'll be well enough to go on our boat excursion tomorrow. It's nice to meet you, Mr. and Mrs. Gav…Ga…?"

"Latif," said Gabor. "I too am glad to meet you and hope to see you again."

After Danielle left, Gwendolyn turned to Gabor and asked politely, "And what is your occupation?"

"I work for German construction firm in Essen," he answered. "I am here to oversee engineering plans for possible airport south of here, at Pachia Ammos." Oh-oh, here we go. I didn't need this in my unnerved condition.

Sure enough, Gwendolyn darkened. "You must be aware that you are interfering with one of the most promising archeological explorations in centuries." Yep, she was going to lay it on with a rhetorical trowel.

"*Ach*," said Gabor, shaking his head. "I of course worry very much about this. I too love the Greek antiquities. But my firm need to build this. The people in south need airport closer than Heraklion."

"Poppycock!" Gwendolyn's eyes glittered behind her steelrims. "You must forgive me if I say that your site should be declared quite unusable. The Antiquities Department is certain we will find the ancient palace in Pachio Ammos. I consult with them, you know."

Poor Gabor was duly abashed. He said meekly, "We of course are worried about stopping plans now that government step in. I hope new information show ancient palace somewhere else."

"It would be scandalous if they had *not* stepped in." Gwen clipped her phrases. "Industry can rarely be trusted not to exert improper influence in cases like this."

Sophie's nose was getting red from being rubbed. "I'm sure this will work out for the best. Airports can be built in many places. Maybe they can delay it until they remove the materials, if they find them. Or maybe they'll just use another site farther away." She didn't really know what she was talking about, but at least she was making conciliatory noises. Gabor looked as though he was about to say something, but seeing Gwendolyn still glowering, clammed up. I was in no condition to say a word and left it to Sophie, the Redfield peacemaker, to handle this.

The attendants were lighting candles and hurricane lamps on the tables and lanterns hanging from cords under the canopies. The soft ambient light soothed us. Some of us, anyhow. Sophie turned the conversation around to the Latifs, asking Samira what she did. Samira tried, but couldn't get what little English she had into gear. Gabor took over to explain that his wife was a social worker in the poor Turkish guest-worker community in Essen. He smiled fondly at the dumpy woman. "Samira has good heart."

I wished the same could be said for Hegel. The surly butthead hardly answered Sophie when she asked him about his plans. Gabor explained that the boy was out of high school, or gymnasium or whatever the hell they call it in Germany, and was going to an American university in the fall.

"I want to be near Los Angeles and Hollywood. It is freer there, I think." What was he going to study? Acting? Lotsa luck, kid. Our son Colin dreamed of becoming a screenwriter in L.A. and ended up teaching high school English in Oakland. Not that he doesn't love it, but Hollywood's a tough place to crack.

But the conversation was doing its job. My image of the bloody bowl was receding, replaced by the reality of the here and now—the cantankerous Frawley, the sullen teenager, and a couple of anxious Turkish parents on an August evening by a beautiful bay. I pictured telling Sophie what I'd found in our room, and wanted to die. The peace she achieved at yoga this morning would be as shattered as my own.

Totally out of character, I was thankful to see entertainers gathering at the back of the stage, testing their microphones and instruments. Anything to delay returning to that room. Soon the music began, softly announcing the performance about to start. A familiar figure dressed in a double-breasted navy suit topped by a florid cravat approached the microphone. It was our own Spiro Santas, with his wavy gray hair and gray moustache with the curled ends. He rapped on the microphone.

"Welcome, my friends, welcome to our special Friday night barbecue. Madame Delphinos asks me to give you her warmest greetings with her hope you are enjoying Astron Bay. Tonight our staff has prepared a special program to introduce you to Greek music and dancing. We hope it will give you great pleasure!" He repeated this in German, spreading his arms, figuratively embracing the dancers that had collected on the stage.

I felt the parallel universe engulf me again. Up on the stage, Spiro looked so jolly, so affable, not the hissing demon spitting venom at Nikos. Not the dark intruder who had served us a cup of blood just this evening. Room service, no less.

"Oh, I hope they do the syrtaki—the traditional dance of Crete," Sophie gushed. She began humming the theme from *Zorba the Greek.* "My heart starts pounding every time I think of Anthony Quinn teaching Alan Bates to do that wonderful dance on the beach at the end!"

"I'm frightfully sorry to disabuse you, my dear." Gwendolyn was still in contempt mode. "I'm afraid the original Zorba never visited Crete, and the syrtaki is not a traditional Cretan dance. Anthony Quinn was too inept to master the steps, so Hollywood had to provide him with something simple." Another frigging replica, I thought to myself. Is there anything real in this place? Hollywood invented the syrtaki?

But Hegel's ears perked up at the name of Anthony Quinn, and he told his folks he was leaving to be near the stage. By now, nearly a dozen young men had gathered there. The hotel's serving men, in toques and white chef's smocks earlier, now wore blouses, vests, and pants matching those of the entertainers. As the fellows formed a line facing the audience, the familiar cadence of Greek music—guitar, bouzouki, flute, drum—filled the air. The dancers chained themselves, each one's arms on the shoulders of the man on either side, and began slow, fluid footwork in unison. Young women in blue skirts and aprons shook tambourines in the rear in time with the music, which accelerated as the dancers moved faster and faster. The dance ended with a great chord on the bouzouki and the line of men raised their arms with a great cheer.

"That *was* the syrtaki—I remember it from the movie!" Sophie said.

After that, the dancers resumed with more acrobatics and variations. I browned out, trying to think of nothing, to float in the music, the movement, and the moment. Sophie and the Latifs were enjoying the show. Even Gwendolyn had turned her chair around to watch. After four or five numbers, Spiro again took the microphone and in unctuous tones invited people to come and join the dancers. People talked and giggled, but no one volunteered until a brave soul finally ventured up to the stage.

It was Hegel, bright in his white tee-shirt and jeans, bouncing up the steps. "And what is your name?" Spiro asked into the microphone. Hegel mumbled something to him. Spiro shouted, "Keanu! Keanu! Let us all welcome Keanu here." The crowd laughed and followed Spiro in applause. Hegel looked sideways, shyly, and smiled. A male dancer took Hegel's arm and showed him how to move his feet, first one shin over the other, then the other over the first. Hegel picked it up quickly, and detached himself, raised his arms, elbows crooked with his hands in the air. I was astonished that he kept time as the music sped up and he faced the audience. Gabor was smiling at his son, Samira was frowning, and I was happy for the boy. He was entirely transformed now that he'd found his métier, and damn, if he didn't look like a young Keanu Reeves up there. Maybe the kid had a future in show biz after all.

Hegel's example emboldened other young people to join him on stage and we were now treated to several exuberant rounds of amateur syrtaki that left the kids elated and the old folks, including me, in a mellow mood. Later on, when they cleared the terrace so the gray guests could dance to their own music, I was still in no hurry to clear out. The music became familiar, with the voices of Sinatra, Como, Engelbert, Carly and Paul McC. My decades. Well, maybe my parents' decades, but still—my kind of culture.

"Dance?" I looked up to see Sophie, bright-eyed, holding out her hand to me, the little sparkles on her sweater glittering in the candlelight. My heart seized up, knowing the evening was coming to an end. I hadn't danced since our son's wedding three years ago, but I would have danced all night, to defer the reckoning waiting in our room.

We went slowly to the terrace and found a place to slow-dance. I looked over Sophie's shoulder, carefully composing a dreamy face. For her part, Sophie was in heaven, hardly noticing that I simply swayed with my legs planted like twin oaks on the floor.

The evening ended around ten o'clock, with a round of fireworks blasted off over the bay from the beach. Sophie looked like she was twenty-five again. And I could hardly breathe as we left the scene and headed back up to the building.

"What's wrong, Red?" I had broken into a cold sweat as I put my key card into the slot of our room with a trembling hand. "Here, let me do it."

"No!" I yelled, and pulled the card in and out and opened the door. Cowardly as I am, the fear of someone leaping out of the dark and grabbing my Sophie freaked me. I reached into the room and turned on the light. It was as I had left it.

"What on earth is going on?" Sophie's face was ashen and she gave me the same look she had given me years ago when I had to tell her that they'd diagnosed Meredith with pleurisy.

So I told her the story of the bloody bowl, sitting on the bench by the patio door as she sat on the bed. The whole story, detailing my anguish at not knowing what was going on and at my stupid reaction to the whole thing.

Like me, she wouldn't believe it at first. "Are you sure you didn't take the bowl out yourself and use it to brush your teeth or something?"

I rolled my eyes. "I know I don't floss, and my gums bleed a little every now and then. But not a whole bowlful of frigging blood, Sophie."

"I wish you hadn't dumped the stuff into the sink. Now we can't be sure just exactly what it was. Maybe there's an innocent explanation, but now we don't have the *evidence* to check it out." Sophie was in Miss Marple mode— much better than having her freaked out over the real or faux gore.

"Nothing would make me happier than to figure out that we did something stupid. Or that I'm losing my mind, for that matter." I looked toward the bathroom and felt a delayed shudder. "But we still haven't figured out how Basket got released in the wild, and this makes two nasty tricks in two days here at Astron Bay."

"Well, you didn't imagine Basket on the road, that's for sure," Sophie conceded. She frowned. "Red, maybe we *have* walked into something dangerous. If you think we should get out of here, let's leave. This isn't the only hotel in Crete."

"Can't right now, obviously. I'll see what we can do about it tomorrow. I feel we've been warned about something, but *what*? And by *whom*? The worst of it is we can't tell anyone about the bowl of blood. Every time I imagine telling Spiro, I see him going ballistic and making a bigger mess of this whole thing than it already is. And I also keep wondering if he had something to do with it?" Hard to imagine, after seeing him as the jolly emcee at the barbecue.

"I'm stuck," Sophie confessed. "But I'm also curious." Brave lady she is. I'd imagined her in hysterics when I told my story, but here she was, bucking up our—or at least my—courage. She got up and got the half-empty bottle of wine from our mini-fridge. I took the glass she offered me, relieved that it wasn't red, and feeling much calmer now that I had my oppressive secret off my chest.

Sophie brought up the question of the next day. "You won't be in the mood, Red, but I set up a date for us to go to the museum in Agnik tomorrow with Gwen." She winced at my explosive "*Whaaat*?" and "*When*?"

"When you were getting my sweater. We had a deal, remember, and I already postponed it for a day."

"So you don't want to change hotels anymore?" I asked. I myself had mixed feelings about the whole thing. The room still spooked me a little but I didn't relish having to negotiate a departure with Spiro tomorrow. Going to the museum would get me out of here for the day and save me a lot of nasty hassle. My natural indolence tipped the scale and I agreed to honor the museum deal.

"Aaaaaahhh!" I jumped up from my bench and spilled the white wine on the tile. A gushing noise from the other end of the room had freaked me, and for a second I expected a Greek figure to leap out of the dark bathroom with a knife in one hand and a silver bowl in the other.

"It's only a toilet flushing next door, Red, for heaven's sake." Sophie came over and put her arms around me. "You sure are jumpy."

Chapter 8
A Museum Mishap

My sleep had been hard-won. Telling Sophie about the bowl full of guck relieved me, and after a refill of the wine, I drifted off soon after hitting the sack. But I awoke around four, according to the clock-radio, with a vivid dream still throbbing in my head. Basket struggling in a bucket of his own blood in Madame's garden. Spiro and Nikos leering from outside the gate, ajar, laughing at me as though I was an idiot. I wanted to nestle up to Sophie but didn't want to awaken her too early. The bowl episode had done its work, and I tried fruitlessly to understand what had happened. I felt mortified by my disposing of the whole matter, red liquid and all, which now haunted me like an impulsive crime. After another hour, I finally fell into a dreamless sleep and awoke feeling like a zombie called up from the dead by eerie chants. Coming out of a fog, I saw it was late and we had to get going.

"Time to rock and roll," I mumbled to Sophie.

"Mmff. Whatimsit?" Most of her head was buried in the pillow, but I saw one eye blink.

"Ten o'clock. Too late for breakfast, but I'll make you some coffee."

"Tnksgd." Many years had taught me this meant "thanks, good." Our wake-up vocabulary was stripped to essentials.

We struggled into our robes and took our coffee and the *Trib* out to the terrace. Another deeply overcast sky, which fit our mood. I tried to remember the fleeting pleasure the music and dancing had imparted to us the night before, but it was no help. I had misgivings about our museum trip in the afternoon. I knew I could sleep-walk the whole thing, past multitudes of dusty broken pots, statues, earrings, coins, and spears. I excelled at mumbling approval and interest and hoped Sophie and Guinevere would ooh and ahh gently enough to respect my walking doze. It was the return that spooked me.

"Sophie, I don't know about this museum trip. I'm almost afraid to leave the room. And if I do, I'm gonna be afraid to open our door when we get back."

"I know how you feel, Red. But I'm not going to become a prisoner to this stuff. The best thing we can do is get out of here like we planned and take our chances. We're going to stick together, like we said last night, and we'll be all right."

Sophie, my heroine. It was good to be able to air my fears to her. "Soph, I hate this place. Astron Bay is beautiful on the outside, but it's a snake-pit on the inside. Madame and Spiro are at war with Nikos. Danielle and Gwen are hissing at each other. Sweet Gabor gets upbraided by Gwen. Hegel hates being here and treats anyone over eighteen like crap. Lyle is a reptile, so he's the only one who feels perfectly at home. Weird things happen to us and we can't tell anyone, even Spiro, about last night. What the hell are we supposed to do?"

"Like I said, I'm not going to let it get to me."

The phone rang, and it was Gwendolyn, all cheerio, checking up on our departure time. "I hope you've had a marvelous rest and that you're looking forward to the museum's splendid collection this afternoon! I was thrilled to hear that you've offered to escort us, and I promise to make it worth your while!" We agreed to meet in the lobby at twelve thirty. I wanted to grumble to Sophie, out of habit, but realized I'd best cling to my new motto, *status quo ante*. Keep things normal like they were before.

Still, I had to be recovering because I was hungry, having had no breakfast and little food for dinner at the barbecue. "Look, Soph, if we're gonna do this, I'm going to need to get some sustenance. I'd like to go to the beach and maybe get a bite at that little thatched place with the fast food. There's time before we go. It's only eleven o'clock. Wanna come?"

"Not hungry. I pigged out at the barbecue. We did a total role reversal last night," she chortled. She gave me one of her sweet smiles. "Anyway, you go on. I need more coffee and a relaxed shower and Gwendolyn will probably be on time."

So I went out alone, dressed for the museum in a polo shirt, slacks, and tennis shoes. The terrace and stage were deserted, the tents, plastic chairs and tables gone, stacked almost out of sight near a shed far back from the beach. I remembered how Hegel danced, having some fun at last, and how comforting it was to dance with Sophie and finally share the secret of the bowl. The clouds were lifting, and there was every reason to think it would be a beautiful day after all. At the beach some hotel guests basked in the open on lounge chairs on the sand, a few even optimistically opening sun umbrellas. But I was still too haunted to take pleasure in the nubile bodies. Even Danielle wouldn't have distracted me.

I reached the cabaña, with its short menu posted under its thatched roof. Only one person sat at the counter on a rattan stool at one end under the eave. It was especially comforting to see this man nursing a beer and smoking a cigarette. A full pack of Marlboros lay on the counter. I had quit a few years before, but I still greatly enjoy second-hand smoke. In fact, this being out in the open, I felt I might do better than that. Sophie wasn't with me and if ever I deserved a cigarette, it was after my ordeal last night. The guy looked seasoned. Curly gray, almost white, hair over a tanned face obscured by sunglasses. Long-sleeved striped polo shirt and jeans. He looked familiar, and so calm that I felt I could strike up a conversation. If he spoke English. I remained standing as I ordered a grilled-eggplant wrap and a beer from the young fellow behind the counter in a tee shirt with the Astron Bay logo. When I got my order, I sidled deliberately down the counter and sat down on a stool not far from my new friend.

I ate my sandwich and took a good sip of my beer. I edged myself a little closer to the man and looked at him. But old Silverhair didn't look back. Frosty. I simply had to have a cigarette. "Morning," I said, "you staying here?"

He looked over, shook his head, and looked away. Rugged fellow, wrinkled. The pack of Marlboros was burning in my eyes. I figured he at least understood English. "Very nice day," I said. Half a nod. "Excuse me, but I wonder if I might borrow a cigarette."

I motioned with two fingers to my lips. Borrowing a cigarette—I knew in my heart that the cigarette would be pretty much unusable if I were ever to return it. My request was a little abrupt, but I didn't have all the time in the world to schmooze. Anyway, he seemed about as ready to schmooze as a polar bear. He looked over again and without a word slid the pack over to me. His shirt cuff rode up a little and exposed a tattoo trailing down from under his sleeve— the double tail of a serpent or whale curling around his wrist. But I was more interested in the smokes than in the curious tattoo. They came with a huge bonus: a pack of matches stuffed beneath the cellophane. I removed a cigarette with its familiar filter, wrapped in cork-like paper. I took the matches, tamped the cigarette and lit it. My hand shook a little, and I pushed the pack back to the man and said, breathing my first puff, "Thank you very much. Very much indeed. That's very kind of you."

He made no further eye contact and stuffed the pack into his shirt pocket. For a moment, I was in heaven, dizzy from the first drag. I nodded to the man. He nodded back, silent. The breath of life. A zephyr swirled around me, and I turned around on my stool and looked out over the beach and ocean, half closing my eyes. My troubles seemed far away. Nothing mattered, nothing at all.

"Red! What on *earth* are you doing!" Sophie. Judge and jailer. I took a last drag and disposed of my cigarette indelicately in the remains of my beer. As I did so, I thought dimly of giving the butt back to old Silverhair, hoping Sophie would understand that borrowing a cigarette was not the same as *having* a cigarette.

My reverie dissipated. I was back in the complicated present. "Sorry, Soph. Just had to. Bummed it from this nice fellow here." I never argue these things.

"Well, Red, I understand—*this once*—but please don't let all this start you smoking again." She was annoyed, but she knew I wasn't going to fall off the wagon. After all, I hadn't bought a whole pack of weeds. And she was cutting me some slack on account of my shock last night. "Anyway, Gwendolyn is going to be waiting, so let's go." She threw old Silvercurls a dirty look, and we took off.

We found Gwendolyn waiting in the lobby when we got there. Sophie asked her to wait a minute while she retrieved her sunglasses from our room nearby. For all of her bravado, Sophie wasn't quite her organized self on this morning.

"Good morning, Red. I do hope you're feeling better. Capital evening we had, last night, don't you think? Even if we did all go at each other a bit." Steelbuns couldn't have been more chipper while I still felt hung-over even though I'd hardly drunk anything, relatively speaking. Maybe some fresh air would do me good.

I drifted outside, to wait for Sophie under the protective overhang outside the lobby. Gwendolyn followed me out. In the drive, a black limousine stood with the driver's door open. The chauffeur was walking slowly on the other side of the vehicle on a little strip of dry grass. He emerged into full view, led by a tiny beige chihuahua on a rhinestone-studded leash. A huge pink bow with glitter on it was attached to its collar, the bow almost bigger than the mutt's head.

"How about that?" I said. "I guess they allow dogs here at Astron Bay after all—provided they're rich and housebroken." Just then the little mutt squatted on her skinny hind legs. "Looks like Chiquita qualifies on both grounds." Banter calms me down.

"To whom do you suppose it belongs?" I couldn't tell whether Gwen meant the little dog or the giant limousine. "Perhaps the resort has a Royal Suite somewhere?" I could have told her we call them presidential suites in the States, but it wouldn't surprise me if old Steelbuns was a monarchist.

Sophie appeared, and we walked to our car, still looking in wonder at the small fancy dog and her miserable chauffeur, hot in his black uniform and cap. It looked like a long afternoon for both of them. Made me feel better about hanging out at the museum. As we left, I almost braked to a stop as I thought we should have set up a trap for detecting any intrusion into our room while we were away. Maybe a chair propped in back of the door, or a string of adhesive tape attached to the door and the jamb. Too late, in any case, and if I had succeeded in rigging something and we found signs that someone had come in, what would we do? Even the maid stocking the minibar could...*Stop it, Red!* I realized we hadn't even hung our *Do Not Disturb* sign on the door handle.

With Gwen's help, we found the museum easily, parked nearby, and went in, paying a few euros at the front desk. The tour began inauspiciously enough with Gwendolyn gabbing with the ticket lady, showing off her knowledge and appreciation of ancient Cretan art. I now wished I were back at the cabaña trying to bum a second smoke from Stoneface.

As we were about to enter the first display room, who should emerge but Samira Latif with a gloomy Hegel in tow? Their sudden appearance seemed to give Gwendolyn a start. Her dinner conversation with Gabor the night before must have disturbed her even more than she let on. Hegel was no doubt bummed that his star turn at dancing failed to translate into celebrity the next day. Here he was, looking like Mom had just sprung him from detention. Mother and son were on their way out. Thanks to Samira's lack of English and Hegel's lack of social skills, we were not delayed by more than a hello and goodbye.

The museum's display rooms surrounded a central court. We went in and dutifully turned left so that we could appreciate the history of Cretan art chronologically in a clock-wise direction. A phallus-shaped Neolothic idol caught my eye in the first gallery, and I checked to see if Gwen displayed any curiosity about it. But she was happily going on about *pixides* and something called a *kernos* to a rapt Sophie. I glazed over at the little cups and bowls until a nasty flashback filled them with blood. I was grateful to tune back into Gwendolyn's lecture. She was nothing if not systematic and she knew more about the habits of people living back then than I know about the private lives of my own children. Which, granted, is *zip*.

I shuffled along behind the girls, half dozing as I usually do during shopping, operas, and company pep-talks. Soon Gwen and Sophie were oohing and aahing as I had predicted over some gold jewelry shaped into ribbons and flowers. They cooed over a hairpin that had a daisy on top. Sophie exclaimed at a tiara decorated with little goats, of all things.

Before long we entered Room II, where the great treasure of the museum stood. *"The Goddess of Myrtos,"* Gwendolyn intoned in reverence. The Minoans seem to have had a weird view of women. Mostly body, a long neck and tiny head. Unusable as a jug, which it was, and ugly as sin as an art object. It was only when old Gwen pointed out the figure's little button tits and painted pubes that I perked up and took a second look at it. But soon I climbed back into my somnolence, an uncomfortable cross between anxiety and boredom.

After an eternity of identical rooms, we were—thank the lord—nearing the end, when Gwen excused herself to go to the "loo," as she called it. This required her to retrace her steps to the entrance. Realizing that this would prolong our tour, I cursed the miserable Brit as she gangled off hurriedly in her high heels. Sophie called me over to gush at a his-and-hers joint tomb. The thought of spending eternity in the same tomb with her—or anybody else for that matter—didn't exactly thrill me. As we waited for Gwen, we checked out a case of jewelry with a weird skull wearing a wreath of golden leaves. A little late to be enjoying your honors, buddy, I thought.

We were startled to hear a loud thud and a scream in a room nearby. Sophie and I both bolted in that direction, back through an angular room with just two cases and into a larger room. Gwen lay on the floor, struggling to get up, next to a case with its top slightly ajar. We rushed over, grabbed her arms, and helped her to her feet. As we did so, a swarthy gorilla of a guard ran heavily in from the next room. No one else was nearby. The guard had a single dark eyebrow reaching over both eyes and the kind of stubbly moustache and beard Anthony Quinn wore in *Zorba the Greek*. He leaned toward us threateningly, which startled me. I expected him to be solicitous, but he was clearly more worried about his displays than any damage to Gwen. He said something in Greek but, when we looked dumb, he barked, "What happen here?" Zacharias Something-opoulos was the name on his ID badge.

Gwendolyn was rearranging her blouse and brushing her tweedy skirt down. "Oh, dear," she said, "what could I have *done*! My heel caught. Silly of me. I hope I'm all right." She straightened her glasses. "Frightfully sorry," she said to the guard, who was looking not at her but at the large floor case next to her with the lid open a crack.

"They are gone," he yelled, "It was opened." We all looked at the slightly raised lid of the display case, dumbfounded. "The figures are gone. What happened to them, the hen, the pig?" What the hell was he talking about?

Inside the case, at the front near the opening of the raised lid, four or five labels lay on the shelf, but fewer objects stood near them. I didn't get it: "Hen? Pig?"

"Animals. Terra cotta from Elounda. Where are they?" He looked at us. We looked back at him, shrugging. He took the intercom from his belt and called someone in Greek. "I have the desk call the police. Stay here with me, you." You, meaning all three of us. After saying a few words more into the phone, he was more conciliatory, but still insisted that Gwen and Sophie open their purses. They were pale and confused but did what he asked. He looked on as the women scrounged around to make the contents visible, with Sophie handing me stuff so that he could check the bottom of her tote bag.

This was weird—even in a place where 'weird' seemed to be becoming the new *normal*. How the hell did that lid get open? All the other cases looked tightly closed, with a detachable lock in a hasp on the wood or metal frame, or a built-in lock like a jewelry shop case. Gwen's fall couldn't have dislodged a lid. It made no sense. But the case was full of miniature animals: lions, tortoises, little dogs. I remembered Gwen had remarked on them when we passed the display, saying something about their symbolizing domesticity or marital fidelity. Some damned thing. But I didn't remember any empty spots. The little objects could have been popped into a purse, I supposed, but they thankfully didn't turn up in Gwen's or Sophie's.

The guard seemed satisfied that the things, whatever they looked like, weren't in the women's possession, but said we had to remain in the museum till the police came. A couple of teenagers in jeans showed up at the door of the room, but Zorba growled something at them and they stayed back and didn't enter. In a few minutes, we heard the blat-blat of a siren. Soon two uniformed policemen entered the room, followed by a solid woman, dressed in a dark skirt topped by a tailored gray tunic. She had penetrating hazel eyes and thick curly dark hair, with streaks of grey, gathered at the back.

The woman said something to Zorba in Greek, then turned and addressed us in British English, seasoned with a Greek accent. "I am Aphrodite Kensington, Inspector with the Ágios Nikólaos police. Please come with me to the front." *Aphrodite?* I asked myself, Aphrodite *Kensington?* Was this Crete, or were we on some other planet? She looked more like an Amazon than Venus in that outfit, but we all snapped to at her no-nonsense tone. Leaving the officers behind, she led us back to the entrance of the museum and into an office off the gift shop. Zorba followed us.

There, Aphrodite asked to see our identification, asked where we were staying, and jotted things down in a metal-covered notebook. After these preliminaries, she addressed Gwen. "Please. Ms. Frawley. Tell me what happened."

"I was returning from the loo…the WC," Gwen said. "I was walking across that room when I stumbled near the large case. Perhaps I wasn't looking and my shoe hooked on something, so I may have knocked against the display case when I fell." She still looked a little shaken and embarrassed. "But I can't imagine that could have opened it."

We all looked at Gwen, as puzzled as she was. She shrugged and said, "Terribly silly of me, not to be more careful with these heels." An understatement, if ever I heard one.

"And then?"

"My friends here, Mr. and Mrs. Redfield, came in and helped me up off the floor, while this *gentleman* dashed in and asked us where the little figures were." She pursed her lips as she pointed to Zorba.

Aphro's wide brow furrowed. "Did you see that pieces were missing when you fell down?" she asked Gwen.

"No, actually, I did not. Selfish of me, but I was busy wondering if I was going to break a leg or a hip as I fell." She looked pee-oed. "I do beg your pardon," she went on, "but I must say I find it astonishing that no one has yet asked whether I might be hurt. Perhaps I could be allowed to return and examine the floor before getting in touch with my barrister."

"Of course, of course." Aphro sounded apologetic. "We will take you to hospital if you believe you have an injury. But you were ambulatory when I arrived, and it did not seem inappropriate to begin my inquiry."

Gwen shook her head, and said, "I am actually all right—at least physically. But the guard quite frightened us when he rushed in shouting. How could he think I opened the case and removed the miniatures as I crashed to the floor? He even searched our *purses* as though we were thieves. I'm certain the objects were missing before I entered the room."

"I understand why you might be puzzled," Aphro said, "but since crimes that involve antiquities are my responsibility, I must treat this as a serious matter." Her accent was slightly Etonian, as though she had learned it well in high places. Maybe she was the child of a Brit, from the days the English supported the Greek government after the war?

"It is not the first time that cases have been opened and small objects removed," she explained. "We apologize for inconveniencing you, of course, but we must take fingerprints and search persons present in the museum at the time. I'm afraid this includes a body search." We all started at this, but she gave us no time to protest. "I shall search the ladies, if you will come with me," she said and led Sophie and Gwen off to the ladies' room.

With the women gone, Zorba closed the office door for privacy and turned to me. This better not involve orifices, I thought to myself, or the frigging American ambassador will hear about it. It didn't, but as Zorba was patting me down, I thought how they got this all wrong, and how I'd much rather be felt up by the mighty Aphrodite.

As the women returned I thought briefly of saying something to the Inspector about my bowlful of blood—okay, soy or ketchup, or whatever—of the night before. I'd be interested in her take on that. But as I formulated it, I realized how utterly inane it sounded and backed off, afraid of really being thought a nutcase by the Greek authorities. Anyway, there was no way that my little bathroom surprise could have anything to do with missing miniatures in a public museum. I let the moment pass.

And so, having been searched, questioned, and fingerprinted, Zorba and Aphro were assured we could not have opened the case or stolen the figures. Or, if we did, we made the tiny terra cotta critters run off and hide on their own.

We were free to go. It was now near the 4:00 closing time. We headed back, glum, to Astron Bay, hoping to recover once again in the Midas Lounge.

We never made it that far.

Chapter 9
Room Service

It was after 4:30 when we pulled into the driveway at Astron Bay. We had to wait while the long black limousine we had seen on our departure pulled past us on its way out. I'd hoped to catch a sight of the occupants or at least the overdressed chihuahua, but the windows were deeply tinted and visually impenetrable. I hate those black windows. Laguna Beach is full of limos like that, no doubt offering cool celebrity sightings if we could only see the riders inside. I was also ticked because we were anxious to get to the Midas Lounge before the free wine and cheese gave out. Lord knows we all needed a drink, and Sophie was hungry.

We walked Gwendolyn to her room a floor below us to be sure she had recovered fully from her fall and the ensuing ordeal. Before leaving her at her door, we arranged to meet in the Lounge in just a few minutes. As we reached the top of the stairs, a loud woman's scream rang through the hall we had just left. Instantly Sophie and I looked at one another as another scream, louder than the first, burst up the stairway like a siren. As we dashed back down the stairs, a third scream produced the awful words: "Help, God, help, he's still alive!!"

We caromed off the wall at the landing as we turned the corner and saw Gwen standing outside her open door flailing her arms and gasping for air between screams. Several guests in nearby rooms had opened their doors and looked out, immobilized. We reached Gwen as she sagged against the wall by her door, and propped her up even as she resisted and pushed toward the door. Her purse had fallen on her doorsill. "Oh! Oh!" she moaned in a harsh whisper. "He's still alive." We eased her down as she crumpled on her thin legs and sat on her shoes with her knees to one side. Sophie held her while Gwendolyn clutched her forehead as though struck by a massive migraine. I almost tripped on Gwen's purse on the door opening as I rushed into her room.

The ghastly scene before me is one I can't forget. A man lay on his back, his eyes bulging. He moved his head from side to side as he clutched at his throat. Blood leaked between the knuckles of his hand, and I was afraid he would choke himself trying to hold it back. Blood trickled from his mouth and his clothes were spattered red. Red spatters dotted the carpet and the side of the bedspread above his head.

I screamed, "Ambulance! Somebody call an ambulance!" A man rushed in the door behind me. It was Spiro, flushed to the scalp, eyes wide open. For a moment we both stood stone still, paralyzed as we stared at the bleeding man flinching on the floor. He rolled his head toward us, unable to focus. He almost took his hand from his throat but a spurt of blood made him clutch it again. Still he lifted his elbow as if to point to Spiro and me. "Gre...gre..." A word or a gargle? It was impossible to tell, but I finally recognized him by the part in the middle of his black hair.

"It's Nikos Gavras," I whispered hoarsely to Spiro, who looked as though he'd been punched in the face.

Spiro spun around as he heard people approach the door. He yelled at them in Greek and German. Then he shouted at Heidi whose accent I recognized in the confusion of responses. Then he was gone, the door pulled partly closed behind him.

By now I was kneeling next to Nikos, whose throat produced another gargle, and reached forward to help him stanch the blood. At that his eyes bulged in terror as though I might be reaching to strangle him. "I just want to help," I whispered. I reached behind his head and shoulder, lifting him so he could breathe more easily. The motion caused his hand to shift from his throat. It had been slit at the Adam's apple. He gagged. A gout of blood spewed from the opening in his throat onto the rug. I recoiled. He slid out of my arms onto his back. A last, awful gargle escaped his wound. Without another movement or spasm, his body was still. Nikos Gavras lay unblinking, staring at the slowly rotating ceiling fan.

I knelt there a full minute, nauseated and shivering at the dreadful sight. I was kneeling in Nikos's blood, and I used my arms, fists in the blood, to help me stand up. My breathing was so shallow I could hardly get any air. I struggled to an overturned desk chair across the room between the window and the door to the terrace. It had been knocked away from the small table against the wall. I righted it and sat down, my knees trembling, facing the armoire by the bed.

I was intensely aware that I was alone in the room, if you discounted the inert figure on the floor. I was shaken by Nikos's valiant struggle to dam the blood inside his body, to hold his throat together while trying to tell us…what? A name? An explanation? What?

The late afternoon light fell through the window at the east. At times of stress and doubt, I focus on small things to stay lucid. Gwendolyn's suitcases stood inside her closet next to tidy rows of high-heeled shoes. The drawers and doors of the armoire were closed, and two piles of books were stacked neatly on her table. Even the notebooks and papers and pens were aligned as though she were expecting guests. I hoped that these images would be all I would remember later, erasing what I had seen and done when I came into the room. In the back of my mind I concluded it must have been a brief struggle, violent as it was.

The door burst open and Spiro rushed in, followed by a large fair-haired man in resort clothes with a leather bag. I could hear the distant music of a siren. The man, a doctor probably roused from his guest room and pressed into service, I guessed, moved toward the body on the floor and knelt down. His bulky back obscured my view for a few minutes, but when he looked up at Spiro and me, he shook his head. He never opened his bag. As he looked at me for the first time, he did a double take. His wide blue eyes stared at the blood on my knees and hands, and I feared he thought he was looking at the killer. He spun to look at Spiro, who gave him a reassuring look. At that, I felt I could leave. Nikos needed no more help from me, and Spiro and the good doctor were in charge now. The siren song intensified as it came closer. As I turned toward the door Spiro warned, "Don't touch anything, sir! The police are on their way." He pushed past me and opened the door with a handkerchief draped over his fingers. I admired his professionalism, given his relationship to the dead man.

In the hall, Gwendolyn was still sitting on the carpet with Sophie beside her. Her purse had been retrieved and she was holding a handkerchief to her eyes, her glasses in her other hand. I thought how weird it was that we got to see Gwendolyn sitting on her bony butt on the floor twice in one afternoon. But there was little other commotion since some staff members were strategically placed to turn guests away toward the elevator or the lounge. A few curiosity seekers were slow to comply and I could hear occasional voices, barely audible and whispery. The operative code word in their explanations was "accident."

I wondered if hotels have a protocol for handling…such things…or if Spiro just had preternatural calm and management skills. I refused to give what I had seen a name. The siren wail had reached a crescendo outside and stopped abruptly. A disoriented janitor equipped with bucket and mop emerged from the elevator. I imagined Heidi at the desk calling the clean-up crew in advance of the medics in yellow jackets, who at last bounded around the corner from the stairs, carrying a light gurney. We now helped Gwen up, along with her purse, to make room in the hallway outside the fateful door.

For the second time today, this afternoon, in fact, we heard the blat-blat of a police siren as cruisers pulled up to the door outside the sixth-floor lobby upstairs. Four uniformed officers came down the stairs and made their way past us to Gwen's room. Twisting his moustache, our pal Spiro, all nervous dignity, opened the door to let them in. Through the crack in the door we could see the yellow-suited ambulance crew crouching on the floor around the body, and the doctor standing over them looking on. The four policemen crowded into the room with them, and in the midst of a tangle of Greek voices we saw the occasional flash of a camera as the police began their work.

A moment later, emerging from the stairs and striding down the hall toward us, we saw—Inspector Aphrodite Kensington. Aphrodite Kensington, phone on her belt, metal notebook in her hand, and sunglasses propped on her head over her gray-streaked curls. An instrument in a black case hung by its strap from her shoulder. She opened her eyes wide as she saw me. "You were just at the museum!" she said, clearly caught off guard. "What are you doing here?"

"I think I just killed a man," I blurted. Sophie took one look at me, her mouth open as the pupils of her eyes glided upward, and fell to the floor in a dead faint.

Chapter 10
Inspector Aphrodite Kensington

Luckily there were medics right there in the room, so it didn't take long for one of them to break open a vial of ammonia under Sophie's nose. She coughed and gasped and a second later opened her eyes. I recognized the smell, which stung my nose and throat as I bent over Sophie, propping her in my arms. Her face was deathly white, and even her freckles looked bleached. I remembered that Sophie hadn't eaten all day. She'd skipped breakfast, and the late lunch we might have enjoyed in Agnik never materialized because of Gwen's fall and the weird disappearance of the little animals in the museum. Did that occur just a few hours ago? I couldn't believe that it was still the same day. It was as if time had become elastic, and this awful day—followed by the gruesome surprise here at the hotel—stretched into infinity like the universe itself.

After Sophie could get to her feet, Aphro delivered some Greek instructions. One of the medics walked us to the elevator, guiding Sophie under one elbow, while another escorted Gwendolyn. When we reached the lobby, I hoped they'd take Sophie and me to our room, but the medics steered the three of us into Spiro's office behind the registration desk. Here we go again with another interrogation, I thought. This can't be happening twice in one day. All of us were in a daze, having no idea what we would be doing now. We were settled in the office, which was blessed with a sofa and comfortable armchairs around a coffee table. Gwendolyn slumped into the armchair and we sat down on the sofa next to her. Sophie assured the medic that she was all right, and he left to fetch a portly staff member who offered us something to drink. I told him that my wife had just fainted and would need some crackers or something to eat. For myself I asked for a martini, but he politely ignored this. Our beverage choice was water, tea, coffee or lemonade.

Sophie rallied enough to ask, "What the hell did you mean when you said you killed a man, Red? You nearly gave me a heart attack!" The policeman, who had sat down in the corner, pricked up his ears.

"I'm in shock, Sophie." How could I tell her about Nikos's ghastly death struggle when she'd hardly recovered from her own shock? I noticed Gwen wasn't reacting to anything. Neither of the women were ready for this tale of horror, and anyway, the cop was listening. "Let's wait till the Inspector gets here before I say more."

Mercifully the waiter returned with a large plate of cookies and zwieback, a pot of hot tea for Sophie and Gwen, and a steaming cup of hot black coffee for me. The coffee did its job, and my head slowly cleared enough to focus on the bigger picture. How the hell did a mortally wounded Nikos Gavras get into Gwen's room? From all we knew, she'd never heard of Nikos before our adventure with the bowls, and here Sophie and I were, five days into our stay, knowing both of them. I clutched vainly at the connection between Madame and Nikos as though it was a life preserver, but I trembled as I looked into our own black hole.

When Aphro arrived with a second policeman, she asked how we were feeling. Gracious lady, she is. "My superior will be here soon," she continued, "but he will be busy in the room downstairs. I know you have had a traumatic day, but I will need to take statements from you while your memories are fresh." She sat down by the desk and took the instrument from her shoulder, which turned out to be a tape recorder. One of the policemen set it up and punched a key to record. The drill would be more elaborate than the one at the museum. After all, even in Greece, the dead merit more attention than ancient clay animals.

"Now Mr. Redfield. We had best begin with your statement, that you believed you killed a man. Did you intend to make a confession?"

I'd tried to formulate an answer to this question, but I was as addled now as I was when I came out of Gwen's room. "I was speaking rhetorically," I said, realizing that didn't make any sense. "I mean, I was speaking literally." Brilliant. I had just confessed to the murder a second time. Gwen, roused from her stupor, looked like she couldn't believe her ears. Sophie looked as if she was about to faint again.

"Let me just describe what happened in the room," I pleaded, "then you'll see what I mean. I saw a man on the floor with his hand clutching his throat and blood coming from his mouth and between his fingers. He looked as if he was trying to hold tight to the wound, like a tourniquet, you know? Like he could stop himself from bleeding to death if he could just hold his hand there tight enough. But at the same time, he was choking himself, if that makes any sense?"

The three women all looked horrified, though Aphro quickly restored her face to its severe calm. I went on. "Spiro was right behind me and the man looked as though he was going to try to say something, but he had to keep a grip on his own throat. I yelled for an ambulance and knelt down to raise him up a little, but that made him lose his grip on his neck. A huge clot of blood came out of his mouth and I nearly dropped him."

I was living the vivid scene all over again, and I realized why I had blurted out what I did. "As soon as his hand was moved, he went still and was dead. I felt I might have killed him by making him lose his grip on his wound." My voice quavered and I stood up and went to the other end of the room with my back to the women. I was nauseated once more and wondered whether I'd ever be all right.

One of the young cops came over and guided me back to the sofa. Sophie opened her arms to receive me. Aphro's voice was subdued. "Mr. Redfield, we will get a medical examiner's report soon. But the preliminary opinion is that someone slit the man's windpipe, missing both the jugular and the carotid artery. He had lost a great deal of blood by the time you and Mr. Santas arrived in the room. He could not have survived much longer."

Thank you, I mouthed silently, thank you. Never had I needed reassurance more. I don't handle guilt easily.

The Inspector continued in her calming voice. "I appreciate your account. It will help in the coroner's estimate of the time of the murder."

I was shocked when I heard the last word. Incredible as it sounds, I hadn't really let the idea of murder penetrate. Even while we were waiting for the police to arrive, I never pictured another person in the room with Nikos. My scientific training makes me reluctant to draw conclusions before all the facts are in. Comes in handy for the practice of denial.

"Are you sure Nikos was murdered?" Stupid question. My cluelessness was fading, but I wanted to hear her say it again for the record.

Sophie gasped, and Gwen stiffened. Aphro looked at me, lightning in her eyes. "You know who he is?" The realization flooded in—how could she know that we knew him? And no one had yet revealed the victim's identity to Sophie or Gwen—including, I now realized, me.

"Uh…yes, it was Nikos Gavras, the owner of a shop in Ágios Nikólaos."

"How do you know Mister Gavras?" Aphro raised her eyebrows, her hazel eyes intense and penetrating. I wanted to say that practically everybody in Crete seemed to know Nikos Gavras, but thought better of it.

"Um. Well," I mumbled, "That's a long story. We bought some goods from him a few days ago in Agnik. In fact, he sort of put one over on us." I didn't like where this might go and my bloody right knee began bobbing up and down. Restless leg syndrome, they call it on TV.

"Forgive me, but I am not certain I understand. Do you mean he cheated you?"

I felt a net drawing around me. "Look, Ms. Kensington, I don't think our shop transaction with Mr. Gavras could possibly have anything to do with this. Everybody knows that Madame Delphinos and Nikos Gavras were feuding about the publication of her memoir. You should be talking to her and Spiro Santas instead of worrying about our shopping trip."

Aphrodite Kensington winced. Sophie glared at me. I'd just made a big mistake. My petulant tone could only serve to tick the Inspector off—plus, I'd just tried to implicate Madame and Spiro.

I braced myself for the Inspector's reaction, but she kept her cool. "Mister Redfield, everyone will be interviewed in due time. Right now I am simply gathering as much information as the first witnesses can provide." She paused as I settled down and went on. "Now, you say you met Mister Gavras in the city?"

"Yes, we went to his shop the day after we arrived and bought some silver bowls that turned out to be just silver plated. Sophie here went back next day to return them, but he wouldn't give us a refund." I prayed that she wouldn't ask about the frigging receipt.

Luckily, Aphro now turned to Gwen for the first time. "Were you with the Redfields on their visits to the Gavras shop?" Gwen shook her head. "I've never met him, and I didn't know who the dead man was until now."

"Did you learn of Mister Redfield's unhappy experience in the shop?"

Gwen looked at me, embarrassed, and nodded. "I was the one who told him that four of the bowls were plate."

Aphro persisted, "Was Mister Redfield upset about being cheated?" It was my turn to be irked. Shouldn't she be asking *me* how I felt? Gwen nodded uncomfortably.

"What exactly did he say?" Aphro pushed.

Gwen burst into tears. "He said he'd like to kill the bastard," she blurted out, and then blubbered, "Do forgive me. I don't want to say that, but that's what he said." She put her hands to her face and her bony shoulders shook for a moment before she lowered them again, her glasses askew, her face red.

Before I could say anything, Sophie piped up with impressive calm. "Inspector Kensington, my husband was upset with Mister Gavras, but he knew we were partly to blame, because I accepted a receipt fixed for a much smaller amount than we'd paid. If Red blamed anyone, it was me. That's why he didn't come along next day when I tried to get a refund. I was the one who had a testy exchange with Mister Gavras, but nothing happened. His sister Elena was there during both conversations with him. You can talk to her and ask her."

"That will have to wait. First we will need to notify her that her brother has been murdered," Aphro said quietly. Oh dear. I remembered Sophie saying Elena was recently widowed. This would be a second blow to the poor woman. Husband and brother, both gone.

Aphro turned off the tape recorder. It was six-thirty by now and she must have realized that she wasn't going to get much more out of her three exhausted witnesses. Gwendolyn still couldn't bear to look at me.

"It has been a difficult day for all of you," Aphro said. "We will need to talk again, but you are free to go now, although I must ask for your passports. However, please remain in the hotel until we take further statements tomorrow."

We went to our room with our escort without saying goodbye to Gwendolyn. We surrendered our passports to the handsome cop, and after he left, I got out of my clothes, wrapped my pants and shirt in a towel and stuck them under the bed till I could throw them away. I took a long shower, almost wanting to shed my skin. Sophie and I sat for a while, not knowing what to say to one another. We had to get something to eat, since Sophie was beginning to feel faint again. Both of us—at least, I—also really needed a drink.

I tried to phone Spiro to ask for an exceptional room service for Sophie, but neither he nor Heidi were at the desk. The person who answered at registration spoke only halting English and failed to understand me. We had to go down to the dining room.

We arrived, got a table, and ordered a double martini for me and a full bottle of Chardonnay for the two of us. Twelve steps or no twelve steps, we needed the extra to take back to our room for later. As we finally gathered our wits enough to go over everything, a voice spoke softly behind me. It was Danielle Tanner, with Lyle. They had just returned from their cruise and felt lucky to have made it back in time for dinner. They looked relaxed and well tanned in their light sporty linens, like people from a different, sunny planet.

As they made motions and moves to join us, Sophie blurted out, "Something terrible has happened!"

"Really? What on earth?" said Danielle.

"Oh, it's *awful*! I hardly know where to start. A murder!" A few people at tables near us turned their heads. They must have heard about the *accident* by now, but not the full scoop, by the look of it.

"Shh," I said to Sophie. I turned to the Tanners, trying to be deliberate because I remembered that this would be a shock for Danielle as well. "It is hard to believe. I hardly believe it happened even now. But when we came back from the museum, Gwen found *Nikos Gavras*…well…*dying* in her room!

I was right. Danielle looked appalled, and so, to my surprise, did Lyle. I figured I'd best spill the news quickly and get it over with and so told them what we knew. "The police questioned us and I don't know what's going to happen. We can tell you more tomorrow, maybe. We're recovering and Gwen is still with the police." Sophie looked into space as though something had just become clear. "They'll have to give her a new room, won't they?"

"Good heavens," said Danielle again, as Lyle looked on, troubled and stern, his bald head reddening. Gone was the sleepy look. His eyes were more open than I'd ever seen them.

"Poor Gwen." Danielle's dark blue eyes narrowed in sympathy. "Is she all right? Can we do anything to help?" Poor *Gwen*? I had expected Danielle would be more shocked about Nikos Gavras, whom she'd known for some years, and whom she'd defended to all of us as a nice, honorable guy. She just met Gwen a week or two ago, at most. But I guess it's natural to identify more with the living than the dead.

"There's nothing to do," I told her, and took a big sip of my martini. "We all just have to stay around. That's about all we know. But I hope you don't mind if Sophie and I eat by ourselves. We've got to talk and settle down." I didn't want an audience when I gave Sophie the full account of my dreadful time with poor bleeding, dying Nikos.

The Tanners understood, tactfully taking a table some distance away. Slowly I filled Sophie in on the events in Gwen's room, and Sophie filled me in on the simultaneous action in the hall outside. We both picked at our meals, urging each other to eat, yet eating little in spite of our hunger. As we left to go to our room, we jealously saw the Tanners, subdued, but enjoying their seafood platters. A day on the ocean, once the sun came out, would make anyone quiet and happy.

Back at our room, we went out on the terrace and sat for a bit, finishing the remains of the wine. We talked of all the things we'd have to tell Aphro in the morning. A great weariness came over us. As we collapsed into bed, we remembered the only good thing that had come out of this whole miserable day. Madame's problems with her memoir were resolved. Half in a dream, I perversely pictured Madame's salon, Zoë pouring champagne, and Madame and Spiro clinking crystal flutes in triumph.

Chapter 11
Serious Questions

Sophie and I woke up, still shaken from the previous day's events. This would be another hard day. We had a date with Inspector Kensington after breakfast with no time to bone up for the exam. That's probably what the mighty Aphrodite wanted. A chance to work us like a therapist looking for the important in the trivial, for veiled meanings and hidden clues. I hadn't been this nervous since my thesis orals. My wish was to leave the Inspector clueless, to coin a phrase, and either get out of Astron Bay or out of Greece entirely in the next day or two.

Nothing would be that simple, of course. I literally had had blood on my hands the day before. I had signaled my wish for revenge, to "kill the bastard," which Gwen had been good enough to stress to the Inspector. Did Gwen have to report it with such theatrical anguish? The woman was a drama queen. But then I suppose Gwendolyn had a right to be unhinged. Finding a bowl of blood in your hotel room was bad enough. Finding a man with a throat full of blood in your room was worse. And at least Sophie and I had each other for support.

"Sophie, don't let me forget to tell Aphro about the bloody bowl I found in the bathroom the night of the barbecue. It may fit in with everything else somehow."

From the bed, where I was sipping my second cup of coffee, I could see Sophie in front of the bathroom mirror. I tried not to look at the counter where I'd gotten my barbecue surprise the night before last. The memory took on a strange intensity now that I had seen copious amounts of the real red stuff the day before, with a cruel reminder of where it comes from.

Sophie came back into the room and poured herself a cup of coffee, all the while frowning. "Red, I've been trying to imagine that story, and it just won't compute. You can tell the Inspector what you told me, but you have absolutely no way to back it up. You have no evidence, you obliterated all signs of the liquid, and you have no witness to corroborate your story. If Aphro asks me to tell her what I know about it, I'll have to say the room looked perfectly normal when we came back from the barbecue."

"Would you really say that?" I felt shocked, like at a betrayal.

"I'd have to, Red. It's the truth. And to tell you the truth, I've wondered if you didn't just imagine that whole fantastic scene. Are you sure you didn't have a second double martini before the barbecue?"

Her emphatic tone reminded me that what I had done with the bowl of blood was about as stupid as a bank robber trying to return his loot in the night deposit slot. I felt guilty erasing the whole incident and then saying nothing about it. Secrets fester, and I wished I had mentioned it at the barbecue. But then, what would I have said? "Hey, guys, I found one of our silver bowls filled with blood in our bathroom. Who do you suppose did that?" Sophie was right: I was probably crazy, and I'd be even crazier to bring it up.

On our way to the dining room, we walked through the lobby. It was alive with activity. The buzz of the throng told us that word of the murder had gotten out, and rumors were spreading like prairie fire. The entire hotel seemed to have been secured, with a half dozen policemen about. Spiro, moustachio quivering, flitted around the lobby trying to appease the guests who wanted to leave for the day and especially those who needed to check out entirely for the morning plane to Athens. We looked at the latter enviously. "Madame Delphinos apologizes to you for this inconvenience," Spiro said repeatedly, as though Madame had miscalculated the trouble a murder would cause.

The breakfast room was just as electric, people whispering urgently to one another. I was relieved that no one stared at me when I entered; I didn't want people to connect me with the murder. But there were the Tanners, plainly anxious to see us, waving us over to eat with them. We would of course be the most reliable people to talk to, given that Nikos had more or less died in my arms. I still couldn't help thinking I might've killed him while trying to help. I didn't really want to join the Tanners, but this would be a brief meal and tables were scarce. So Sophie and I went to the buffet for an uncharacteristic Continental breakfast, in spite of how little we'd eaten the day before. If this kept up, I was going to actually end up *losing* weigh on this vacation.

A decanter of coffee awaited us at the Tanner's table. "So, good buddy, tell us about your ordeal." Lyle hadn't lost his sleepy, mocking smirk nor his exquisite lack of tact. I noted that their breakfast was even more low-cal than ours. Lo-fat yogurt, whole-grain cereal, fresh fruit, creamless coffee. I hate those crunchy-granola types.

"It must be terrible to find yourself mixed up in this." Unlike her husband, Danielle's purring voice carried concern. For a moment my libido flickered.

"I'm all right," I said, giving her a woebegone look. Might as well milk her sympathy. In truth, I was about as all right as a witness to an execution. Shoot, the day before I practically *was* a witness to an execution!

"Do you feel comfortable telling us about it?" Danielle put five slender fingertips on my arm. "There's much talk going on, but we don't understand what people are saying. I wish I knew German."

I gave them a sketch of the events in the fewest words possible. When I came to Nikos's struggle, I stopped. I really couldn't talk about this at frigging breakfast.

"What on earth was Nikos doing there? And how did anyone get into Gwendolyn's room?" Danielle brushed her sweep of blonde hair to one side. "It doesn't make any sense." Tell me about it, I thought. I'd seen a bowl of guck in my bathroom that didn't make much sense either, but I kept that to myself.

"Well, we all know *somebody* who would have had access to all the rooms, don't we?" Lyle's voice drawled. I could tell Sophie didn't like his tone. "Do you mind if I smoke?" Without waiting for an answer, Lyle took a Danish cigar from its tin and lit it. I didn't mind a bit. Blow some smoke my way, fella, and it'll be all right with me. Sophie glowered but didn't say anything.

"I mean, it's pretty obvious what's going on after all that feuding between Madame what's-her-name and Nikos Gavras."

"Nothing's obvious to me." Sophie's voice was uncharacteristically sharp. "What are you saying?" She's a stickler about calling people on innuendo when she hears it.

Lyle leaned forward across the table toward us and lowered his voice to a smoky rasp. "Think about it. Nikos and the old lady are having a blow-up about her memoir. Santas invites Nikos to the resort to meet and talk about it. He needs an unoccupied room and sees you guys going off with Gwen. *Voilà*, they walk into Gwen's room and Nikki gets his throat slit. Piece of cake."

"That's ridiculous!" Sophie put her coffee cup down with a clatter. "Spiro may have been angry at Nikos, but he's not stupid. Why would he risk ruining his business and draw attention to himself as a suspect? The *only* suspect, if he does it here." Sophie was so indignant that I had to shush her before everyone nearby heard her. "It's completely crazy," she whispered.

If Lyle took umbrage, he didn't show it. He looked lazily at his Rolex, gauging if it was time to leave, took a puff of his little cigar, and let his point stand. But Danielle, who had been studying her pearl-painted nails during the exchange, now leaned toward Sophie and spoke to her in an urgent whisper.

"We have reason to think there's much more to it than that." That got our attention. "They say that Nikos was threatening to reveal an embarrassing family secret if the memoir wasn't stopped. Apparently he was going to go public with the information that Spiro Santas is actually Madame's illegitimate son."

Sophie choked on her coffee, and I too was dumbfounded. "Where on earth did you get *that*?" I was mentally calculating if the ages added up, and decided they did.

"On our cruise yesterday. Someone mentioned it. He was born in Switzerland, Spiro, I mean. Apparently Madame gave the baby to a friend of the family to bring up. It may be a rumor, but you never know." Danielle shrugged and took a bite of her last strawberry, holding the stem delicately with three fingers. "But it makes sense, doesn't it? That she'd want to cover something like this up and yet still have Spiro around later to take care of things when her husband died."

She leaned back and let this new information sink in, studying us with her indigo eyes. Secrets do fester, I thought to myself, the second time that morning. And even Sophie, who looked intensely unhappy, clearly found the speculation difficult to refute.

"Pardon me, Mr. and Mrs. Redfield." The voice behind us came from the young officer who had been with the Inspector yesterday. Good looking dude. "I am Stavros Marcaris, Inspector Kensington's assistant. She has asked me to bring you to the conference room off the Midas Lounge when you have finished your coffee."

Sophie looked back at Adonis and gave him a dimpled smile. "We're ready to go." We took abrupt leave of the Tanners and went to meet the formidable Goddess of the Inquest. A vague guilty feeling was coming back as we approached the conference room, and my stomach knotted as it did when I was led to the principal's office from my third grade classroom. On that occasion, I had farted in class, and I remember the lady principal as even more Olympian than Aphro.

94

The conference room was large and oblong with many chairs around a long oval table. Aphro sat at one end with her equipment and greeted us cheerfully as we walked in. There were no windows, and a large full-color aerial photo of the Astron Bay Resort made me wish all the more that we were out on the beach rather than stuck in here. Or in an airplane taking a last picture as we left.

"Please have a seat," she said, gesturing to nearby chairs. The Inspector looked surprisingly unofficial this morning. She wore a long black dress, cinched at her waist with a belt of silver squares, each with a different classical design. If the outfit was meant to put us at ease, it didn't.

She started the tape recorder, which hummed softly thereafter, and opened her metal notebook. We went over the whole silver bowl fiasco with her again. Conflicted, I omitted the peculiar use to which our one silver bowl had been put. When Sophie got to her second trip back to the Gavras shop, she remembered to tell Aphro about Nikos's phone conversation, apparently making a date at Astron Bay with someone—in English.

This clearly interested the Inspector. "To your knowledge, is there anyone else at Astron Bay who knows Nikos Gavras?" I'd already blundered by mentioning Madame and Spiro the night before, so I didn't name them now. But we had to mention Danielle. I felt like a rat saying that the lovely Danielle Tanner knew Nikos better and longer than any of us.

"Did you see Mrs. Tanner anywhere before you left on your museum trip yesterday? Breakfast? The pool, the beach?"

"No. We didn't see them till dinner yesterday, after you questioned us. They'd been on a cruise and hadn't heard about the murder."

"Did they say where? Where they went?" Aphro asked.

Sophie answered. "No, but it may have been off the beaten track." She turned to me. "Didn't they say they were going to charter a boat from that skipper they were talking to before the barbecue?"

"Something like that." I was blank on the Tanners' destination, but I remembered the skipper, sort of. I looked at Aphro. "You should know that Danielle said only good things about Nikos when we talked about him. She defended him even when she heard our silver bowl story. Created a bit of conflict since we frankly disliked him after that… And so did Wally," I added.

Sophie's glare functioned like a kick under the table. Had I reinforced the idea that we had a motive, or had I stupidly brought Wally into the picture?

Aphro looked at us shrewdly, understanding our body language. She pressed on. "This individual you just mentioned. This is someone who also knew Mr. Gavras?"

Sophie, bless her, intervened. "Oh, Wally. He's a sweet Australian fellow who wanted a reproduction of an antique piece and got different quotes for it from Nikos and the shopgirl. Or was it Elena? We met him afterwards at lunch. What was his last name, Red?"

"Peacock, something like that. I have it here." I looked in my wallet for his card. "Pinnock."

"May I see the card?"

I handed it to Aphro, who read the name and smiled. I guess it is a funny name. She made a note and handed it back to me. "I believe this takes care of my questions. Is there anything I can answer for you?"

Sophie looked thoughtful for a moment and shuffled in her seat in her Capri pants. "Well, yes, I do," she said looking directly at the Inspector. "I'd like to know who was in that big limousine that was here yesterday afternoon. We saw it as we headed off to the museum, and it was leaving just as we came back."

"Sophie's right," I said. "The limousine was here during the time of the murder in the afternoon. We saw it before we left and it was just pulling out when we came back. Who came in it?"

Aphro was not forthcoming. "I am sorry. But I cannot discuss other aspects of our investigation."

Sophie was not put off so easily. "Well, you know, this might be very important. If Nikos kept an appointment with someone here at Astron Bay, it makes it look as though the killer could be a guest."

"Or someone who works here," I interjected. I couldn't seem to get Spiro out of my mind. Lyle's insinuation was weaving its way into my brain, whatever Sophie thought. My face must have turned red, because Sophie came to the rescue.

"What Red is saying is that it's pretty scary to think that there might be a killer on the premises." She squirmed in her seat again. "That's why we're a little freaked out at being locked down here today. It means we're potentially trapped in the hotel with a killer."

Sophie was right, but I didn't get what she was driving at. "That's why I asked about the limousine," she went on. "Here's someone from outside who comes to the hotel for the exact interval we were away and during which Nikos Gavras was murdered. Could the limo have brought a hit man here?"

At this Inspector Kensington gave a most unprofessional snort of laughter, though she quickly regained her composure. "Forgive me, Mrs. Redfield, I do apologize. Your concerns are completely reasonable. But the image of a hit man in a limousine with a chauffeur and a tiny Mexican dog…" The thought tickled her funny bone again and she again had to compose herself. "We actually do know the identity of the mystery guest, but we cannot release it to the public."

Sophie looked embarrassed and a little annoyed. "Okay," she said, "but it would be helpful to know who it was. Mysteries like this don't help us feel more secure."

Aphro, trying to make up for her amused lapse assured Sophie solemnly that the place was crawling with security forces. I don't think it occurred to Sophie that the other guests would want protection from *me*, if they knew *my* role in the business.

The Inspector closed her notebook. The interview seemed to have ended. "We are allowing some guests to leave the hotel today, once we've verified their destinations with passports and tickets. But because you are witnesses, please stay in the resort for the rest of the day." She made it sound like an honor. "Hopefully, by tomorrow you may be free to move normally." Not exactly. *Normally* means we'd have our passports and could get the hell out of here, like the crowd in the lobby.

"Well, it'll be a relief to leave the hotel tomorrow," Sophie told her. "We only have two weeks of vacation here and this first week hasn't turned out very well." She can say that again. We've enjoyed a crook with a slit throat, blood all over the floor and my hands, his sneaky deal with the bowls, one of which turned up with fake blood, and let's not forget the Basket-napping. Oh yes, and a sweet little museum trip that ended with a Greek gorilla putting his paws on my privates. And that was just the beginning of our wonderful, sun-drenched vacation in beautiful Astron Bay!

Sophie went on. "We haven't seen any of the sights yet and we're dying to get to Gournia and Elounda, and Knossos, and down the coast to Pachia Ammos and beyond. We hear there's a new dig down there that we'd love to see, although it's apparently not open." Who's *we*, Tinkerbell?

"Actually, it's an old excavation," Aphro said. "They are taking a last look for ruins before the airport is built in that location. We generally restrict such sites because they are magnets for looters. I arrested a small ring of Germans five years ago who were mining and removing antiquities near there."

"Yes, we know about the controversy over the airport," Sophie said. "Gwendolyn Frawley got into a big argument with Gabor Latif at the barbecue the night before last. She accused his company of destroying the site and interfering with the archeological work."

Aphro opened her notebook again, asking, "Who was that?" Nice work, Sophie, ratting out another of our friends.

"He's a Turkish fellow with the engineering company working on the airport," I said. "Gabor Latif, with a German firm. Gwendolyn Frawley has a bee in her bonnet about him." I was getting a bee in mine. It was time to go.

Aphro noted the name in her book, and we confirmed that he was a guest at the hotel. "My main professional responsibility is looking into the underground trade in buried antiquities," she volunteered. Was that a joke? Underground trade? Were we seeing more of her sense of humor?

"Then you're not a homicide detective?" I asked.

"Not primarily, although I have dealt with murder more than once since I became Inspector."

"So why were you assigned to this case?" I asked.

"Nikos Gavras dealt in replicas of antiquities. And you yourselves are involved in that other unsolved mystery." We looked baffled, and Aphro, surprised that we didn't get it, raised her eyebrows. "The animal figures missing from the museum yesterday. You have no further ideas about that museum theft, do you?"

"Not a one," I said, frankly pissed. The phrase 'museum theft' sounded like an accusation. I tend to forget things like that after a man dies at my knees. Give me a break, woman. I now realized that Aphro had been questioning us all the time. All this background talk was still being recorded.

"You know," I said, "a lot of people are saying that Spiro Santas is the killer! They've heard about the memoir feud, which was in the paper a while back. And now they're saying that Spiro might have silenced Nikos for trying to blackmail him."

Aphro was clearly displeased at this news. "Where did you hear this? Who is saying this?" She opened her notebook again.

"Um…" People. Two people, I guess, to be perfectly accurate. "The Tanners told us. At breakfast. They heard it on their trip yesterday."

"Go on." Aphro stopped jotting and held the pen up, waiting for more.

"Well…what they heard made it sound as though Nikos was threatening to reveal that Spiro is Madame's…well, you know, her…what do they call it nowadays, her *natural* son."

Aphro scowled. "I hope this rumor stops with you. It is very difficult to clarify wrong information that damages the reputation of innocent people."

Innocent people? "How can you be sure Santas is innocent! He's been raging at Nikos to everybody in earshot ever since we got here, claiming that the guy's been making threats to Madame. And here we are with a fu…with an airtight alibi—an alibi you yourself can swear to—and we end up having to spend hours defending ourselves."

I knew I'd lost it by the sight of Sophie's horrified look and Aphro's surprise. But I just couldn't stand all this bullshit anymore.

"I think one way or another you're going to make sure it's not a Greek who gets nailed for this—that's why you're harassing only us foreigners." As soon as I said it, I knew that was irrational and I instantly mumbled an apology, pleading shock from my trauma yesterday, and at least getting clucking noises out of Sophie.

But the interview was over, and I left the conference room a chastened man. As I reached the door, Aphro added a postscript to our interview. "If you go touring tomorrow, do be careful in Pachia Ammos."

I turned around. "Why?" I asked.

"There has been some sabotage at the airport exploration sites and security is not perfect there."

Chapter 12
Gabor Has a Problem

The waves lapped the shore with a slow rhythm. The sun stood behind the umbrella and I inhaled a deep cloud of cigarette smoke, exhaling exultantly as the warm breeze blew the smoke inland toward the cabaña. A guy with silver hair smiled approvingly at me, before Sophie and I boarded the helicopter that rose slowly off the beach above Astron Bay. The resort spread out below us like an aerial map. Tangled lanes marked a hedge-lined labyrinth, where tiny figures skulked along the paths, pouncing around corners and preying on each other. A crocodile, a weasel, a stork, a walrus, a cat, and a hobbit. A poodle and a chihuahua raced around among them. The helicopter went silent and fell away from us, leaving us to plunge into the Aegean. Miraculously, Sophie and I sprouted wings to fly away from this accursed island. Sophie, giddy with pleasure at being aloft, flew closer and closer to the sun which melted her wings and then… I awoke in terror.

I was in bed, breathing into Sophie's hair. What time was it? More to the point, what day was it? The day before had been so clouded by the unpleasant ending of our morning interview with Inspector Kensington that we never recovered. Sophie didn't reproach me for my foolish accusation because she judged that the murder had left me unhinged—a bit more unhinged than usual, at any rate. I, in turn, had caught her point that a murderer might be on the loose among us here in Astron Bay. What should have been a day of blessed indolence on the beach turned into an oppressive experience of house arrest that I resented like a grounded teenager. Especially now that Astron Bay felt like a dangerous place. I was spooked by every noise on the water, every shout at the pool, the shadow cast by every waiter who approached asking if we wanted a drink. I scrutinized the face of every guest for a sinister sign or a knowing grimace, including the few nubile young women who sunned on towels on the beach. My Merl Reagle Crossword puzzle remained unsolved, and *Twilight in the Ruins* lay in the sand unread. I did nothing all day except exert myself mentally to keep us alive—and wish I had a cigarette. Dinner alone with just the two of us was no better, as Sophie and I obsessively rehashed the murder and the interrogations—continuing into the small hours when we finally turned out the light. No wonder my sleep was beset by angst and turbulence.

But this morning the sun was shining, in contrast to yesterday's mood. And a phone call from Aphro's office told us that we were free to leave the resort—if not the island.

"We're going to stop moping and get on with our lives today," Sophie announced firmly as we headed out to breakfast, having decided to skip coffee in the room. "We need to get out of here and clear our heads of all this miserable business. Maybe we can get Gwen to go with us to Gournia or Elounda." Instead, we found only Gabor Latif and Hegel, among our acquaintances in the dining room. "I'm going to ask them about this Pachia Ammos thing the Inspector warned us about," Sophie said as she headed to their table.

Gabor glumly invited us to join them, looking about the way I felt yesterday. "Samira stay in room ill with worry," he explained when Sophie inquired about her absence after pouring us a round of coffee. "The Inspector talk to us about murder for an hour yesterday." Sophie frowned in distress at this news. Well, she did sort of gratuitously rat him out in our own interview, albeit only to show off what she knew about the airport controversy. "We tell her Samira and Hegel visit Museum in Ágios Nikólaos and have late lunch in city on day of murder. But when she ask me where I was, I tell her here—in my room at hotel." He knitted his bushy brows and looked down at his unfinished plate. "Inspector then point out I have no alibi." Bummer. No wonder he looked upset. If we didn't have our ironclad alibi—well, I hoped it was ironclad—I'd be even more of a basket case than I was.

"That's ridiculous," Sophie said firmly. "Why on earth would you need an alibi? You didn't know Nikos Gavras, did you?"

Gabor shook his head vehemently. "I never hear of man until yesterday. I never even hear his name."

Hegel, finished with his omelet and sausage, interrupted to ask if he could go to the gift shop for a magazine. He looked as if he'd had enough of his folks obsessing about this stuff and needed a mental change of venue.

Sophie waited until the boy had gone to ask, "Gabor, are you sure you can't prove that you were never near the murder scene?" This was assuming, of course, that he *had* never been near the murder scene. But she clearly felt real urgency to clear things up since she had inadvertently dragged the Latifs into this. Then again, if Aphro knew about the Pachia Ammos dig, she would've learned Gabor's status as a guest here at Astron Bay sooner or later.

"Maybe if you tell us what you did on Saturday, we can figure out how to clear you of any suspicions," Sophie offered, while my stomach growled and I looked enviously at the scraps of egg and sausage on Hegel's abandoned plate.

Gabor looked up, surprised by her willingness to help, and brightened a little. "As I tell Inspector, I was in room at hotel. Working on computer, writing reports for my company."

I perked up at this. "Computer! Did you use the internet? With some sites, your own computer should record everything you do. Time and everything. Did you tell anybody about that?"

"Yes, Inspector Kensington ask about that. She smart lady. I did, but only one internet search early in afternoon. No good as alibi."

I had thought I was pretty smart, too. "How about your writing? The backup system in the computer has a history of recent use, opening files, working times, everything."

"Also not good. Inspector point out I could have left room with computer on. Some long times I read and check notes and figures and not write. Computer not able to see I am always in room."

"Well, the whole thing is ridiculous in any case," Sophie pronounced. "You have absolutely nothing to do with Nikos Gavras, so you shouldn't even have been questioned at all."

"The Latifs are Turkish, Soph." I said this with some heat. I knew my accusations of national bias were problematic, but they were hard to suppress. "Everybody knows Nikos Gavras feuded with Madame Delphinos, and Spiro Santas was furious with him. Yet he's free as a bird while the rest of us are grilled and put under house arrest." My voice had gone up in octave and volume and folks at nearby tables perked up their ears. Gabor blinked, trying to understand.

"Cut that out, Red. You're going to get us in trouble with that kind of talk and then we'll never get out of here!" Sophie turned to the baffled Gabor in exasperation. "Red is convinced the police will pin this murder on foreigners in order to protect their Greek friends here at Astron Bay." She gave me a severe look. "But he's just upset by everything that's going on."

Hegel had returned from the gift shop with a magazine in hand and looked with disdain at this domestic skirmish as he sat back down with us. This shut us up, and we made moves to get up and head for the buffet.

"Wait a minute!" Sophie yelled, as she got up. The cover of Hegel's magazine had caught her eye and she reached over and asked the boy if she could have a look at it. It was a *People* magazine, and on the glossy page a very slender, very tall young woman with very straight and long blonde hair was smiling at a companion. She cradled a tiny dog in her arms—a toy chihuahua with a giant, glittery pink bow on its rhinestone-studded collar. "That's the one!" Sophie exclaimed. "That's the little dog the chauffeur was walking by the limousine the day before yesterday!"

"You seem to know every dog you see, Soph. Do you recognize them by smell? Or is it their wardrobe?"

Irony is not one of Sophie's strong points. "That's the dog, Red!" She was as excited as if she had spotted a live celebrity. "And I'll bet you a hundred dollars that that's yesterday's Mystery Guest. Remember the photo Madame showed me of Elizabeth Taylor and Nicky Hilton? It makes perfect sense!"

"Funny. She doesn't look like a hit man," I chortled. Sophie rolled her eyes and returned the magazine to Hegel. Like I say, irony is not one of her strong points.

The Latifs seemed to have missed the limousine of two days before, so Sophie filled them in briefly. Hegel freaked out that he had missed the sighting and said something gruff to his father in German. Blame for making him go to a stupid museum with his mother when there was a celebrity around, I guessed. Gabor shushed the boy wearily and rose to leave. "I must go to Pachia Ammos today," he explained. "Someone try breaking into the construction trailers again. I don't know what my firm will do, but we guard it all hours now." This confirmation of Aphro's warning pretty much scotched any plan for a drive down the coast for us on this day.

With the Latifs gone, we got our breakfasts—omelet and sausage for me, natch. Back at the table Sophie—still feeling a little guilty—continued to vent her outrage that Gabor could even remotely be considered a suspect. But I was becoming more thoughtful on the subject.

"I feel the same way, Soph, but I hope we're not being too trusting. What if something is going on with that whole airport and archeology business that we don't really understand? Gwen has been hinting around that there's some sort of corruption going on."

"Oh, I think she's just upset because the Antiquities Department hasn't called her in for consultation yet, and she's getting antsy about waiting around. But that doesn't mean it's Gabor's fault, for heaven's sake."

Sophie had a point, of course. "Still, as far as I can tell, Gabor's the only person who's been questioned so far who was in the hotel without an alibi." I took a last bite of omelet and washed it down with the coffee dregs. "Of course, we don't know about Spiro."

Sophie shook her head vehemently. "Red, if that celebrity visitor of Madame's is who I think it is, there's no way on earth Spiro would plan a murder right here at the hotel during an incredibly delicate moment like that!"

"On the contrary, can you think of a better cover? There must've been all sorts of distraction for the staff with Spiro highly visible, bustling around and officiating all over the place. Looks like a perfect set-up to me."

We were at it again and as a result deferred discussion of what to do today until we got back to our room. As we entered we noticed the message light lit on the phone. I picked it up and recognized the unmistakable voice of Wally Pinnock. "Red and me dear Sophie! How ye be today? Heard ye've been havin' a bit of a hullabaloo there at Astron Bay, is it? I'd be chuffed to have some lunch wid ye so y'can tell me about it. Little bistro on the lake serves the best snag on three continents. Give us a jingle. Ta."

To my surprise, Sophie jumped at the proposition to go back to Agnik, albeit not before offering me one of her deals. First Mother Sophia would need to check on Gwendolyn Frawley and Madame Delphinos, and then—when we got to Agnik—we could check on Nikos's sister Elena. "Two bereavements in one year…" Sophie clucked and shook her head in sorrow. She phoned Gwen and got no answer, but left a concerned message. She also called the front office to ask about Madame Delphinos, and left another concerned message. After that we were on our way to Agnik. "I wonder why Aphro smiled when we told her about Wally the day before yesterday?" Sophie asked in the car. I had no idea but marveled yet again at Sophie's elephantine memory.

Chapter 13
The Widow's Business

In Agnik, we got tied up in a bit of city traffic, but found parking near *Gavras Greek Arts*. On the way to the restaurant, we passed the shop, whose door had a sign in Greek and English: "Closed." However, we saw a small light and Sophie spotted the young shop girl she had met on her second trip, inside, seated at the counter and busy with papers. We passed on, resolving to revisit the shop after lunch.

At the restaurant, Wally sat at a table in the open by the water, conspicuous in an argyle sweater with his canvas bag over the back of his chair. He waved us over as we entered. "'G'day, mates,' he said, bobbing his round head with its glad eyes. "Dandy to see ye again, Red, Sophie, m'dear. Have yourselves a seat." I sat down next to him and shook his hand, and Sophie took a chair across from us to have a view of the lake.

"So our murder at Astron Bay is in the papers already?" I said to Wally. "Didn't know you read Greek."

"Don't, mate, but news gets 'round. Thought I'd get details from another of the Queen's old subjects. Not many crimes of that sort about here. Odd doings, to me mind, and a bit of a shonky deal. It's a wee world we live in, i'nt it?" It was a wee world, all right, but big enough for me to want a translator.

Wally ordered a chard for Sophie and two amber fluids, which I fervently hoped would turn out to be beer, for us. Before the drinks arrived, Wally lowered his voice again and rasped conspiratorially, "That Gavras was a bad lot, more likely to play divil than victim, what? But ye still hate to see him go down like a brindled bull in the bush. Poor bloke. And the poor lass. His sister, was she?"

"Widowed as well, just last year," Sophie said.

Wally looked up in surprise. "I c'n guess how she must be feelin'." His light blue eyes lost their baby-face brightness for a moment. "Me dear Mandy left me just two years ago, never well, now she's gone. Could hardly put meself together again. Thank the lord for me potting or I'd be out of me mind still." He reached into his canvas bag and pulled a photo of a sweet, plain, brown-haired woman from his wallet.

"Sorry to hear that, mate," I said. A little Aussie talk might be the best way to show sympathy. Looking at him with his brow down, I realized that like everyone, our droll friend had a more serious life than we might have guessed.

"Well, now, it seems ye've had a bit o' nasty interruptin' your holiday. Da says to keep the divil in the dark if ye leave home for a week or he'll be at the foot o' yer bed the first night away. So the lady loses her brother as well." He tisked quietly to himself.

Sophie nodded. "Her name is Elena. I feel so sorry for her. Have you been back to the shop? It said *Closed* when we passed by today, but the shop girl is in."

"Ah, if Nia's in, I'd not much mind droppin' by there after lunch. The sister's deserving of our respects, even if Nikos did have a shark's eye for business. I'd also fancy a gander at the business if she'd let us. Ye wouldn't be up for joinin' me, would you? Then in the arvo I'd show you around the old burg." Our drinks arrived, a white wine and two beers, thank the lord.

"Great idea," I said. "We—Sophie—had a mind to do the same thing." I was a little surprised at his interest in the business—a little forward on the occasion of a condolence call, I thought. But I was curious too, though I felt like a buzzard, circling the dead on the ground.

Our lunch arrived, less than three hours after we'd had breakfast, and a bit of a reprise of the same. Great skordalia dip with pita, and more sausage, or *snag* as they call it in the land of Oz. You can never have enough snag, I always say. And zucchini. Great grub. I was mending. My appetite had returned, at least until we narrated for Wally our version of the murder scene at Astron Bay. Not a nice lunchtime topic. As I told him what had happened, I could hardly believe I had been through such a gory experience. "So what gets a guy like Nikos murdered?" I asked Wally when I had finished. "Any ideas?"

"None I'd be puttin' in the bank, mate." I noticed he'd not shaved today. Made him look older and wiser, more grizzled than gnomish.

"Well," said Sophie, picking at her salad, "You remember we mentioned the feud between Nikos and Madame Delphinos when we had lunch the first time?

People seem to be betting on that, and Red is more and more convinced it had to do with that." She gave me *the look*. "But I can't believe it. Not right *there* in the hotel."

"Mebby Nikos was too sharp for his own good. Knew how to turn a customer 'round, din't he? Me Da always says 'Watch ye dun't get landed by the trout at the end of yer line.'" Wally winked at me. He sounded like he was hinting that we be careful in our involvement in the case.

"We seem to have gotten ourselves snagged twice," I said ruefully. "First by Nikos's rip-off with the silver bowls, and then because I lost it and threatened to 'kill the bastard' when our friend Gwendolyn Frawley back at the resort confirmed that the bowls were plate." If I hate anything more than confession, it's having to confess over and over again. But I figured I'd best get it over with.

Wally looked sympathetic, not gloating like Lyle. "Hard to dance with a fellow has his hand in yer pocket. Must be a cargo of you bilkies out there, mad as a cut snake at Gavras."

"But scams like that surely wouldn't get a shark like Nikos killed!" I took my jacket off. The day was warming up.

"Mebby he had shonkier dealings, selling things he'd no call to be selling."

Sophie's eyes widened. "Drugs? Is that what you mean?"

Wally shook his head. "Dun't seem very likely, does it? But mebbe he was circulatin' beauties a few centuries too old to be on the market." Wally was turning out to be a bosom buzzard.

"You mean antiquities?" Sophie asked.

"I mean antiquities, luv," he said.

"Well!" Sophie said, "we saw some lovely ones in the museum the afternoon Nikos was killed." She suddenly looked at Wally in astonishment, realizing that he didn't know this part of the story. "Did we tell you we had a brush with crime there, too?" Having given herself an opening. Sophie took over the museum story, ending with Gwendolyn Frawley falling on her butt next to an open cabinet. "They actually accused us of stealing the little animals! Got the police and everything! Can you imagine?"

"Why, ye don't be telling me!" Wally looked genuinely amazed. "A right magnet for misfortune, ye are! I'd best be careful around the two of ye."

"Well, anyway," Sophie went on, "We were still rattled about the whole thing when we got back to the hotel and Gwendolyn finds Nikos dying in her room. It was terrible! And if you can believe it, the same policewoman, Inspector Kensington, showed up again! I almost had a heart attack!" Sophie could have been on stage.

"That's quite a yarn, little lady." Sophie took this as a compliment. "Aphrodite must've been flummoxed to see ye twice in a day," he said.

"Aphrodite! Do you know her?" I asked.

Wally looked to his side, then at the ceiling, then grinned at us. "Oh, she's made a fine rep for herself here in this shank of the island. Cracked a lootin' ring a while back, she did. Germans they were, nabbed 'em cold. Can spot a thief by just skeezin' at him." It was Wally the Peacock's turn. Of course, he wasn't explaining which side of the law he met Aphro on. I realized this might be another time when the Redfields were showing themselves a tad green and gullible.

"How do you happen to know her?" Sophie asked. The mystery of Aphro's smile at the mention of his name yesterday had been solved.

"Well, let's say we share an interest in replicas and antiquities. Me line of work crosses hers on occasion, and I sometimes see her when I visit these shores. Charming lass, with a good eye for telling a replica from the dinky-di artifact."

"So we understand," I said, not sure if we understood. "Good at murders, too—we hope. From what you say, I wouldn't be surprised if she had her eye on Nikos before this." My famous nailing-the-foreigners theory of Aphro's sleuthing was beginning to feel a bit shaky.

"Wouldn't doubt it, t' be sure." Wally looked up at me puzzled. "So who's this Frawley bird that's been turning up at all these crimes?"

"Gwen, Gwendolyn Frawley, she's a wonderful person." Sophie smiled, thinking of Gwen in happier moments. "She's an antiquities expert from England, an authenticator who knows a—what did you call it?—dinky-doo doo—artifact when she's seen one."

"Dinky-di. Means genuine, right out of the ground," Wally translated. He shook his bobbing head at what he'd heard, however. "That's a tight tangle you're in there, at your Astron Bay place. Murder, theft, and knowing all the people. I'm surprised the good Inspector be lettin' you out at all. " He looked around theatrically and chuckled. "Wouldn't surprise me if she has ye staked out."

On reflex, Sophie and I looked around uneasily at invisible police lurking under the counters and behind the cupboards in the restaurant. Wally laughed.

"Why don't we finish up, me friends, and pay a visit to our little shop on Main Street?"

The day had turned into a hot, hazy afternoon and few people were in the streets. We reached the *Gavras* shop in no time, and through the door we saw the shopgirl, Nia, still working at the counter. Wally looked in with cupped hands and knocked tentatively. She rose, apparently recognizing Wally and maybe Sophie, and came to the door. She opened it a crack to talk to us. Her black hair with its bronze sheen was mounded in a pinned pony tail on top of her head and she was dressed like an American teenager. A sad expression belied her perky get-up.

Wally greeted her with friendly sincerity. "G'day luv." She gave him a tentative little smile. "Heartily sorry, young lady, for what happened to Mr. Gavras. Me friends and I stopped in to pay our respects. I hope you'll be telling us the lady's all right?"

"Ah, yes," she said, relaxing a little but still talking through the cracked-open door. "She named Mrs. Mylonas. So sad, she is not very well feeling. And now there is many things to do. But you are kind and nice." She looked a little uncertain. "Mrs. Mylonas is in back. I ask if she see you." She let the door close and disappeared through the curtain in back of the display counter.

In a moment, Elena emerged from behind the curtain, clearly a little under the weather. She wore a black dress, her hair somewhat undone as though her combs could not secure the wisps. She had heavy glasses on. I felt this visit was probably a mistake, but we were on the spot now.

Elena opened the door and waited for us to speak. "Mrs. Gavras…ah…Mrs. Mylonas, is it, we are so very sorry," Wally said solemnly. "Me friends have told me about your loss, and we wanted you to know our concern. Will ye be all right, now?"

Her sad eyes softened a little. "Yes," she said, "please come in. I am glad to see you again." She looked less glad than relieved at a chance to talk. She opened the door and we all stepped over the sill, feeling out of place. Here we are visiting the sister of a guy that gulled us out of a few hundred bucks a few days ago. And died a violent death a couple of days later. What the hell was there to say?

"Death is always terrible," Elena said, "but I cannot understand the killing of an innocent man." The word 'innocent' gave us all an awkward moment.

Wally had unusual finesse. "You were very good to me," he went on, "and

I can speak for Mrs. Redfield, who appreciated your concern when she was here last. So we wanted you to know we care. We'd gladly help ye if we could, if you'd let us know?" We nodded compassionately. I wondered where Wally's Strine had gone.

"Yes," Sophie said, "We're especially upset because my husband discovered your brother at the hotel. We knew right away what a terrible shock this would be for you." I held my breath, praying that Elena wouldn't ask for details, and praying that Sophie wouldn't give them if she did.

Elena took off her tortoise-shell glasses and silently passed her hand over her eyes. Sophie too looked ready to cry. But Elena recovered and said, "Thank you very much, you are kind. I cannot believe he went to the hotel and did not come back." She shook her head. "He almost didn't go. We were very busy and he was upset that he would be late for an appointment."

"Did he say who he was meeting?" I asked, stunned to think that Elena might actually know. But she shook her head sadly.

"We're surprised to see you here with the shock you've had," Sophie said, "but I'm glad we found you in."

"That we are, Mrs. Mylonas." Wally went on, earnestly. "You've only been here for a year, I'm told, and now it's all in your lap. You should get away for a bit, you should."

"There is nowhere to go. I live upstairs." Elena motioned us to step further into the shop, but there was nowhere to sit down. "Yesterday I take time off for family. We make plans for funeral. But today Nia and I have to work in the shop." Nia nodded at the lists and forms spread out all over her counter space. "People telephone about orders, but the police take Nikos's computer, and we do not know what to tell them. So we take order forms and try to find things in inventory."

"There, there, now. Ye'll soon be managin' the business like a pro, I'm willin' to wager," Wally was back in buck-up mode.

"No. Nikos send objects to England and America, but he take care of export business while Nia and I take care of customers in front." No wonder she had dark circles under her eyes. She should be grieving for her brother now, not struggling with the burden of the business. I remembered Sophie telling me that Elena's late husband was a controlling sort, not one to bring Elena into his dealings at their Athens shop.

"I have no practice with exports, so that makes difficulties. Especially because the computer is hard for me to understand," she went on.

110

"Well, as I'm tellin' ye, be sure to let us know if there's any help ye be needing. Even with the computer. We'd do our best to try." Was Wally just blowing good Aussie cheer, or was he actually offering her our help? If so, he might've checked with us—although Sophie would have agreed in a heartbeat.

He hesitated a moment and then said, "'T'would be grand to see some of the export goods some time. Some businesses hold their best stores back to sell abroad, I'm told." Did the Pinnock have an angle he was working here? I hoped our new friend wasn't planning to exploit the grief of a bereaved woman. I felt in her state she was being much more open to us, strangers as we were, than she should be.

But Elena showed no signs of distrust when she answered Wally. "At the moment, we do not know what is to export and what is not. Without the computer, I do not know where the export goods are sent. Some are packed, some are not. We must send boxes but we don't know what is paid for yet. But in few days we will have computer back and hope to know much more, Mr…"

"Pinnock," Wally said and reached into a shirt pocket under his sweater to take out a card.

"Mister Pinnock," Elena repeated, looking at his card through her glasses.

"So, I'll hope to return sometime soon and look over items ye've not yet committed, once ye've got a better handle on the business." Ingratiating customer, that Wally.

Elena smiled, just a little. "Yes, do of course come back, even if I am not here myself." Seeing Wally look perplexed, she explained. "Some people have phoned, asking about buying the shop."

"Buying it?" I stared at her. Nikos was not yet in his grave—barely cold, in fact—and vultures were already collecting. I couldn't believe it.

"Yes, I too was surprised," Elena said. "I did not speak to them yesterday. It is not respectful to Nikos. But business alone is too difficult for me. So I telephone them today to say I would meet them later, when all this is over."

"Might I ask who it might be?" Bit nosy of Wally, I thought, but he went on. "It's been me good fortune to trade here as a happy customer for some time. So, of course, I'm hoping the shop keeps up the tip-top quality of the merchandise."

Elena brightened. "It will do so, I am certain. It is the people in the workshop that makes our products who ask about possible purchase. So the artworks will stay the same."

"Boffo news," Wally beamed. "But are these blokes local? Work around here? I'd be grateful for a peek at their works, how they do it. I'm a potter meself, y'know, and I've been bowled over, if ye'll pardon the phrase, by the repros and replicas I've bumped into in yer shop."

But it was becoming clear that Elena was getting a little tired. She offered to look up the information for Wally another time. We sensed we'd overstayed our welcome and that it was time to leave. Just as we began our good-byes, Wally addressed Elena with abject humility. "Excuse me, m'dear, I'm embarrassed to have to ask. Would you be having a loo in back I might use?"

"Loo?"

"W.C."

"Uh…uh." Elena was at a loss. "I…Nia," she said, looking at the shop girl. She spoke in Greek, and Nia came forward and led Wally through the curtain to the back. Elena looked embarrassed and turned back to Sophie, who again launched into her inimitable heartfelt condolences as Nia returned. "No matter how terribly upsetting this has been for everyone, it is clearly hardest for you," Sophie said.

"Everyone?" Elena looked puzzled.

"Well, I guess I'm thinking of Gwendolyn Frawley. Her room was the one where Nikos was discovered, and poor Madame Delphinos, who must be feeling terrible having this happen in her hotel." I was just about to have a conniption about where this could go when, thank goodness, Wally reappeared through the curtain offering apologies and we were able to resume our farewells.

We walked to the door with Nia, who unlocked it from the inside. As we stepped outside, we confronted a bulky gray figure walking toward the door, sporting familiar wavy gray hair and a substantial moustache with its ends curled upwards. It was Spiro Santas, carrying a thin black briefcase. He was as surprised to see us as we were to see him, but he recovered his composure, bowed to us, and addressed Nia in Greek. She looked confused and closed the door, and we all stood there for an agonizing moment, wondering what to do. For all my suspicions of Spiro, it seemed impossible to stop him from seeing Elena if he wished. What could I do? Tackle him, pin him down, and yell, "Oh, no you don't!" into his walrus face? Just then, the door opened and there stood Elena, solemn and large-eyed, looking at him while he spoke to her rapidly, urgently, in Greek, his face reddened and his eyes bulging. Then, improbably, she opened the door wider and he entered the shop. The door closed, and we stood on the street alone.

Chapter 14
The Wild, Wild West

"Blimey! Who was that tall poppy?" Wally thankfully waited until we were out of earshot of the shop to ask. After he explained what a tall poppy was, we told him that the prosperous looking fellow was Spiro Santas, Madame Delphinos's godson. "What d'ye suppose he's doing skulking around poor Mrs. Mylonas?"

I had exactly the same question, but told him it was unwise to speculate. I was torn between wanting to stay and be sure Elena was all right, and wanting to clear out so we wouldn't embarrass either one of them.

"Come on, be reasonable." Sophie had sensed my unease. "Spiro's not going to do anything to Elena with Nia there. And besides, he knows we saw him enter the shop. If anything happens, we can testify he was here."

Sophie didn't see that testifying would be cold comfort if Spiro and Elena's conflict took a physical turn. But I conceded she had a point and we tacitly agreed to let the matter drop and get on with our afternoon, or *arvo*, as Wally would have it.

He had promised us an arvo tour of Agnik, but something else was bothering Wally.

"I have a whiff of danger, mates. Elena shouldn't be talking with anyone about selling the shop just now, least with the blokes that kept Nikos in pots and pans. A little fast in more ways than one, I'd say."

"I thought so too," I agreed, "but there's not much we can do, is there?"

"I have a plan," Wally announced after a minute. "M'thinks the lass needs an advance party to check the place out for her, and we'd make a trio of pretty fair scouts. I'm saying let's hop down and take a squizz at the shop where the goods are made. What d'ye say?"

"How do you know where they are?" Sophie looked at Wally, squinting against the sun. She'd forgotten her sunglasses.

114

"Well, now, I did a wee bit o' research in the back room when I skipped to the loo, and sure enough, there's boxes and such, sure to be from there. I saw an address in Gaitani on the labels and Gaitani's not far. We'll find it if we keep our sniffers in the air." He reached in his canvas bag and pulled out a slip of paper with an address on it. "Gaitani's off the road past Astron Bay. And you have a car and time on yer hands and mebbe a map of this part o' the world?" His light blue eyes glittered with mischief. "How'd ye fancy a wee road trip into the outback?"

I looked at Sophie. Awkward, not being able to consider this in private. The little sneak had something up his sleeve, I could tell now, snooping in the shop. I read Sophie's brow and she seemed to have her own doubts.

"Well! I don't think we can just show up down there, even if we could find the place." Sophie's a sensible lass—compared to Wally, at any rate.

Wally gave us a reassuring grin. He had an honest face, all right, but only an obscure plan. "Elena's never been there or seen these folks, so we can always tell 'em we're there on the widow's behalf, seeing as how she's so busy. And if worse comes to worst, I'll just tell 'em I'm wanting to take a wee peek at how they do their work. Fine work it is, and they'll be proud to show it, I'm sure."

I still didn't like it, but Sophie looked at me and nodded, as if to say it was okay with her. Braver than I am, she seemed willing to put Elena's interests before our own and have us take Wally down to Gay Tawny or whatever the place was called. I'd be doing the driving, giving me a bit of control, so I concurred.

"Okay, hop in, Wally. Front seat if you think you know where you're going."

Wally sat in the front seat with our local map from the hotel as his guide. I saw him writing on a piece of paper as I turned east on the highway, going on south after a bit to Astron Bay, a route we all knew. Sophie didn't see it, but I was shocked to see that he had a piece of letterhead paper from *Gavras Greek Arts*. Did he steal that from the back room?

He noticed my interest. "Just scribbling ourselves an introduction, or the best I can do. Best way in this country. Suspicious of strangers, they are."

The day was bright and the land and air were dry, with dust behind us as we passed the hotel and drove further into this ancient world. Few dwellings appeared by the road, the view of the distant hills unobscured even by roadside vegetation. Every now and then we passed a metal road sign pierced with bullet holes. Reminded me of the American West—a place I like better in the movies than in my back yard.

Ten minutes beyond Astron Bay, Wally hunched up to get a better look over the dashboard and checked the map. "We're getting closer, mates. I do believe that's the road." A rude sign in Greek stood by an isolated, weathered section of wooden fence, a picturesque mark of an abandoned orchard or farm. A herd of goats grazed on a low hill curving up against the horizon. In Laguna Beach we use goats as living lawn mowers to clear flammable brush from the steep canyons in summer. I imagined these little critters produced the great tart feta we got at cocktail hour.

I headed the car down the side road. After a few miles, we saw a group of trees clustered around a little town with a few houses along the road and a store with a dusty gas pump. "Gaitani," said Wally, "let's go on a mite more to see where this takes us." We saw another road off to the right, and took it since the road beyond was rough and rutted. We drove for another two miles before we reached a large ramshackle compound of four or five buildings, all surrounded by high, sturdy fencing. The whole scene reminded me of California's backcountry, with the odd isolated farm by a creek or a sun-weathered house and shop selling junk as antiques. We even have ostrich farms back home, if you can believe it. Wally would feel right at home in our state.

But this place looked about as inviting as a back-country prison. The protective fence around it told me we were out of our home territory and perilously close to someone else's.

"I have a feeling these guys want privacy." Since no one was expressing any concern, I figured I'd better.

"They're just shy." Wally said, flashing one of his gnomic grins. "We've come all this way, mates, let's tell 'em we're here. Sure they'd love to see us." Brave bluff irony for a guy that short.

We drove up to a main gate in the fence, accompanied by our cloud of dust and stopped the car. Beyond the locked gate a short driveway led to a large main building beyond it. It looked fairly new, though the other structures were cruder, sheds connected by passages covered with corrugated metal, supported by unpainted two-by-fours. Piles of dirt lay about the area, with boxes and building materials stacked and covered with tarpaulins. Messy-looking place. Two trucks and a black sedan were parked near the main building. A large conical kiln stood apart in the back, with smoke emerging from the top, the air around it shimmering with the heat. Several workers stood by, tending what we assumed was the firing of pottery. Nothing romantic about this place.

Wally and I lumbered out of the car and went toward the fence. The gate had a steel plate with a lock that secured it against ordinary tinkering. Sophie followed us, putting on her broad-brimmed straw hat to protect her fair complexion from the sun. A small sign on the gate identified the place in Greek and English as "*Onarchos Replicas and Reproductions.*" A sign on the fence next to the gate, in Greek, made no sense to me, but its exclamation points were hardly meant to attract customers. Nothing about this place called out "C'mon in! Pots for patio and garden! Bring the kids!" Not like the cheerful emporia along South Coast Highway in Laguna Beach, with their clumsy clay urns and Mexican terra-cotta chimineas. I thought fondly of the Pottery Shack where Sophie and I had bought our colorful everyday dishes. Then I saw something designed to rebuff visitors even more. Beyond the main building a dark board on two posts showed a white outline of a body with a circular target painted over its heart. Target practice. Holes in the target. Hard to believe we were only ten or fifteen miles from the saunas and fitness center and aromatherapy of Astron Bay. Good place for an NRA retirement home.

A man in a brown uniform emerged from the main building and walked over to the gate toward us. Not a meeter and greeter, by a long shot. His holster, gun and all, showed he was ready for other kinds of visitors, not the glad-handing likes of Wally. No hospitality at all, in fact, an impression deepened by his one Greek eyebrow, like Zorba's at the museum, the one who pawed me all over for the little animals he thought might be hidden in my briefs. The man's single brow darkened his hooded eyes.

Wally'd better be good if we were going to see any artwork. "G'day," he said, nodding, smiling. Brave little bugger. Affable as a Disneyland guide. His short stature and round face made him look about as threatening as a puppy. Sure enough, the guard relaxed, his shoulders slumping a little bit, his arms akimbo. "We've come from Nikos Gavras's shop, sir. I wonder if ye'd be kind enough to help us." The guard seemed not to understand, but reacted to Nikos's name. Wally held out his sheet of *Gavras Greek Arts* letterhead paper. This couldn't work, especially if he'd tried to forge a letter of introduction in English! The guard took the paper and turned, motioning us to wait. A superfluous gesture with his locked gate. He walked back to the main building and went inside.

"Wally, how do you expect to get away with this? This place is a dead zone." I prefer my adventures in vicarious form. The place made me feel I should be looking out for a machine gun nest and a sign saying: "Intruders may not leave this place alive."

"Worry not, me lad," Wally replied. "The Greeks warm up to me once they know I'm not after their daughters. And I'd venture there's few daughters in this charming spread, much as I'd welcome them." True, I said to myself, the Greeks *and* their daughters would think Wally more a pet than a threat. But good luck with the pistol-packing guard, all the same. What the hell were we doing here? I looked at Sophie. She had her "What have you gotten us into this time, Ollie?" look on her face.

We stood in the sun for a few minutes, then moved into the shade of a scraggy olive tree nearby. Another man emerged from the front building and came up to us, so we went back to the gate. No smile, but a much more urbane specimen than the guy with the gun. "Yes?" he asked. He was dressed in pressed black slacks, white shoes, and a silk shirt. Striking outfit for the outback. He held Wally's note by his side. "I am Theo Onarchos."

"Forgive me, sir," Wally said, "We've come from Nikos Gavras's shop in Ágios Nikólaos on recommendation of Mrs. Gavras—I'm sorry, Mrs. Mylonas, she is. I'm sure you've heard the unhappy story, sir, of Mr. Gavras's sad end. His sister was good enough to accept our help in her time of sorrow…" Wally trailed off as the man shook his head. I couldn't tell whether it was to share the sorrow or to indicate disinterest.

"I am aware of Mr. Gavras's accident," the man said, "but what have you to do with it?" His English was good, despite his exotic look, and his voice was completely even. It was unclear whether he was asking a question or delivering a challenge. He handed Elena's note back to Wally through the fence. I noticed Wally had written down only Onarchos' name and 'Gaitani' and some numbers.

Wally took the note and said, "To be honest with ye, sir, it's been me pleasure to visit the shop when I'm in Crete—many times in me travels over the years. When we last spoke to poor Elena, Mrs. Mylonas, widowed as she is, said we might pay ye a visit, and gave me this note to show where ye might be. She's new to the Gavras shop, don't you know, not more'n a year if that.

Asked us to find out for her what she'll be needing to do now, seeing as you've been supplyin' her shop."

"And who are your companions, here?" Good question. Sophie, in her white pants and embroidered turquoise top didn't look like a business agent.

"Do forgive me, sir," Wally said. "These folks are Mr. and Mrs. Redfield, from America." His voice became somber and he knit his brow. "They are vacationing nearby and were kind enough to drive me here."

The man looked sharply at Sophie and me. I felt like kicking Wally, forgetting that he had to improvise to explain what the hell *we* were doing here. But Onarchos recovered himself and flashed us a B-movie smile.

"Mr. and Mrs. Redfield," he said, bowing slightly. "And Mr…"

"Pinnock." Wally pulled out one of his cards. "Wallace Pinnock." Wallace? I thought. The card he'd given me read W. Pinnock. I wouldn't have figured Wally for a Wallace.

"Very well, Mr. Pinnock. But I don't understand your business here."

"Ms. Mylonas is a tad at sea about her brother's business." Wally was cranking up the Aussie charm as best he could. "She's run a shop before in Athens but dun't know beans, as it were, about the Greek ceramics business. She's had some inquiries about selling the shop, ye may have heard"—here Wally gave Onarchos a knowing look—"and she needs to know soon all she can about her suppliers. That would be you, we understand." I couldn't quite figure out Wally's strategy. Why didn't he come right out and say he knew Onarchos was interested in buying the shop? He was making even me suspicious. In any case, it was not a winning performance, judging from Onarchos's look.

Onarchos shook his head and said, "I appreciate your wish to act as Ms. Mylonas's agent here, but I believe these matters can be worked out in good time. I would rather deal with her myself. Thank you." He began to turn as if to end this unprofitable discussion.

"To be very honest once again, sir," Wally went on in an ingratiating leprechaun lilt. "I have some interest on me own account. I'm a potter meself and a great admirer of your work. On account of me own purchases from the Gavras shop, I'd hoped to get a look at how they're made." This seemed an even lamer tack than the earlier one, although Wally managed to infuse it with great sincerity.

Onarchos turned back and looked as though he was about to refuse and put an end to this business once and for all, when who should pipe up but my own bold bride.

"Mr. Onarchos, we agreed to drive down here with Mr. Pinnock because I would just *love* to see how your beautiful pieces are made! Could we have a look, just to see the finishing touches?" Criminy, Soph, what are you thinking? We ought to be getting the hell out of here. Much as I liked Wally, I was losing confidence in him by the minute, and it was less and less clear what this place was all about.

But Wally, grateful for Sophie's intervention, broke right in. "That was me very question." He now positively beamed at Onarchos. "We've come a way to visit you, and perhaps we could just have a peek into yer workroom. Mind, we're not asking for a tour to see the whole business of firing, painting, and glaze and the like. Just a wee feel for the place so Mrs. Mylonas can trust our word on your wonderful work and how you'll hopefully be keeping her supplied till she decides what to do."

Onarchos considered this silently, visibly reluctant to let us into the shop. Snakes are used to slithering off after a rattle, but his own cold courtliness stopped him. He hadn't even unlocked the gate to his compound, guarded, we remembered, by a man with one eyebrow and a pistol. All this time we had been talking to him through a hurricane fence, as with a prisoner in his own jail.

To our surprise, he relented. "Very well," he said. "Come with me." He removed a batch of keys from his belt and unlocked the gate. "We sell only to dealers and have no visitors. But to please Mrs. Mylonas, we will satisfy your curiosity—only briefly, however, since we are quite busy." Good point. He couldn't really afford to run afoul of Elena if he was trying to buy her shop, and a report from Wally telling only of fences, pistol-toting guards, and a rude refusal could put the kibosh on the deal.

Onarchos led us up toward the main building. "We prefer to remain little known, and owing to our remote location, we must guard the grounds at all times." He looked at the shot-up target on the board as we neared the structure. "We had several break-ins before we fully secured the compound."

We followed him inside to a cool, dark entry area. We stood there, momentarily adjusting to the darkness after our time in the bright sun. To the right, a dim, frosted-glass cubicle stood with its door ajar. Inside, the man we recognized as the guard sat at a table smoking and joking in Greek with another man not visible to us. Zorba II looked up as we passed, still laughing at something, and I noticed all of his upper front teeth were gold rather than white enamel. As I looked, a hand from inside reached across the gap to grasp the door handle to close the door. I first saw the wrist, the fluke of a whale, or a fish tail, wrapped around it, and then saw that it belonged to a mermaid extending right up the arm to the elbow. The tail was like the motif on the wrist of the silverhaired fellow who slipped me a cigarette at the Astron Bay cabaña the day—the day we went to the museum. *That* day. I knew that lots of men have tattoos like that but my heart nonetheless skipped a beat.

Onarchos ushered us through an office to the door of a large workroom. My head was now swimming from the combination of surprise, cigarette smoke, and the trouble my eyes had adjusting to the darkness. Like an idiot, I now remembered to take my sunglasses off. The large room was filled with benches, tables, and work stations. Pots, plates, and urns, reproductions in all stages of finish, were laid out on the tables like an assembly line. The three or four workers hardly looked up as we poked our heads in. I hoped Wally was satisfied. The place was what it said it was. Now let's get the hell out of here.

"This is our factory, as I call it," said Onarchos, with his drawstring smile. He led us around the tables so that we could assure ourselves that the place was indeed creating reproductions of Minoan artifacts. Wally, staying in character, pointed to the occasional piece and commented on its dinky-di finish. Onarchos didn't rush us, but didn't encourage us to dawdle either.

We turned back the way we came and Onarchos escorted us to the entryway. "There's little more to see, but you can tell Mrs. Mylonas that we are more than happy to continue our business relations in one form or another." He proceeded toward the exit. "Please give her my condolences. I've done business for several years with Nikos Gavras, and I know she must miss him." A pretty oily line, and pretty late to be saying it. But fair enough, the dude was smooth.

After shaking hands, he stood on the steps leading from the back door as we walked toward the gate. A sudden pair of noises—Crack! Crack!— exploded in my ears. Sophie made an incoherent cry as we all ducked and looked up to see the guard not fifteen feet to our right, with his pistol held in both hands at chest level. He turned and looked at Onarchos on the steps, and both men broke into a grin. The gold glinted in the guard's mouth like a flash. For a moment the gun he held at chest level was pointed straight at us, but then he slowly turned back and faced the target and we heard another loud double Crack!

We looked at the silhouette on the board. One irregular hole in the heart area. It was a Gotcha! moment for Theo, still smiling as we left. We walked quickly through the gate, which mercifully we could open, and it closed and clicked behind us. Wally and Sophie were ashen. I didn't have a mirror to see how my ruddy good looks had survived this strange episode, but my throat was dry and I had a lightness of the head and a shiver of the body. We found our way to the car. We got in, looking briefly for Onarchos, who had already disappeared into the building. I started up the Renault and hustled it onto the road back to Gaitani. None of us said a word. Sophie and I were suppressing our reproaches at being taken on a stupid and dangerous wild goose chase. Wally sat hunched up, thinking. Thinking *real* hard, as though to absorb and make sense of what had happened back there.

We'd gone less than a quarter of a mile when a cloud of dust came toward us, stirred by a convertible heading our way. The driver wore sunglasses and a Stetson, like a cowboy. The woman's gauzy head scarf and sunglasses qualified her for a fashion magazine. They passed without looking and disappeared in the dust visible in my rear-view mirror.

"That was Lyle and Danielle!" Sophie exclaimed. "What are they doing here?"

"Who?" asked Wally.

"The Tanners, our friends at the hotel," I said. "They've dealt with Nikos for years. They're probably checking on business, like we did for Elena."

I saw Sophie scowling in the rear-view mirror. "We ought to warn them not to go there," she said. I wasn't about to turn around and go back. "Soph, don't worry about it. Lyle can take care of himself."

"I don't like this for another reason," she said, after a minute. "It's like they're picking Nikos's bones, getting to his supplier before Elena's even gotten on her feet."

I didn't like a lot of things about this adventure and wished I could shed the fear that had enveloped me back at the compound. That fear made me wary of telling either Sophie or Wally that I'd spotted a mermaid's tail winding around a man's wrist. The arm of a smoker, I figured—a Marlboro smoker. Sophie would lock onto that image and put it in her kaleidoscope of scenarios. And I was no longer sure I should be putting such guileless trust in Wally.

When Wally finally spoke, he was grim. "Elena shouldn't swim with sharks like that. We'd best give her a report before she dives in."

I wouldn't have minded a report myself, especially one that sorted out the sharks from the dolphins in the Cretan whirlpool in which we found ourselves.

Chapter 15
The Big Baboon

A fitful night. I awoke periodically, feeling like I was being dragged behind a car into some pretty dark territory. All the people we had befriended seemed to have their own agendas. It was unsettling to have Spiro pop up at Elena's like that, then have Wally lead us to that sinister compound in the wild—only to see the Tanners breeze by. But we were too deep in this disquieting world to back out. Sophie, brave girl, didn't want to and Aphro so far said we couldn't. But even Sophie was getting queasy, able to trust almost no one except possibly Elena.

"How'd you sleep?" I rolled my head to see Sophie, penetrating me with her green eyes.

"Not all that well." I said, "That business at the Pottery Shack was scary. Seeing Wally and Onarchos negotiate was like seeing a puppy playing with a scorpion. He's bad news."

"I'm not all that sure about Wally, to be very honest." Sophie rubbed a sleepy seed out of her left eye with a crooked knuckle. "Sneaking around in Elena's back room like a hyena. What's he after?"

I decided not to defend Wally. We'd see him again if we were to help Elena, and I—and Sophie, it turned out—thought it would be best if we didn't let Wally help Elena all by himself. He might be up to something after all.

It was our eighth day at Astron Bay, and Sophie and I had been together enough in the last few days that we wanted to do our own things. Like flab out at the pool for me and let Sophie take a hotel-sponsored tour to the windmills of Elounda or some other pile of stones.

After breakfast, I found a message on the phone and listened to it. I heard a cracked voice say, "Mrs. Redfield, Sophie, dear. This is Madame Delphinos. Spiro tells me you are concerned about me—how very sweet of you! Won't you and your husband join me for coffee this morning? Please call if you are free. My private number is 1600."

This sent Sophie to heaven first, then to the phone, establishing on the fly that it was all right by me if we went down. If I'm too confused to make a fast decision, she assumes it's a 'yes.' Madame told her we should come down at 10:30, calling ahead, and Zoë would open the garden gate, now barred, to let us in. Sophie cast a baleful eye at my Coors Beer tee shirt, when she got off the phone. "That's hardly better than no shirt at all. Let's try something nicer." Nuts. She was probably right.

Even before we reached the gate, we heard Basket bark, and as soon as Zoë let us in, Basket was in Sophie's arms. Zoë led us through the garden into Madame's sunny salon, where she was already seated in her chenille chair. The room looked and felt quite different this morning. It took me a minute to realize that it was suffused with perfume and adorned with flowers—vases and baskets of orchids, lilies, pink roses, and mixed bouquets on tables, windowsills, even shelves. Some blooms were wilting a little, making the place look like a provincial florist's shop. Madame waved her lorgnette at us and Sophie gently spilled Basket next to Madame in her chair. She was dressed in a sequined dress the color of deep red roses, setting off her bright white hair, immaculately done up for the day.

"I'm so glad you could join me," she said as Basket settled beside her. "Many friends have sent these lovely flowers for my ninetieth birthday on Saturday. They live far away and many are infirm, so this is what they do now. Ninety is a round birthday, they say, and deserves to be remembered."

"Well, wow! Happy birthday, Madame!" Sophie beamed her most radiant smile at the old lady. "I wish I had known! We're so honored you thought of having us down to see you!" I thought back and realized that Madame's birthday was the day of Nikos's death. Nasty coincidence. I *prayed* that it was a coincidence.

"*Merci, ma chérie,*" said Madame, waving us to the divan where we had sat before. "But sadly, as you know, my birthday was spoiled by murder—*murder!*—in my own villa. Spiro did not tell me until after dinner, and I was destroyed. Simply *destroyed.* Such a beautiful day I had, and then this terrible news." It was unclear whether she was ticked at Nikos for ruining her birthday or whether she was genuinely distressed at his untimely end.

Zoë brought a simple tray of coffee in a gleaming china pot, milk and sugar, and a plate of vanilla wafers—thankfully a more businesslike offering than *tisane*.

"We've been very upset about this too." Sophie poured Madame's coffee and mine before taking her own with a wafer. "I wish we could help in some way, but we hardly know what to do."

"I try to think of everything now but it is too much." Madame closed her eyes and touched each of her temples with two fingers in a stagey gesture. Nothing wrong with her little gray cells, as far as I could tell.

"I had just seen my visitor out, and it was such a refreshing visit!" Madame leaned forward, looking at Sophie myopically. Sophie's eyes sparkled, anticipating word about the mysterious visitor. But Madame took a different tack. "I lay down on the chaise for a *petit* nap before dinner, when Spiro phoned to say he could not join me this evening because there had been a terrible accident. I shouted *'Mon dieu! Basket,'* but Spiro assured me no, no, a person, and I cried *'A guest?'* And he assured me no, no, not a guest. I was terrified for a moment that it must be my dear visitor, but Spiro again said no, no, and said he had to go, leaving me with *terrible* uncertainty!"

She paused, nearly overcome by her dramatic narration. By then I was at the edge of my seat, wondering how the news that it was Nikos Gavras had gone over with her. So far this whole thing had been about *her* rather than him.

Madame took a sip of coffee, fanned herself with an embroidered handkerchief that appeared out of nowhere, and continued. "Spiro finally *told* me that Nikos Gavras was found dead in one of the rooms, when he came by later. An exhausting day, a terrible day! I could scarcely leave my bed the next morning. Spiro wanted to call the doctor." Basket hopped down off the chair and had to go out for a moment. This gave Madame a brief intermission until the little mutt returned.

"It is worse when you know the person, *n'est-ce que pas*? A stranger killed is very sad. But a person, even an enemy, is worse. Worse for me and worse for my Astron Bay. Even worse for my memoir. How do I write about Erasmo's grandson now?"

The gal may be an old lady, but she needed a reality check. "I think you're going to have to wait until the police figure out who did this before you can write anything about it." I hadn't planned to insert myself into this conversation, but somebody had to remind her that there might be a murderer basking by her pool or doing yoga on the lawn outside her iron gate.

Madame seemed to have heard only one word in my caution. "The *police*! The *police*!" She spat the words. "The police have treated me shamefully! They tell me nothing, so I must rely on Spiro, and he has not a moment for me."

She now addressed herself to me, and although she wasn't calling me *mon chéri*, I sensed urgency in her voice. "I have asked you here to tell me what you can. Spiro tells me *you* found Nikos Gavras! You must know more than I can find out from him or the police!" She may have been ranting, but I could see her point. Without knowing the details, she must be more anxious than if she knew the whole ugly story.

"Surely Inspector Kensington should have told you the details," Sophie said. "How could she keep you so in the dark?"

"She? Kensington? I know nothing of her. This was the Chief, from Agnik, a terrible man with the manners of a bull. No skill, no grace, no sensitivity to my condition. He acted like an army officer invading a home. He treated me like a—a—*babushka*." I didn't know what the hell that was, but I could tell it wasn't a compliment. Sounds like Madame got the Zorba treatment rather than the Aphrodite touch.

"Everyone knows of my dispute with Gavras! Now this ape, he grins at me and says, 'So it seems the problem with your book is solved.' Can you imagine? Such a thing to say the day after Nikos Gavras has died. I thought he was going to ask if I had killed him myself! 'Of course,' I would have told him, 'I go on the elevator with my cane and walk in and hit him on the head. Is that how you think it happened—you *baboon*?'"

Sophie and I couldn't even look at one another. Her report was breathtaking. I would love to have been there.

"Then he asked what my Spiro was doing!" Her voice rose further, and even Basket lifted his head and looked at her. "What he was doing at the time of the murder, that afternoon, he asked. I could not believe my ears: the brute was accusing Spiro! I told him about my visitor, how Spiro was busy with her, with her chauffeur, her little dog, my birthday flowers, my beautiful birthday cake, the candles. I asked the beast to leave"—here she pointed to the door in a gesture of eviction—"and I have not seen him since." She delivered this last line on a note of triumph, victorious in her agon with the Greek police chief.

Madame sat back in her stuffed chair, breathing hard, and Basket, sensing that the theatrics were over, rested his head back on her lap. Murder on the premises clearly suited her sense of self-importance, but she needed an audience to witness her response to it. Hence the Redfields' command summons to coffee this morning. In fact, she never asked further about our role in the discovery of Nikos.

After a few sips from her *tasse*, Madame sat upright again, her sequins glittering, and looked at us shrewdly through her lorgnette. "It is important that you advise me. Why was Nikos Gavras in my hotel? Do the police have ideas? I would never have permitted him to set foot in my villa."

Sophie broke in. "I don't think anybody knows. But oddly enough I might have been the one to hear Nikos make an appointment to meet somebody here at Astron Bay."

Madame gasped, almost choking on her coffee. "*You* know Nikos Gavras? How in heaven do *you* know Nikos Gavras?" I felt again like saying that as far as we knew, *everyone* in Crete knew Nikos Gavras. But I could see why she was amazed by Sophie's admission, in view of our arrival only a week ago.

"It's a long story," Sophie said apologetically. She then proceeded to tell about our visit to the shop, although she shrewdly downplayed the rip-off, not wanting to give Madame further cause to disparage Nikos. When Sophie reached the overheard phone call, she conceded with some embarrassment that she'd actually hoped that Nikos might be seeking a *détente* with Madame. I was dying to ask the old lady what language she and Nikos would have used, had they spoken, but figured it was none of my business. At least for now.

"Ah, Sophie, Sophie," Madame sighed. She was settling into a more familiar mode with us. "How sad it is that I *cannot* now arrange anything with Nikos. It is too late, everything is too late." She rested her shoulders against the back of the armchair and touched her brow with the back of her hand, as though she lay on a deathbed. Mimi, I thought, with Puccini's somber chords crashing around her.

"Madame," Sophie interjected, all business. "Was that what Spiro was trying to arrange yesterday? He was at the Gavras shop in the afternoon."

"Spiro? My Spiro? Where did you see him? Impossible! He was here, I am sure!" She revived quickly, sat up and leaned forward. "He would have told me! I would never approve!"

Time to back up. We were walking into traffic against the light.

Sophie, bless her, was up to the challenge. "Madame, I am sorry. Please don't distress yourself. We thought it was Spiro, but maybe it was some other gentleman with gray hair and the moustache." Sophie simulated a twirl with her hand. "We didn't get a very good look at him, and it sounds as though we were mistaken."

"I will have a word with him to be sure my Spiro keeps nothing from me." Sophie had averted an immediate crisis, but Madame, under her powder, was still a bit pink of cheek.

"Madame," Sophie said, breaking the awkward silence, "can you tell us who your visitor was? We saw the limousine and the little chihuahua. Was she a gorgeous thin blonde woman?"

"No, no, *chérie,* I must not say, I promised her. Our families are connected, and she was here on a private errand, and so asked to keep her visit a secret. If others knew, the press would swoop down on Astron Bay like vultures." *That* would have added a bit of zest to the day of the murder, I thought, a celebrity with an entourage of paparazzi on top of everything else.

Sophie looked disappointed not to get more information, and decided to push her Nosy Parker nose in just a little further. "Is she from a family of famous hoteliers, by any chance?"

Madame simply smiled her crinkled smile. "I cannot say, *ma chérie.* But I tell you that she came to tell me of her engagement to the grandson of my dear Pierro's brother, and to celebrate my birthday, of course."

She now leaned forward again and looked directly into Sophie's eyes. "Can you guess her birthday gift for me?" Sophie looked clueless, and Madame wrinkled her nose and sniffed the air.

"Perfume!" Sophie cried triumphantly.

"*Oui, oui.* The perfume of her great-aunt *Eleezabeth.*" Now Madame struggled to rise from her chair. "I have said too much already, and you must be eager to be in the fresh air and enjoy a beautiful day." I stood and helped her up. Since we'd gotten her off the subject of the murder, the police, and even the possible complications with Elena, I thought we'd done a pretty good job on our diplomatic mission with the old dame.

"Basket, stay." After a last pat on the mutt's little head, we took our leave, and went out through the scented garden and off to some much needed diversion.

Chapter 16
Cruisin' for a Bruisin'

After the visit with Madame, I wanted to relax. Maybe forever. Back in our room, there was another phone message. I feared it might be Aphro. But the message was from Gwendolyn, who had recovered a bit and wanted to get out of the hotel. After Sophie and I agreed that we could both use some time to ourselves, Sophie called Gwen back and they made plans to see Gournia. Sophie would drive, and it seemed they could have a fine time. I muted my delight at the plan; it's not a celebration of marriage to glory in the absence of one's spouse. But Sophie gave her blessing to having me park at the resort and pig out if I wished. "But no smoking."

Sophie left after a scramble to get properly dressed and to gather guide books. I changed into a swimsuit and terry-cloth robe, gathered my crosswords, *Twilight in the Ruins* with a bookmark on page 18, flip-flops and sunglasses. Putting on my Kriti cap, I headed for the pool. I got a towel, spread it on a chaise, and sat down. I had just started my puzzle when I noticed Danielle across the way. Alone. Bikini. A welcome sight, proving that the Tanners— or Danielle at least—had survived the Onarchos firing range. Remembering seeing her near Gaitani made me tense up a bit. I really didn't want to think about all that. But just then she saw me and smiled. I nodded and smiled back, cool as sorbet. Then I leaned back against the chaise and tried to think of the crossword clue—the seventh planet. I thought of Lyle as I began to doze and suddenly I had it: *Uranus!*

A few minutes later, a shadow crossed my face. I took my cap off and saw Danielle, the sun behind her head making a sparkling halo of her blonde hair. She looked down at me, not smiling but with a generous look. I would rather have looked than talked, but I would have died before being impolite to this sailor's dream. "Hi there," I said, lowering my voice half an octave. "Have a seat." I moved my feet off the end of the chaise, and she sat down, stretching her long tanned legs in front of her. Now what?

"I imagine you must feel pretty bad about Nikos," I said. She deserved some condolences since Gavras *was* a business associate.

"Yes," Danielle said. "It's very disturbing. I'd like things to go back to the way they were."

"Don't we all."

"I want to do something today to put it out of my mind." She turned her face up toward the sun and arched her back. The gesture flattened her trim ribcage and stomach. "Lyle's busy trying to figure out how to settle things so we can go home. But that policewoman made us leave our passports with her, of all things. Just because we had business with Nikos." She almost pouted. "Lyle will be on his laptop all day to see if we can put things on hold with the Gavras shop. I don't think the sister can deal with any of that yet."

No, I said to myself, she probably can't. Danielle clasped one of her knees and pulled her foot up on the chaise. She smiled, closed her eyes for a moment, and shrugged. "That leaves me at loose ends for the day." Poor baby. She was hardly in mourning for poor Nikos. Not a word of regret except where she was concerned.

"Well, so am I," I said, not thinking it through. "We're pretty upset about things ourselves, witnessing the crime scene and all. Sophie and Gwendolyn went to Gournia so I could lie here trying to forget what I saw."

The pool glittered blue in the sun. "Tell you what," Danielle said, touching my arm, "how would you like to take a short boat tour on the Gulf of Mirabello? It means 'beautiful sea.'" She was smiling again. "The hotel has boats that go along the coast down to Pachia Ammos and back. They'd stop there long enough for us to walk around a bit and maybe get a drink. Good distraction, not long, two or three hours. I think they have a departure at one o'clock."

"Sounds like a good idea." So good that I felt the hair on the nape of my neck rise. It would blow plans for lunch, but what a way to spend my free day. Days ago I would have felt both thrilled and guilty to arrange an excursion with this lissome blonde. But now I had an excuse. If I could not forget about the murder, I might have some luck in getting more information about Nikos from Danielle. I could legally enjoy her company by setting aside a flirtatious purpose to see what might lay under that blithe exterior. I took Danielle's invitation to mean Crocodile Man wouldn't mind if his better half and I had a little outing. So we agreed, and she returned to her chaise to bask some more.

I went back to our room after a short time and put on chinos, a black polo shirt, running shoes and a light windbreaker. I wished I had a Stetson like Lyle's to wear instead of a stupid baseball cap. Besides spiffing up, I strategized. I didn't want to tell the sun-lit sylph about our visit to Elena the day before, or our fleeting glimpse of her and Lyle in their convertible in the backcountry. But even if I didn't take her into my confidence, I might learn more about Nikos's business dealings with Onarchos. Sophie will be proud of me, I thought. I'd morphed from window shopper into super-sleuth.

We met at twelve forty-five at the larger dock at the north end of the beach and boarded a small tour boat with seven or eight other guests. We headed out to sea, seated on boards by the gunwale under a striped canopy, the breeze in our hair and the sun in our faces. Danielle wore huge sunglasses, a clingy coral sweater, and tight white shorts. Instead of the appliquéd canvas totes Sophie favors, she carried a square leather affair with thin patent straps that presumably held her wallet, camera, compact, and other things wholly unknown to men. "Prada," Danielle said, when she saw me looking at it. Whatever that meant, Prada to you, too.

She looked thoughtful. "What happened after you all found Nikos?" She squinted against the bright light, even behind her sunglasses. As she moved to face me better, her leg brushed in light contact against mine. For a second I wished I were wearing shorts. "It must have been a dreadful shock, especially with that woman from the police interrogating everyone right away. Poor Gwendolyn! I hope she's all right."

"She seems to be," I said. "Sophie said she sounded okay this morning." I remembered there had been some snarking between Danielle and Gwen the night of the barbecue, but I guess a murder makes arguments like that seem petty in retrospect.

"That's a relief. I would have died. What a thing to find in your *room!*" Danielle shook her head and turned away, as if to dispel the vision. "What did it look like?"

It? I thought. How about *him*, for old time's sake, Danielle? "His throat was sliced. He was still alive, on his back, choking, struggling, looking up at the ceiling fan." I couldn't bear to go into more detail.

"Poor Nikos! I knew him, but not very well. I don't know what's going to happen to his shop, with only his sister there. She should sell the place. She's not a business woman."

I realized I'd have to yield a little to get a little. "Actually, we visited Mrs. Mylonas yesterday to offer our regrets and see how she was. She was very nice to Sophie in spite of our problem with Nikos."

Danielle turned and looked at me again. "I'm surprised you'd want to have anything more to do with that place after your experience there. You are really too kind."

She paused, looking out to sea as the boat turned and headed south. A Greek goddess could have had Danielle's profile. She pointed to a large crag rising from the shore, saying they could see it from their room at Astron Bay. The sea was calm and through the gentle ripples, we could see the sandy ocean floor beneath the boat. We lost sight of the white façade of the hotel as we moved on south.

"Anyway," Danielle said, turning to me again and this time grazing my shoulder, "what did the police have to say after the murder? It must have been very unsettling."

I shrugged. "The Inspector did most of the talking. A lot about who saw what, when, the timing, but there wasn't really much to say."

"I suppose not. Still, it must have been weird."

"The weirdest thing was that we had seen Aphro about an hour before in the museum in Agnik."

"Aphro?"

"Aphrodite Kensington, the police Inspector. She's the one that held us up at the museum after Gwendolyn fell and there was some stuff missing from a display case. Did you hear about that?"

Danielle looked uncertain for a moment. "Yes, actually. Gwendolyn told us about that the day before yesterday on the phone. Poor woman. She was very upset. It wasn't her best day. But did the cop-lady say anything about how all this happened?"

"You mean the missing things in the museum?"

"No, no," Danielle said, shaking her head. "About Nikos."

"I'm afraid not. Except that we aren't suspects, thank heavens. Gwen neither. We were all at the museum—with the Inspector, as luck would have it. Gave us all a handy alibi."

"Speaking of alibis," Danielle said, "I can't figure out why they don't just book the manager, Santas. He was there all afternoon and he had a glaring motive." She was at it again.

"But that gives him an alibi. He was working at the desk, visible to everyone."

Danielle looked over my shoulder, out to sea, then back at me. "How long does it take to go down a floor and slit a guy's throat on a slow afternoon?"

Coming from Danielle, this question was grotesque, to say the least. "Good point," I said. Bad point, I thought to myself.

Danielle went on. "I've also heard that Turkish fellow I met at the barbecue was at the resort all day."

"Gabor Latif? What could he possibly have to do with Nikos Gavras?" Danielle was beginning to give me the creeps, hypocrite that I am. It's okay for me to suspect Spiro, or Gabor for that matter, but when you hear somebody else doing it, they sound mean-spirited.

"Well, Gwendolyn thinks there's something fishy about the company he works for," she answered. "Corruption, you know. Maybe Nikos knew something he shouldn't have known about their excavations."

I wasn't pumping Danielle for information, I realized. Instead, she was feeding me scenarios. And I was miffed that she and Gwen were on the phone Sunday, even though Sophie and I couldn't rouse her. On instinct, I moved my leg and torso slightly away from hers. Danielle still looked gorgeous on the outside with the rays sparkling off her smooth hair and high cheekbones, but I was beginning to dislike what emerged from inside.

I decided to go on the offensive. "So what were you up to that day?" I asked. A little blunt, but anything she said would be of interest.

"Believe it or not, we were visiting a leper colony."

"You've got to be kidding!" I said in real surprise. "I should think you'd be wearing a bell, like in the old days."

"It's perfectly safe, Red," she said. "Former leper colony, actually. Spinalonga Island, which is relatively deserted these days. Lyle and I took a boat we hired and walked around. It's an interesting place."

Danielle must've seen the skeptical look on my face—marveling at why this business-like fox would be interested in an abandoned leper colony. She launched right into a brief lecture.

"Many Cretans fled to Spinalonga when the Turks took over this island around 1800. After the Turks left Crete, Spinalonga was turned into a leper colony that was closed in 1957. Hardly anyone lives there now, but the fortress and the remains of the colony are interesting."

For the first time on this trip I felt grateful that Sophie's interests veered to art and antiquities after all. Pharmaceutical chemists on vacation don't really fancy visiting graveyards full of spores from incurable diseases. I'd seen *Ben Hur* with Charlton Heston on the old movie channel one night. Those disfigured women with their eroded faces gave me the willies.

"Actually, I have some pictures on my camera, if you'd like to see them." Danielle reached into her sleek handbag and pulled out a digital camera. "Here, have a look." We got under the striped canopy to reduce the sun's glare. She turned the screen to me. "Here's the guy that took us over. He was really nice. A real Greek boat man. We left from Ágios Nikólaos and the trip takes less than half an hour."

I said nothing, but my heart skipped a beat as I looked at the picture. It was a guy with silver hair, standing next to Danielle in one shot and next to Lyle in another. He had a white captain's hat on this time and what looked like a uniform, complete with a white jacket and gold buttons. I'd seen him before, not once, but twice—no, three times. I was pretty sure this was my Marlboro Man, but also the guy talking to Lyle at the barbecue. I took the camera, and with Danielle narrating, the picture show went on as I clicked forward. Pictures of Lyle and Danielle, individually or together in various poses, standing before the fortress, the cannons, the dwellings, and, of course, the cemetery of the leper colony. Other people showed up in the background of some of the pictures, presumably residents or tourists from other boats.

I circled back to the beginning of the series because I could not free my mind of the skipper. If this was the guy at the cabaña, the one I thought of as Silverhair, he was turning up like a bad penny. The mermaid tattoo on the wrist handing me a cigarette—did it belong to the *Arm* reaching for the door knob at Onarchos's compound? And was this him? I couldn't be sure, since he didn't show up in any of the other pictures. He wore aviator sunglasses and. his jacket had long sleeves, so no mermaid tattoo was visible. But my instincts told me that I shouldn't ask Danielle about him.

Instead I asked lamely, "What on earth would make you want to visit a leper colony?"

I could see one eyebrow raised over the frame of her sunglasses. "Maybe there's more to me than hanging out at the spa."

That brought me up short. "You're right," I apologized. "As a scientist I should appreciate your curiosity. I guess you were pretty surprised at what lay in store for you when you got back."

"Yes, it was certainly a shock seeing you and the other people so upset. We're still trying to figure out what happened. Kensington asked us a lot of questions the next day, wanting to know everything about our business dealings with Nikos. But she couldn't ask much more, since we were away. She went on so long, we were afraid we'd miss lunch."

"I can imagine. Anyway, I hope you and Lyle manage to straighten everything out on the business end. It must be difficult in foreign territory." I wasn't ready to get into the Pottery Shack sighting, so we ran out of things to say. I thought of changing the subject, maybe asking her where she grew up or whether she was a cheerleader in high school, but the mood just wasn't right any longer. We remained silent and soon reached Pachia Ammos.

We debarked near a waterfront café and walked inland a little bit. Pachia Ammos looked shabbier than I expected, though the rows of little painted tables and chairs with old guys in shirtsleeves and suspenders sitting around talking had an Old World charm. A spiffy yacht stood at a pier some distance away, looking out of character with all the rude fishing craft and colorful sailboats moored in the cove. I could almost read the name on the stern, but I couldn't tell whether it was in Greek or Roman alphabet. Maybe both, like the Ikaros we saw in Agnik. In the distance we could see a cleared expanse inland, with various heavy trucks near several sheds and a fenced area with more equipment.

Danielle took a few pictures of the cove and the bleached white houses with blue doors and shutters by the shore. "You know," I said, "I envy people like Elena, living near a place like this. I wouldn't be surprised if she sold her shop and settled down here. She should get out of the city." I had decided to get back to my main business on this trip. "You said earlier that you think she should sell it."

"Well, I think it's only reasonable."

"What are you going to do if she does? You depend on the shop pretty heavily, don't you?"

"We do. Or did."

Time to play my trump card. "Is that why you went down to Onarchos's place yesterday, to check out the new buyers?"

Danielle visibly started at this. "No! I mean yes." She seemed confused. Clearly Onarchos hadn't discussed our visit, or at least hadn't mentioned our names. That was reassuring. "I didn't see you there," she went on when she recovered. "We just went down there to be sure of our suppliers. I didn't know they wanted to buy the shop." She looked out to sea. "How do you know about Theo?"

"Theo. So you do know him. Elena, Mrs. Mylonas, told us about him. We went down with a friend of Elena's. He buys at the shop and wants to know whether he can keep buying stuff there, just like you."

"I see. Small world." She looked up at me and smiled. "I think we need to get a table if we want to get some wine. The boat leaves in a little while."

We walked back to the waterfront and took a small table at the café and ordered a couple of glasses of wine.

"A local airport could perk this place up commercially," I told her, "but it would play havoc with the local color. I like it as it is."

"You're right, Red. I find this place really charming. A nice contrast to the posh resort we're in." She smiled one of her generous smiles.

"Well, it looks like they're about to begin the heavy work here," I said, looking back in the direction of the sheds and quonset huts in the distance. "I'm guessing that's Gabor Latif's company over there."

Our wine arrived soon after we ordered, a Cabernet called 'Metsovo.' I lifted my glass to Danielle and put it to my lips. Suddenly a scruffy mongrel barked sharply nearby and a split second later a loud explosion rent the air. The table shook and I almost spilled my wine. Danielle dropped her glass, which spilled on the way down on her trim white shorts. The glass shattered at her feet as she stood up abruptly, using her napkin to wipe her shorts and legs.

"Oh!" she cried, "what was *that*?"

I looked over to where the blast had come from and saw men running from the construction firm's shack toward a dissipating cloud of smoke. "Jeez," I said. "that can't be the beginning of construction, can it?" The dog was still barking, and I wondered how animals can sense an explosion or an earthquake before we lowly humans hear them.

"Maybe the Germans are rushing the project," Danielle said bitterly, seated again but still dabbing at her shorts and legs. "Maybe they're removing artifacts before they get stopped by the Antiquities department, like Gwendolyn Frawley says."

"You can't mean that, Danielle. If it is a valuable site for antiquities, they can't clear it with explosions like that!"

"Well, business is business, even in Greece."

I didn't feel like arguing with Danielle, who looked upset—whether because of the explosion or the spilled wine, I couldn't say. I wanted to go over to the source of the blast and have a look, but the boat would be leaving soon. Our fellow tourists were already returning prematurely, while the good people of Pachia Ammos headed in the other direction to see what was going on. I pushed the surviving glass of wine over to Danielle in a silent offer to share, but she shook her head. Before long the bell from the boat signaled that it was time to go and so we rose and headed down to the dock.

On board the guests buzzed about the explosion, some saying that it was not trivial. They claimed a small drilling rig on or near a truck blew up somehow, and at least one person was injured. As the boat glided back out into the sea, the afternoon saw a chill breeze in the air, and Danielle and I seemed to feel it between us without quite understanding what caused it. Attempts to resume conversation failed. Danielle still insisted that the blast was most likely a sinister move on Bohnen-Essen's part to advance their interests in the airport construction. I tried to make less of it, telling her that these things happen to industrial machinery once in a while. But I did not tell her that Aphro had warned us, and Gabor had confirmed, prior incidents of sabotage. The event today raised the stakes in the whole business if it *had* been done on purpose, and speculation and blame were becoming serious matters. So we let the topic drop, and after some desultory small talk, Danielle and I remained silent until we reached Astron Bay. The cruise had been a dud both on the flirting front and on the inquisition front—with the exception of Danielle's weird digital camera slide show.

We went into the hotel at the ground floor door by the pool and stood by the elevator. Danielle handed me her chic purse to hold while she fixed her hair, disheveled by the wind. She was holding a small compact mirror up to her face when the elevator door opened, revealing Spiro. All three of us stood still, unaccountably embarrassed. In an awkward move I thrust the Prada purse back at Danielle and smiled weakly at Spiro. Instead of replying with his customary bow, he looked as startled and ill at ease as he had when we surprised him by emerging from Elena's shop. The red wine stains on Danielle's shorts made us look as if we'd returned from some revel. My face must have flushed with the color of my name as he finally nodded and moved past us, heading in the direction of the pool.

We got into the elevator. Danielle's hair was still in disarray, and we exchanged only a brief goodbye as she exited on her floor. I wondered if she was going to have as much 'splaining to do as I did when I next encountered Sophie. Just then the elevator door opened on the sixth floor, and there she was, greeting me with her dimpled smile.

Chapter 17
The Shoals of Marriage

"Hey, strangers." I said to Sophie and Gwen. "What a coincidence. Enjoy the trip?"

"Hey there, Red!" Sophie was glowing. "Yes, we had a fine time." Gwen nodded, but she seemed preoccupied. Not surprisingly, given what she might have on her mind. Like whether the hotel had installed a fresh body in her new room. Heidi appeared from a door behind the desk, tossing her single blonde braid behind her. Gwen turned to speak to her.

"Well! Why don't we go for a drink and we can tell each other our adventures," Sophie suggested. "Gwen locked herself out of her room and has to get another key. Gwen…oh, sorry." She turned and stopped, seeing Gwen talking to Heidi. We all waited while Heidi activated another key for her.

"Silly old me." Gwen gave us a wry smile. "I always seem to lay my key down in the room when I come in and forget to take it with me next time. And they only gave me one key for my new room." Being a couple is nice that way—you always have a spare key in the family.

"I'm rather tired, I'm afraid," she went on, "so you chaps run along. Red, I must say Sophie's a splendid student, and I hardly tripped on the rocks this time."

We parted from Gwen and went down the hall off the lobby to our room. Sophie was bubbling over about her journey. "Gwen knows all about Minoan history. Did you know it might have been the earliest European culture, even earlier than the Hellenes?" Hellenes? Sophie spends a couple of hours with Miss British Museum and I end up getting a pop quiz.

"You don't say." I put on my best enthusiasm as we reached our door and let ourselves into our room.

"Yes," Sophie went on as she took off her canvas sun hat and got rid of her tote bag. "Gwen thinks early Crete might have been a kind of utopian society ruled by women. That's why so many of the artifacts are based on nature or domestic life, household objects and pets and things."

"Really," I said. "I guess that explains all those hens and pigs and dogs in the Agnik museum. Makes you wonder if old Gwen filched the critters after all, given her interest in the stuff."

"Cut that out, Red," Sophie said, giving my arm a little poke, and flopping down on our settee. "Gwen is a serious scholar. She thinks it was the rule of women that made Crete a place of peace and prosperity for such a long time. Until the island was invaded by warriors from the mainland who destroyed everything."

"Leave it to Miss Oxford to find a feminist angle in archeology," I said.

"Don't knock it," Sophie retorted, her bubbly mood waning. "You guys haven't exactly made this a peaceful world for the last two thousand years."

"*Us guys!* Remember, Soph, I work on pharmaceuticals. Medicines, painkillers, cures for cancer." I could have gone on to all our redundant nasal sprays, pimple balms, sleep aids—not to mention erectile dysfunction meds— but didn't out of respect for my tattered conscience. The conversation had taken a political turn—not our forte during cocktail hour, and we hadn't even started drinking yet. If Meredith were with us, she would already have assailed me with a lecture on the ethics of the pharmaceutical industry—'such as they are,' as she puts it. Rowan Redfield is hardly a hero in his own home, truth be known, notwithstanding his efforts to bring home adequate bacon. I longed for a martini.

"Let's change clothes and go over to the Lounge," Sophie said, reading my thoughts. Or maybe there was a twitch of my upper lip that gives me away when thirst comes upon me. But much as I longed for the hard stuff, instinct told me to delay until I'd had a chance to come clean about my afternoon tryst with Danielle.

"Listen, Soph. It's a beautiful late afternoon, with the Aegean as blue as I've ever seen it. Shame to pass it up for a smoky bar. Why don't we get ourselves comfortable with some wine on the terrace before we go down to dinner." I made my voice low and romantic, and by George, it worked. Sophie looked at me with a gentle smile as she went off to change out of her denim outfit, duly softened up for the coming revelations about my cruise with Miss Nevada.

"So, what have you been up to?" Sophie settled herself into one of our rattan chairs and began sipping her *vino* and popping mixed nuts. "Partying by yourself all day at the pool?" She looked at me, still smiling warmly. "You look red, Red." She says that every time I'm embarrassed or sunburned. Sophie too has a punny bone. "Did you forget to wear your Angels cap?"

"It's more than that," I said, both sunburned *and* a little embarrassed. "I spent the day with the lovely Danielle, of all people." Sophie's eyebrows shot up, still smiling but now in mock surprise. "In fact, I joined her on a short cruise down to Pachia Ammos. It was her idea."

As though a cloud had swept over the terrace, Sophie lost her sunny look. "Red, what's going on? You were going to spend all day at the pool and now you tell me you ran off with a pretty blonde!"

My earlier thoughts about the day came back to me. It was impossible to forget Danielle in a bikini this morning and her gentle touches during our boat trip. But this was real life, not fantasy. "Not even window-shopping, Sophie," I said. "It was a research expedition."

"I'll bet," said Sophie, "like finding out how low her standards are for later reference? How come she was on the loose today?"

Did this reference to low standards have to do with my girth? A few years ago, Sophie said I looked like George Clooney. In the last year she's gone over to John Goodman as a point of reference, and the word 'pudge' has entered her vocabulary. I decided to ignore the barb.

"I meant I thought I could find out more about why they were down at the Pottery Shack yesterday. Lyle was busy trying to figure how to work out the business deals they'd made with Nikos, and Danielle was alone. She suggested we go down south on one of the small tour boats. I was really bothered about seeing them yesterday, so her proposition was a golden opportunity to find out what the hell they were doing there."

Sophie was not to be disarmed so easily. "If it weren't for your flab and your blood-shot eyes, I'd be downright jealous. I can't even take comfort in Danielle's shitty standards. It's not like Lyle is any kind of stud." Ouch again. When Sophie starts cursing, watch out. She's can be both mean and unfair in a mood like that.

I took a couple sips of wine and kept my mouth shut. Don't complain, don't explain. Just listen and wait for a break in the weather.

"And I bet you bought cigarettes to look cool on your little sleuthing gig." Sophie gulped her wine.

"'Course not, Pumpkin." Time for some sweet talk before I ended up on the rattan settee for the night. "Why don't you let me tell you about my afternoon, and you'll see that it wasn't a whole lot of fun. There were some pretty disturbing revelations, if you want to know the truth."

A pause. "All right." It was Sophie's way of backing off from a rampage. She knows what 'Pumpkin' means. It means she's won, as if I'd said 'Uncle.' And she never rubs it in. Animals like us wouldn't have survived if we couldn't negotiate truces.

So, as the light faded over the Aegean, I described my late-morning encounter with Danielle and how my failure to relax led me to join her on the trip to Pachia Ammos. In deference to both of them, I omitted mention of the bikini. Or what was in it. I reported Danielle's probing for what Sophie and I had seen, what we knew, and what Aphro had asked us. As I recounted the story, I again regretted that I'd told Danielle about our visit to Elena after all. But, I told Sophie, I had finally asked Danielle straight out what they were doing the day of the murder. Their leper colony trip surprised Sophie as much as it had surprised me. Then I told her about the photo of the skipper that looked like Silverhair.

"Who?" She looked puzzled. I remembered then that I hadn't told Sophie about *the Arm,* with the mermaid tattoo, reaching across to the door of the smoke-filled cubicle at Onarchos's place. I told her now, although in her mood she was less interested in the skipper than in why I had waited until now to tell her.

"I just didn't want you to jump to conclusions. There must be a zillion Greek men with mermaids on their arms. Anyway, even if it was the same guy that was at the cabaña and the Pottery Shack, I figured that that in itself didn't make him sinister." I was less convinced as I listened to my own explanation.

"Except, Red, he just happens to be showing up everywhere!" Sophie makes everything more significant. Unfortunately, I saw her point.

I fell in with her concern. "Well, that's what I'm wondering too. What was he doing at Onarchos's place—way the hell inland—if he's really a tour boat skipper working the customers here at Agnik and Astron Bay?"

"Do you think the Tanners went to the Pottery Shack specifically to see him?" I could see Sophie's mind was racing.

"Who, the skipper or Onarchos? I don't know myself. But I didn't want to let on to Danielle that I've been tracking that mermaid tattoo. I just asked her straight out what she and Lyle were doing there."

"And?"

"You were right, Soph, they were trying to get to Nikos's suppliers, just like you said." Sophie likes to get credit for having been right. Don't we all.

I got up and poured us another round of wine. It was comforting to talk to Sophie about these new connections, but troubling to think about what they might mean.

"I've got a worm in my stomach, and it won't go away till I know more," I said, as I handed Sophie her glass. "I think those Tanners aren't what they seem. Except Lyle the reptile. He has predator written all over him, a real bottom feeder. But at least you don't have Danielle to worry about. I mean with me, if you ever did." I looked at Sophie with hangdog appeal. "I mean, we *do* have Danielle to worry about—just not in *that* way. She's a sly fox. I'd just like to keep my eye on her for other reasons."

I probably should have dropped it, but Sophie's 'low standards' crack still rankled. In my mute, lusty heart, I hoped she was jealous and yet grateful for my nobility in the face of temptation.

She didn't give me that satisfaction, but she did reach over with her free hand and pat me on the leg after she took a sip of wine. "I never really worry about you, big Red. There aren't many women who'd put up with you the way I do. And after twenty-five years I know you're not going to turn into a crude, creepy cretin overnight." I was relieved. Sophie was being fair again. Alliterative to boot. "So what else did you find out?"

The effort of artfully minimizing Danielle's attraction had distracted me from the memory of the explosion at Pachia Ammos just before we left. "Believe it or not, we were hanging around waiting for the boat to go back and there was a big bang, an explosion in the area, the place where Gabor's company is working on the airport." Did I really have to tell Sophie that Danielle and I were having a cozy glass of red wine when the wine glass fell out of her hand at the blast and spilled all over her short shorts and long legs? No, I *really* didn't. I went on. "The people were coming back to the boat and we didn't have time to go over and investigate it, but they said there was an injury. What struck me was that Danielle right away said it was Gabor's company that was blowing up evidence that the *palace* was right there where the airport was going to be built."

"That's what Gwendolyn kept talking about when we were at *Gournia*! She's on that kick really bad." Sophie frowned. "This thing has really knocked her for a loop."

"You shouldn't be surprised," I said. "Even if Ms. Frawley would like a guy to share a room with, she probably prefers one who's warm and up to the right moves."

"Oh, Red, for heaven's sake. What an awful thing to joke about." She shot me one of her schoolmarm frowns.

"Sorry. How *was* Gournia anyhow?" I was enjoying my wine and beginning to relax. The marital sun had broken through, and Sophie had the floor.

"Well, at first it was fun." Sophie now propped her feet up on the outer wall of the terrace as she sipped her wine. "Gwendolyn enjoyed telling me all about the Minoan matriarchy and its prosperity. But as we neared Gournia, she suddenly turned glum and started in about how much she hated the thought of the airport. She started carping about Gabor again. She still thinks he's trying to interfere with the work of the Antiquities Department, and that this may be why she hasn't had follow-up calls for consulting at the site."

"Well, that might explain her snit the night of the barbecue. Not that Gwen isn't prone to being a little snitty."

"It's bigger than that, I realize, now that I've seen Gournia." Sophie looked thoughtfully at the setting sun. "There really is a major discovery at stake."

Oh-oh, here it comes. I refilled my glass and settled myself more deeply into my chair. I could hear the classroom bell for Archeology 101.

"I wish you could have seen the place, Red," Sophie said, forgetting my strong feelings about ruins. "It's really big, an entire town, excavated so you see low walls, all that remains of the houses and things, laid out along paths and streets. You can see everything since nothing is above eye level. It must have been a huge community, built on a long low rise, and the houses had kitchens and water reservoirs and everything. Gwen says its heyday was in 1600 years BC. But it wasn't discovered until the turn of the century."

Fascinating. I was delighted I hadn't gone there to be bored for a whole day. I would have hated it even 3500 years ago. No plumbing, bad food and dirty neighbors. "So what's this big archeological stake Gwen is stewing about?"

Sophie repeated the notion that the farming community of Gournia must have been attached to a palace of some sort, presumably near the ocean around Pachia Ammos. I realized I'd heard it before.

"Sort of a Knossos South," I opined. Got to grab my points when they drop into my lap like this.

"Exactly," Sophie exclaimed.

"And Gabor's firm could derail the exploration of the site and then pave it over." The barbecue discussion had registered better than I thought.

"It's not just that," Sophie said. "Gwen and I stopped to get a cup of coffee shortly after we left Gournia, and now she went off on a really hateful tack. She's heard that Gabor doesn't have an alibi."

Oh lord. I could well imagine what Gwen would make of that.

"Gwen has the whole scenario worked out. She thinks Gabor sent Samira and Hegel off to Agnik to get them out of the way and then waited for his chance. 'Murder requires motive and opportunity,' she said. 'Gabor had both.'"

The truism was no surprise coming from Gwendolyn Frawley, a Brit from the land of Marple and Holmes.

Sophie's brow was still wrinkled and she took another sip. "I reminded Gwen that Gabor had no connection to Nikos at all, but she flew into her bribery and corruption charge again. She thinks Nikos may have found out about this somehow and tried to blackmail Gabor or his firm."

"That's pretty farfetched," I said, although at this point nothing seemed totally impossible anymore.

"Well, Gwen admits there's no actual evidence for any of this but she keeps coming back to two things. Gabor doesn't have an alibi, and Nikos must have come to Astron Bay to see someone about some deal. She says no one else has a motive either so Gabor is left by a process of elimination."

"Only if you discount Spiro." We were down to the last few peanuts in the can and out of wine, and I was beginning to feel cranky toward just about everybody again. "Gwen is totally out to lunch. How the hell would Gabor have gotten into her room?"

"She thinks he might have taken one of her keys at the barbecue. She had two of them and maybe left one on the table where we ate."

"She could have just lost it. Or anybody could have taken it. One of the waiters, for cryin' out loud, not even on purpose. And some of the staff have keys to all the rooms, if it comes to that."

"Whatever." Sophie tipped a last drop of red wine out of her glass. "But the fact remains, Gwen says, that the murderer must have gotten one of her keys and the police found it on the floor on the other side of her bed in her room. And she sat with Gabor the night before the murder." I didn't remember seeing a key on the floor.

"It's still crazy," I said. Of course, someone had gotten into *our* room on the night of the barbecue, although it wasn't Gabor, sitting right there next to Gwen. Was it? The Latifs *did* show up at the barbecue only in the course of my bloody bowl excursion, come to think of it. But Gabor didn't know Nikos, and didn't know anything about the silver bowl scam, did he? It didn't compute, as Sophie might say. It didn't compute.

Chapter 18
Blowups

By the time we went down to dinner, I was in a great mood. The wine had mellowed us out and washed away the last residues of jealousy and sheepishness over my excursion with Danielle, and I decided to work hard to ensure an agreeable meal.

Gwendolyn turned up looking far more relaxed than I expected. She had neatened her bun and her steelrims sparkled. She had on a loose, flowing print dress that went well with her reddish hair. It made her look more like a young dowager rather than an old dowager. It turned out that she'd been cheered by a call from the Antiquities Department. A guy named Krispofritos (at least that's what it sounded like to me) had left a message on her phone, telling her he had some sort of great news. She looked forward to meeting with him next day. I gathered he'd been tactful enough not to acknowledge her current situation. Just how, I thought, *would* you acknowledge her current situation? 'Hello, Ms. Frawley. If you've got the dead body thing under control, perhaps you might drop by and check out some cracked pots tomorrow. See you soon?'

"Sounds like you'll be able to get started on the serious professional work you've been looking forward to," Sophie said. "Any idea what the great news is?"

"I'm sure I don't know, but it must be frightfully important if Mr. Christophoros phoned me himself. I know most of the chaps on the team from the last time I was here. I consulted with them on Gournia materials and even earlier on the Thera excavation on Santorini. They've been awfully slow on the current site, but it's clearly heating up now with the airport. I'm *awfully* keen to hear they've had a break-through there."

It sounded like the occasion warranted a little celebration, and I offered to spring for a bottle of champagne. It did the trick, and old Gwen became downright convivial as she held the sparkling flute and sipped her bubbly. All through dinner she told us stories about some of the Oxford eccentrics she'd worked with and surprised us with a real flair for mimicking stuffy dons and toffs. I had to admit it was one of the more enjoyable dinners we'd had at Astron Bay—although that's not saying much, given our circumstances.

As the meal came to an end we ordered a fabulous *Sachertorte* for dessert along with some vintage port. But then who should come over to us but Gabor Latif? He must have been emboldened by the guffaws and jollity at our table to make his approach, although he looked like hell with scratches on his left cheekbone and the swarthy left arm revealed by his short-sleeved shirt. I could not help think his injuries were connected with the explosion at Pachia Ammos that afternoon and dreaded the thought of having to return to disaster themes in the midst of our festivity. He had left Samira and Hegel behind at their table and smiled nervously with deference as he approached. "May I join you, please? For a few minutes?"

"By all means." I spoke instinctively but not happily, remembering the bad chemistry between our friends. Hoping Gwen might extend her good mood and soften up a little, I pointed to the empty chair.

"Good evening, Miss Frawley," he said, as he sat down next to Gwen. He seemed oblivious to our curious stares at his injuries. "I am sorry we argue some nights ago. And I know you have difficult days behind you. But I have good news. I think you will feel good." I brightened up. He wasn't coming with tales of sabotage, and if his news coincided with what Gwen expected St. Christopher to tell her tomorrow, we might have to order a glass of port for Gabor too. Under the influence of the champers, Gwen actually remained civil. I thank Bacchus for many favors.

Gabor relaxed a little and loosened his tie as though to talk and gesture more freely. "I could not speak of this before although I wanted very much, because Antiquities Department say they must tell about new information first. They say they try to call you today." He was now all smiling eagerness, but this threatened scoop of her news had an immediate chilling effect on Gwendolyn. She stiffened and sat up from her relaxed pose. "You know my firm offer last year to make sonic surveys and drillings for Antiquities Department—after authorities in Athens and Heraklion tell them their concerns. They say now that Pachia Ammos does *not* show sign of central palace."

"For heaven's sake," Gwen sputtered. "How on earth could they decide that on the basis of just a few drillings? This is absurd. The initial findings were extremely promising." Sophie and I looked in wonder at the renewal of hostilities. Out of the corner of my eye, I noted that Gwen had eaten none of her *Sachertorte*. I calculated the chance of getting a crack at it if she got too cheesed off to eat it herself.

Gabor continued, foolishly undaunted. "The sonic survey was very thorough, over much larger area. No evidence of big structures or regular patterns. We compare findings to records of older excavations—but nothing additional appear. Our work cover much larger area than older surveys and our modern techniques make it more certain. I think you will be pleased our firm is not threat to a valuable site."

"Well, that does sound like wonderful news," Sophie broke in, trying to salvage the earlier good mood. "Everyone wins in this, it seems to me. Except the people that don't want an airport—and phooey on them!" Her smile faded as she looked at Gwen.

"I will certainly ask my friends in the Department about this," Gwen pushed her plate away. "Christophoros should have informed me much sooner. I am their consultant, after all."

To our surprise, Gabor, though nervous, kept his equanimity. "I am sorry, Miss Frawley, but they are afraid of publicity because there is another—*another wonderful*—thing." He leaned in toward us and whispered in excitement. "Antiquities say they have more evidence now that palace may be inland, away from ocean, more protected."

"That's perfectly ridiculous." Gwen's shoulders bobbed with vehemence. "You can't tell a thing like that from your few drillings and sonar and magnetometry. I simply don't believe it."

Gabor clouded up. His eyebrows twitched in a spastic frown. "There is archeological evidence also," he said. "I cannot tell much, since it is new and we wish not to make public just now. But some pieces also turn up at possible palace site away from Pachia Ammos and more inland." He began picking nervously at the scratches on his arm. The great dinner mood was shot to hell.

"Wow," I said gamely, "from what you've told Sophie, Gwen, that would be a real find." This had to be great news for her. Surely she would get into the spirit of the thing.

But after a moment that seemed to hang in the air, Gwen looked sharply at Gabor. "Mr. Latif," she said, "how can you possibly know all this? *I* should have been informed of these findings and decisions. *I* am a senior consultant, trained at Oxford, and *my* advice should have been solicited." Whoa, I thought, Her Highness was insulted. No matter how good the news, if you're the last to hear, it's bad news. I expected her to spread her stork wings and soar off in a huff.

"Miss Frawley, please forgive them, and my firm. Antiquities say they tried to telephone to you. We first need secure the inland area because looters may come if publicity get out. So everything kept confidential until evidence is clear and certain." He was now making self-deprecating gestures with his hands and looked twice as distressed as he had been at the barbecue.

"You say 'we,' Mr. Latif. It is completely inappropriate that your firm, hoping to build an airport, is the very company that tells the Antiquities Department that the government can go ahead with construction. It is a blatant conflict of interest, and I will not trust this decision."

"Gwen, it's all right." Sophie put her hand on Gwendolyn's arm in a calming gesture. "I'm sure your friend was calling to tell you about this and surely you trust him."

"I am so sorry. I thought this news be very good for all of us." Gabor said, dumbfounded.

Gwen took her arm from under Sophie's hand, adjusted her glasses and rose majestically to her feet. She turned toward Gabor. "It is difficult not to suspect that people have been bribed. Once commerce gets involved, archeological work becomes riddled with graft, like everything else. This matter reeks of corruption. Palm oil, we call it." She rubbed her fingers together in an ugly gesture, as though feeling grease.

Without another word, she snatched her small purse from the table and stalked off. She stumbled on the step leading out of the dining room. She swept her dress about her theatrically as she recovered and went out the door, taking long strides, without looking back. She did not even acknowledge the Tanners as she passed their table near the door.

"Well, my goodness," Sophie said. "I am so sorry, Gabor. Ms. Frawley has been under a lot of strain lately, and she's not very well, I'm afraid."

Gabor looked stricken. "I apologize to disturb your meal. I thought I had glad news. I must go. Please, I am sorry." He rose with a mournful look and turned to go back to his family, who were looking on with concern and impatience from across the room.

"Gabor, wait," I said, "Stay for a minute. This is so embarrassing. Please have a seat and tell us what this is all about." I gestured toward his chair but he remained standing, indecisive. "What is the story of the palace? Why would Gwen be so upset?"

"And whatever happened to you, with all those cuts on your arm and face?" Sophie's voice was nurturing rather than inquisitive, but Gabor was no longer in the mood to confide.

"I will tell you maybe another time." He jabbed his hand forward as if to shake, but withdrew it and started to move away. "I am sorry. I tell you later about this. My family wait for me. You are very kind. I am sorry." I rose to see him off, partly as a courtesy and partly to prevent Sophie from leaping up and giving him a hug. She looked pained at his distress and I sensed that her earlier suspicions about Gabor had been put on hold. My own faith in him, paradoxically, had suffered a blow, if only because Gwen *did* have a point about Gabor's conflict of interest, and his injuries remained unexplained. Why not tell us about the sabotage—unless Bohnen-Essen *was* eradicating the last traces of the Minoan palace, as Danielle had charged?

As we sat down again, I turned to Sophie. "What the hell is going on? Gabor seems to have lit Gwen's fuse. It makes no sense that this news would make her so mad. It should have been good news, and she acts as though he's bulldozed Stonehenge."

Sophie sat stunned. In silence, I made good on my threat to Gwen's unconsumed dessert and cordial. Her cake was just as rich and delicious as mine. But we both remained glum, looking out the window at the darkening sky and the lights coming on along the shore in the distance.

A voice sounded behind us. "Please Mr. and Mrs. Redfield. May I have a word with you?" Spiro had approached the table and seemed almost as deferential as Gabor. But he stood erect, his maroon blazer and name tag reinforcing an important mission.

"Of course, of course. Have a seat." I swept my hand toward Gabor's vacated chair, praying that he wasn't planning to mention seeing me with Danielle outside the elevator a few hours ago.

"No, no, please. I see you have finished. I hope you can meet with me privately. I will take care of the billing." He picked up the slip that we normally signed. "But please join me on the terrace."

I didn't know the dining room had a terrace, but we rose and followed him to the end of the long room. On the way, Spiro paused to say a few words to one of the waiters. As he did so, I noticed Hegel's soccer jacket draped over his seat, forgotten as the Latifs hastily left the room. We continued, and Spiro pulled apart drapes concealing French doors to a tiny outdoor bay with four metal chairs around a small table. We went out, and Spiro with silent courtliness seated Sophie. Deftly, he lit an oil lamp with a lighter and turned on a small electric heater built into the outside wall. I took my seat, and noted a spectacular view of the cove, mostly in darkness now, with the glow of city lights from Agnik on the northern horizon. Then Spiro partially closed the doors and seated himself at the table. Sophie and I looked at him and at one another, wondering what the hell was coming next. I felt chilly, although it was a warm night. He was a large man, too big for the metal chair, and looked all the more awkward as he repeatedly cleared his throat and fingered his moustache. He was clearly stalling until the waiter arrived with a tray, set down three cordial glasses on the table, and left, closing the doors behind him.

"Walnut liqueur." Spiro raised his small ornate glass toward each of us. "Produced locally by the family of our chef. They make too little to distribute commercially, so they give Astron Bay only a small subscription. We offer it only to special guests." He smiled for the first time, though his shoulders remained tense. I took a sip, relishing the smooth earthy flavor. Hopefully I wouldn't stumble to the elevator on our way back to our room. Two ports and a liqueur didn't equal the martini I had passed up tonight, I calculated, but they still packed a small punch.

"I must tell you something, Mr. and Mrs. Redfield. We have not been able to speak since you saw me at the Gavras shop in Ágios Nikólaos the day before yesterday, and I find I must ask for your help." Alarm instantly flashed on Sophie's face—with worry that his news might involve Elena, I guessed. She drew her light shawl around her and I too shivered a little, feeling the net of our involvement gathering about us. Don't agree to anything, Tinkerbell, I tried to telegraph Sophie. Just listen.

Spiro leaned forward on the table. "A week before Nikos Gavras was murdered, I received a letter from him. He writes a very bad thing. He tells me I am… I am…the illegitimate son of Madame!" We couldn't tell if his face was red, but in the dark it seemed to glow in embarrassment. "It is a damnable lie. I am Madame's godson, son of her dearest friend, Sonia Santas, whom she met in Switzerland." He delivered this as a statement of proud fact, as though to clarify any confusion about the truth. "But Nikos writes he will tell everyone

I am Madame's son if her memoir is printed and published. And he will tell the world that Erasmo Gavras is my *father!*"

My liqueur almost spilled as my hand shook. I steadied the glass with my lips and then put it down. Good grief! Scandal upon scandal. We'd heard half of this rumor before—from whom?—but not the punch line.

"I said nothing to Madame," Spiro continued. "It would kill her, to have such an evil rumor become public. I thought of paying Nikos not to do this thing, but that would appear to confirm his accusation. So I said nothing to anyone until the police..." He could hardly go on. His managerial composure had collapsed, and he looked away from us for a moment.

Sophie, steady as usual, leaned toward him. "The police? You mean just now, or earlier?" Comforter of the afflicted, she was in overdrive on this night, replete with distressed men. I could see her hand itching to pat the sleeve of his blazer, its gold-embossed button glinting in the lamplight.

"The police received a copy of the letter before Nikos was murdered. But there was no crime and nothing for them to do. Until Nikos Gavras died at Astron Bay. They showed me their copy of the letter the next day, and my heart almost stopped. The Chief himself questioned me and I told him the story was not true. I begged him not to tell Madame. But he did, and Madame was furious and almost chased him out of her room." For a moment his eyes crinkled in a faint smile at this image of his inimitable godmother, afraid of nothing and no one. I was less amused, remembering that the old lady had left out this part of the story when she gave us her own comic rendition of the scene. Trusting Americans that we are, we'd been played for laughs.

Sophie must have felt this too and decided to shed our gullibility, because she now made a surprisingly bold move. "Mr. Santas, forgive me for asking this. But if the police had Nikos's letter, why didn't they take you into custody? As they say in detective novels: murder requires motive and opportunity. That letter made you the prime suspect with both."

Spiro seemed relieved that we had shifted from his murky family history back to the murder. He now took a sip of his liqueur, wiped his moustache bristles from center to tips with both hands, and went on with his story. "They of course took my passport, as they did yours. But I had limited opportunity on the day of Madame's birthday celebration when I was almost always with my staff. So instead of arrest they simply kept me under close observation until the letter could be tested. They learned, to my great relief, that it was not written by Nikos Gavras."

"Wow!" I almost choked on my last sip. "How did they determine that?"

"There was no copy of the letter in Gavras's computer, and the printer is different. And the signature does not match Nikos's handwriting perfectly. That they can tell. Also, there are no fingerprints on the envelopes or the letters that match Nikos Gavras's. They agree that the letter is false and the signature was forged."

"But if Nikos didn't send the letter, who did? And why?" The truth dawned on Sophie even as she asked. "You were being framed!" She paused to let this sink in, and then turned to Spiro in full Marple mode. "Is that what you need our help with—to find out who framed you?"

"No, no, my dear," Spiro said sadly, smiling ruefully at Sophie. "My request has to do with a terrible mistake I made, and for which I am now ashamed."

A silence followed as he composed his request, giving us another chance to take in the beautiful starry night over the bay, with its glowing hills on the horizon.

"Before I learned from the police that Nikos did not send the letter, I decided to confront Elena Mylonas to demand what she knew about this. That was when I met you coming out of the Gavras shop." Spiro struggled visibly to tell us what came next. "Elena was shocked when she saw the letter. She had never heard of this, she said. Never. No one in her family has ever said this, that I was the son of Erasmo and Madame Delphinos. Nikos could not have said this, she was certain. 'You are lying,' I screamed at her. 'Your family wanted to blackmail Madame to keep her from publishing her memoir.'" Spiro shook his head in embarrassment. "I was very angry. 'You lie,' I shouted at her again, and she began to cry."

Spiro's voice cracked at this point, and he struggled to go on. "The shopgirl rushed from the back room and stood between us and told me to leave or she would call the police. I left but I could still hear Elena weeping behind me as I went out the door."

No wonder he was ashamed. Even if he was upset, he'd been pretty brutal, confronting Nikos's grieving sister like that within two days of his ghastly murder. I hoped we hadn't offered our help too compliantly in advance, if he was going to ask what I thought he was going to ask. But, of course, Mother Sophia jumped right in.

"Is that what you need our help for? To explain all this to Elena?"

Spiro looked grateful for the preemption. "Yes. Yes, it is. I have telephoned to apologize, but the shopgirl says Elena will not speak to me and asks me never to come to the shop again. I will write a letter, I think, but I thought if you could also tell her how very sorry I am for my terrible mistake and my…my…" He could not bring himself to say it. For a gracious dude like that, an act of despicable rudeness must hurt like hell, like a self-inflicted saber wound. Spiro reminded me of a policeman I'd seen on a TV documentary once, crying after he had shot a man by mistake.

"Of course, Mr. Santas, of course. We'll do what we can." This time Sophie did put her hand on Spiros's sleeve. The sky was entirely dark now.

Spiro's body shook only once. He then rose, stood at his full height and once again became the manager of Astron Bay. "Thank you. Thank you for Madame and myself." We too rose and all of us returned to the dining room. Two waiters were clearing the last dinner dishes and setting tables for the morning. Hegel's jacket now hung tidily on the coat rack by the door.

Chapter 19
Hegel in Hot Water

Needless to say, I woke with a headache next morning. There's something pure about gin and vermouth, some transcendent simplicity that cleans your brain and sharpens it for serious thought. That's why I'm a martini man. Cordials and liqueurs, on the other hand, are polluted with fruits and spices and even flowers, for crying out loud, and loaded with sugars that clot your acuity and perception. I'm a chemist, and I should have known better than to be seduced by chocolate cakes and walnut elixirs the night before. I could hardly move until the coffee and aspirin Sophie brought me did their work. Only then did I let her open the drapes so the morning sunshine could flood our room. By the time I staggered out to the terrace in my black pajama shorts and Angels cap, the coffee had warmed my spirits a little. But I still felt lousy about the way a nice evening had been unaccountably spoiled the night before, and I remained baffled by Spiro's confession.

"What the hell does Spiro think we can do to patch things up with Elena?" I asked Sophie. "Doesn't it seem weird to you that a bunch of Greeks living in a relatively small community need foreigners to act as their go-betweens?"

Sophie was surprisingly unscathed by the evening's dissipations and looked crisp and cool after her shower. "Well, the Gavras family stayed mainly in Athens, except for Nikos, I gathered from Elena. So I doubt if the two families had any social interaction. But I also wonder if Spiro isn't setting us up for something. I mean, he sure got my sympathy last night, but how do we know everything he told us is really true?"

She got up and took my coffee cup to refill it inside, and the receding sight of her cute rear end in her denim shorts cheered me up. Dang, she looked good for a grandma!

"Red, I think we should call Aphro before we do anything," Sophie said, as she settled back in her rattan chair across from me.

"What for? We don't know anything she doesn't know already."

She was holding her mug with both hands and squinting at the horizon. "Well, for starters, we could check out Spiro's story about the forged Nikos letter, and make sure it checks out before we talk to Elena."

She had a point. Elena could verify that Spiro confronted her with a letter and its allegations, but only the police could verify that they also received a letter and that it was a forgery.

"I also thought of something else," Sophie went on. "How can we be sure that the day of the murder actually *was* Madame's 90th birthday? What kind of coincidence is *that*—having a murder and a birthday party both occurring at Astron Bay on August 10? Madame and Spiro could have set up a phony celebration to give themselves alibis."

I was shocked. "Sophie, how can you even think such a thing?" Yesterday Sophie was in love with the old dame, and here she was accusing her of murder after her godson spilled his guts out to us last night.

"Well, Madame fibbed when she told us her little story about roughing up that police chief baboon—isn't that what she called him? She didn't mention anything about Nikos's letter to us." So Sophie had picked up on that little discrepancy too. "With that letter, the police *had* to question her and Spiro. So why wouldn't she cooperate? That makes me wonder what else isn't true— like that whole birthday show. Aphro could verify her birthday from Madame's passport. And she could check the local florists. Madame could have ordered all those flowers for herself, you know, to distract the staff and everybody from what was going on in room 534."

Sophie was marpling. "You've been reading too many Sue Grafton novels, Soph. This is real life—not some fantastic plot festering with evil motives and lies and conspiracies." Sophie made me read one of those California mystery books a while back. Made me long for the days when I could still cuss like that foul-mouthed detective—before Archie came into our lives and I turned into Grandpa.

"Red, think for a minute about all the weird stuff that's going on. Basket kidnapped. That bloody bowl in our bathroom—provided, of course, that that wasn't just one of your martini hallucinations. Wally's wild goose chase into the middle of nowhere with the Tanners turning up there. And that skipper of yours popping up all over the map. Last night you tell me there was an explosion down at the place where Gabor works, and he won't tell us about it. Gwen accuses him of bribery. Shall I go on?"

Sophie was right. Seconds after I contradict her I begin to see her point. Once her trust is shaken, she doesn't recover easily. Me, I'm a professional at denial if anyone tries to disturb my equilibrium. Sharks? They're *dolphins* till I see blood in the water. But now, with Sophie on the case, the water had a distinct tinge of pink.

"We're going to go down to breakfast and keep our eyes and ears open." Sophie had made up her mind and was taking charge this morning. "After breakfast, we call Aphro and ask to meet with her. I'd call her now but it's too early. I need to get my thoughts straight and I need stronger coffee for that. And after we've phoned Aphro we're going to the spa and get a massage. If ever we needed one, today's the day."

Whoa, whoa. Who's *we*, Tinkerbell? But before I had a chance to protest this massage bullcrap, Sophie disappeared into the bathroom to get ready. Oh well, I'd have at least a half-hour to come up with my excuse.

At the door of the dining room, we looked in and saw the Tanners in one of the smaller booths just inside. They avoided our eyes as studiously as we avoided theirs. Well, except for the metaphorical dagger or two Sophie shot in Danielle's direction. Hegel's soccer jacket still hung on a coat rack next to them by the door. Its yellow arc of letters on the back spelled 'Latif.'

It was only 8:30, but the place was already surprisingly full. People must be taking tours this morning. We went over to the window and seated ourselves at one of the larger tables, just being vacated. Shortly afterwards, the Latifs showed up, Hegel and all. And wouldn't you know it, Sophie waved them over. Hegel had his sullen face on, alert and resentful, but at least he was quiet as he took a chair beside his parents.

"Good morning, friends," said Gabor. He had dark circles under his eyes as though he hadn't slept well. "It is very kind of you to invite us. I am sorry again for disturbance last night with your friend. But I am shocked by her accusation against me and my firm. People in restaurant hear her and if they believe, my name could be ruined. Why would she do cruel thing like that?" Good question. Maybe it's because she's a cruel, scurrilous and slanderous nutcase.

"Oh Gabor, it's we who are sorry," Sophie said. "I know this is no excuse, but we have to remember that Ms. Frawley has simply been devastated by these events."

"What events?" said Hegel.

"The murder," I said. "Ms. Frawley found the man's body in her room."

"Oh, *Ja*, that—cool." Hegel looked around checking out the breakfast buffet across the way. *Cool?* I thought. Well, I suppose Nikos wasn't one of Hegel's pals and kids that age don't relate much to strangers. He mumbled something to his mother beside him and started to get up to go to the buffet. "Hey, Hegel, you left your jacket in the restaurant last night. It's over there on the coat rack," I called after him. He mumbled something I presumed was thanks and took off. The waiter brought us a large pot of coffee.

"How is Hegel?" Sophie asked as she poured herself a cup from the decanter. "Is he having a better time now? He seemed to perk up at the barbecue. I hope he's found some more friends and is beginning to enjoy the resort."

Samira, busy pouring Gabor's coffee and doctoring it with a big spurt of cream and three little packets of sugar, looked up. "He more happy. But his friends..." She shook her head and compressed her lips. Hey, Samira spoke a little English after all! Maybe she was just shy at first. I could see Sophie was pleased that she trusted us enough to open up a little.

Gabor took over. "Samira still worry. Hegel make some friends at resort but young people want to get away from *Elderhostel*, they call it. Go out all day and at night, sometimes come back late." I caught their concern. Been there, done that.

He actually looked just as worried as his wife. "Young people take bus from here to Pachia Ammos, has soccer field and nightclub. We do not let him go Ágios Nikólaos—too big. But even Pachia has...rough people."

"Oh dear." Sophie sympathized with clucking noises. "It's tough being a teenage boy these days." As though she'd know. "They face so many hazards and it's hard to protect them from everything." I had a flashback to the smell of weed coming out of Colin's room when he was that age, the big jerk. And he had the nerve to throw my smoking in my face when I yelled at him about it.

"We make Hegel take his *Handi.*" Gabor gestured to indicate a cell phone. "To phone my company if he has problem."

"Well, that's good, given what's been going on at your construction site." I pointed at the place on my cheek and arm that corresponded to Gabor's Band-Aids.

Gabor sighed, took a sip of his ruined coffee, and asked, "How you hear of this so soon?"

"I was down there on a hotel tour boat. We were having a glass of wine when I heard the explosion." I didn't like the sound of 'we,' and neither did the frowning Sophie who also winced at the mention of 'wine.'

Gabor looked at Sophie and me—in his mind the touring couple. "One of our mobile drill units was—what you say—blown up. Our technician was near blast, and he unconscious and taken to hospital. He have broken arm and ribs. I was behind him and fell on ground. Lucky. Hospital say this morning he will be okay."

"How could that have happened?" Sophie leaned into our conversation. "Why would anyone do that?" Plainly, she did not think it was an accident.

"We not know who did it. More sabotage now than before. But was never before this bad, with injury. Just tires cut, and equipment pushed over. Our work inland we do with unmarked trucks now. It is very difficult. People still think we destroy palace site in Pachia Ammos."

"What people, exactly?" I remembered a second later that both Gwen and Danielle belonged to that camp. But Gabor just shrugged and shook his head. It still made no sense. If the Antiquities people were working with Bohnen-Essen, they wouldn't blow up their property, surely. So who would? Antiquities terrorists? Attic-terrorists—is that what we'd call them? Hard to picture them. Greek teenagers, incensed about classical palace ruins? Middle-aged Greek women working in an antiquities cell, laying in dynamite and locating targets on a map? Didn't compute.

Hegel now approached our table with a full plate, nearly colliding with Gwen, who had just come in. She threw Gabor a nasty look, and I was glad he had his back to her and didn't see her.

"Well!" Sophie said, "anyone else want to get some breakfast?" On our way to the buffet, I saw Gwen join the Tanners, who were getting ready to leave. We gathered ourselves a pretty nice breakfast—not hard to do with that marvelous spread—and returned to our table.

Hegel, who had wolfed down his breakfast, asked to leave. He was planning to play soccer with some pals in Pachia Ammos, and needed to get his duffel bag. His father wouldn't be giving him a ride. Gabor was taking the day off to celebrate the Antiquities Department decision to give the green light to the airport construction. It turned out that the Latifs were going to scout out flats and apartments in the area—now certain they would be staying in Crete for a year or two.

And so we soon parted, the Latifs returning to their room. As we headed upstairs, Sophie turned to me and said, "Doesn't it strike you a little quick for the Latifs to be making plans to move here?"

"Why? What worries you about it?"

"I don't know. It just seems sudden, if they got the news only yesterday. I'm remembering what Gwen said last night. If Gabor's firm has been bribing people, maybe he's known all along they'd be staying? Maybe that's why he's easing up on Hegel, knowing the kid's going to need friends if they'll be staying here in Crete for a few years." I had nothing to say to that, but she was right— it was one more thing to wonder about.

I suddenly realized we had reached the lobby and I hadn't gotten myself out of the massage yet. I needed a massage about as much as I needed a high colonic. Both are egregious invasions of privacy, equally ineffective in accomplishing their aims. Which, as I understand it, is the purification of the mind, the body and, if you have one, the soul. While a colonic may have some attractive attributes, a massage has an amazon beat your flesh, a mere towel to protect sensitive parts thereof, and a mystique that makes no sense. But I share such opinions with Sophie only after my second martini, when she thinks I'm joking.

This morning I had no such out. "I'll give it a try but only this one time," I told Sophie, unhappily sober as we stepped up to the front desk to book our torture. There we met ol' Keanu, or Hegel as he was even more improbably named, ready to take off with his duffel bag. He was about to join two pals at the bus stop but was asking Heidi about return schedules and writing down times on a pad of notepaper. I was glad to see that he wore his jacket. As we waited for Heidi to finish with him, the phone on the counter rang and Spiro, coming out of the back room, picked it up. He looked up saying "Latif? Yes, just a moment."

Hegel heard him and said, "Room 343."

Spiro looked at him, surprised. "You are with the Latifs?"

"*Ja*, Hegel Latif." It took the boy a minute to figure out why the Greek manager looked confused. "Hegel *Keanu* Latif," he clarified. Spiro smiled. Did he remember the boy's syrtaki at the barbecue?

"Are your parents there?" The boy nodded and Spiro put the call through as Hegel left the building for the road with the bus stop. Heidi now turned her attention to us and began checking the spa calendar for massage reservations.

Just then a police car pulled up to the hotel door and two policemen got out. A minute or two after they entered the lobby, Gabor and Samira came up the stairs, puffing from the climb. It took a second for us to realize that the police were there to see them, or more precisely, to see Hegel. They quickly established that the boy was on his way to wait for the bus near the head of the driveway and went to fetch him. When they returned to the lobby, and in full view of his terrified parents and his two baffled friends, they put on latex gloves and wordlessly and carefully searched his duffel bag, then his pockets. Reaching into his pants pocket, the policeman on his right evidently found something. He carefully pulled out a pack of cigarettes. Hegel looked as if he was going to die.

I couldn't believe it! They were busting the kid for a pack of smokes? Sophie would probably approve, but I was shocked. Then the policeman to his left reached into the pocket of his jacket and drew out two tiny clay figurines, each smaller than a shot glass.

One was a little pig. The other was a hen. I could see, since I was getting too close. The policeman holding the jacket asked me to step back, if I would be so kind. Hegel said, *"Was sind diese?"* He was clearly too rattled to remember to speak English.

The two policemen looked at Gabor and Samira. "We must ask you to come with us to Ágios Nikólaos."

Hegel said, "What *are* those?" Getting no answer the first time, he had switched to English. "What are they doing in my jacket?"

Looking at the stricken parents, the policeman said, "They are pieces missing from the museum in Ágios Nikólaos. We think your son was there the day they disappeared." The Latifs, all three, were wide-eyed and mute. Hegel could say nothing, imploring with his eyes for his parents to do something. The poor kid had lost his hard-won cool.

I couldn't believe this. So they had something to hide after all.

We followed the group outside as the Latifs were shepherded into the back of one of the vehicles by the police. Sophie called to them as they got into the car, "Samira, Gabor, let us know if we can be of any help."

I turned to Sophie after the police car had driven off. "Can you believe Hegel would *do* something like that?"

She looked incredulous. "Why on earth would he steal some mini antiquities?" she asked. "That's crazy."

"Well, you know kids. He's got new friends and his folks keep him on a pretty short leash. Maybe he needs money for cigarettes, and beer, and girls, and maybe drugs." At least Colin never got hauled off in a paddy-wagon. We were probably spared more than most parents.

Sophie was thinking, deeply. "I could swear that that case in the museum was okay when we passed it and didn't have the lid open or anything missing. Isn't that what you remember?"

"I agree, but with everything that's been happening, I'm beginning to wonder if I'm remembering anything correctly," I said.

"Well, that's what I remember." Sophie seemed to have no doubts. "It was after Gwen tripped that a theft became clear. And Hegel and Samira were long gone by then, so this whole thing makes no sense." She stopped and ran her fingers through her curls. "Unless."

"Unless *what*?" I asked.

Sophie was thinking with fierce concentration, the sun lighting up her freckles. "If I'm right, it raises even more disturbing questions. How did the police know whom to search, and where to look, unless someone tipped them off? Why didn't they suspect Samira and check the Latifs' room before messing around with Hegel's duffel bag and his pockets?"

"You think those babies were planted?" I was floored at the thought.

She nodded. "Hegel was as surprised as we were."

Screw the massage. This was getting too worrisome for distractions. I wanted a drink by the beach. Maybe a cigarette, too. In the shade, in private, so Sophie and I could think out loud. Sophie complied. Except for the cigarette.

We returned to the lobby and cancelled our massage. I looked ruefully at the pack of cigarettes from Hegel's pants pocket that lay on the reception counter, abandoned.

Chapter 20
Living on in Cyberspace

When we got back to the room, we tried to reach Aphro. No luck, which was just fine by me, since I was pretty embarrassed about my outburst at the end of our last interview with her and now felt I'd made sort of a fool of myself. Also, I was pretty confused about what we would say to her. Not because I didn't think we had things to tell her, but because so much new information was piling up. The last one, with Hegel accused of stealing museum pieces, and Sophie arguing they were planted, was so peculiar that I almost lost sight of the big ugly picture of Nikos clutching his slit throat with an agonized look in his eyes. I just couldn't make sense of all the things that had been happening. I kept telling myself to stick to facts, like the scientist I was. Unlike theories, facts don't have to make sense, and you'd better not confuse the two.

Since we'd just had breakfast, we stayed in the room for a while in case Aphro called back, which the station assured us she would. They said she was busy. She was probably giving Hegel the third degree. I hoped he was both innocent and more gracious with Aphro than he was with the rest of us. Little punks like that deserve to be taken down a peg or two. But a police interrogation seemed a bit excessive for a lesson in manners. If they scared him straight too early he might never be able to cut those apron strings.

Finally we decided to go down to the beach, lie on a towel and think about what to do before having a cool beer at the cabaña. As we were about to leave, the phone rang. Aphro at last! My mind was racing.

"G'day Red, how ye be?" Wally's cheery accent was unmistakable.

"Wally! I'm fine. I thought it would be someone else, but it's even better to hear from you. What can we do you for?"

"I come to ye with an odd proposition, me friend—prob'ly not to yer liking since it involves some hard yakka. But I thought I'd put it past ye in case ye've been bored out of yer noggin'. 'Twould keep ye outta mischief and we'd be beholden for yer help."

"We?" I asked. Sophie looked at me quizzically. I shrugged to let her know I didn't yet know what Wally wanted.

"Ms. Mylonas and meself. That lady's feelin' the weight of the world on her wee shoulders. Police gave her back Nikos's computer. Copied all the files, they did. Gave it back so she could crank the business back up. But the poor lass dun't know her Excel from her e-mail—no better than I do meself. At sixes and sevens she were, when I shambled by the shop this mornin'."

"That does sound tough. But what could we do to help?" I remembered making a perfunctory offer when we were there last. But that was frankly more condolence patter than a serious gesture.

"Ye'll be glad to know Ms. Mylonas's holds ye in high esteem. Yer Sophie's a sensitive lass who put the poor widdie-woman mightily at ease on her last visit. And me she likes on account o' I don't haggle and I admire the goods of the shop, familiar as I am with the trade, don't ye know? I also b'lieve turnin' to us shows she's a wee bit friendless since she left her home in Athens."

Although I noticed I wasn't singled out for my own sterling qualities, I had to admit Wally was a persuasive little devil. And I was still persuadable in spite of the wild goose chase into Crete's barren West the last time we fell in with one of his schemes. "Go on, then," I asked, "what's your proposition?"

"Do ye know computers, lad? Handy with them, are ye? I'm a tyro meself, and so's Elena and her girl there." Thankfully I do crossword puzzles or I'd never know what the hell a 'tyro' was.

Wally went on. "We thought ye might make sense of the sales records and mebbe match orders while we get inventory ready to ship. Y'know, deal with the finances, bills due, and all that lot. I wouldn't be asking and she wouldn't be asking, but the Greeks don't always trust one another, 'xcept fer kin. Better the divil ya dun't know than the divil ye know, me Da likes to say. That way ye can send him packing' without a twinge when he's made a bingle of yer bizzo." Wally's Strine was hard enough to follow when he wasn't talking business.

"Wally, I know zip about bizzo." I hoped I was using the right word. "I balance the checkbook to keep the generous and imaginative Sophie from exploding the family funds, but that dun't make me a fiscal officer." One week around Wally and I was getting the hang of a foreign language for the first time in my life.

"We'll give ye a fair go then, lad, and I know ye'll be brilliant. Ms. Mylonas is an old hand at runnin' a shop, don't ye know, as long as the bizzo's on paper and not on the cyber. Ye'll make a smart team with the lass, I'll warrant."

This was a most peculiar request. Diving into the computer of a dead crook, doing a digital autopsy. But, in truth, I was intrigued. An opportunity to learn a bit more about the oily Nikos, one step behind Aphro and her crew. After all, it wasn't that big a shop, and tracking his business to the point Elena could deal with it shouldn't be all that hard. At least we could try.

"You're on," I said. "I know Sophie will go along." I looked at Mother Sophia to make sure she was on board, even without knowing the details. "When do we begin?"

"Ye'll need some tucker to keep yer strength up. Let's meet at the shop after lunch. Mebbe around one o'clock?"

"Do we get a martini out of it?" I asked.

"Better n'that, lad." I could hear a smug chuckle on the line. "I seem t' remember the charming Sophie would fancy a visit to the grand palace at Knossos. If ye like, I'd take ye round there tomorrow, if we finish the Gavras bizzo today. I know the place like the back o' me furry paw. Have ye had a gander at it yet?"

"No," I said, "You've got yourself a deal." Better Knossos with the droll Wally than an Amazon massage.

I told Sophie what was up, and—memories of Wally's western junket repressed or forgotten—she was delighted. I felt myself empowered. Wise, generous, capable, a cyberhacking guru. No more stewing. Action. Better than watching our backs at Astron Bay, where silent foreign creeps might pounce out of the shadows. And I didn't mean the police.

"Red." I turned to Sophie who was looking straight at me as I hung up. "What should we do about Spiro? We more or less promised to talk to Elena about how wrong he was and how guilty he feels."

"Hm. I forgot all about that with the commotion over Hegel in the lobby."

"Can we be sure Spiro told us the truth and isn't just using us?"

"Maybe not. But I'm willing to regard him as a blood brother, if you'll pardon the expression, and give him the benefit of the doubt." Bad choice of words because for a second I was back in Gwen's room with Spiro right behind me, watching Nikos use his hands as a tourniquet to stop the bleeding from his throat. But we tacitly agreed that if the opportunity offered, we'd present Spiro's case to Elena.

After a brief nosh at the cabaña, we drove to Agnik and got to Elena's shop ten minutes early. Nia was there, waiting on a dilatory couple, probably American, who looked around in a perfunctory way and left with barely a nod. She then fetched Elena from the back.

"Oh, Mr. Redfield, thank you for coming. And Mrs. Redfield, I am happy to see you again." Elena smiled warmly at Sophie, who reciprocated. Although she still wore black, Elena looked less distraught, more business-like than the last time we were there. Nia stood back, deferential as ever, but smiling with her bronze-tinted pony tail bobbing on top of her head.

"Mr. Pinnock told you we need your help?"

"Yes," I said, "I'll certainly be happy to have a look at your electronics." But a disturbing thought hit me: what the hell would I do with a Greek keyboard? Produce Greek text? "I'm sorry, are your computers in Greek letters?"

"No," said Elena. "So many foreign sales make the English alphabet needed. And with many European clients, English language is best. Everyone understands, that way." Whew. I may be Phi Kappa Phi, but that doesn't mean I know what it means.

"Nikos learned computers in America, but I know only a little. Some e-mail with my nieces and nephews in Athens, but not much more. You can help teach me a little, I hope?" Elena appealed with her dark eyes.

"I hope I can help, and Mr. Pinnock will come soon, I think." It occurred to me that if we were going to broach Spiro's apology with Elena, we should do it before Wally arrived. But speak of the little devil, just then he came tripping into the store, all smiles, swinging his canvas shoulder bag.

"G'day, Sophie, m'lass, Red, mate, a pleasure as always! Ms. Mylonas, Nia, grand to see ye. Let's begin." Wally and Elena had had seemingly consulted about where to start. "Let's go in back and have ye meet the dreaded computer."

"Oh lord, don't let it be Hal," I said.

Wally laughed and lowered his voice, "Don't worry, Dave. Everything will be fine, Dave." He laughed again, this time in his own Ozzie voice. "Don't be gettin' yer knickers in a twist, lad. We'll first get ye a feel for the cyber-scape, in a manner of speakin'."

Nia remained in front, and the four of us went behind the curtain into the back room. To our surprise, it was a large, cool room with a door leading out to a rear courtyard, shaded by trees with a weathered wooden table and chairs. Elena turned on lights to reveal rows of shelving against the wall on each side of the room. Some were filled with binders and ledgers, and others were crammed with all kinds of pottery, brass, crafts, and silverware (including, I remembered ruefully, silver decoys and silver-plated follow-ups). A number of boxes were stacked up against the back wall, some open and empty, others nailed or taped shut, a few others open with one or more pottery objects resting in wood shavings, sawdust, or polystyrene peanuts.

"I was expecting real confusion," I said. "But this is really pretty orderly. Nice spot outside, too."

"This was the family home, you see, and now I live again in my old living quarters upstairs." Elena smiled at the cool enclosure in back of the office. "I played in this courtyard as a child before Mother and Father went back to America."

I looked around for the computer. It was on a large oak desk that held a small lamp, monitor and keyboard, with the CPU underneath. Papers littered the table next to the screen. The computer was on, with a screensaver of painted dolphins cavorting in ocean waves. I have little clownfish Nemo on my computer screen back in Laguna, so I felt right at home.

I was relieved that the computer was a PC, with older versions of Microsoft Office. As I clicked around, the files and directories on My Documents seemed straightforward: Sales, Overhead, Orders, Inventory, Sources, Domestic, Export, and others less obvious or less related to the business. The Export directory had over a dozen folders of destinations by country—Austral, Austria, Fr, Ger, etc., all the way down to UK, USA. Under USA, sure enough, I saw Tanner LV. A voyeuristic rush came over me as I realized I might get a peek at the Tanners' financial knickers, as Wally might put it.

The e-mail system was unfamiliar to me, but the browser was good old Netscape. "I think I can work with this," I said to Elena after a few more minutes. "What shall I look for? What do you need?"

"I think I know the shipments needed to fulfill the orders," Elena said. "I have contents and addresses for most of the packages. But I don't know order numbers and payments. I think they are there in the computer."

This didn't sound too difficult, so I got to work. Sophie, enchanted by the courtyard, had drifted outside and was sitting on one of the chairs under the large tree, enjoying the strange feeling of an arbor in the middle of the city. But Wally soon put her to work. He had Sophie go through the recent paper receipts and order them by date for later filing in the computer while he worked on the packing. He clearly enjoyed handling the objects, admiring their craftsmanship before sealing and addressing the boxes. With all of us busy with the orders, Elena returned to the front of the shop to help Nia with some customers who had drifted in.

It was weird to be actually *working* like this on our vacation. Sort of like doing a Habitat for Humanity project in your spare time. Only how many philanthropists send volunteers in to work on dead people's finances?

We worked happily at our tasks for a good part of the afternoon, with Elena occasionally popping in to offer help and explain things we couldn't figure out. The shop did a surprisingly good business out front this afternoon. At least there was a fair amount of traffic, from the sound of it. I got a pretty firm handle on the pending orders, their status, and method of delivery and payment. It wouldn't be very difficult for Rowan Redfield, Computer Guru Esquire, to teach Elena Mylonas the setup so she could process her own orders in future.

Gavras Greek Arts was a pretty lucrative business from what I could tell, with the sly Nikos selling items for hugely more than he paid for them. However, his profit margin was considerably less on the export business. Clearly he did better when he turned his oleaginous charm on his customers in person rather than by e-mail and correspondence.

Sophie showed up with a bundle of recent receipts she had sorted. Wordlessly, she held up two of them. The first one, dated 7 August 2005, was for our blasted silver bowls. Sure enough, it had the bogus price of $150 marked "Pd." on it rather than the $350 we actually paid. Beneath this was, in ink, not carbon copied, " 80." I jumped to the conclusion that this was the price Nikos had paid for the set. I was ticked all over again. It wasn't enough for him to gyp us—the creep had to go and rub it in. Of course, he hadn't planned to be dead and have his fleeced lambs nosing around in his bizzo within days of his decease.

The other receipt Sophie showed me was for "10 bwls, 10 figs," and a list of other semi-coded items in various quantities. The total came to 850. The pieces had been ordered by LD Tanner, Parthenon Hotel, Las Vegas, NV USA, signed by a barely legible "D. Tanner." So Danielle was indeed doing business with Nikos during her stay here. I no longer referred to her as luscious.

The afternoon wore on. We were all getting fatigued, and Sophie noticed a setup for making tea in a corner of the back room. Elena, still distracted in front, delegated Sophie to use the hotplate and brew us all tea. Wally, busy with a list of items that appeared ready for shipping, was opening some boxes that had not yet been taped shut, waiting for me to print up the invoices. Sophie took mugs of tea out front to Elena and Nia. When she reentered through the curtain, I heard her give a little gasp. Wally, bending over a box, did not hear her, but when I looked at Sophie's face she was bobbing her head and gesturing forcefully with her eyes toward Wally. Wally looked up at me and said, "Ye get them invoices yet, mate? Me time's almost up. 'Pointment with another potter bloke for a beer, as I may've mentioned."

"Don't you want your tea?" Sophie's voice sounded strangled.

"Me best thanks, but no, luv," he said. "But I'll tip me beer to ye and Red for yer good work this arvo. Ye've done heroic service for our damsel in distress!" Cheerful as always, he was, and I couldn't imagine what was eating Sophie, who seemed turned to stone all of a sudden. But my instincts told me not to ask until Wally had cleared out.

I got him the last of his invoices, and he finished sealing the last of the packages. Sophie had gone out to the table in the courtyard and was sipping her tea, frowning in silence. When Wally finished the last box, he eased his swag over his stocky little shoulder and popped to the door to bid Sophie farewell. "I'll be seein' ye around ten tomorrow for our safari to Knossos."

"Well, I am a little tired from all this work today." She sounded more wary than weary. "Maybe we should rethink Knossos tomorrow."

"Suit yerself, lass." Wally waved cheerfully as he headed toward the curtain. "Only give me a buzz before ten if it's no go."

Elena emerged through the curtain, and Wally spoke his goodbye to her. "Mr. Pinnock, what a kind gentleman you are." She took both his hands in hers and her face glowed in gratitude. "Thank you, thank you so much." Wally looked warmly at her, nodding. His face was crimson as he left through the front.

I was dying to know what Sophie was bugged about, but Elena now stayed in the room to consult about the files and the boxes Wally had sealed. Sophie shook her head silently when I looked at her. Whatever it was, she didn't want to discuss it in front of Elena.

In another five minutes, Elena was done with the boxes, and asked if we would like to stay for a glass of wine in the courtyard. She seemed to want an opportunity to thank us for our help, and a glass of wine sounded pretty good to me. Then I had a brilliant idea. If I could get Elena off into the courtyard with Sophie, I could buy myself a little more time on Nikos's computer alone. That would give me a chance to do a little private sleuthing in the files, on behalf of the firm of Nosy Parker Redfield, Inc.

"What a lovely offer," I said effusively to Elena. "I'm sure Sophie would very much enjoy a glass in the shade, and if I could take mine here at the computer, I could finish up the last of the filing." Sophie looked displeased at this, but my expression told her that she should play along. They left, and I turned back to the computer.

First, I went to the Onarchos file and scanned through the copious correspondence. It looked pretty business-like and ordinary to me. Only the file dates stopped abruptly about ten days before the murder. Nothing more was filed, as though all communication with the Pottery Shack had come to a sudden halt. That's the problem with sleuthing. Even if you find something interesting, what the hell do you make it of it?

I had to leave the Onarchos file at that. Next I called up Netscape and looked in the bookmarks. A couple looked unmistakably pornographic. Nikos—you randy little devil! I yearned to check them out, but I stopped myself, realizing one of the gals could come in and catch me in the act. If Sophie goes ballistic when she sees me smoking, don't even think about her response if she ever caught me surfing porn.

On the browser, I noticed a bookmark that started with "Parthenon LV Archeocenter—licensed to sell..." and called it up. And what do you know. I didn't get Athens—I got Las Vegas. The Parthenon Hotel and Casino. A gallery in the Parthenon Hotel and Casino. The picture of a very old looking sculpture in the shop of the Parthenon in Las Vegas. Offered for sale at a mere $47,500, and described as "1600 B.C Minoan. Provenance Eastern Crete. 13 × 3.5 cm. Terra cotta. Good condition, missing nose, unrestored. Authentication G. Frawley, Dalrymple Ltd. London UK." The figure didn't look worth anything like forty-seven five to me, but who was I? Mr. Phil E. Steen of Laguna Beach, connoisseur *extraordinaire* of the smooth legs and hooters of marble sculptures of females—but not much more.

"Holy shit," I said, out loud, hoping Elena and Sophie, talking outside, hadn't heard me. I just got it! G. Frawley. Gwendolyn Frawley. Ms. Steelbuns was the authenticator for that piece, and it was bookmarked in Nikos's frigging computer! And then Whammy No. 2. From the paper receipt Sophie had showed me, I remembered that the Parthenon was the name of the Tanners' Las Vegas hotel. My heart went pit-a-pat and rose to my mouth. I felt light-headed and my breath came fast and shallow. Our friends must have known one another before they came to Crete! And who the hell is Dalrymple?

I was excited, but succeeded in slowing my breath. I would have to move fast to find out something, anything more. I searched the Excel Sales journal, neatly dated as the entries were. I began with the May date of the Parthenon exhibit and moved rapidly backwards in time, past many orders from LD Tanner, Las Vegas NV USA. Ten of them went via "Dalrymple Ltd., UK." Only two of them appeared to be statues. "Stat. sm. Quantity 2. Cost 400. Shipped 03-11-05." Could it be that one of these Sm. Stats. now sold for $47,500? Kind of pays the expenses if you can parlay about $260 bucks each into over forty-seven thou minus shipping and handling. And authentication? I was learning a helluva lot more than I'd bargained for without being able to put it all together on such short notice.

I found no more information in the Export files for Tanner and Dalrymple, just a repetition of the information in the Sales journal. Very neat. Redundant. Good businessman, Nikos old boy, crooked as you were. Good records: liars can't depend on memory.

Elena and Sophie were getting up from the table outside and making moves to come back in. I shut down the programs as quickly as I could, and gulped down my untouched glass of wine. It was going to take a lot more than that to calm my nerves after the colonoscopy I had just performed on Nikos's digital guts.

Elena was as effusive with her thanks to us as she was with Wally, almost as if she wanted to give us a hug. But first we'd have to get her to call us Red and Sophie instead of Mr. and Mrs. Redfield. We promised to return in a few days to teach her how to use the computer, and she again showered us with gratitude as we went through the curtain to the front of the store. Nia was gone, and had turned off the lights. It was 5:15, and the store was closed. After a last flurry of thanks we were out on the street.

As we got out of sight of the shop, Sophie whirled around and grabbed my arm. "Red! Something awful happened. When I came back after I stepped out, I saw Wally take a pottery piece and put it in his canvas bag! He's a thief! He was casing the joint. That's why he wanted us to be with him, so we could distract Elena and he could take stuff from the inventory!"

Criminy! With all the other complications and suspicions, Sophie had to dredge one up with Wally. "C'mon, Soph, that just can't be true."

"But I saw him!" We had reached the car. I was too distracted to say anything about it. This would have to wait.

"You ain't heard nothing yet, Soph. Nikos had a computer bookmark to the gallery at the Tanners' hotel, and it was selling a frigging Minoan artifact for $47,500! They bought two of them from a guy named Dalrymple for around 400 euros. And you'll never guess who authenticated it for them."

Sophie's jaw dropped open. "Wally?"

"Get in the car, Sophie, and buckle up. You'll need to be secured in your seat when you hear this."

She obeyed mechanically and stared at me with wide eyes.

"G. Frawley. Gwendolyn Frawley, herself," I said. "Now don't that beat all!"

Chapter 21
Trouble in Knossos

Instead of driving back to Astron Bay, we decided to stay and have dinner in Agnik. After visiting with Elena and probing Nikos's business affairs, a peculiar loyalty to both of them stole over us. Going back to the scene of the crime would be like visiting Nikos's funeral with the killers. Not that we had adored Nikos, but he was a victim and would do no more harm. Most of our new acquaintances, including ones we liked, now had a cloud of suspicion swirling around them like a swarm of bees. We didn't want to get stung, innocent as we were. I wanted to find a fine restaurant, begin our cocktail hour and talk over what we knew. And what we didn't.

Most of the elegant places we saw weren't ready to serve dinner yet, so we settled for a place on the lake in the center of Agnik called *Aristo's Bistro*. It was small, quiet and informal, and we could have a cocktail at one of the small tables outside while they set up the rest of the place for dinner. We had a view of the little rowboats moored on the lake, and the water sparkled in the late afternoon light.

"Soph," I said, "I don't believe you saw Wally take a piece from the shop. Are you really sure? It bothers the hell out of me."

"I think so. I was just coming in and when I pulled the curtain aside, he was stuffing it into his canvas bag."

"You *think* so? What did you actually see? It might have been some notes. Maybe he made some notes on the craft of the stuff, for his pottery business back in Oz." How could that sweet little guy have a dark side? I hadn't felt quite so kindly toward him at Onarchos's shooting gallery, but after quietly working side by side with him at Habitat Gavras all afternoon, I was back in his camp.

But Sophie held firm. "Wally stuffed something bulky into his bag. It was painted in black and rust colors and I'm pretty sure it was a piece of pottery. I didn't see its shape but it wasn't paper."

"Soph, you saw something, but you can't be sure what it was. I didn't see it."

"You were engrossed in the computer, Red. Don't try to gaslight me on this."

I sipped my martini and shook my head, still in disbelief. "I can't afford to lose Wally; he's on our side. Or so I thought. Can you table this for a while so we can go to Knossos with him tomorrow? You'd be missing a chance to see it with an expert."

Sophie smiled in spite of herself. "I can't believe you're begging to go to an archeological site! I love the role reversal."

I took advantage of her lightened mood. "Give Wally a chance, even though he left in a hurry. I think it's an important sign that he himself isn't trying to avoid us."

"Let me think about it till morning," she said. "I do really want to see Knossos, but not with a shoplifter for a guide."

A table was ready for dinner, and we moved and looked at the handsome menu. My appetite was back and I ordered the stuffed chicken. The restaurant was pretty and cool with a breeze off the lake. The sound system played French music that reminded me of old Leslie Caron movies. Sophie too gradually brightened. Our Chardonnay was poured, and Sophie picked up her goblet to clink with mine.

"I actually managed to accomplish something else I haven't had a chance to mention yet." It was good to see her bright again after her frowning mood since leaving the shop. "I broached Spiro's apology with Elena, while we were having our glass of wine in the courtyard. She sounds skeptical about his sincerity, but she's relieved that Spiro's backed off from his blackmail accusation."

"Did she say Spiro could call on her again?"

"I didn't want to press her on that. Let her take it one step at a time. But at least we can tell Spiro we tried to start the healing process." Curious choice of words, but oddly appropriate. As new moral fissures opened up in our circle of friends, it felt good to hope that others might be sutured. This train of thought unfortunately led us back to the mare's nest I'd stumbled onto in the computer. Did Gwen and the Tanners know each other before they came to Astron Bay? They claimed they met there only a few days before we arrived. Did Gwen know Nikos after all? If so, that skinny lady was in a whole lot of trouble.

"I just had another troublesome thought," Sophie said—reaching over with her fork to take a taste of my stuffed chicken. "Could Wally's pilfering of a pot at the shop have anything to do with Hegel filching those little animal things?"

I almost dropped my butter knife and roll. "Sophie, I can't believe you just said that! You're the one who's positive Hegel was framed." She shrugged, chewing my chicken, silently conceding my point.

"Anyway, try to picture little Keanu and old Wally in some sort of cahoots. Wally has to be the most *uncool* dude on Hegel's planet—or anybody else's, for that matter. It just won't compute."

We finished our meal with no resolutions on anything. When we returned to our room in Astron Bay, we checked our phone, hoping Aphro might have left a message. She did, though it was an accented male voice that told us: "Inspector Kensington has your message and will call you when she returns tomorrow." Returns tomorrow? Where the hell would she go off to in the middle of a murder investigation? And instead of spending all day waiting for her call, I hoped we'd be away most of the day tomorrow. We went to bed early and spent a fitful night.

Sophie was already awake when I opened my eyes "I don't want to go, Red."

I was frankly more distressed by the prospect of having to avoid Gwen and the Tanners this morning than I was by taking old Wally for a ride. So we drank our coffee on the terrace and argued. I was ticked at Aphro for putting us on hold, and told Sophie it might be time to see the American consul, assuming there was one in Heraklion. I wanted to make sure we got our passports back so we could leave next week as planned.

The phone rang and I came back in from the terrace to answer it. "'Top o'the morning and glad t'know yer still breathin,' as me Da likes to say. Are ye ready for a little sightseein' then?"

"Hey, Wally!" My reserve faded in the light of his cheer. "How are you this morning? About Knossos…" What was I going to say? What might he be hiding under his blarney? I looked at Sophie, who frowned but shrugged, as if to say it was my call. "We're ready to go anytime you are. Just give me directions to your place."

In a little while we were ready for our outing to the most famous landmark in Crete. Sophie wore a pink outfit this morning with small colorful butterflies embroidered on a light cotton jacket—a sharp contrast to her sour mood. As we got into the Renault, she said, "Wally sits in front with you on the way to Knossos. Then when he pulls out an Australian knife to slit our throats, I'm making my getaway from the back." I couldn't tell whether she was kidding.

We found Wally standing with his swag on his shoulder, smiling and bouncing on his toes in the shade of his building. He got into the car, politely doffing one of those Crocodile Dundee hats with the brim pinned up on one side.

I was pretty tense as we headed north and west toward Heraklion on the hot, dusty road. Except for a banged-up Mercedes behind us, the road was clear. To my relief, Sophie sat in stony silence in back. Wally, in front, rocked from side to side like an English garden gnome on speed, leafing through maps and guidebooks.

"Hope you'll fancy a bit of yabber on this here Knossos, me friends." With that he launched into a colorful and disjointed lecture on the place. "'Twas scoped out round and about 1894, but the main excavation was done by a bloke named Arthur Evans early in the century."

"The last century," Sophie interrupted. Wally frowned, turned around, and thought for a minute, "Right y'are, lass," he said. "I do keep forgettin' we be livin' in the space age now. So let's say: old Evans was plowin' the site at…the end of the Victorian Era." He paused to see how this went over with Sophie. "We still call it the Victorian Era, don't we?" I could see Sophie in the rear-view mirror, looking loaded for bear.

Wally continued, intrepid. "Now this Evans bloke fancied he knew just how folks lived in days of yore and so took a few liberties, he did, with the restoration. But even if it's not fair dinkum, 'tis as fine a place as ye'll squinch in Crete or even all of Greece. Temples, palace, living quarters, all laid out for a grand walkabout. Spiffy civilization that, early on with King Minos, said to be a peaceful bloke."

"Our friend Gwendolyn says it's because women ruled Crete that it prospered so well," Sophie interrupted. She wasn't going to confront Wally, it seemed, maybe picturing that phantom knife in his shoulder bag. But she wasn't going to let him give his lecture in peace either.

"Right ye are again, lass. We'd all be better off with the ladies runnin' the guv'ment, to be sure." It was hard to get a rise out of him. "'Twas Minos gave his name to Minoan culture. Now that story about Queen Pasiphaë havin' the palace artist build her a fake cow so that she could have a naughty with her husband's prize bull…" Wally shook his head in disbelief. "That's gotta be a furphy."

"What'a *furphy*?" I asked.

"Minoan bull." Wally guffawed, cracking up. Sophie, in the backseat, was not amused. Her schoolmarm expression reminded me of old Mrs. Hepplewhite's in fifth grade.

Our doughty docent went on, "When he saw his plowed ruins snakin' over five acres, old Evans thought o' the legend of the labyrinth where the carnivorous beastie were kept. The hairy Minotaur, munchin' on mainland virgins for his din-din. Imported by old Minos himself."

Wally was clearly enjoying teasing Sophie, and I braced myself for another feminist counter-offensive. But she let him go on about earthquakes and Mycenaeans, as we tooled down the road, slowly drawn in by his sure grasp of history under the Aussie patter. Meanwhile, I noticed that the black Mercedes with the bashed-in headlight was still trundling along behind me, even though we were now in a passing zone. Polite, these Greek drivers, even if they treat a fine car like crap.

"I'd surely fancy a time-travel back to 1900, doin' a yakka with old Sir Arthur and his blokes during the excavation. Ripping, it must've been." Wally glowed at the thought. "In me London studies back a bit, I had the fortune to meet one of Evans's jackaroos at the museum. Old man he was by then, and a real earbasher. But his stories of adventure stirred me, I tell ye, and made me daft about the art of the gentle Minoans."

I looked in the mirror to see the gentle Sophie looking confused but moved.

"Been gone on it ever since," Wally continued. "And when I got home to Canberra after that, I devoted meself to the craft of faithful reproductions. It's a bit o' sport beside overseeing me pottery business, but I'd be the poorer without me Minoan passion."

Sophie broke in. "And you get pieces to copy any way you can?" Oh-oh, I thought.

"Oh no, luv," Wally said. "The ridgy-didge pieces can't leave Greece, so I copy the copies, like the kylix I bought on the day of luck when we met. 'Course, there's originals in Australia, too, in museums, and some spiffin' replicas once in a way. But I prefer doin' me research right here in old Kriti."

"Replicas, what's the difference, that and reproductions?" I asked. I knew he'd discussed this with us before, but the fine distinctions of archeological art will never be my strong suit, I'm afraid. He repeated that replicas recreate the artifacts with all their flaws and wear at the time of excavation, while reproductions look like new.

"So what is it they make at Onarchos's place again?"

"That's what's been tickling me brain cells, mate. Ye'd think they'd make mostly fine repros in small lots. And their work is aces, I'm obliged to say, 'specially now I've had a close squint at the pieces in Elena's shop. But some of the pieces in Onarchos's biz when we were there looked like replicas to me. Makes ye wonder if he dun't do a lurk in copies of museum pieces or private collections. Legal or not."

"Lurk? Is that something illegal?"

"Illegal—or at least shonky," he answered. Half an answer—but better than none.

This whole conversation was getting interesting indeed, and gave us glimpses of what might have prompted Wally to head into the wilds of the west a couple days ago. I could see Sophie in the mirror. Her narrowed eyes and focus told me she was taking mental notes.

"Well," Sophie said, "and what did you get out of Nikos's shop?" I held my breath. Go slow, Soph. "I mean, you had quite a long time in the back room…squizzing at his wares." Even Sophie was catching the Strine bug.

Wally was silent for a minute, and I held my breath again. Then he said, brightly, "The good news of no news, lass. Scads of repros, most packed and ready to go, and the shelves groanin' with more. Nikos done a good trade, as Red no doubt scoped from the dockets."

The conversation stopped as we neared the turnoff for Knossos. I had been so distracted that I hadn't noticed till then that the car that followed us out of Agnik was still behind us. Not surprising, given our destination. Doubtless culture hounds like ourselves. After a few miles, we came to the entrance to the palace and grounds. The Mercedes turned off with us and parked near the road, while I drove on to get closer to the entrance.

Getting out of the back seat, Sophie cheered up instantly. Once inside the grounds, she was thrilled to see the main palace buildings and surrounding structures. The palace looked just as it did in the guidebook, but the extent of the whole complex was breathtaking. It seemed to spread a quarter mile or so from side to side and it spilled down the hill. To my surprise, the structures were high, with broad roofs on the lower structures, stairs to nowhere, stairs to the upper levels. Awesome, as our son Colin would say.

"Well, me friends," said Wally, putting his outback hat back on, "here we are in the presence of the oldies. Come with me and I'll give ye a speedy walkabout and then ye can explore on your own. But first, d'ye fancy a bit of tucker?"

Having skipped breakfast, we agreed readily. Wally led us down the hill to a small concession shed against a wall selling gyros, lemonades, and ices. It was cool in the shade of some conifers. We were also relieved, to coin a phrase, by the restrooms nearby. Wally declared that lunch was his "shout" in return for the ride, so after he paid we got our camera ready for the great tour.

Visitors were relatively few, but varied. A Nordic couple with a tow-headed kid were hiking around, and an African family in colorful robes, the women with head turbans, struggled to negotiate the higher steps, cautiously gathering their gowns about them. We saw Americans in aviator glasses and Asians carrying tripods, and one guy who looked Greek, but was clearly a tourist, wearing a blue Hawaiian shirt and carrying a camera around his neck. A few guards in gray, with visored hats, stood around. Knossos was certainly an invitation to the whole wide world.

"Let's be off, friends." And Wally literally charged off as fast as his short legs would take him. We scurried dutifully behind him, surprised at his speed, especially up the steps and the structures with some height to them. He was more organized this time as he narrated the tour, telling us what was what— outbuildings, little palace, main palace with its throne room below, the north propylaeum or whatever, and, of course, the bull fresco.

Luckily he slowed down in front of the frescoes, which were captivating, even if they were only copies. Sophie loved the frieze in the throne room, with its strange reclining hybrids, like birds with lion's bodies, their crests and tails shaping lovely white curls against the cinnamon background. Happily photography was permitted, and she snapped away in every direction.

"Terrific, Wally," I said, when he finished our tour. I really meant it. He might be a crook, but as far as I was concerned, he was *our* crook. I began to appreciate Sophie's interest in this place, where you could get a feel for what it was actually like a zillion years ago.

"Ye're on yer own, now," Wally finally said. "I like to squinch at sites at me own pace, and you're the same, I can see." Not true, since he hadn't seen us explore ruins before. But it was gracious of him, since I wanted to slow down and wander around at something less than a fox trot.

We agreed to meet in an hour at the same place. Wally wandered off toward the palace areas, and at a more leisurely pace we went the same way. Sophie was busy with her camera as we checked out rooms on the lower stories, with their mosaics, frescoes, columns and lord knows what else. Coming out on the higher levels, we looked at the stairs to the upper rooms of the palaces. Sophie suffers from slight acrophobia, so we declined to go all the way up. We noticed Wally, nimble Wally, bounding up the steps to a landing on the way to the parapet and waved to him, but he didn't see us.

Sophie turned to me and gave me the camera. "Red, take one of me against this building. It's a lovely color, so be sure to get some of the sky for contrast. Maybe we can get Wally to take one of both of us later on."

I took the camera and in the bright sun had to get the pose through the view-finder. As I clicked the shot, we heard a multiple shout, as if from a crowd. Sophie turned on reflex to look behind her, and saw Wally was gone from the parapet. The man in the Hawaiian shirt came hurriedly down the steps. At the back side of the building people were shouting and we ran toward the noise around the corner. A female German tour guide was shouting "*Hilfe! Krankenwagen! Eile!*" and guards in gray came running.

We stopped abruptly. I didn't want to see. I didn't want Sophie to see. But we did. Wally lay inert on a canopy, which had collapsed over a restoration area. It must have broken his fall, a good fifteen feet. His legs, arms, and bag were splayed out on the canvas. His outback hat lay on the pavement nearby. The canopy revealed mounds of something beneath, whether bricks, stones, or some other materials we couldn't tell. My god, I thought, he must be dead!

"Wally," Sophie screamed as she ran down the few steps to the area.

Two guards had arrived, one of them already on a cell phone. The other knelt down and felt Wally's neck for a pulse. I ran up shouting, "Do you speak English? He's our friend, he's with us." Both guards turned to me, speaking Greek. The German tour guide said, "They say he is alive and they've called for an ambulance." Sophie pushed to kneel beside Wally but the guard, still on his knees, waved her away. I took her arm and led her back. She was ashen and red-eyed. We saw the guard open Wally's shoulder bag, take out his passport and wallet, and jot something on a notepad. No evidence of Sophie's phantom knife, of course.

No one moved Wally, and Wally did not move. Some blood seeped from under his head and his left arm and shoulder formed a disjointed, unnatural position. At least I could see him breathing. "What's taking so long?" I asked urgently.

"The hospital is in Heraklion, but hopefully there is an emergency unit in a village nearby," the German tour guide said.

Sophie had left all of her suspicions of Wally behind, appalled by this event. She turned to me suddenly and whispered loudly, her voice strained and unsteady. "Red! Red! That man coming down the steps! I think he pushed Wally over the rail! I've seen him before! He looks Greek. I've seen him before! Get the guards to stop him before he gets away!"

"Sophie! Stop! Calm down! We've got to first see to Wally! Just hang on!" Sophie can get like that when bad things happen. She has an explanation before she looks twice. She strained to extricate herself and I was afraid she was going to take off after the guy herself.

"He had on a flowered shirt and a camera. Blue with red blossoms. Guard!" she yelled. The tour guide said something to the guard but he shook his head and held his palm up to Sophie, distracted. We heard the sirens. The ambulance and a police car stopped in a cloud of dust at some distance, then edged forward as close as they could get. The medics flew out of the ambulance, opened a gurney, and raced toward us, followed by more policemen. The crowd had swollen and the men had to fight their way through to Wally.

The medics went about their work quickly and professionally, finally moving Wally gingerly from the canopy to their gurney. Not a motion from Wally. The police waved the crowd back and beckoned to the German guide and questioned her. She pointed to us, and we were motioned over. Fortunately, one of the policemen spoke good English, so Sophie could finally talk to someone.

This time, it was serious, short sentences. "He was pushed. You must find him. A man in a blue Hawaiian shirt with red flowers. And a camera."

She suddenly looked at me wide-eyed. "The camera," she shouted at me. "You were taking a picture of me when it happened. Look at the picture!"

I had never closed the digital camera, still slung around my wrist by a cord. I held it up quickly and moved the replay switch. There it was! A picture of Sophie, smiling, standing with her back against the wall. On top of the parapet, outlined against the sky, a man's back in a blue Hawaiian shirt, a burley arm slightly extended, touching the back of a short male figure pressed against the railing. His bag swayed away from him in the air in front of him. No faces were visible, but it sure as hell didn't look like an accident. At the very least this was hit and run—at worst, attempted murder.

I held the camera for the policeman who instantly opened his cell phone and yelled into it in Greek. He did this twice more, and then quickly used the phone again for a rapid conversation in an urgent voice. "Your name?" he asked, as he looked at us. "Redfield," I said. "Sophie and Red Redfield." He went back to talk into the phone.

The next few minutes were a blur. We didn't know what to do. More police had arrived and were fanning out. The search Sophie had cried out for was now in progress. In a poignant moment I saw Sophie walk over and pick up Wally's hat. I was torn between wanting to stay and see if anything happened, and push on to the hospital to be with Wally when he arrived. But I didn't even know *what* hospital or where it might be. Wally's observation a few days ago that we were magnets for misfortune came back to me. He should have known better than to travel with us.

Finally, the English-speaking policeman approached us and said, "You know Inspector Kensington?" I was floored. This wasn't exactly how and where I expected Aphro to return our frigging phone call. "Yes," I said, although I really felt like saying, "It's about bleeping time."

"Can you go to Heraklion to meet with her?" he asked.

"If you give us directions, yes."

"She will meet you at the ticket counter of the Heraklion Archeological Museum," he said. I felt like saying, 'What the hell is she doing there?'

He gave me directions on a tour-guide map. As we left him, Sophie said, with a little tremor, "Is Wally going to be all right?" Whatever the case, Wally was *her* crook now too.

The policeman shook his head. "It is too early to know, madam."

When we reached the parking lot, we were gratified to see policemen checking IDs as people left the Knossos grounds. We got in our car and drove out toward the road. The dinged black Mercedes stood in the shade under a tree at the outer end of the lot. I had an impulse to stop, go back, and tell the policeman to check it out. But I felt I was turning into Sophie, with suspicions running amok, forgetting for the moment that her wild suspicion about the guy in the Hawaiian shirt turned out to be true. But if Flower-Shirt belonged to the Mercedes, he was still inside the compound. They'd find him.

Unless he fled on foot.

We drove on to Heraklion, dreading the near future. How much misfortune would follow us there?

Chapter 22
Camera—Not Obscura

It took us only a short time to find the Archeological Museum in the city center, and the parking was easy in the visitors' lot. We went to the front desk, asked for Inspector Kensington, and waited while the clerk called for her. Aphro appeared shortly and welcomed us with concern. I was relieved that my snit at the end of our last investigation, when I practically accused her of planning to nail a foreigner for the murder, seemed to be forgiven or at least momentarily forgotten.

We went around the desk and headed toward the stairs to the upper floor. Sophie slowed her pace as she looked through the open doorways to the museum displays. She walked wordlessly by, gazing at enormous pottery works, bronzes, a female figure holding snakes, a vase entwined with octopus tentacles, marble statues. She had loved the Agnik museum, but this aroused new dimensions of wonder. Even I was impressed.

On the upper floor she looked into a room with gorgeous frescoes, and here she couldn't contain herself. "Stop, please," she said urgently. "It's the 'Parisienne'!" I didn't know what the hell she was talking about, wondering if she got her museums confused. This wasn't the Louvre, for cryin' out loud. But Aphro smiled and followed Sophie into the room. They stopped before a fresco of a young woman in profile, with large eyes—okay, only the right one was visible—and black curls, one of which looped and dangled over her forehead.

"She is beautiful, isn't she?" Aphro said softly. Aphro might have looked like that once, twenty years and twenty pounds ago.

Upstairs, Aphro showed us into a comfortable room with two sofas angled in the corner with a coffee table serving both of them, and a desk and chair in front of the window overlooking a courtyard.

"Please," said Aphro, pointing to a sofa. She was business-like as usual, but offered some tea. We gratefully accepted although I could've used a martini. But this was neither the time nor the place to request one.

"Now then, I know you are concerned about Mr. Pinnock. I can tell you only that he is still unconscious and they have not yet fully evaluated his condition."

"But how seriously hurt is he?" asked Sophie, "I can hardly believe he's alive after that fall."

"He fell on a canopy, which fortunately covered stacks of burlap sacking," Aphro said. "He's a very lucky man. The officers said the sacks were not there yesterday and arrived only this morning for removing rubble from a restoration site. They broke his fall. Thankfully he fell on that side of the parapet and not the other."

"*He didn't fall.*" Sophie said this sternly to convey her conviction. "He was pushed and we can prove it."

"Quite," said Aphro, seating herself next to the desk. She clicked on her tape recorder and opened her metal-covered notebook. "Why don't you tell me what happened."

Sophie leaned forward. "Well! We parked and went into the grounds and had a sandwich and some lemonade after the drive from Agnik. We were a little hot and dry, you know, and it was nice to look around for a few minutes before Wally led us on this quick tour he promised us. I was just bowled over by the sights, following after Wally. I could hardly keep up with him and look at the map at the same time…"

I waited for Aphro to growl 'Just the facts, ma'am'—like Sergeant Friday on TV.

"Mrs. Redfield, can you remember anything relevant to Mr. Pinnock's accident?"

Sophie nodded and now gave a more focused account of the end of Wally's tour followed by our photo shoot in front of the wall. "We waved to Wally, who was going up the steps, but he didn't see us, and I turned around so Red could take my picture. Then, just as he snapped the photo, the man pushed Wally over the railing and…"

"Mrs. Redfield, you couldn't have seen this with your back to the wall, could you?"

"Oh, no, I did see it, but not until afterwards." It all made perfect sense to Sophie, if not to the incredulous Inspector. "You see, we showed the photo to the police when we realized this must have happened as Red was taking my picture. And sure enough, there was Wally about to fall with the man in the colorful shirt right behind him."

"Really!" Aphro's eyes had opened wide. "I assume the police took your camera."

"No," I said, "we have it right here."

Aphro shook her head, amazed but grateful when Sophie pulled our camera out of her tote bag and handed it to her. She brought up the picture, and looked at it closely—expertly pressing the menu button to zoom in on details. She whistled softly as she studied the magnified image, which she showed us across the table. The image revealed little more to identify the man in the colored shirt. But his arm was clearly extended toward Wally, whose canvas bag was swinging slightly away from his body.

"I must ask for your camera, or at least the digital card, until we can get copies," Aphro said. She took the little disc out of the camera and made an urgent phone call in Greek. "I am having an officer come to copy the files and print this picture."

Fast, good work, I thought. Printed large it might yield a better view. But the guy's face wouldn't be visible, whatever other techniques they could use. A woman arrived with a silver pot of tea, three china cups, sugar, and cream. A familiar figure followed on her heels—the handsome Stavros who had escorted us to an earlier investigation. Sophie dimpled for the first time since I took that photo, as the dude took the card from Aphro and left.

Aphro now turned back to Sophie. "Did you see the man who did this? Later? Or even earlier?"

Sophie frowned with concentration. "What I remember, right after Red took the picture, was a man hurrying down the steps and hustling off. I didn't get what had happened, and by the time I did, he was gone. It wasn't until I saw Wally lying on that pile of stuff that it hit me. So I said to Red, 'That man in the flowered shirt, he pushed Wally!' I said it even before I thought it through. I'm kind of intuitive and these things just jump into my mind."

"Why would you think it was that particular man if you didn't see him on the parapet? There might have been others there. Were there?" Aphro was looking at Sophie a little skeptically.

Sophie took a sip of tea and thought for a moment. "There wasn't anyone else coming down those steps." She hesitated for a second. "Also, I think I saw him earlier, and I don't just mean at Knossos." She gave Aphro a slightly embarrassed look. "Maybe I'm too intuitive for my own good, but that man looked weirdly familiar—like the guard at the Agnik museum that day, you know, on the day Gwendolyn tripped. Or maybe like the guard at the place where Nikos got his pottery."

Aphro stood up and walked around for a minute, seeming to sort out this new information. She sat down again and looked at Sophie. "Now think very carefully, Mrs. Redfield," she said. "How well did you see the man and how sure are you that he resembled Zacharias Stephanopoulos? Greek men share characteristics, some quite prominent, and a foreigner might think they resemble each other more than they actually do."

"Aphro's right, Soph," I said. "You might be doing some profiling here without realizing it."

Aphro's frown was instant and pointed directly at me. "Aphro?" she said.

I blushed. "Forgive me," I said. "'Inspector Kensington' is a bit of a mouthful and so Sophie and I have a shorthand for you. I'm sorry to sound familiar. No disrespect intended." I was born with my foot in my mouth. And in California everyone's on a first-name basis.

Inspector Kensington let it go, thank goodness, and went back to the point at issue. "Your husband is right, Mrs. Redfield," she said. "Zacharias Stephanopoulos has worked many years at the museum as head of security. He is a trusted employee. He took the place of his father when he retired."

"Well, maybe you're right." Sophie looked intensely into space, as though conducting a mental line-up. "The man in the flowered shirt had one black eyebrow across his forehead—you know like the Mexican painter, Frida Kahlo? That's what caught my eye." Political correctness goes by the wayside when we're under stress, I guess. "That kind of—you know—linear eyebrow." Here Sophie drew her finger straight across her forehead. "The museum guard had one like that and so did the man at the Pottery Shack near Gournia. But maybe they just looked alike because they both wore uniforms."

Aphro looked hard at Sophie. "Zacharias Stephanopoulos does have a brother. He worked at the museum until he took a position elsewhere several years ago." She pondered. "Where did you see this other man? Near Gournia, was it?"

I broke in, finally. "It was near Gaitani. We call the place the Pottery Shack because there's a place named that in Laguna Beach where we live. But the place we visited is a factory of some sort that makes reproductions of antiquities. It's run by a fellow named Onarchos, and it supplied Nikos Gavras's shop with objects. He was the guard there, I mean this other person Sophie is talking about. He *did* look like Zorba. Zacharias, I mean. Neither of them very friendly."

Aphro let the Zorba gaffe go, but looked none too pleased. "I am aware of the Onarchos firm. Why did you happen to be down there?"

"We went with Wally Pinnock." I summarized the day we had stopped to give our condolences to Elena, and how Wally had gotten—surreptitiously— the location of Onarchos's place from her. "As far as we knew, Wally just wanted to see how they made the reproductions. He's a potter, and he admires the work and the techniques. I don't know if that was his real reason to go down there. In fact, I'm wondering if that trip put him in danger." I shuddered as I thought about the connection. "If the guard was the guy who pushed Wally at Knossos, Wally walked into some pretty deep...ah...doo-doo." Having a three-year old grandson ruins your vocabulary.

"It's not a coincidence," Sophie blurted out. "I thought that place had something to hide. It was all fenced in with this armed guard and his pistol, shooting at targets outside. They hardly let us see anything inside and we almost got shot—accidentally—when we left." Sophie made little quotation marks in the air around the word "accidentally." She looked at me for a moment before she went on. "I also now wonder if Wally was interested in something besides pots. I'm sure he knew more than he told us."

"Why do you say that?" Aphro asked.

Sophie stood up and turned to look out the window. I saw her tug at her earring, something she does when she's uncomfortable. She was clearly struggling with something, and I knew what it was.

When she turned around she looked straight at Aphro and speaking very deliberately, told her of yesterday's joint venture with Wally at *Gavras Greek Arts.* "When I came in from the front of the shop, after bringing Elena and Nia some tea, I saw Wally do something. I—I hate to say this—but I saw him put an object, I think a small pot, into his bag."

Sophie looked relieved to get this off her chest. "I don't know who to trust now. I didn't even want to go to Knossos with him today, but Red said we should. Now he almost died!"

"That's why we've been trying to reach you," I explained. "To get your advice on what to do."

Sophie sat down again and slumped against the back of the sofa. "If we hadn't gone to Knossos, all this wouldn't have happened. And I still don't understand why Wally would steal!"

Aphro looked surprisingly calm, like a middling poker player. I would've thought she'd jump on the new information and run with it.

"I'm sorry I was not available yesterday or today. I've been here in Heraklion to test some artifacts at the museum's research facility. They have specialized equipment for dating samples. This case almost certainly involves antiquities traffic." No answer to the question about Wally, although I could see why it wasn't immediately relevant. Wally wasn't going anywhere, especially if he died. The thought made me shiver.

Aphro finally sipped her own tea and turned to Sophie. "If this occurred yesterday afternoon, why did you telephone earlier? What else did you wish to tell me?"

"We have so many conflicting suspicions about the murder," Sophie shook her curls, "it's hard to remember all the clues." She was falling into Marple mode again. "We wanted to ask about Hegel, the Latif boy, and the little animals. Why was he arrested like that?"

"We had a tip and took him and his family in for questioning," Aphro said simply.

"*Gwendolyn*," Sophie cried in her Eureka voice, and pointed straight at Aphro. "It was Gwendolyn Frawley who called, wasn't it?"

Aphro looked nonplussed. "No," she said, "it was a man. He refused to identify himself, but he gave information that would have compelled us to speak to the Latifs in any case."

"How could Hegel have taken the figures?" Sophie said. "We were there after he and his mother left the museum, and there was nothing wrong with that case full of little animals when we passed it the first time."

Aphro nodded. "It remains a mystery," she agreed. "But we have other questions about the Latif boy. He spends much time in Pachia Ammos, and we now believe that he may have been bribed—with cigarettes or with money— for information and access to Bohnen-Essen's buildings and equipment."

"By whom, for crying out loud, and what for?" I interrupted.

"We are not certain even after talking to the boy. He is either afraid of disappointing his father or afraid of betraying someone else, so we get only confused answers from him. But the young Latif seems implicated in the recent sabotage at the Bohnen-Essen compound. We are therefore keeping him in custody—for his own safety—until we understand what is going on."

"Poor Samira!" Sophie always feels more sorry for the mother than for the father, as I learned from our experience with Colin when he was acting up. But I saw a major cloud hovering over the Latif family and their dreams.

"We hope to release him in another day or two," Aphro said.

"Well, that's a relief." Sophie relaxed into a smile, but Aphro turned and looked at her sharply, as if suddenly remembering something she said. "Why did you ask if Gwendolyn Frawley accused Hegel Latif of stealing the miniatures?"

"She hates the Latifs." Sophie tugged at her earring again. "Gwen thinks Gabor is bribing the Antiquities Department to get permission for the airport in Pachia Ammos. She thinks there's graft and corruption at the heart of it." Sophie unfortunately went on to another of her friend's nutty accusations. "Gwen also thinks Gabor might have taken one of her key cards at the barbecue the night before the murder when she sat next to him."

"What do you mean, one of her keys?"

Sophie explained Gwen's double key practice, and her suspicion that one of the card keys went missing the night before the murder at the barbecue.

Aphro found this interesting and jotted something in her notebook. "We know that Ms. Frawley originally requested two keys and that one was found in her room the afternoon of the murder. But she had not mentioned a possible Latif connection."

"I hate to say this, but I even wonder if Gwen phoned Nikos and asked him to come to Astron Bay?" Sophie was on a roll. Gwen was no longer a bosom buddy.

"Why would you think that?" Aphro looked surprised.

I wanted to be part of this conversation. "We told you about this, didn't we? That Sophie overheard Nikos on the phone, making an appointment with someone at Astron Bay in English, the day she went back to get a refund for our bowls?"

"Yes, of course. But why would you think now it was Ms. Frawley who made the call?"

"Holy shit!" I yelled, and then, quickly, "I beg your pardon, Aphro—Ms. Kensington. Sorry," Sometimes I feel too stupid to live. "That's the other thing we wanted to talk to you about, you see. The bookmark. When I helped Elena with the computer yesterday, I found a bookmark to an announcement by a Las

Vegas gallery that they were selling a $47,500 Minoan sculpture. And it was authenticated by a 'G. Frawley.'! And Nikos sold it for a fraction of that. So don't you see, Gwen knew Nikos after all!"

"Or Nikos knew *about* Ms. Frawley." Aphro said this calmly without any sign of surprise. "We too found the bookmark in Nikos's computer files, but it proves only that he was aware of her work as an authenticator. Not that he had business or other dealings with her."

"Oh." I felt a little deflated. I make a dramatic announcement about my major discovery, and it lands in the conversation like a dead pigeon.

Then I remembered the other part of the bookmark. "The Tanners, you probably know, may have a financial interest in the gallery in Las Vegas. If Gwen authenticated a sculpture for the Tanners, then doesn't that mean she knew the Tanners before coming to Astron Bay? And Danielle Tanner for sure knew Nikos. Someone could make a lot of money on things like that. I mean the markup."

"That too occurred to us," Aphro said, "and it remains a question we have not yet resolved." I wondered what she meant by that. Did she get evasive answers on that point from Gwen and the Tanners? I was beginning to be impressed that Aphro had gotten much deeper into things than we realized.

Now she seemed to consider for a moment and then asked, "Have you told either Ms. Frawley or the Tanners of your so-called bookmark discovery on Gavras's computer?"

"No, we haven't spoken to them since we stumbled onto it."

"Mr. Redfield." Aphro looked at me earnestly. "It would be extremely helpful if both of you kept that information to yourselves for the time being. We must proceed cautiously in view of the many obscure aspects of this affair. "

"Oh dear," Sophie said. "Red can't keep a secret to save his soul."

"Sophie!" I snapped. "What a thing to say!" As I mentioned, Sophie can be both mean and unfair.

"Sorry, honeybug, but it's a fact. You're just too open and trusting for your own good."

"Well, look who's talking?" Sometimes it's a real pain in the butt being married to Sophie. There was little I could do to salvage my *cojones*—incidentally, the only Spanish word I know. "My lips are sealed," I said with exasperation. "Okay, Inspector Kensington?"

She smiled. "Why don't you call me Aphro. Some of my friends do." I wanted to hug her, although I didn't quite get what she meant by 'some.' Her friends who are yahoos, like me, maybe?

We heard a knock on the door, which opened without any response from Aphro. Stavros gestured from the hall. Aphro went to him and bent over a large photo he was holding. He spoke urgently for a few minutes and left. She returned to us with the print, beaming.

"Well done!" she said to me, "well done! Good news!"

She held out an enlarged photograph over the coffee table for Sophie and me to see. It wasn't the one of Wally being pushed. Instead, it showed a handful of tourists emerging from the throne room at Knossos. Wally was in the background. I was in the middle of the picture. A man on the side was just leaving the room, partly facing the camera. His vivid blue Hawaiian shirt with its red hibiscus blossoms stood out. So did his single, dark eyebrow over both eyes.

"The murderer!" Sophie gasped.

"Attempted murderer," Aphro said, grinning, this time with visible relief. "Stavros says the hospital phoned to say Wallace has regained consciousness. He'll be all right." She closed her eyes and bit her lower lip for a moment.

"What a relief," Sophie squealed, and clapped her hands. "You look relieved too. Do you know Wally—Wallace—well?"

"I knew him in London. But that's another story for another time." Aphro was all business again, as she clicked off her tape recorder, put on her jacket, and began collecting her phone, notebook, and computer case. "I must be going," she said.

Sophie and I were floored. Just as the case was beginning to come together before our eyes, Aphro walks out! No discussion, no interest except for Wally! Bless his wee soul.

The sun was about to set and we were pensive on our way back to Astron Bay. The day had been dramatic and traumatic, ending with a rich, taxing conversation with Aphro. We were haunted by all the things we'd still forgotten to tell her—especially about running into the Tanners at the Pottery Shack and my cruise with Danielle. In the rear-view mirror, I was shocked to see the black Mercedes following us. I realized I hadn't mentioned that either. But as the sun went below the horizon, both of the Mercedes's headlights came on. It was not the one-eyed car we'd seen earlier. In my fatigue, my mind was playing tricks on me.

Chapter 23
A Nordic Massage

"I've had enough for a while," I told Sophie at breakfast the next morning. I hardly looked up as I ate. I'd had a gruesome dream in which Wally fell from the parapet clutching his bloody throat. After yesterday, I had new anxieties about people's uncivil friends in high places, to speak literally. I felt uncomfortable in the hotel restaurant, not knowing how to greet our erstwhile pals. The Latifs were now in actual trouble, and I still hadn't sorted out the possible connection between the Tanners, Gwen, and Nikos. Wally's experience had told us to beware of Greeks bearing gripes.

"Well, I've had more than enough too, Red. And now that we know Wally is on the mend, we're going to chill out today, as the kids used to say. First we're going for a swim in the pool before it gets too hot. And then, big guy, we're going to get that massage! It'll do you a world of good!" I had hoped that one murder and an attempt at another would distract Sophie from this sort of thing. But she was in therapy-mode today.

"And then," she chirped on, "a nice dry sauna or a cool waterfall shower, a lean lunch with some wine at the cabaña and a long nap in the afternoon—possibly with some hanky-panky, if you're feeling up to it." Her eyes twinkled and she flashed a come-hither smile. That's why I don't mind Sophie's therapy jags as much as I might. She has a pretty liberal sense of the therapeutic. And she was hoping to salvage just a little of our savaged vacation.

"We'll just forget everything today," Sophie burbled on. "We'll call Gerty and Ezra later in the evening when they're up. Well, when Meredith's up, anyhow. Tomorrow, we'll pressure Aphro to give back our passports and confirm our reservations for our flight home next week. After yesterday's help from our camera, she owes us." Sophie had her customary energy back and had finalized our plans without detouring for a consultation with me.

But her scenario was pretty seductive, and I didn't want to dent her good spirits. So I decided to let her plan stand. But then, as usual, she went too far. "I'm going for the Citrus Body Polish," she said, "And I'm going to order a Hot Towel and Eucalyptus Infusion Therapy Massage for you. Deep breathing, hotel towels steeped in eucalyptus essence…"

"Just a cotton-pickin' minute, Soph," I interrupted. "I don't remember any doctor prescribing frigging eucalyptus therapy for me. You know I'm allergic to that kind of stuff—perfumes, rotten eggs, swamp gas, public toilets." I had visited a winter resort in Snowbird with Sophie two years before and walked past some of the rooms at the spa. Even outside, the eucalyptus smell was strong enough to choke a koala. I never wanted to visit Australia after that— at least not until we met Wally and I learned how to speak Strine.

"Oh, Honeybug, I'm only kidding. Just get a regular massage and you'll enjoy it more than you expect. And it'll make a good vacation story to tell your friends at work. Grist for your grump mill." As though I didn't have enough vacation stories for a lifetime after all that had happened.

"Okay," I said, "I promised, and you did me a good turn by going to Knossos. Just don't expect me to like it. And be prepared for my impressions of it afterward." It was an empty threat. My grouching slides off Sophie like a yodel off an Alp.

"Deal," she said, and we went off to our morning swim, followed by the dreaded massage.

I had hoped without admitting it to Sophie that the massage might have some side benefits. Like a gorgeous Swedish masseuse. I was thinking Anita Ekberg. To my surprise, the place wasn't a big parlor with a bunch of folks getting themselves patted and kneaded, but a series of discreet private rooms, salons, and baths leading off from an airy glass-domed reception area. The place smelled like a perfume shop with hints of exotic blossoms—and yes, eucalyptus. To my further surprise, Sophie got hooked up with a masseur rather than a masseuse: a young hunk who looked like a cross between a Viking and a surfer. Mr. Washboard Abs led her, happy as a goldfish, into one of the massage rooms. It was then that my masseuse arrived to greet me in the outer area

Lord, she looked like a Greek statue commissioned by a rich, horny noble in the glory days of Sparta. She was about six feet tall with great proportions. Flaxen hair in a pony tail, setting off a refined face with pale blue eyes. Loose white tee shirt and white shorts. Exquisite breasts, heavy under her shirt. Very short white shorts, with firm, shapely legs extending all the way to the floor. Clogs. As she led me into the massage room, I blocked an impulse to feel her back to see whether she wore a bra. Like the former President who is my marital role model, I was about to commit adultery in my mind. Only the thought of Sophie with the Viking dampened my nascent fantasies.

The name embroidered on her shirt was actually Bibi, but to me she instantly became BB, the Brigitte Bardot of a cooler, more serious, less slutty generation. She led me into a low-lit room with a well-padded massage table, Naugahyde or something, with a big doughnut headrest. "You can put your clothes down here." She spoke in a low voice with a Nordic accent, and pointed to a chair. "Here is your robe and a towel." She handed them to me and laid another towel on the table.

"Um." I said. "Um." Did she mean *all* my clothes?

She smiled. "If you like, leave your shorts on. Some people do."

Whew. Just *some* people? I guess Norwegians were, well…uninhibited when it came to that sort of thing. I knew that my boxer shorts were less embarrassing than what hung beneath. I turned and removed my plaid bermudas and polo shirt and left them, along with my wristwatch, by my flip-flops under the chair. I began to put on the robe, but quickly realized this wasn't the protocol. Maybe I should just get on the table or something. Or something? She saw my confusion and motioned me to the table.

"Lay down on the table, face down." Not wanting to ask any more embarrassing questions, I did what I was told. "No, with your face into the headrest," she said as she put a towel over my ass. I scooted and craned around to see her eyes on me. Her eyes were—well, professional, darn it. A job to do with expertise and no warmth. What the hell was I doing here? Dammit, Sophie: no more deals!

Before I could think up a run of expletives for later, BB dimmed the lights. She turned up the music, which I had not noticed before. Beautiful, soft panpipes music, the sort advertised on TV late at night on obscure cable channels. I felt a warm liquid on my back and soon hands—her hands—were spreading it strongly over my neck, shoulders, spine, as they moved slowly toward the edge of the towel.

"Just relax," she said, "I hope you feel comfortable."

I now realized that I was literally in the hands of one of the most gorgeous creatures that had ever touched my bare skin. My face was in the hole of the headrest; my eyes closed. My soul melted as I listened to eerie pastoral melodies. Images came to mind involuntarily. Women. Danielle in that bikini, but I moved on hastily as I pictured her holding a .45 with a silencer. BB went on with my thighs and calves, oiling them and kneading them slowly. Julia Roberts in *Pretty Woman*. Samantha in *Sex and the City*. Scarlett Johannson in *Lost in Translation*. No sex in that one, darn it. Swimsuit models and centerfolds. BB went for my feet, flexed my instep, got between my toes, for heaven's sake! Oooh! Back a bit in time, Sophie coming toward me at a dorm party from across the room, lighting up my life. Honey curls, golden freckles, and a dimple in one cheek as she smiled. I'd seen her poring over her notes in class, but never like that. A perfect opening. Weeks later I held her in my arms. No boxers this time. She—we—were good!

"Now you can roll over on your back." *What? Already?* Bibi had caught me off guard.

"Maybe a little more on the back, the neck?" I played for time, hoping to regain my control. Finally, finally, I could roll over without embarrassment.

She smiled at me and began to talk as though she knew she had to keep the client's mind on higher things. As she spread oil on my chest, she said, "Have you been to Greece before, Mr. Redfield?"

"Yes, for a meeting, but not to Crete."

"Oh, then what is your business?"

"I'm a research chemist with Prentham Pharmaceuticals. In California." That's really going to impress her. Sheesh. Maybe I should invent a sexier vacation profession for myself—like tennis coach. Yep, she'd go for that, all right—with the curve of my paunch under her palms.

But in actuality, BB asked intelligent questions about my job and made nice observations, even though it was all somewhat mechanical. She was practiced at professional small talk.

"How long have you been working here," I asked when we'd pretty much exhausted pharmacology as a topic.

"About four years," she said. "I was anxious to live in southern Europe. Away from the snows, the dark winters, the men, the sex. I wanted a more meaningful life. There are many resorts in Greece that need physical fitness and holistic wellness personnel. Here I teach yoga too, and I can meditate at an ashram nearby. I think I may never leave. My inner life has become serene and rewarding."

So BB was into spirituality. The one subject on earth I know squat about. I groped for a response. "Well, that's wonderful," I said lamely.

"Next I train in the art of *Ashiatsu*," she said.

"Ashi—what?" I asked.

"Ashiatsu. It is an ancient Buddhist massage using foot pressure on the muscles."

Foot pressure? I asked myself. You mean like walking on the—what, chest, abs, the lower stuff? I didn't want to go any further with this. Lying on my back as I was, even the thought of a Nordic goddess walking all over me terrified me. Thankfully, the session was coming to an end. As it was, she was already down to my kneecaps and about to work on my loose left patella. Starting with Anita Ekberg and winding up with the Dalai Lamess was an unwelcome transition. But I had to admit, for all of my grousing, the massage was not that hard to bear. All my resentment had been rubbed out of me. Bibi was just plain nice.

"All right," she said, "you can get up now. Put on your robe and slippers, take your clothes and the towel and you'll find the showers and the sauna down the hall through the door to the left as you go out." She handed me a blue cotton drawstring bag with the Astron Bay logo on it for my clothes and wristwatch.

"Why would I want a sauna in this heat?" I asked.

"It's not a wet winter sauna. In summer the sauna is dry with very low humidity. The dry heat makes you perspire, which cleanses your pores and makes you feel cool. You will enjoy it," she said, with a little smile.

"My pores don't need cleansing." I sounded defensive—the product of years of parrying Sophie's moves on my hygiene.

"Oh, it will be good for you. We sometimes find our towels brown from smokers. Their pores ooze tar." BB sure knew how to gross a guy out. I bet Sophie put her up to that one.

At the reception desk, Sophie's Viking said my wife had already gone on to the waterfall shower. No thanks, a plain shower would do just fine for me. At that moment my old pal Lyle emerged from one of the massage rooms in his robe. Damn, I said to myself, where's he headed? We both needed a shower, glistening with oil under our robes—or shorts, as the case may be— but I couldn't bear the thought of showering with the Reptile. So I ducked into the sauna wing to avoid him, forgetting that Astron Bay's showers were almost certainly more private than the ones in the locker room at Millard Fillmore High School.

I stowed my robe and bag in a locker and went into the sauna. The room was empty and surprisingly large, with cedar-planked walls and benches. It was hot, but not unpleasantly so. I sat down and felt almost light-headed, my body immersed in the foreign atmosphere.

After three or four minutes I wondered if it was safe to leave, when Lyle came in with a white towel around his loins and carrying a bottle of water. He must have decided on a pre-shower sauna.

He seemed not to mind our meeting as much as I did. He nodded a greeting and sat down wordlessly on a cedar bench across from me. He looked perfectly comfortable, but I couldn't stand just sitting there like that. The silence echoed around us. I was dying to ask him about the 47 K statue sold at the Las Vegas hotel, but in the nick of time remembered that Aphro had told us not to discuss that with anyone. Maybe Sophie was right, that I can't keep a secret to save my soul.

"Lyle, I understand from Danielle that you're…um…trying to deal with Nikos's supplier. That Onarchos place south of here. Any luck in getting to do business with them directly?"

Lyle looked at me, sidelong, the dim lights of the sauna glinting off his bald head. He was trim, no belly fat or creases. Strong chest and arms. Stayed in good shape. I imagined him preening in all those Vegas hotel fitness centers with trainers and treadmills and bench-pressing equipment. I looked down at my stomach and its sad sag.

"Seems it's going to work," he said. Not a man for long answers.

I wished I had a towel on instead of my boxers. When you want to spar with another guy in a sauna, you want to be wearing the regulation uniform.

"I understand," I went on, "that they make some replicas as well as reproductions. Stuff that looks like the real thing, just out of the ground."

Lyle took a second to look at the far wall. There aren't too many places to look in a sauna. "I wouldn't know," he said. "We only shopped reproductions from Gavras. Did you get that idea from Onarchos?" He turned and looked at me with his heavy-lidded eyes. "He said you'd been down there." Did he really hear that from Onarchos or from Danielle?

"No, we were just helping Nikos's sister Elena a couple of days ago. We spent some time in his office processing his inventory and it all came from Onarchos's place. Some pieces were really realistic. Looked like museum pieces."

This time I noticed his eyelids flicker. Did the image of me snooping around in Nikos's paperwork give him a little jolt? "Well, what's wrong with that?" he asked, sounding casual. "Gavras was a businessman. His job was to sell objects that look like antiquities from this area. I hope you're not accusing him of anything. The poor slob just got murdered." I could almost hear an inaudible "you creep" at the end of that sentence.

Both of us were beginning to glisten with sweat. It was good to see him sweating a little, metaphorically speaking, so I persisted as I perspired. "I'm not accusing anyone of anything. Not that Nikos was an honorable guy, in my opinion. For that matter, Onarchos may not be an honorable guy either." This was pushing it a bit, and I hoped my little defamation wouldn't come back to haunt me. "If I were you, I'd be careful," I advised him. "That murder case put us all under a cloud, especially if we knew Nikos. I'm just glad I have an alibi, since I was the one who discovered the body." Not strictly true, but what the hell.

Lyle's face was tightening up and he took a long, deliberate swig from what must now have been bottled warm water. Then he looked at me directly with his narrowed eyes. "I don't like the sound of this, Redfield. What's your game here? We have an alibi too. And if you're under a cloud it's probably because you threatened to kill the bastard." Ouch. Flinching, I groped around for a quick save.

"Maybe that's why I think it's fair to suspect Nikos of dealing in shady replicas. If he was in the business of gypping customers, why not go for bigger game?"

Plainly, Lyle did not enjoy this conversation. "That would be stupid, and Gavras wasn't stupid. But if you're really on this jag, talk to Frawley. She was just asked to evaluate a piece taken from Gavras's shop after he died."

What? Could he be talking about Wally's piece—the one Wally filched from the shop? Who asked Gwen to look it over? Not Wally; he'd spent the day after his little shoplifting with us at Knossos and then in the hospital. Did Wally really take a piece that had to be 'evaluated'? To whom had he given it? Or sold it? Was he helping Elena or taking advantage of her? I tried to calm myself down. I was thinking like Sophie, not like myself.

"Take it easy, Lyle," I said, "I'm just saying there's a lot of bad trade, like you say, in antiquities—theft and looting and everything."

"That's a fact, friend," Lyle said coldly. "I have to be careful of that sort of stuff myself in the shops and galleries in Vegas." He took another swig of warm water and pushed the cap down to close the bottle.

Then he volunteered something. "Gwendolyn thinks Latif could be the source of any real antiquities Nikos might have been trading. She says Latif's in bed with the archaeologists." That was a new one. Old Gwen had accused Gabor of bribery before, but not exactly of collusion with looting.

"Is there any evidence of that?" I asked.

Lyle shrugged. "His kid stole figures from the museum, I hear. Chip off the old block. If Latif's game was getting too obvious, he might not have minded seeing Gavras disappear." Lyle paused. "No alibi either."

I should have kept my mouth shut, but Lyle's trashing Gabor made me see red, pardon the expression. I didn't think anyone would take Gwen's ravings seriously, but here was Lyle, spreading an even darker version of her rumor. "There were no fingerprints on those animals or any evidence that Hegel took them." I practically hissed this through my teeth, aware I had just made it up.

Lyle's lids flickered again for a second. "Doesn't prove he's innocent. Or his old man." He looked as if he'd had enough. He rose and adjusted his towel, saying, "I've got to get going."

I was now working on impulse. It might be my last chance to ask Lyle about the skipper. "That guy who took you and Danielle to Spinalonga on the day of the murder—you know, the boat guy? What's his name?"

Lyle headed for the door. "None of your fucking business, asshole," he said when he got there. He shot me a venomous look. I realized I'd blown it. Then came a last shot. "How's Pinnock?" he said. The door slammed and he was gone.

I was stunned. He didn't even *know* Wally. 'How's Pinnock?' How the hell did he get to ask that? Wally wasn't exactly well, but how could he know that already? I remembered I'd told Danielle about Wally taking us to the Pottery Shack on our cruise down to Pachia Ammos. Onarchos could have told the Tanners about Wally's visit too. But Lyle's question could only be a warning. As though he'd added, 'We've got plans for you too.'

The temperature in the sauna was rising with steam becoming visible. I was having trouble breathing. What the hell was going on? I stood and went to the door, suddenly panicked that Lyle might have locked it behind him. But thank god it opened and I stepped out and ran to the reception center in my boxers. "There's steam in the goddamn sauna," I snorted. "I thought it was supposed to be dry!" Sophie's Viking beveled around the desk and sprinted off, while I shook my head and hoped Sophie wasn't around to hear me cussing. Lyle's foul mouth was infectious.

He came back in a minute or two. "It's all right," he said. "Someone accidentally switched the water on over the volcanic stones in back. There is no cause for concern."

I went and took my shower. Lyle, I thought. That sonofabitch was trying to fucking *braise* me. Like the pork ribs Sophie makes for Sunday dinner.

Chapter 24
The Bingle

I strode out of the spa in a huff. I looked for Sophie at the pool. Sure enough, she was waiting for me, dangling her legs in the water and looking forward to that lean lunch we'd promised ourselves. I shucked my flip-flops and sat down next to her. Putting my own feet in the water, I told her about my testy session with Lyle in the sauna. "What the hell did Lyle know about Wally? It was only yesterday he almost got killed, and today Lyle's making snotty barbs about him."

Sophie frowned. "It may have been in the news, or someone in the hotel might have talked about it."

"Not likely for Lyle to pick up local news. In Greek, yet. He's a tourist, for heaven's sake." Sure, Onarchos could have told Lyle about Wally's visit. But how would he know about the Knossos incident so soon unless he had something to do with it?

"Let's get a sandwich and go to the room so we can talk." I felt we could hardly ever eat or talk in public anymore for fear of being overheard.

Upstairs, the back of the terrace was in shadow by then and we could eat our grub in its cool air.

"So how was the massage, Mister Lincoln." Sophie almost slid into the chair beside me, utterly relaxed after her experience.

"Not bad," I conceded. "Did you arrange Bibi for me?"

"Yep." She smiled sheepishly, picking up her tuna sandwich. "Had to, after I knew I was getting Sven."

I hated to trouble her relaxed and cheerful mood, but even the blue Aegean failed to calm me down after my sauna experience. "Look, Soph, let's go back to Lyle. He's a baddie. He practically accused Gabor of murder."

Sophie put her sandwich down, and made a displeased face while chewing with her mouth full.

I went on. "He not only made the same noises as Gwen about corruption and graft, he accused Gabor of funneling antiquities to Nikos. And then killing him when things went awry. He brought up Hegel's arrest. I tried to defend them all, but he wouldn't buy it. No alibi, he said. So I got mad and asked him about *his* little alibi trip with the skipper to Spirochete Island."

Sophie swallowed and passed a napkin over her lips. "You *didn't*!"

I took a sip of my beer. "Tell you the truth, Soph, the minute I said 'skipper' I knew I'd blown it."

"You may have. But Lyle didn't know you saw the skipper at the cabaña before the murder. Or even that you saw him at the Pottery Shack." Sophie had the whole thing in view, as usual. If she's watching, you don't need overhead cameras for the record.

She crumpled her napkin and took a sip of her bottled lemonade. "I'm more worried about the Latifs than anything, after what Aphro told us yesterday, and now with all these rumors swirling around them."

"I say we let them fend for themselves and mind our own business. We're not the frigging Red Cross."

The phone rang and I went in to answer. Speak of the devil. "Mr. Redfield." I recognized the accent. Gabor sounded constrained. "I am glad you are there. I wish to speak with you, please."

"Is it about Hegel?" I really didn't want to hear this. I had yet to recover from Lyle ruining the effects of my great massage, and I didn't need Gabor to ruin the effects of my beer.

"My boy will come back, but I am…" He broke off. "I need to talk with you. You have been kind." A tight, sad voice, urgent, pleading. "Can we meet outside?"

"Sure." Sure? Talk about letting the Latifs fend for themselves. Just call me "Red" Cross. I muffled the phone and told Sophie that Gabor wanted to talk privately, outside. Interested as she was, she motioned with a wave that I should go down alone. I arranged to meet him in five minutes.

Gabor was waiting by the shop and we went outside. I could see children and fat people playing in the pool, glittering in the sun. Gabor steered me to the right, down the paths toward the beach. He wanted to avoid people we might know as much as I did. Zoë, walking Basket on a leash, greeted us as we walked along a balustrade. Basket sniffed my ankles and looked curious and disappointed that Sophie wasn't with me. Sophie would be glad to hear that they were keeping tighter control over the little mutt. I realized we hadn't seen Madame in a few days.

I followed Gabor, who had gone on, preoccupied. When we reached the lawn area back of the beach, he stopped and turned to me, indicating a small concrete bench to sit on.

"I hope you can tell things that help me and my family," he began. I now saw that although the band-aids and gauze patches were off, he still had red scrapes and small gashes on his face and arms. The guy had had his world shattered in just a couple of days.

"When will they release Hegel?"

"They say by evening today."

The kid was busted two days ago with the critters in his jacket. That meant he'd been in custody for two nights—a helluva long time to ask him a couple of questions. I decided to come right out with it.

"Gabor, what did Hegel do? This isn't just about the museum animals, is it?"

He shook his head. "It is about sabotage. I did not know this, but Hegel…" He sighed, shaking his head again. "Hegel meet people, bad people, in Pachia Ammos. Inspector ask him very hard questions. I am ashamed. I am glad Samira not understand much."

"What sort of bad people?"

"Few days ago when Hegel was in Pachia Ammos with friend, he met man. Nice man, he thinks. Greek friend he meet at barbecue translate for him. The man was official, like a policeman, with gun and uniform. He ask Hegel how our firm work, about drilling and airport. He offer Hegel cigarettes and money to have look later, after work stop. Hegel think it not bad to do, but never tells me this."

I looked over at the cabaña, where a less than friendly man had given *me* a cigarette one day not too long ago. Smokes are appealing lures—and not just to kids. "I can't believe they'd go so far as bribing kids and sabotage just to stop your airport project."

"That is the problem. They do not harm equipment needed for airport. They harm drills, coring machines, and things we use to look for palace out in west. It is archeological search in west they disrupt, not airport planning. The drill they explode in Pachia Ammos is one used for exploring western area."

"So someone already knew what you were doing in the west, near the new palace location? Do you think Hegel told them about this?" I suddenly remembered a man with a gun and a uniform I'd seen a while ago, but Gabor didn't have to know this.

"Yes." Gabor, stricken with second-hand guilt, could not look at me. "I should have told my son firmly not to talk about inland palace to anyone." He shook his finger at an imaginary Hegel, to impress on him the need for discretion. I felt for Gabor, deep in the purgatory of parenting a teenager, but I also worried a little about having my sympathy enlisted for some sort of complicity. The Latifs were by no means out of the woods, as far as suspicion went, and I didn't want to be played for a sucker.

I heard a low familiar voice behind me and turned to look. It was Danielle, walking up a parallel path some distance behind us, leading toward the tennis courts. She was carrying a racquet and telling a story. Lyle walked easily beside her, tanned and toned, his bald head glistening in the light. I heard his lazy chuckle. They were having a great time, while poor Gabor here had his heart broken.

"Hegel take man into Bohnen-Essen compound after hours. Show him equipment. Maybe even show him drilling maps and records if we did not keep office locked."

"What maps and records?" This whole thing just didn't compute. I could see people not wanting an airport or worrying that the airport would destroy an archeological site. But if I was getting this, somebody was bothered enough by the firm's exploring the ancient stuff in the west to blow up their drilling equipment. It made no sense. Who would mind anybody discovering signs of a buried palace in a totally undeveloped place? Not the anti-development folks, surely. And not the antiquities activists and crazies, whoever they might be. They should be throwing parties and dancing the syrtaki. And having old Gwen join them. The image of Gwen executing Greek folkdancing moves in her high heels flitted through my mind for a second, and tickled my sense of the absurd. I needed a laugh just then, even a silent one.

"Is hard to explain, Mr. Redfield," he said. "But I could show you. I have some time until later this afternoon when I hope Hegel return. Samira take sleeping pill to rest and not need me. You would like to come with me to see these places? We can talk more in the car."

Quandary. Part of me really wanted to get a fix on what the hell was going on with this whole airport and archeological stuff, which I still didn't quite understand. Yet part of me also resisted going on another wild goose chase into the Cretan west. Promised to be even less fun with the gloomy Gabor than with the wily Wally. But my instincts told me that this is where the mystery lay— out there in that nebulous geography where ancient culture and modern commerce intersected. Just then I caught a glimpse of Spiro in his blazer near the barbecue area to our right, pointing out some dead branches on a large tree to one of the gardeners. He reminded me that the whole Delphinos-Gavras feud remained unresolved as well. But right now Gabor's offer to enlighten me was powerful bait, and I bit.

"Please call me Red," I said, "and I'd enjoy that ride. Let me just tell Sophie where I'm going."

I went up to our room, telling Gabor I'd meet him in the lobby in five minutes.

"You're crazy, Red." Sophie was not pleased, when I told her the plan. "What if he takes you down some garden path and snuffs you?" She was no longer the Latifs' social worker. "It's crazy for you to put yourself deliberately in danger like this, especially after what happened to Wally yesterday!"

As she said this, I remembered the black Mercedes that followed us to Knossos yesterday.

"Sophie, stop it! You're catastrophizing," I said sternly, "Get a grip." There's no other way to deal with Sophie's 'brush-fears,' as we call them— or my own, when they flare up. Sven's relaxing morning massage had clearly worn off and so had BB's, for that matter. All that serene talk about meditating in an ashcan seemed a million years ago. For a day that started out with all sorts of erotic promise, this was turning into another day of tense encounters and uncertain adventures.

"I won't ask you to come with us, Pumpkin," I said soothingly. "But this is a chance to break through that whole web of innuendo and rumor everybody's been weaving around the Latifs, and I don't want to pass it up. And there's really no solid reason to distrust Gabor. His lack of alibi isn't evidence."

Doth Red protest too much? Sophie certainly looked as though she thought he doth. "Well, if something happens to you, don't say I didn't warn you."

I met Gabor in the parking lot and we got into his car. I let him drive, but Sophie's concerns had made me aware that I would have had more control over the situation if we had used my tinny Renault. It was his company's car, he said. I was relieved. Gabor wouldn't bring bloodstains back to Bohnen-Essen, would he? Would he?

We soon reached Pachia Ammos. "Thick sand," Gabor said.

"What?" I asked, not understanding.

"'Pachia Ammos' mean 'thick sand' in Greek." Yes, I'd heard that before, though I couldn't remember where.

I'd not seen much of the place from the beachfront where I had shared the fateful red wine with Danielle. It was a small town, a few major streets, two or three restaurants and hotels, and some really nice dwellings overlooking the ocean. We turned from the ocean inland to a large open space with a line of trucks and utility vehicles parked in a fenced area nearby. The name Bohnen-Essen GmbH stood out on some of them. His firm. It was early afternoon and few people seemed to be about. We got out of the car and walked around a little.

"They stop work here a few days ago." Gabor swept his arms around toward the northwest, over an empty plain dotted with test digs, little flags here and there, drilling equipment on small carts. "We leave this site for now to begin planning for next phase. Finances not yet set, since we have waited so long. And environment issues remain problem. But we have verbal permission and soon sign contract to begin."

"How did you convince them there was nothing under this area?" I asked. We had stopped by a Quonset hut, which had a rough wooden bench in its shade, but we didn't sit down.

"My company pay for technology to map what is underground in entire region. Infrared aerial photography, drillings, magnetometry. Sonic probes. Some important sites found that way, like Sybaris, Greek city in Italy. Much faster than old digging and drilling. Even good archaeologists work very slow."

I looked at the barren surroundings. "I'm surprised that this went on so long if there was no evidence of a palace or whatever."

"Pieces of clay tablet found in Gournia many years ago have signs of palace. So people dream of palace and no one can build airport. We think just politics. But maybe not. We would still have problem if map tablet was not put together."

"Map tablet? Was this the big thing that just happened that you were telling Gwen about?"

Gabor brightened for the first time that day. "Come inside and I show you with photographs." He pulled out a ring with a half dozen keys and unlocked the door of the trailer-sized building with its corrugated metal roof. Inside was a dim, stuffy office with desks and shelving littered with rolls of blueprints and other papers, and with huge maps tacked to boards on the walls.

"Many years ago, pieces of stone tablet found by Canadian archeologist look like plan of area around Gournia." Gabor began rifling through rolls of paper on one of the large desks. "They kept in Heraklion museum, but make no sense as map. East and west not right, not like modern map." He had pulled a file out of the mess and now opened it to reveal a black and white photograph. "Then, this summer," he went on, "two new pieces found inland were joined with map tablet in Heraklion, and map now make sense. Show palace to west of Gournia, not east."

"Fascinating." I'm not crazy about archeology, but I like geography and atlases. Weird to think of Gwen's ancient Minoan ladies messing around with map tablets if they were indeed running the show in those days. The photo Gabor held up didn't make much sense to me, although it was easy to see how the four or five stone pieces with lines and marks etched into them would fit together to make a whole.

"So my firm offer to help test and excavate western sites now," Gabor continued, "and results very positive so far." He beamed again, the way he had done that night at the table with Gwen, before she ruined our *Sachertorte* with her snit. "I will stay to help with new search in west. If government give contract, we help finance excavation for a time."

I wanted to say it sounded fascinating, but it also sounded a bit shonky to me, as Wally would say. The deal would look like the German firm bought off the government by offering to fund excavations at a place removed from the proposed airport site. But I desperately wanted not to be cynical just now. Even a drug scientist loves a discovery. I had a weird flash, years from now bringing Archie over here to look at the palace ruins and telling him that Gramps had been around for its discovery.

"So where is this place? Have your guys found anything to prove they're in the right region?"

A glow had returned to Gabor's sallow dark complexion. "We keep this secret and leave no sign of drillings. Attract looters otherwise. But I can show you some locations we tested west of here. You like to drive there? Not far."

We got in the car and headed north toward Gournia. Then, to my surprise, Gabor turned off at the small section of fence that marked the road west to Gaitani. Unmistakable: it was where Wally had us turn on our trip to the Pottery Shack. We passed Gaitani and its few shops, gas pump and dwellings, and the side road to Onarchos's place. We continued past a sign with a strange icon:

a cross on a dome. I figured it probably pointed forward to a church. Below it was a long name in Greek, and below that, a short name I could make out: Asari.

As he drove, Gabor again spoke with feeling of his appreciation for being in the midst of the remains of an ancient civilization. If his culture hype was an act, it was a great one. It probably *would* take an expert like Gwendolyn Frawley to see through it. Or Aphro. But I was as happy to swallow it as I was listening to Wally's blarney. Tinfoil bowls weren't the only things in danger of slipping right by me.

The road was wretched, rutted and stony. The car lurched from side to side, and we slowed down and stopped by a barren area off the road. Gabor pointed out an unmarked old van a bit off the road in the field. "There is one of our vehicles. We use trucks without our name to bring drills for borings. It will be gone tonight. Several drillings each day, we move around, not make us obvious."

I could see his point. The area was so barren and deserted that it wouldn't be hard to abscond with antiquities from obvious drillings and diggings. Of course, the same principle would also make the company and employees like Gabor vulnerable to suspicion—particularly if you wanted to pin a theft or murder rap on him.

Gabor turned to me. "It is good there are very few people near here. This is where we find possible wall or roof patterns running deep under ground."

"But how do you know there is anything there?" I asked. "I don't see any markers or any of those little flags archeologists use to mark sites."

Now Gabor grinned broadly and motioned me to get out of the car. He opened the back door and took a zippered leather folder from the seat. He opened it up and pulled out a large folded piece of paper. He unfolded and flattened it and held it up. It looked like the kind of weather map you see on the evening news, curvy lines and things, only not in color.

"It is a grid," Gabor explained. The vertical lines were rows of numbers over which densely curved lines were superimposed. "Grid show magnetic..."—he groped for the word—"*anomaly* under soil, and that indicate building structures below surface." I noticed Gabor's technical vocabulary surpassed his regular vocabulary, and his explanation made perfect sense.

Fascinating. You'd think old Gwen would jump up and down if she could see this.

We walked around a bit to the edge of the area that would correspond to the edge of the grid. Suddenly it all made visual sense to me. As Gabor pointed to various details on the grid, I now pictured walls rising from the ground, with stairs and parapets and irregular roof lines, like the magnificent complex at Knossos, the home of a whole civilized community of builders and artists, royalty and priests, dancers and scribes. For a moment the stakes of this whole business took on life in my imagination, and I saw them spread into the domains of contemporary Cretan life—culture, heritage, politics, business. And crime. The figure of the Greek man who had bribed Hegel to enter the Bohnen-Essen compound at night remained shadowy, but his motives were coming into focus.

Gabor looked gratified to see I understood, and to give me a sense of the size of the whole area, we got back in the car and drove forward for another half mile or so. By now the road was no longer passable, at least with any safety. The whole archeological field was certainly immense, and there was even more of the site beyond. But Gabor had to spare his company's car and with some difficulty turned it around. I noticed the gas was low. Not knowing how far he planned to take us, I pointed this out to him. "*Ach*, yes," he said. "I knew I need petrol but forget. We stop in Gaitani."

We soon got back to Gaitani and its local store with its single gas pump. We pulled up there, beyond the junction of the side road to Onarchos's place. We left the car and went into the store. Gabor prepaid the gas, and I got a bottle of soda. Gabor began pumping gas. I stood next to the building, sipping my drink and watching a little boy pulling a small goat by a rope on the side of the dusty road. A great scene for a photo or a painting. It could have been a hundred years ago. A car approached in a little cloud of dust and I watched carefully, hoping the boy and his animal would be safe. The car came closer, the dust on its black paint muting the sun's reflection. It was a Mercedes. With a smashed headlight. It reduced its speed, passed the boy, and went on slowly beyond us toward the intersecting lane to Onarchos's place.

I threw my bottle down and ran to the car. "Gabor," I yelled, "We've got to go! Stop with the gas. Get in the car and drive! Hurry!" There was no time to tell him why. He looked baffled, but put the hose back quickly and screwed the gas cap. "We've got to go. Get in." Thank God I had gained his trust. He moved quickly into the driver's seat as I buckled myself into my own. As we lurched into the road, I looked up toward the lane and saw the Mercedes turning around. I was all Sophie now, intuitive and scared as hell.

"Speed it up, if you can," I hissed to Gabor. He accelerated and we were off. The hilly terrain forced turns in the road, and Gabor kept his pace fast, but safe. The Mercedes was indeed behind us but still at a little distance.

"That car that passed the gas pump and turned around followed us to Knossos yesterday," I said. "And our friend was almost killed there!" We flew around another curve and the black car disappeared for a moment.

"Why would it follow you?" Gabor looked wild-eyed as he speeded.

A thought struck me. "Why would they follow *you*?" I said.

I saw him look in the rear-view mirror. He threw his head back, gesturing for me to look behind us. The Mercedes was now approaching rapidly and was soon close enough to be tailgating us. "Hurry!" I yelled to Gabor, "It'll ram us if we don't get out of here."

Gabor looked in his side mirror again and realized he would have to swerve if he were not to be hit. We almost drove into the rut on our right as we did so, and the Mercedes fell slightly back on the narrow road. It sped up again and the road, curving, didn't allow a pass, but it was too late. The Mercedes, as it came abreast of us, suddenly fell to our left. As it jogged off the road, the driver struggled to right the car, accelerating to achieve an impossible jump back onto the road. We heard a loud thump as the car disappeared down the rise. Gabor braked to a stop fifty yards up. We got out of his car and went back, walking gingerly in a cloud of our own dust on the outer edge of the road. The Mercedes lay on the driver's side about ten feet down the hill, its right front wheel spinning and steam seeping from the hood. It could have rolled another two hundred feet if the rocks had not stopped it.

"Do you have a phone?" I was out of breath. "Call the police!" As Gabor quickly unclipped his cell phone from his belt, I felt a moment of panic that we were too remote for reception. But in a second I heard Gabor speaking urgently in Greek. I'd forgotten he spoke Greek. He clicked off and began to descend the short distance to the Mercedes.

"Gabor, wait! That man may be dangerous." I hurried behind him, but he didn't stop. He reached the car and hunched himself over to look in the passenger seat window. I followed fearfully, although there was no movement inside the vehicle. Courage is not a prominent Redfield gene. The car had only the driver, crumpled in a heap against the driver's door.

As we made a futile effort to right the car, a truck approached, parked near us, and two men got out. I had a moment of terror—but they simply wanted to help. Together we pushed the car up and over onto its wheels. The driver's body slumped away from the door onto the passenger seat. Even through the bloody window, the single black, straight eyebrow running across his forehead was visible and unmistakable. His open mouth revealed a glint of gold teeth.

Chapter 25
An Evening with Elena

"Do you know this man?" one of the officers asked in good English as he pointed to the body. The police had pried the passenger door of the wrecked Mercedes open, lifted the body out, and laid it on its back. He wore a brown uniform with a holstered gun on his belt.

Gabor shook his head. "No." The policeman turned to me.

"He's dead, isn't he?" I asked before he could say anything.

"An ambulance is on its way. Do *you* recognize him?"

"I think I know who he is," I said, "You must contact Inspector Kensington in Ágios Nicólaos. She may be able to identify him better. I believe he's the security guard at the pottery plant down that road back there." I pointed. "And he may also have been involved in an incident at Knossos yesterday." I was careful how I put this, since the word *crime* might raise a red flag that could get me detained. I'd already spent more time shut up with police here in Crete than in all my previous forty-seven years in the States.

The two men from the truck who had helped us right the car were also being questioned by another policeman. I wondered if they recognized the dead man as a local and knew his name. The ambulance arrived as Gabor and I were being questioned about the accident. We described the car chase, but I was cagey about the weird web that might connect the driver in some oblique way to the shop and possibly the death of Nikos Gavras. Like I said, if I was going to end up in police custody again, I'd rather it be with the friendly and sensible Aphro than with the baboon who had interviewed Madame after the murder.

While we were giving our descriptions, the police checked tire tracks and skid marks. It was pretty clear that we were the chasees and not the chasers, and the whole thing looked as though it might even have been accidental rather than malicious. So the cops finally took our names and contact information and told us we could leave. All this time the medics had been inspecting the body for vital signs, but Zorba II was clearly gone. Before we started the car, Gabor phoned the hotel. He asked them to let Sophie and Samira know we were on our way back, saying we had been delayed by an accident we had witnessed on the road. I didn't look forward to my return to Sophie who has a hundred ways of saying 'I told you so!'

But the scene played out a little differently than I expected. Sophie greeted Gabor with a big smile when we entered the lobby—and announced "Hegel's home!" She then impulsively gave him a hug. "He's with Samira in your room."

When we got to our own room, Sophie put her arms around my paunch and gave me a squeeze. She was clearly glad to have me safely back home too. I kissed the top of her head and freed myself. "Let me get a martini and a cool seat on the terrace, and I'll tell you about it. I'm still a little shook up. You'll be very surprised to hear what happened."

"I'll get you that martini," she said. "Just sit down and take it easy for a minute." I was glad she was in nurturing mode. When she came out with her wine and my martini, I told her about the Mercedes, the chase, and the crash.

Of course, she freaked out. "Red, you had me convinced nothing was going to happen and then you go and almost get yourself effing *killed*!" When Sophie swears, even in abbreviations, she's really upset. But I was grateful she seemed more upset *for* me than *at* me.

"You're not going to believe who was driving," I said.

Her eyes were wide open. "Zorba Two?" she said.

We tried to reconstruct the information Aphro had given us yesterday and its relation to the two dramatic incidents we—I—witnessed in the last two days. As far as we could recall, the security guard at the museum, Zacharias Stephanopoulos (Zorba I in our parlance) had a brother, also a security guard (Zorba II) who left the museum to work for Onarchos. This was the guy in the Hawaiian shirt who pushed Wally off the wall yesterday. Today he reappeared in the same black Mercedes that had followed us to Knossos and tried to drive Gabor off the road. It all made perfect sense—except for the why? Why go after Wally? Or after me or Gabor for that matter?

Sophie took a sip of her wine and frowned. "It's got to have something to do with that pot Wally stole from Elena's shop. But what? And how could Zorba Two be running around today in the same Mercedes after he tried to kill Wally the day before?" Sophie said. "I thought Aphro's people would have grabbed him by now!"

"We never told Aphro about the one-eyed Mercedes, if you remember. We couldn't really be sure that it was Zorba Two's car at the time."

"Well, I still don't know how the police missed him at Knossos. But today proves that he wasn't just after Wally. He was after you too," Sophie said.

"I think he was trying to intimidate us to keep us away from the Pottery Shack. Soph. He couldn't have done much today." God, I felt stupid. Now Sophie is going to say he was going to murder us.

"Red! He was going to murder you! He had a gun, you were in a deserted location, he could have got away with it. You and Gabor couldn't have said anything if you were dead, and he'd be free to get off the island!"

She was ticked again, and there wasn't much I could say to contradict her. Sometimes hysteria makes pretty good sense. Like when you're next in a serial rub-out scheme.

Finally she looked at me with exasperation. "And on top of everything, we have to go to Agnik to dinner tonight."

"Whaaaat!" I yelled, and almost dropped my empty glass. "You're crazy, Sophie! Do you realize what I've been through? What *we*'ve been through, if you count yesterday? I don't care what happens but I'm not going anywhere tonight."

"We've got to, Red," she said seriously, and took a sip of her wine. "It's about Elena."

"Nuts. Has something happened to *her too*?"

"No, but she found that a bowl was missing and that puzzled her. When she called Wally to ask about it, he didn't answer. I realized nobody had told her about Wally's fall, and of course she doesn't know about his little larceny. When I told her Wally was in the hospital she almost went to pieces."

Sophie was for sure back in nurturing mode, thank god, but I was still damned if I was going to Agnik. "The woman should read a freakin' newspaper once in a while," I said. "Give her a little distraction from the shop."

"Don't be mean, Red. The fact is we went off and got massages this morning and forgot all about Elena, and it looks as though Aphro didn't bother to fill her in either. She's very upset, and she also found something in Nikos's files she wants to talk to us about."

"Did she say what it was?" This might be interesting.

"No. She said it was complicated and she'd better show us. She also wanted to thank us for our help by inviting us to have supper with her. Around six."

I still didn't want to go. My mind went its own way. I took a minute to try to imagine what I *really* wanted to do tonight. It had something to do with floating down the Nile on a barge on a balmy evening, and involved a harem and a bunch of eunuchs waving palm fronds. "Can't this wait till tomorrow? This just isn't a night I want to go out to dinner."

Sophie narrowed her eyes, and twenty minutes later we were in the car driving to Agnik.

The shop was closed when we arrived, but with a few knocks we heard Elena walk down the stairs in back. She greeted us warmly, and we followed her back to the courtyard with its nice table and chairs. Before any of us sat down, she asked urgently about Wally as we stood in the late afternoon light.

We assured her that Aphro had said he was going to be all right. I was too tired to go over the business at Knossos. I had even less appetite for reporting my own adventure on the road back from Gaitani. Instead I plopped down unceremoniously into one of the hard garden chairs round the painted wooden table.

"Oh," Elena said, "you must be tired. Sophie told me you were out all afternoon. Let me get you some wine. I have a Dafnes that I think you will like." She went in the back room and returned with a tray of glorious goblets and a carafe of ruby red wine, slightly dewy with the humidity.

"How did Mr. Pinnock fall?" she asked after she sat down. "Such a serious accident. They should have more fences and rails at Knossos. I believe other people have had accidents there, but not as serious as this."

Clearly Sophie had left out the guy in the Hawaiian shirt when she talked to Elena on the phone. Just as well, especially since with Zorba II now dead, it made no difference. So we told her how Wally's fall was broken by a canopy over a restoration area, with burlap underneath, and how he was unconscious when he was taken away by ambulance. "I think he'll be all right," I said, trusting the assurance Aphro had given us.

"Who will look after him?" Elena said. The afternoon light cast a gentle glow over her melancholy face. I guess being a widow she knows what it's like to be alone when you're in ill health or in trouble. In the aura of that golden sunset, she looked a little like Irene Papas—serious, with a heavy heart.

Sophie asked, "Elena, you mentioned something about a piece—a piece of replica art, was it?—that seems to be missing from your shop." Oh lord, Sophie, not yet. I wanted to kick her under the table but was afraid I'd get Elena instead. Sophie seemingly wanted to take Elena's mind off Wally although this was precisely the wrong question.

"Oh yes," Elena said, coming out of her distraction. "It seems not so very important now and I can probably get another from Mr. Onarchos. But I could not find a bowl that was already paid for after you and Mr. Pinnock left on the day before yesterday."

"Really," I said, feeling embarrassed, as though I'd been a lousy bookkeeper. "Do you have any idea what might have happened to it?"

"I don't know how anyone could take it," she said. "I know it wasn't Nia. Or anyone who came to the shop. The bowl was in back. I always lock up shop at night and there are no signs someone came in. Maybe it is in a box where it shouldn't be. Maybe Mr. Pinnock put it in the wrong one. It is difficult to know because many are sealed shut."

I was impressed with Elena's reasonableness. She wasn't jumping to any conclusions or making any accusations, unlike you-know-who. I looked at Sophie, who betrayed nothing. She looked steadily out at the sunset over the lake. I figured she must've decided that the wily Wally was the bloke who was going to have to solve this little conundrum, now he was on the mend.

"Well, hopefully you'll be able to get a replacement," I said. "But didn't you tell Sophie you had something else to show us. A file or something?"

"Yes," she said, "Let me get more wine, and some light, and I'll bring it."

The sun was close to setting and the shade of the courtyard was deepening. Sophie had gone with Elena and they returned from the back room, Sophie with another carafe of wine and Elena with a kerosene lantern. She put it on the table and lit it, then went back to the office and returned with a manila folder. She pulled a bunch of papers from it.

"I found this in one of the recent ledger books, in the back." She held up a print-out of the Las Vegas gallery announcement with its photo of the statuette, the very one I found bookmarked on the computer two days ago. She handed it to me. On the back were hand-written figures, $200 \times 1.3 = \$260$. $47,500? The last was underlined twice, emphatically.

Elena then handed me two glossy photos of the same figure. One was intact, while one had a broken nose like the one offered for sale by the Las Vegas gallery. Very curious. The backgrounds and display surfaces didn't match the one in Las Vegas. The two pictures were not computer print-outs. They were glossy photos, made elsewhere, independently.

Now Elena pulled out copies of e-mails, the first dated 10-4-2005. I realized that in the European style, this was April 10, not October 4. "Were these in the file," I asked, "or did you print them out?" She confirmed she found them in the file.

The messages were short and Sophie brought her chair around so she could read with me by the fading light. The first was addressed to "dalrymp@ltd3.uk."

> *Sir,*
>
> *I need to speak to you by telephone at once. I have an urgent matter regarding an American export to discuss with you. Please give me a telephone number where I can reach you today.*
> *Nikos Gavras*

The second was the reply:

> *Dear Mr. Gavras,*
>
> *I do not speak to clients directly, as you know. Please contact my American agent D. L.Tanner about any business matters. I believe you have her telephone number.*
> *Sincerely,*
> *G.M.D.*

The next message was dated the same day:

> *Sir,*
>
> *I need to speak to you and not to your agent. If you do not give me direct access to speak to you, I will contact appropriate authorities and ask them to contact you.*
> *Nikos Gavras*

A last message, without salutation or signature, read: "Very well. I will telephone you after close of your shop this evening, about 17:00 hrs."

Beneath the printout were handwritten words
"Terms"
"D.T."

"Theo"

"Elena," I said, "This *is* important. Did you verify that these e-mails were in the computer?" The glow of the wine had burned out and my brain was sitting on cold concrete.

Elena nodded. "Yes, but that is all. No more e-mails to this address later. But I have telephone billings, because Monday I must talk to recent clients, questions about orders. I am glad Nikos was careful, always keeping bills and records for over a year. That's how I see a large number of calls in spring."

She handed me a bunch of phone bills, held together with a large paper clip. I began to riffle through them and saw right away repetitive entries to London, UK, with the same number. They began on 11-5-2005—May 11. Among them in the next week or ten days were calls to Onarchos's place, which Elena identified, and to Las Vegas.

"I need to just think about this for a few minutes," I told Elena. She nodded as though she understood. "I saw it was important, but thought I would ask you rather than the police." I took this to mean that she recognized a serious irregularity implied in the e-mails but without being able to quite put it together with the photos or with its possible implications for Nikos's murder. And anyway, the police had had the computer in custody for a couple of days.

She rose. "I must prepare supper, so please excuse me. It will be ready soon, and I will turn on more lights so you can see better."

It was getting darker and Elena turned the upstairs lights on to illuminate our courtyard more brightly. With a last glow from the clouds turned gold by the setting sun, it was strange to be dealing with this dry, grim correspondence in such a lovely scene.

As Elena left, Sophie turned to me with a frown and said, "Red! This is bad. No more e-mails, just phone calls. Whatever it was, it was too delicate or dangerous to put into writing. I now think Nikos *was* involved in dishonest traffic in antiquities. Not just replicas. That statue is a giveaway. Especially with the print-out of the web picture, and the calculation of prices." Sophie is always stealing my best thoughts. There was no escaping her inferences. But I saw a small problem with her conclusions.

"You're good, Sophie, and I agree. Except I don't think Nikos *knew* he was conveying antiquities. And that's what those e-mails must have been about." We tried to put the story together. Nikos sold something for a few euros, then found it marked up to forty-seven kilobucks. If this was a surprise, he would have been pissed. So how would he react? Call the cops or get in on the deal? He had acted on his sudden knowledge by phoning around. But to what purpose?

"How could Nikos not know about his role in lucrative traffic till so late in the game?" Sophie wondered.

"Maybe the replicas were so good he didn't know. Remember how Wally was always oohing and aahing over them." I fervently hoped Wally wasn't just putting on an act when he did that. But I put that thought aside. "Just think. If real antiquities were mixed in with the replicas, Nikos wouldn't have suspected. He's licensed to export replicas and has all the necessary customs clearances. *Voila*! You've got looted artifacts traveling around the world as replicas with legitimate paperwork from a respectable business. Great way to get them out of the country without alerting the authorities."

Sophie nodded to indicate that she found this convincing. "How do you know some were the real thing?"

"I don't. But the price on that thing in Las Vegas is too steep for a replica, don't you think?"

Sophie considered the implications of our scenario. "When he saw that exorbitant price on that noseless Las Vegas thing, it must have made Nikos drool. You know Nikos as well as I do." She paused to consider. "Which isn't very well, I know, but you know what I mean. He didn't shrink from shady deals. And I bet it infuriated him to be used like that. But by whom?"

"Looks like Lyle and his sweet, innocent bride," I said. "I've gotta hand it to you, Soph. It makes sense." Then I remembered something she wasn't going to like. "I hope you haven't forgotten Gwendolyn in all this. She authenticated that thing with the broken nose. She's gotta be in on this too."

"Not so fast, Redster." Sophie's confidence was up and she was sounding like Sam Spade. "If that noseless statue is real, and Gwen authenticated it as real, it proves only that she had a concealed connection with the Tanners. Not that she knew anything about the smuggling." Sophie was going to bend over backwards to be fair to her friend.

"I know this is hard for you, Soph, but Gwen's no innocent in all this. If she authenticated that piece in London, she plainly overlooked the possibility that it was an illegal export. She pretends to be a stickler for *provenance*, but she couldn't have looked into the origin of the imports very carefully in this case."

"Would she do something like that on purpose?" Sophie's doubt was at last giving way to regret.

At that moment, Elena, with a tray, called from her balcony where she had finished setting a small table. "Supper is ready," she said, "Please bring your glasses and the lamp."

Chapter 26
Erasmo's Story

Carrying our wine glasses and the lantern, we went up the outside stairs to join Elena on the balcony. From there, we could overlook the courtyard below and the lake beyond. The table was set with placemats and condiments, oil, vinegar, salt, pepper. Bowls of chick-pea soup were ready for us, and we were ready for them. White linen napkins wrapped neatly around stainless silverware lay next to the bright orange dishes, and we saw salad plates and a colorful salad in the center of the table. It was lovely, a word I learned from Sophie. Informal and gracious. We took our places and sipped our soup quietly as the light in the sky faded into a deeper and deeper blue. Points of light came on across the lake, one by one, like the stars becoming visible in the sky.

As we finished, Elena told us "Now I will get the fish. We will have only salad and fish. It is not much, but I hope you like it. You would like more wine, no?" I had become relaxed again, if still alert. It was so cozy that I thought I was simply out to dinner with a new friend.

"Maybe a little." I can handle wine if I space it out, but I realized I hadn't even finished my second glass. Rarely happens except during great football games when I can't take my eyes off the tube—and then it's usually a bottled beer at issue. I'd had a rough day, braised in a sauna, followed by a wild goose chase with me as the goose.

"What a lovely supper," Sophie said, "and what a lovely setting." The afternoon light was gone now, but we enjoyed the soft glow of the lantern and the way lights were coming on all over Agnik. Elena came out with more wine and the large platter of fish. It was a surprise: squid stuffed with a rice and tomato mixture, served with lemon wedges. I found it delicious.

It was difficult to return to the troublesome business of the e-mails and photos of the replicas, and Nikos's financial calculations and that slew of phone calls. It seemed too early to share with Elena the burden, heavier by the hour, of our suspicions. On the other hand, it seemed wrong to treat her like a child, holding back information more important to her than to us.

Sophie, always the one to get to the point, braved Elena's innocence. "Elena, we feel Nikos stumbled on to something illegal in his business, and he didn't know whether to go to the police or deal with the people involved directly. He may have been afraid that if he went to the police with his information, the people would get him in revenge." Sophie was putting as good a face on the situation as she could. I noticed she had also slipped into a first name format with Elena, who was nodding as she listened, not offended or alarmed as we feared she might be. Something of the same sort must have occurred to her independently.

"I can maybe learn more about this when I meet with Mr. Onarchos," she said.

A jolt of alarm shook me. "When will you see him?" I asked.

"The day after tomorrow," Elena said.

"Elena," I said urgently, "please call Inspector Kensington tomorrow and show her the things you showed us. You really should not meet with Onarchos before calling her. If you can't reach her right away, insist that her office contact her."

Her brow furrowed and she asked "Why?" I realized we hadn't filled her in on our trip to the Pottery Shack, perhaps assuming that Wally had done so. But it now looked as though Wally hadn't done so either.

Sophie again tackled the difficult issue. "Elena, we're not sure just exactly what is going on. But if this whole thing that led to Nikos getting killed was about antiquities smuggling, it's very possible that the Onarchos business played a role in it. If so, they may have a bad motive for offering to buy your shop." For someone who can't tell an anecdote or a story without a trillion digressions, Sophie can be surprisingly focused and concise when the need arises.

Elena still looked perturbed, but she promised she would speak to Aphro before moving ahead with the Onarchos negotiation. It suddenly occurred to me that this might be the first time that even a hypothetical name or entity had been attached to the image of her brother's murderer. That had to be an immensely disturbing thought.

But after a minute, Elena sighed, her shoulders relaxed, and she leaned back in her seat. It was as though we'd given her permission to put off something she'd wanted to postpone anyway. We too wanted no worries to cloud this gracious scene, with an Aegean breeze cooling us above a bay ringed by twinkling city lights below and stars above.

With business out of the way, we were able just to enjoy a social visit. Elena brought us some herbal tea and honey, and began trading stories with Sophie about her nieces and nephews in Athens in return for hearing about our grandson Archie. Regretfully, Elena had no children of her own, but she doted on her sister's little boys and girls. I warned her that when kids grow up and become teenagers they turn into punks—a point I illustrated using old Hegel. I included mention of the kid's transformation at the barbecue in Astron Bay— of course, leaving out the story of the filched critters in his soccer jacket.

The mention of Astron Bay must have jogged Elena into making an astonishing revelation. "I visited Astron Bay yesterday for the first time. What a beautiful villa!"

Sophie was instantly on the *qui vive*—though she proceeded cautiously. "We're sorry we missed you. We were in Knossos, you know, or we would loved to have shown you around."

Elena took a sip of tea and smiled. "I was given a tour, by Spiro Santas, you will be glad to hear." Whoa! Now that's a picture to conjure up—the lady and the walrus peacefully strolling the paths of Astron Bay!

"And did you also meet his godmother, Madame Delphinos?" Sophie asked. "She invited us to tea the day after we arrived, and served us a tisane, just like this one." That's my quick-witted gal. When she sees an opening, she lets it fall into her mitt like a fly ball at a baseball game.

Elena paused to take another sip. "My errand was with Madame, and it was a difficult one, as you can imagine, after my painful argument with Mr. Santas. But it was time to make peace, I felt. You have heard of Madame's argument with my family over her memoir?"

Sophie blushed. "She told us just a little about it. It sounded as though it had to do with the connection she had with your grandfather many years ago."

I could see Elena struggling with how much to tell us. Maybe it was the serene setting that created a feeling of intimacy among us, but after taking another sip and looking out over the sparkling shoreline, she began to tell us her version of the story.

"My grandfather had once been in love with Angelina Delphinos," she began. I almost choked on my tisane. *Angelina*! If ever there was a woman who warn't no angel, it was surely Madame.

"He was married to my grandmother at the time, and already had three children. I know that Madame thought our grandfather was a seducer, a Casanova—a *roué*, I believe she calls him. And it seems that is how she describes him in her memoir. My brother was furious when he heard this, and threatened to go to court and accuse Madame of slander and libel."

"Then it wasn't true?" Sophie asked. Reasonable question, since we were clearly dealing with a little contradiction in the man's character.

Elena paused again, trying to order her thoughts and choose her words carefully, it seemed. "Grandfather would gladly have married Angelina, I think. But he could not and would not leave our Grandmama and their children. They were married very young—a marriage arranged by their parents. That was the custom in those days. And soon after the wedding it became clear that grandmother was—how do you say it—ill in her mind. She was a beautiful woman, and when her mind was clear, she was kind and warm. But when the darkness covered her thoughts, she became angry and full of despair and threatened to kill herself."

Oh my. A sad and not unfamiliar story, and I don't just mean Jane Eyre and the madwoman in the attic. Even though I get a lot of crap about my pharmaceutical job, people forget how much psychotropic drugs help people with mental illnesses these days.

"Oh dear," Sophie chimed right in. "I know exactly what you mean. James Joyce's daughter was ill like that and the family tried everything. They got her the best medical care available then and even sent her to Carl Jung in Switzerland. But there just wasn't anything much available to help in those days."

Then, bless her, Sophie patted me on the arm and told Elena, "You know, Red here is a chemist who works for a drug company and they make all sorts of medicines nowadays that would have been like a miracle for your grandma. What a shame they weren't available then."

Elena smiled at us. "I am glad you understand. And I am glad to say that Madame Delphinos seemed to understand as well—much to my surprise."

Wow. I could see Sophie practically jumping out of her chair with excitement. "That's wonderful! What did she say?"

"No one had ever told her this. The family kept grandmother's illness secret because insanity was a shame on the family in those days. There was enough money to have nurses take care of her at home and keep her and the children safe, although much of the family money was used up by Nona's care. In this way she lived a long time, until she was nearly seventy-seven. She died only six years before Grandpapa passed away in 1988."

"I guess that explains why your grandfather couldn't be honest with Madame when he fell in love with her," Sophie said. "He couldn't betray his wife's secret to her. And Madame, who was young and a little wild, might not have appreciated what a wrenching predicament he faced." It's weird how you need all the information, in any situation, to get a fix on how to make a fair judgment. Here poor Erasmo sounded like a total jerk in Madame's version, but like a hero in Elena's.

"So what's going to happen with Madame's memoir?" Sophie asked.

"I do not know yet," Elena shrugged. "But Madame believed my story, I am quite certain. I now wish Nikos had explained the problem to her when all this came up a few years ago. But Nikos hated Madame. To him she was a terrible woman telling her scandalous life in a lying memoir to make a fortune by dishonoring the Gavras name."

"Well, that's not totally unreasonable, it seems to me," I said. Unlike Sophie, I too saw Madame as a self-centered diva.

But Elena added a surprising footnote to her point. "My brother was also desperate to make the kind of money the family had in the old days. His divorce in New York eight years ago was very expensive for him. If Madame had not asked his permission to print her story, Nikos could have sued after the book came out and maybe received much money. But he lost that opportunity when she asked his permission to publish the book. If he agreed, he would get nothing. If he refused and she published it anyway, he could still sue. So he refused, hoping she would go on and publish."

The logic of this left me a little dizzy. But I took her to mean that family honor wasn't Nikos's only concern in the matter. The masterbilker was in hale and oily form when negotiating with Madame.

Elena shook her head sadly. "My brother's life did not go as he wanted. In the end, money was more important to him than honor." For a moment I was afraid she was going to cry. "I think this cost him his life."

Sophie was shaken by Elena's grief. "It's hard to lose someone you love and not be able to save them from themselves," she said and reached over and touched Elena's arm.

However, Elena pulled herself together and although her eyes were still glistening, went back to Sophie's question about Madame. "I think hearing the story of Erasmo and Grandmama touched Madame's heart. And I now think she understand him and his love for her in a different way. I don't know if she will still publish her memoir, but I think she will think carefully how to tell this part of the story."

It was dark now and I was beginning to feel that if we didn't break up soon, I'd fall asleep at the wheel driving back to the hotel. It had been an exhausting and emotionally charged day, and I'm not exactly equipped to handle this sort of life—even with the martini and the great wine I'd enjoyed tonight. So Sophie helped Elena clear the table, and after a warm good-bye, she drove us back to Astron Bay. Please, I prayed, let me spend a little time at the pool tomorrow snoozing under my cap with a puzzle and a novel on my chest.

Chapter 27
Healing

We phoned Wally in the morning after a late breakfast, following a call from Aphro telling us that he was out of the hospital. After a crash and fumble on the other end of the line, I delighted in hearing his voice.

"Bit of awkward here, mate, with one arm in a sling and another with a mind of its own. Dropped the phone, I did. How be ye, and what's the latest news and gossip? Our friend Aphroditty tells me ye had yerself a bingle in the bush yest'day."

Aphro*ditty?* Sheesh. More syllables than Kensington. "We'll let that go till we see you," I said, "but how be you?" Wally's cheer was improbable and highly infectious, easy to fall in with. "Aphro told us that you're home and wanting to see us. Not as much as we'd like to see you, I bet."

"Now that's a grand thing to hear, and I'd be chuffed to see ye both."

We settled on lunch time, and I asked if we could bring him anything.

"Well, me landlady made up a lovely eggo for me brekky, but now that ye be mentionin' lunch, a little tucker bag would be dandy. It's me arm and shoulder that's buggered, and me poor aching head, but not me innards, thank the stars."

"Anything your wee Aussie heart desires," I said.

He paused for a minute, not to take umbrage at this shot at his size, but to consider the menu. "How about ye stop at a Macca's for a burger or two, and some chips."

Macca turned out to be McDonald's and chips turned out to be "spuds of the French persuasion," otherwise known as French fries.

"Urban picnic coming up, Wally!" I said.

"Ace! Ye're a ripping cobber, ye are." I took it he thanked us, but that was only my best guess.

We turned up at his place a few hours later, armed with a McDonald's bag. At Sophie's insistence, we also brought a carton of salad, a small tray of spanikopita, bottles of iced tea, jars of olives, nuts, and dried figs—things he could get at easily if we opened them before we left. At my insistence we added a six-pack of beer in case he was up for some. Wally was dressed but propped up in bed, with a collapsible TV table beside it covered with newspapers and books. He was wearing glasses and looked like hell, with dark circles under his eyes and part of his head shaved and stitched in back. His right arm was in a cast up to the shoulder, and held in a sling, presumably to immobilize his collarbone. He was dressed in shorts and an unbuttoned shirt with his left arm in the sleeve and the other side roughly draped over the cast on his right. His chest was as hairy as his legs and feet.

"Ye'll have to wink at the mess," he said. "Me housekeepin's always a bit wantin' but now it's downright hurricane." Actually, the place was a compact but cheerful studio apartment with windows on two sides and a door leading outdoors to a scrubby looking common area. "Could ye help me to the chair there, mate," Wally asked. "It'll save time and wear on me knackered bod if ye give me a bit of a hand." I went over and hoisted him off the bed by his good arm and led him over to the seating area. While I was getting him propped up on an easy chair with an ottoman under his feet, Sophie spread napkins on the tile end-table and set out his lunch. At a silent signal from her, I stowed his beer in the fridge for later consumption.

"Hey, here's hopin' you're copin'" I said, lifting my iced tea to him in a toast, after I settled myself on the sofa. "What's the prognosis after Knossos?" Hard to be anything but playful around this pup, even as Sophie looked askance at me.

"Oh Wally, we're so sorry about all this," she said. "Just think if we hadn't gone to Knossos, this would never have happened!" Sophie Nightingale tisked and looked sympathetic. I hoped she wouldn't make the visit a deathbed scene. "Who's looking after you? You look like you should still be in bed in Heraklion."

"Wouldn't have it, even if I'm still a little unsteady on me pinnocks." He laughed softly and winced. "Hurts only when I laugh, as they say. They thought I had a concussion. But Aussies and Irishmen don't get concussions—their heads is mostly bone as I'm sure you know. Helps when ye tussle with the roos."

Sophie dished a spanikopita and a little salad on Wally's plate next to his burger and fries. "Will you be going home to Australia now?"

"We'll speak o' that another time," Wally said. "Ye haven't come to trade small talk, have ye? So let me finish up me Mac, and let's compare some notes. Aphroditty tells me the sod that sent me flying went after you and some other bloke in Gaitani, and racked off in the pursuit. Richly deserved, to me mind. But I'm still tryin' hard to wrap me mind around it all. For a start, why would he be after you?"

"Hey, tell me first, why would he be after *you*?" It seemed to me that we ought to be tracking the sequence of events in order here. "We meet the fellow guarding Onarchos's place and a few days later he's trying to kill both of us just for showing up? What's your theory, and what's Aphro's slant, assuming she's talking about it."

Wally looked sly, but didn't answer. Instead, he just shrugged his left shoulder. "I'm still letting the facts roll in, but as they say on the Reef, be sure the shark's dead ere ye be countin' its teeth. I'm sure we'll know more before the sun's up tomorrow." Not exactly an answer, but I guessed it would have to do for now. And who's 'we', Ozzie?

Sophie turned to me, frowning. "Red, there's something I've got to put on the table." She turned back to Wally. "I don't know how to say it, and you may not like it, Wally, but there's something in this whole business that really bothers me." She took a deep breath and a sip of her cold tea. Facing Wally squarely, she said, "Elena said there's a piece missing from the inventory when she went over it after we left…"

"Aye, lass, ye saw me steal the wee pot, din't ye?" Wally smiled. "Ye're a sharp-eyed lady, Miss Sophie. I tried to spare ye a tussle with yer conscience by pinchin' it out of yer sight, but you've a quick eye, ye have. It's the first thing I've pilfered since I raided a quid from me Ma's purse when I was a tad. Had to do it. I mean the pot."

"So? Why?" I said, spitting out an olive pit and taking a few more from the jar.

"To be honest with ye, Aphroditty's been leery of the goods comin' out of the Onarchos plant fer some time now. And she figured most of them went through Gavras's shop. The Gaitani bizzo makes replicas on top of the reproductions, as we reckoned."

"We know you think their craftsmanship is really superb." Sophie likes to remind people of what they already know.

"Aye, lass. The afternoon we were all at hard yakka in Gavras's shop, I saw a set of three pots in one box, as brilliant as replicas can be. Like Museum pieces, they were, all pretty much the same. But a close squint and a wary heft told me one of them was different. Like mebbe four thousand years older than the others."

"Well, even if it *was* an antiquity, that didn't give you the right to steal it." Even Wally's bunged-up shape didn't spare him from being lectured by Mrs. Hepplewhite—just like on the drive to Knossos.

"Right ye are, lass. But me friend Aphroditty wouldn't clap me in irons even so. After Gavras's murder she asked me to keep an eye cocked for shonky bizzo in his shop, and I felt it me duty to oblige. She was needin' clues to Nikos's sad end, and to hear her tell it, the road to Nikos's murder was paved with Greek antiquities."

"But why didn't you just ask Elena for the pot," Sophie persisted. "I'm sure she would have given it to you if you'd explained why you wanted it."

"Ah, luv, that would be flippin' a cart in front of the horse. I'd have bought the pot if it hadn't been boxed and paid for accordin' to the invoice. If I told Elena me suspicion, that the thingo might be antique, 'twould insult her late brother and mebbe have gotten back to Onarchos and his hoons, seeing as she was now dealing with them."

I had to admit I was relieved to have Wally forthcoming like this, thanks to the straight-shooting Sophie. "But Wally, you're making it sound as though you're in cahoots with Aphro on this. As though you've been doing a wee bit of spying for her?"

"We've been pals since me London days, we have. Met in an art history class at the University." That was a good one. How the hell would Wally ever pass an exam written in the King's English?

He went on with his voice and eyebrows slightly lowered. "I'll let on a wee bit more, if ye be prudent with what I tell ye. When I brought the bowl to Aphroditty, she looked to get it dated. You know, scientifically. To see just how old it really was."

Sophie broke in. "Why that's like the statuette on the Web site. It went out of Nikos's shop as a replica and wound up in Las Vegas as an antiquity! Forty-seven thou!"

Wally whistled. "That's some big bickies, I'd say. For a statuette, is it?"

"Yes," Sophie said. "A statuette with a broken nose, authenticated by Gwendolyn Frawley."

"The lass with the knack for finding dead men sleepin' in her room?"

"The very one," I said. "And we're beginning to wonder if she's a link in an antiquities export scheme, along with Onarchos, Nikos, Dalrymple, and the Tanners."

"And who might this Dalrymple bloke be?" Wally asked. I realized we'd never filled him in on our computer finds because we weren't sure we could trust him. Now we also told him about the strange e-mails and phone call clusters Elena showed us last night.

"It smells like Nikos got the short end of the scam and was making noises to Dalrymple," I concluded, mixing my metaphors like crazy.

Wally looked anything but confused by this. "Ye've hit the nail right on the thumb," he said, "Yer theory's brilliant, but yer players are still a muddle to me aching noggin. Tell me again who this Dalrymple might be?"

"He's a London dealer. Gwen works or consults for him, I think." I hoped Sophie wouldn't mind my helping myself to the last of Wally's brined olives. "Here's what we're wondering: does Onarchos find antiquities, make replicas of them, then ship them together with a bunch of replicas out of the country through Nikos? The replicas are the decoy. If the real thing is authenticated somewhere else, like England or America, big money is made by all—except maybe Nikos."

Wally took a chip from its paper chute and munched it thoughtfully. "I'm going to risk telling ye that the pot I pinched from Elena was a real antiquity. Aphroditty had thermoluminescence done on it the day ye were kind enough to drive me to Knossos. That's why I needed a ride up there. Me plan was to offer the charmin' Sophie a squint at the Heraklion museum, and while the two of ye be tourin' the exhibits, I'd be consulting with the good Inspector about me pot."

"That reminds me of something." I rummaged for a last French fry but found the chute empty. "Lyle Tanner told me that Gwendolyn Frawley was asked to authenticate something when I saw him in the sauna."

Wally looked startled for a second—probably at the thought of me in a sauna—but he didn't miss a beat. "That would probably be me pot. The very one I nicked and Aphroditty had tested! But I can't reckon why she'd need it tested again."

"Oh, but don't you see," Sophie exclaimed. "It's very clever of Aphro. I bet she wanted to see if Gwen would say it was real or a replica. If she says it's real, she only confirms the Gavras shop as a smuggling conduit. But if she says it isn't real, then she's covering for the actual smugglers, and that would mean she has to be in on their deal." As always, Sophie doesn't have to think. She just *knows*. Some chemists are like that. Know it first, prove it next.

But Sophie wasn't at all happy with her conjecture. "I really hope Gwen's not involved too deeply in this. Underneath, she's a nice person, and she's so nervous about everything already anyway."

Wally, silent through this, said thoughtfully, "There's not much innocence left here, me friends. Even if ye don't have yer paws on the whole of the pie, it's the divil to keep clean hands once ye've picked up a slice, me Da says. Ye can't be just a little pregnant." Now there's a mixed metaphor for you: a pregnant slice of pie.

"Where do you think they got the antiquities," Sophie asked.

"Probably dug 'em up near the pottery place. Real outback that, as ye squizzed with yer own eyes. The thingos could be right there under the brogues of the blokes making replicas of them," Wally said.

Of course. Wally just made the connection I'd been trying to forge between Onarchos's Pottery Shack and the grids and maps and things Gabor had shown me on our fateful trip to Gaitani. "Wally, you're a genius. That would explain the fence and guards and no trespassing signs around the pottery compound and why they were so reluctant to have us come in. And it would also explain why Onarchos's thug went after you and after Gabor Latif and me yesterday. It's not just smuggling, don't you see. They've also independently discovered the palace site."

Wally took a deep breath and the curly hairs on his chest glinted. "Was that car in the bingle yesterday after this Latif or after you?"

"I don't really know," I said truthfully. "I don't even know whether it was trying to scare us off or just off us. Why do you ask?"

"Your friend Latif might be in on the lurk. Either with Onarchos or with another lurk tusslin' with his," Wally said.

"I'm sorry, Wally," Sophie said with a little hint of exasperation. "You're going to have to speak English because I'm just not following this."

"Sorry, lass. Ye and Red have become such grand cobbers of mine, me mind's forgettin' that yer Strine's not up to snuff. What I meant to say was that if this Latif bloke is in cahoots with Onarchos, then the point of the car chase might have been just to scare old Redfield here. But if Latif is in cahoots with the politicians, then he'd be taking antiquities out of Onarchos's hands and the goon might've been after him. Ye savvy now?"

I did, maybe. "I guess one way or another, we've all simply gotten too close to Onarcho's bizzo for comfort." That Strine just sneaks into your language.

"Right ye are, laddie," Wally said. "Those bloody blokes got a big problem and they're running around like headless chooks."

Before I had a chance to ask him what 'chooks' were, I heard a knock on the door. Wally called out his cheerful "It's open, luv," apparently expecting his landlady. But instead Elena came in carrying a clay casserole. She was surprised and glad to see us. She'd left Nia to tend the shop and had come to see if Wally needed any help. I wanted to ask if she got in touch with Aphro and shelved her meeting with Onarchos, but strangely the mood had changed with her arrival.

Wally smiled warmly at the sight of the casserole, and Elena looked as comfortable putting things down in his little kitchen as she had in her own place the evening before. We realized our work was done for the day, and it was time to let the second shift take over.

Any further sleuthing was going to have to wait. It was time for Marple and Clouseau to hit the road. We took our leave, and soon were on our way back to Astron Bay.

Chapter 28
The Crowd Gathers

When we returned from visiting Wally, Heidi hailed us in the lobby. There was a note in our box. Aphro wanted to meet with us in the conference room off the Midas Lounge at "20:00" that evening. The typed note was cold and impersonal, like a mass mailing. We went down to dinner later than usual and were glad to see the Tanners and Gwen at one table, the Latifs at another, all preoccupied enough to ignore us, as we did them. We took a table and I let the martini go for once before ordering. Sophie and I speculated about what Aphro wanted of us at that time of day. We hoped we might be able to get our passports back after all, and we then argued about what to do if we actually got them. Sophie felt that our lives were in peril and that we should go home. I felt that others' lives might be in peril if we didn't see this thing through. We often reverse roles like this, with Sophie suddenly becoming the survivalist, and me turning into Albert Schweitzer. But her reasoning made sense. If things were coming apart for whoever ran the antiquities scam and killed Nikos, they might be more dangerous now than before. And they might be right here in this dining room.

Dinner was fine and we signed our bill and got to the Lounge five minutes before 8 o'clock. To our surprise, Gwendolyn Frawley was also there, fidgeting outside the conference room door. We were joined at 8 o'clock by the Tanners, and then, as if this little party wasn't already awkward enough, by the Latifs, Hegel and all. And then, to our surprise, it became even weirder when Spiro turned up and not only opened the conference room door, but came in with us. We could all do little more than look at each other and nod, aware that the meeting would be stressful at best and fateful at worst. It occurred to me that if Aphro had called the usual suspects together, we might all have to perform tonight. I had an excited moment hoping that Madame Delphinos would show up. The old lady gives a helluva performance!

Another five minutes saw us assembled around the familiar oval table with Aphro at one end in front of her ubiquitous recorder and metal notebook, and the dashing Stavros and another of her henchman guarding the door. Did she expect one or two of us to make a dash for it in the course of the meeting? I noticed something else on the table: a laptop computer.

"I must thank you very much, very much indeed, for coming," she began. "I hope tonight to straighten matters out so that I can return your passports." Good old Aphro—acting her part like a cross between Hercule Poirot and everyone's aunt. I had an irrational hope that she would produce a surprise, information that Nikos was killed by the husband of a secret girlfriend, say, or some other hidden killers out in left field. Maybe that chauffeur with the chihuahua, after all. But that stuff happens only in cheap mystery novels. If we were the usual suspects here—and I counted nine of us in the room—the surprise wouldn't be who it was, but how they managed it, and how everybody would handle things when the truth was revealed.

The proceedings began with Stavros pushing a button to lower a screen at the opposite end of the room from Aphro, then inserting a flash drive into the laptop computer on the table. After clicking at the overhead gizmo in the ceiling the computer icons came on the screen. "Thank you, Stavros," the Inspector said. Besides looking like Adonis, the young cop was a Greek geek.

When the first image popped up on the screen, a little gasp ran around the table as everyone realized what was happening in the photo. Familiar as it was, I too caught my breath. It was our photo of Wally being pushed by the man in the flowered Hawaiian shirt. Aphro asked me if I recognized him.

"Yes, he was at Knossos. Sophie took an earlier picture that shows his face."

"This one?" asked Aphro as she pressed the forward key. Zorba's brother was unmistakable. His physique and shirt betrayed him as the man seen from the back in the shot of Wally headed for his fall from the palace roof. I snuck a quick peek at Gwen to see how she reacted to seeing the double of the guy who had upbraided her in the Agnik museum, but she wasn't even looking at the screen. Instead it was Hegel who caught my attention. He was riveted by the image of the man whose slightly open mouth showed a bright glint of gold.

I confirmed that I had first seen the man at Onarchos's compound in Gaitani. Aphro then asked Gabor if this was the man who tried to drive him off the road yesterday.

"Inspector, I do not know. I have not seen this man in my life. A black car was driving very fast behind us, as if to crash into us. This may be the driver in the wrecked car—I believe I saw a gold tooth—but I am not certain."

"My father is innocent!" Hegel jumped up and blurted out. "I was the one who helped this man see my father's compound at night. He said he just wanted to protect ancient ruins." So, Zorba's brother *was* Hegel's cigarette pusher.

"Thank you, Hegel, and do sit down." Aphro said this kindly but firmly, and Hegel sat. "This is why we kept Hegel in custody for two nights," Aphro explained to Gabor. "If Hegel identified Fotis Stephanopoulos, we feared your son might become a target for the man. But since Onarchos's guard also infiltrated Bohnen-Essen, it is not unreasonable to ask if you know him."

"I have never seen him before car crash," Gabor said again. "I have no contact with this person Onarchos. I have never met him. My firm does not deal with him or his firm. We are careful with rules, Antiquities people will confirm." Gabor said this with dignity and a trace of anger, casting a sidelong look at Gwendolyn Frawley.

It hit me that Aphro needed to know something we had not told her before. "Aph...Inspector Kensington," I said, breaking in, "The car chasing us near Gaitani was the one that chased us to Knossos!"

She turned to me sharply. "What do you mean 'chased you to Knossos'?"

"I don't really mean chased," I said. "More like 'followed.' When I drove Wally Pinnock and my wife Sophie to Knossos three days ago, I noticed a black Mercedes with a broken headlight following behind us. When we got to Knossos it pulled into the parking lot as well, and we saw it there on our way out."

"Why did you not report this to the police or to me?"

"We had no way of knowing it had anything to do with Wally's assault when we talked to you in Heraklion," I said.

"And after the Gaitani accident?"

"I was too shook up, I guess, But you're absolutely right, that I should have mentioned it. It was seeing a black Mercedes with a broken headlight drive past the gas station that made me yell at Gabor to get in the car and get out of there. Seeing that car was like seeing a phantom. After the accident, it probably looked like the headlight was broken then rather than before. But I'm sure it was the one that followed Wally and us to Knossos."

"Did you see this car at the Onarchos compound when you were there earlier, perhaps near the buildings?"

"No, but we weren't there to look at the cars." I noticed Lyle had gotten a cup of coffee from the set-up on the sideboard, and that Danielle was rummaging for something in her big purse. "But you can ask the Tanners if they saw the Mercedes in the Onarchos parking lot." Danielle looked up instantly, and if looks could kill, I would have been assassinated.

Without showing surprise, Aphro jotted something in her notebook and pressed a computer key, bringing up another image on the Powerpoint. It showed the statuette with the broken nose bookmarked in Nikos's computer. A caption gave the catalogue description and its authentication by G. Frawley. Gwen visibly started at this, and moved her bony glutes as though she wanted to get the hell up and out of here.

"Ms. Frawley," Aphro said, moving the cursor to the description. "I assume this is your name, well known in antiquities circles. I wonder if you could tell us for whom you authenticated this *Kore*. Was it Mr. Dalrymple, with whom you may have had some dealings?"

"Really, I have no idea," Gwen said stiffly. "I do many authentications and I'm simply ghastly with names. My records are back in Oxford—but I will check them as soon as I have my passport and can return there." Her tone betrayed more than a trace of impatience, emphasized by her darting eyes and restless movements of her arms and hands.

"Ms. Frawley, the web page where this picture is shown was bookmarked in Mr. Gavras's computer. The exhibit took place at the Parthenon Gallery in Las Vegas, in the United States." This was getting interesting. I noticed that Lyle's heavy eyes flickered and Danielle looked up from her purse where she had been playing with her lipstick. Gwen's teacup rattled on its saucer after she took a sip.

"Now, Ms. Frawley, on the day of the murder you insisted that you had never met Mr. Gavras, and had heard of him only recently from Mr. and Mrs. Tanner and from Mr. and Mrs. Redfield. Had you nevertheless any business dealings with him? By e-mail or correspondence or by telephone?"

"I believe I have stated most clearly," Gwen said icily and in a slow cadence, "that I have had no direct dealings with Mr. Gavras. Of course, that does not preclude the possibility that we may have shared clients and contacts." The fidgeting stopped and Gwen was suddenly all control. I had to hand it to old Steelbuns. I would've laid odds on her going bananas at this point but she was earning my nickname for her.

"You may be interested in this," Aphro said, bringing up the image of the companion statuette, the one with its nose intact. Everyone looked intrigued or startled at this, especially Gwen. Aphro shuffled papers she took from her notebook and began to read e-mail messages between Nikos and Dalrymple. To my surprise, they were not the ones Elena had uncovered. The first explained that the small replica *Kore* that Dalrymple had ordered had been damaged and disfigured. That explained the broken schnozzola on the thing. Nikos apologized profusely for the accident—"a very rare occurrence"—and offered Dalrymple an intact effigy. Aphro now moved the slides forward to another one of the figure with the broken nose "Mr. Gavras sent both images to Mr. Dalrymple so that he could judge the extent of the damage, but surprisingly his client opted to purchase the broken figure."

Aphro paused a few moments to let the implication of this information sink in, before asking Gwen, "Now, Ms. Frawley, do you stand by your authentication of this *Kore* as a genuine antiquity?"

"I authenticated only the one displayed in Las Vegas, the one in the first picture you showed," Gwen said shrewdly.

"There was only one with a broken nose, Ms. Frawley. It was damaged by Nikos Gavras, who sent it on to Mr. Dalrymple after that gentleman requested a discount to compensate for the damage. The *Kore* left the Gavras shop as a damaged replica and surfaced in Las Vegas, nose still very much broken, as an antiquity authenticated by you, with a mark-up in excess of a thousand percent."

"I know nothing of its provenance," Gwen insisted stubbornly. I still couldn't believe her cool. She should be having visible conniptions by now.

"Let me now ask you if the small pot you were asked to examine two days ago is authentic or a replica, as far as you can tell?"

"Yes, well, I'm afraid I've had some difficulty with that." Gwen smoothed one of her non-existent eyebrows with a thin forefinger. "I've been frightfully distracted, you know, and it would require more thorough tests in my UK laboratory to be certain. I simply don't have the equipment here to render a definitive professional judgment." Cool response from a professional authenticator, I thought to myself. "Unless you wish me to take it back to England, I had best return the piece to you. The people at the Heraklion museum can surely give you a quicker result." Seemed to me that Gwen had just blown her consulting job in Crete.

"Very well," Aphro said. She reversed the sequence and went back to the bookmarked picture. "Mr. Tanner, you have a connection with the Parthenon Gallery in Las Vegas, I believe? This is where the picture was posted, and your wife has dealt extensively with Mr. Gavras."

"Yes, ma'am," Lyle said, sliding his bulging eyes for the first time at Aphro. "We buy for the hotel gift store there, but the gallery is a separate enterprise. We had nothing to do with that exhibit or the display of that piece on their web site. And we'd have no way of knowing that thing came from Gavras's shop."

"Mrs. Tanner, in what capacity do you serve Mr. Dalrymple?" Aphro asked Danielle.

Danielle snapped her purse shut, and looked up, suddenly all business. "We are one of several agents in the United States who scout objects for him in the Mediterranean. I come to Crete to locate pieces I think he may want and direct shipments to him through Nikos Gavras's shop. Gavras had the export license and produced the necessary customs declarations. I do the same for a number of shops and galleries in Las Vegas, as you know."

"Do you remember assigning this particular *Kore* for export to Mr. Dalrymple?" Aphro asked. "It was shipped earlier in the year."

"I've just explained that I'm only one of several people serving Dalrymple." Danielle brushed the curve of blonde hair on her forehead to the side. "And as Ms. Frawley said earlier, we too have many different clients and don't have our records here."

"Let's look more specifically at the transaction," Aphro said. "Could you in fact have been the broker for this statuette? We know that it came from Onarchos's place and was transmitted through Gavras's shop to Dalrymple."

"We don't control where Dalrymple ships his objects," Danielle snapped. A pause. Then she snapped again, "And why would Nikos sell a genuine antique as a replica? It makes no sense." The cool Danielle was no longer quite so cool. Her transformation on the cruise came back to me.

"Inspector Kensington," Lyle intervened. "My wife and I deal only in reproductions and replicas. As far as we know, this piece is still a replica, whatever Ms. Frawley says."

Ouch. Gwendolyn shot Lyle a cutting glance. A reputation was at stake here, although as far as I could tell that reputation had been shot to hell a little earlier.

"Why did you visit Mr. Onarchos," Aphro asked Lyle.

"We needed to see him in light of Nikos's death. We didn't want to have our supplies disrupted." Lyle's lids looked heavy again, as he added an afterthought. "We thought it inappropriate to disturb Ms. Mylonas in her mourning."

"When you visited Mr. Onarchos, did you notice a black Mercedes? With a broken headlamp?"

"No," said Lyle and Danielle, almost in unison, while Danielle shot me another dirty look.

"Mr. Tanner," Aphro went on, "were you aware that Mr. Onarchos's firm sold antiquities as replicas?

"Inspector, I have no idea. That doesn't mean they didn't. But I'd be very surprised if they did." Lyle's drawl served him well, drawing his words out slowly and giving them unearned weight. "When you buy replicas and reproductions at the cheap prices we do, why would we authenticate them to make sure they're not more valuable? Makes no sense." Cool dude, that, although as Lyle himself might say, it looked to me as though the cops had him by the short and curly. Then he added, "Are you really sure that thing without the nose came from Onarchos's place?"

"Yes, according to Gavras's records." Then Aphro added very slowly. "But we will be able to verify this further. We have warrants to search the Onarchos compound this evening and take computers and records into custody."

Dead silence hung over us all. You go, girl, I cheered Aphro on. Nail the snake, or at least give him a run for his money.

It worked—if not the nailing, at least the giving him a run.

Lyle took a Danish cigar out of a pack from his jacket pocket but saw no ashtray when he looked around.

"Begging your pardon, ma'am, but aren't we all forgetting something here?" He stayed cool even without lighting up. "It's Mister Santas here who had a grudge against Nikos Gavras. When are you going to put him in the hot seat?"

The familiar signs of agitation instantly swept over Spiro's face, red color, trembling moustache tips, and dew behind his specs. But although his body visibly stiffened, he wisely kept his yap shut.

"Mister Santas has been questioned several times about his dealings with Nikos Gavras. We are satisfied that he took no action against him."

"Took no action! Are you crazy?!" Yes, the croc was losing it, yes! This was better than an American football game! "He went ballistic when the old lady's dog went missing. And what about that silver bowl of blood in the Redfield's bathroom. What was that all about? Looks to me like Santas was trying to frame Nikos while we were at the barbecue!"

I thought Sophie was going to have apoplexy. If she did, I was going with her. We had told no one—absolutely no one—about the silver bowl filled with fake blood. Not the Tanners, not Gwen, not Gabor, not Wally, not Elena, not even Aphro. And, for the record, I now remembered that Lyle Tanner had missed the barbecue.

I braced myself for high drama with all eyes turned on us, but Aphro merely gave us a piercing look that clearly warned us to say nothing. "Spiro Santas has an alibi, Mr. Tanner," she said calmly.

"We have an alibi too, as you know perfectly well," Danielle hissed. "And we have pictures of our trip to Spinalonga to prove it. I'm sorry we didn't offer you more than our boat receipt in our interview, but we didn't realize it would be necessary."

Wow. I had to hand it to Aphro. She was a master. With everybody tired and cranky, the figurative fan was on, and taking a direct hit. Even the imperturbable Stavros by the door stood up, as though Danielle might make a dash for it.

Aphro improbably smiled at Danielle. "I will be happy to look at your camera and its digital card to verify your alibi. Stavros will accompany you to your room to fetch them, and he will return them to you tomorrow."

Danielle, shaken by her outburst, rose and left the room with Stavros. A great looking couple—like something out of a vodka ad.

And that was the anticlimactic end of the meeting. No revelations. No arrests. No real drama except for that tiny slip on Lyle's part, betraying his role as the phantom who slipped into our room to surprise us with a bloody bowl when we returned. Spiro, still flushed, left the room first, then the Latifs departed followed by Lyle, and so did Gwen after making some noises about wanting her passport back.

We too were almost out the door, when it hit me. It was me, Rowan Hercule Nero Morse Redfield himself, who possessed in his martini-drenched brain the shreds and tatters of diverse images and scenes and knowledge that together provided the missing piece of the puzzle, the missing link, the key to the mystery of Nikos Gavras's murder.

I went back to the table and leaned across to Aphro, who was collecting her electronics and notebook while her other assistant retracted the screen.

"Aphro," I whispered to her, even though only the fellow and Sophie remained in the room. "The Tanner's camera reminded me to tell you something. The skipper of the boat they took to Spinalonga was at Astron Bay the day of the murder. I saw him before we left for the museum. Then we saw him again when we went to visit Onarchos at his Pottery Shack!"

She looked dumbfounded. "How can you be sure of that? You weren't on the boat to Spinalonga."

"No, but Danielle showed me the pictures you'll see when you get her camera. There's one of her and the skipper. It was definitely the same guy at Astron Bay the day of the murder and later at Onarchos's place."

For the first time Aphro sounded tired and impatient herself. "*How do you know? Who is he?*"

"He has this tattoo. On his arm. I asked him for a cigarette at the cabaña, around noon the day of the murder. He had on a long-sleeved shirt, but when he handed me the cigarette pack, I saw a tattoo that looked like the tail of a whale. You know, two *flukes* or whatever they call them, winding around his wrist. Then, at Onarchos's place, someone closed an office door when we were touring the place with Wally. I saw a whole arm as it closed the door. It had a mermaid with a curled tail wrapped around the wrist." I knew this sounded weak.

"*Did you see his face,*" Aphro hissed. It was the first time I'd seen Aphro lose her composure.

Sophie broke in. "Red calls him Silverhair, since he has shiny white hair."

"Excuse me," said Aphro. She said something hurriedly to the policeman and they swept out the door without saying goodbye. By the time we followed them to the lobby they were gone.

Sophie looked miffed. "Did you tell Danielle about your bloody bowl on your boat cruise?

I put my arms around her. "No, Pumpkin," I said, as I kissed her curls. "I never told a soul about the bloody bowl except you."

Chapter 29
Gordon Gryoka

What a night! Sophie was so tired she drifted off to sleep like a life-long narcolept. I had to move her aside to get into bed myself after 10:30, having downed a glass or two or maybe three of wine. And there I lay beside the sleeping beauty, stewing about Aphro's strange interrogation. What was the point of that whole business? She never said a word to Spiro, Sophie, or Samira, and there were no dramatic revelations except maybe why Nikos went ballistic at seeing his busted *Kore* sell for 47K. But Aphro became tense as a runner at the starting block when we told her about Silverhair. Where'd she run off to? I never had a chance to tell her that no one—absolutely no one—knew about the bloody bowl except Sophie.

I finally went to sleep around 3:00. By that time the moonlight had stolen into the room, since I'd forgotten to close the drapes. As I drifted off, I felt Sophie stirring and hoped she wouldn't rouse me. She didn't, so when the phone rang at 8:30 I was in the depth of some dark dream, following someone into a hole in the ground where everyone was waiting for me, while blood oozed from the ground between their toes.

"Hello?" Sophie said in her sleep-drugged, morning voice. "Aphro!" Pause while she listened. "Well, yes, I suppose so. But please wait a few minutes till I tidy up and make Red presentable."

"*Now* what?" I asked, feeling the creases embossed on my cheek by the bedsheet. "What's up?"

"Aphro's coming here in just a few minutes. She says it's important and shouldn't take too long. Get yourself ready while I put on some coffee and some fresh clothes." I realized that Sophie was still dressed in some of last night's clothes. With her hair mussed and no make-up she looked like hell. I threw on some jeans and a shirt while she got the coffee started. I was headed for the bathroom when Sophie intercepted me. "Let me get into the bathroom first to fix this face," she said, dispensing with marital courtesies. I heard an *aaaargghh* as she caught sight of herself in the mirror a minute later.

I threw the empty wine bottle into the wastepaper basket, tried to do something with the bedcovers, and kicked our sandals under the bed. I'm not much good at housework, but I get away with it because I'm a great cook. I got a crack at the bathroom minutes after Sophie emerged, almost human. Just as I came out, she was adjusting her fresh top and we heard a soft knock at the door.

Sophie opened the door. Aphro strode in, computer bag and purse slung over her shoulder, crisply dressed but looking a bit weary.

"I have news for you," she said.

"Let me get you some coffee," Sophie said. "Like Red says, we don't start breathing until we have a cup, and he just woke up." Aphro sat down on the cushioned bench by the door to the terrace, and propping her stuff on the floor next to her, waited for her coffee to arrive. She took a sip and made a grimace but didn't say anything. Why do Europeans always think our coffee tastes like dishwater? Ruined by espresso, I suppose.

"First," said Aphro, rummaging in her computer case, "here are your passports. I hope you won't make flight plans to leave immediately. I may need you for a few more things in the next day or two."

"Oh, thank heavens," Sophie said, taking the passports over to the little safe in the night table that I had checked on the night of the bloody bowl. She wasn't taking any chances on Aphro taking those babies back. "I can't tell you what a relief this is. Our return flight is on Wednesday, three days from now. But we won't finalize anything before we check with you again." This sounded accommodating enough, but Sophie looked as if she'd like nothing better than to kick Aphro out of our room and start packing.

"Let me bring you up to date," Aphro said. Sure, I said to myself, lots must have happened in the last ten hours. "I feel I owe you some explanation for the help you've been so good to give us. It has been indispensable." She poked around on the keyboard and finally turned the screen toward us.

"Fuchrist's sake," I said, using a verbal save to disguise my expletive. "It's the skipper! Where did you get *that*?" The black-and-white mug shot, showing his face and torso, his arms crossed over his chest, looked as if it had been taken some time ago. His hair was substantially gray but not yet entirely silver. His light eyes looked out defiantly from his swarthy face. The tattoo on his arm was like a signature.

"He's an old acquaintance of the police," Aphro said. "Your description last night of his tattoo and hair—on the same man—reminded me of him. He has a record of several arrests on the mainland and has twice evaded conviction for murder, the last time about five years ago in a prominent case in Piraeus. His name is Gordon Gryoka. He has been largely out of sight since then, but has evidently been working in Kriti."

"Did you nab him, then?"

"Not yet," Aphro said. "But we have Mr. and Mrs. Tanner in custody."

"Wow!" Sophie gasped, nearly choking on her coffee. "How did *that* happen? Where?"

Aphro began to look like her old self. Cool, with a hint of pride. "The meeting last night was designed less to produce information than to provoke a reaction. The aim was to let the Tanners and Ms. Frawley know we were onto them. The meeting also put them out of commission for a few hours while we raided Onarchos's compound."

"So the rest of us were just there as decoys?" Aphro had sure jerked us around if she had used us mainly as props in her little suspect round-up.

"You played your part rather well." She smiled at me like a teacher bucking up the self-esteem of her class dunce. "At any rate, the exchange with the Tanners provoked the desired reaction, though luck played an important role."

"What do you mean *luck?*" Sophie asked.

"I knew nothing about the Tanner's photos, which they had cleverly not offered during the earlier interviews. They had already established their alibi by signing on to a private cruise and producing a receipt. Putting them on the 'hot seat,' as they put it, prodded them to offer further evidence of their trip on the day of the murder."

"Why didn't they just show them to you the first time?" Sophie asked.

"I can't be sure. Perhaps because they knew the image of Gryoka carried some risk. However, even if I had recognized Gordon Gryoka in the photo, I might not have pieced him into the puzzle of the Tanner's plot. That depended on your memory of seeing the 'skipper,' as you call him, at the cabaña here and at Onarchos's place." She smiled at me warmly again.

"But how can you disprove the Tanner's alibi?" asked Sophie.

"We can't. They did indeed spend the afternoon in Spinalonga, as the digital date on their image file proves. But the sky in the photo with Gryoka is overcast, and the sky in Spinalonga was bright and clear all day. We saw the discrepancy right away and checked the weather reports for that day. In Agnik, Mirabello Bay had clouds early that morning. We suspect that's when and where the photo with the 'skipper' was taken. He never went to Spinalonga, we now think, even though the photo was presumably intended to provide his alibi as well."

"When did you figure this out?" Sophie asked.

"Last night, after we left the hotel with the camera. I drove to my headquarters with it and studied the images with two of my colleagues. We confirmed the weather records and found an old picture of Gryoka in our computer files within an hour. I might say this left little time for sleep."

"Tell me about it," I said sarcastically.

Aphro pointedly ignored my plea for sympathy. "Stavros and his partner had no sleep at all. But they had a most productive night. We instructed them to guard the exits from Astron Bay and at four o'clock in the morning they saw the Tanners struggling up the bluff on the side of the building with suitcases to get to their car without going through the lobby.

"So they were leaving!" Sophie almost spilled her coffee at this news. "How on earth could they get off the island at that hour without passports?"

"By private boat." Aphro took another sip of her now cold coffee and winced again. "They drove to Pachia Ammos and our men followed without headlights at a distance. They stopped near the base of a small pier where a yacht lay tied up with its running lights on. The Tanners had clearly arranged the yacht to take them off the island, although how they could do this on such short notice is hard to imagine. We thought they might try to leave by boat, but had no idea where or when."

Aphro, I thought to myself, you're wasted on antiquities. They should make you Greece's Columbo. You *are* Greece's Columbo!

"So what happened?" Sophie exclaimed. "They didn't get away?!" Sophie never goes to bed before she finishes a mystery. I got up for more coffee for us all while Aphro raised her voice so I could hear her at the other end of the room.

"My men apprehended them as they hurried toward the yacht. Costa caught up with Mrs. Tanner and stopped her. Lyle Tanner kept running and almost reached the pier when the boat powered up, cast off, and left for the open sea. He shouted at the boat to come back, then turned to see that all was lost."

"Did they freak out?" You would've thought Sophie was actually watching *Columbo* on TV rather than hearing it narrated.

Aphro politely refused a refill. "No, they simply said they wanted to contact their attorney. They have good nerves and a steely dignity." Lyle, Lyle, going out in style. Personally, I never liked the dude.

"Did they really think they could get away?" I poured more coffee into Sophie's mug. "It's an island and a launch on an open ocean is no place to hide."

"If you have enough gas, time, and luck, even Karpathos, 130 kilometers away, can be reached in five or six hours. Rhodes or the Cyclades could be reached thereafter in stages." Aphro moved her hands as if to draw an imaginary map of Greece in the air. "The Tanners had a good deal of cash. If they had reached the mainland, they could have gotten false passports there."

"So what about the skipper…what's his name, Gecko?" Even Sophie gets names wrong.

"Gryoka," Aphro said. "He's still at large, possibly piloting the escape vessel. Their own photos connect him to the Tanners, so we assume they hired him to kill Nikos Gavras."

That silenced us for a few seconds. Aphro had just attached a face to the hand that wielded the knife. It was a disturbing vision, especially the image of a mermaid under the sleeve of the arm that lashed at Nikos's throat.

"Do you think you'll catch him?" Sophie asked.

"Possibly. Our men saw the name of the escape yacht. Gryoka will have to cover or disguise it to escape notice."

"What was the name of the yacht?" I asked.

Aphro smiled and said, "*Ikaros.*"

It took us a minute to remember why that rang a bell, and then Sophie burst into a laugh, her first in days it seemed. "The son of Daedalus, who flew too near to the sun! You don't think they have a helicopter stashed on that yacht, do you?" We told Aphro of the coincidence, that we had seen the vessel on our first trip to Agnik after our arrival.

As Aphro zipped up her computer case, her cell phone rang. She took it quickly from her purse and listened, then took a sharp breath. "*Efkharistó,*" she said quickly. Thank you.

Aphro whipped a look at us. "Put on your shoes and a jacket. You are coming with me and my men. Elena Mylonas just called the station. She's been taken hostage and your help may be needed. Hurry!"

Chapter 30
Walking the Plank

Two policemen hustled Sophie and me into a police car outside the lobby, along with Aphro. With sirens wailing, it sped toward Agnik.

"Where are we going?" Even after two cups of coffee, Sophie's mood and appearance remained crappy, and the sirens didn't help. "What's happening?"

Aphro turned around and spoke loudly so we could hear. "Our raid on the computers and records of Onarchos Reproductions last evening must have shocked Onarchos and his people," she shouted. "They appear to have made hurried plans with the Tanners to leave, but we disrupted their escape. I'm afraid this prompted them to take a hostage."

Aphro closed her eyes and opened them again. She looked pained. "I'm terribly sorry it had to be Elena Mylonas." Interesting question. Whom would she *not* mind seeing taken hostage? Hegel Latif? Gwendolyn Frawley? How about big Red Redfield?

"Poor Elena," Sophie cried. "Why on earth her?"

"She lives alone by the harbor, and Onarchos knew where. That made her an easy target."

"But what now?" I asked. "You said Elena called from Agnik. Where are they are holding her?"

"On a yacht in the harbor. She was told to call us and ask that we send a civilian on board to negotiate with them. They don't want a policeman, and the only way they can be certain we don't send someone undercover is by having it be someone they know. They seem to have thought of you, Red, as a safe choice. That's why you're here, I'm afraid."

"*Whaaaat?*" I said.

"Yes. We did not expect this at all."

"Why the hell not?" When you're being offered as a hostage, you dispense with courtesy.

Aphro looked embarrassed. "We raided the compound, got computer and office materials, but found Onarchos's place poorly protected. The buildings were guarded by an inept fellow who ran away. We were looking chiefly for evidence of looting and smuggling, and may have underestimated the possibility of violence." She must've forgotten that their armed guard tried to send Wally flying before going to his just reward off the road near Gaitani.

Sophie persisted. "Aphro! Why didn't they just take off at night and leave Elena alone? They could have just disappeared without risking a direct police confrontation."

"Money. They need money. The Tanners carried the cash they needed. They want two million euros and hope to get away with it to another country." Aphro had to shout to make herself heard.

"Will you give it to them?" Sophie yelled back.

"We'll try. We won't let them take Elena, and we can't risk her life. But they seem in a panic, tripping over themselves to escape. I can scarcely imagine how they can get away with this. That makes them more, not less dangerous, I'm afraid."

I noticed she seemed perfectly okay about risking *my* life in this harebrained adventure. This whole stupid scheme on both sides seemed chancy at best, fatal at worst. Thanks, Aphro. Delighted to serve the republic. I needed some excitement in my fat middle age. I felt as if I'd been dropped into Act III of Aphro's drama, this time on a trap door in case I forgot my lines. At least Sophie, shivering next to me, seemed to be taking the risks to old Red with the seriousness they deserved.

The driver turned off the siren and drove more slowly through the town as it approached the harbor. We passed through a cordoned area leading to the docks. A small crowd was gawking from behind the police tapes, unable to see much. We approached other police cars surrounding the area. Officers with rifles stood around a large motor launch with an upper cabin and below-deck quarters. The gunwale stood well above the dock. A wide improvised gangplank led up to the deck. The word *Ikaros* was inscribed in graceful Greek and Roman letters on the stern.

Aphro jumped out of the car and went over to the officer in charge. I guessed it was Madame's Chief: he *did* look like a baboon. Sophie and I stepped warily from the back seat. Both Aphro and the Chief gestured intensely as they spoke. It took some minutes before she returned to us.

"They will have the money here shortly. But, Red, I'm afraid that much depends on you now." She looked at me directly and significantly and took a deep breath. I wondered if she doubted that I could pull it off. I certainly did.

"Please listen carefully, because I may not have time to repeat this. The Chief has negotiated with Onarchos by phone, agreeing that you will take the bag of cash and ascend the gangplank. Elena will be allowed to come down at the same time so you will pass her on the ramp. You will go on up and wait at the top until she is safely on the pier. You will then enter the upper cabin and deliver the money. They will verify the amount and allow you to return to us. That is all. Do you understand?"

Oh boy, did I ever. I was going to get to walk the plank, right into the lair of that eel Onarchos! Urbane fellow, hopefully serves chilled wine and steamed lobster on his yacht. I really looked forward to spending some time with him. It reminded me to ask, a shade below a scream, "What the hell says he won't take *me* along as a hostage?"

"The boat itself is surrounded. If you're not allowed to return, they lose their only chance of leaving. We have assured them a safe passage out of the harbor only if they allow both you and Elena to come back to us."

"Why should they trust you if the boat is surrounded?"

"Look around. This is a Sunday morning with many small pleasure craft out in the harbor. Onarchos's group presumably has guns. They know we won't risk a shootout in an area like this. They must also know we'll try to apprehend them later on the open sea, but I imagine they think they can elude us there."

"Aphro, I don't feel comfortable with the role. Do you have an understudy?" I did not smile.

"You're the star." She smiled, but ruefully and with worried eyes.

I couldn't bear to look at Sophie, who must have been dying at this point. When I did, her face was a mask of paralyzed conflict. I could imagine what was going through her mind. She could refuse to let me do this, but then what of Elena? Her eyes were squeezed almost shut in a frown and she was biting her lip. When she spoke, she said only two words: "Your call."

I put my arms around her and held her tight. "It won't be all that hard," I said. "Just keep it together and things will be fine." What the hell did I think I was saying? Doing? Life goes on, right? At least for the majority. I kissed the top of her head and hoped it wasn't good-bye.

I looked up at the yacht where I glimpsed a shadowy outline through the cabin window. Then a curious movement on the pier. An unarmed policeman slowly approached the boat near the prow and put a black box the size of a cigarette pack on the hull, to which it adhered. He stepped away and took up his former position after his rifle was returned to him. That's one they didn't think about in their haste, I thought hopefully. A tracking device, maybe a GPS unit. They're doomed. But if they take me with them, I'm doomed too. I hate dilemmas with no good options.

Another police car drew up. An officer got out, bringing a satchel over to the Chief. Aphro took me over to them. Too bad they found so much money so fast, I said to myself. They must have had to hold up the central bank of Heraklion. They spoke in Greek. Going over my instructions, I supposed.

Aphro turned to me. "Red, the money is here. Take it to the gangplank, step onto it, then stop. When Elena appears on the deck, walk up the ramp as she comes down and passes you. Be sure she is on the pier before you move up to the deck." That freaked me even more. Bad enough to have my own hide to worry about without another innocent life depending on my uncertain cool.

"Then go ahead as I told you," Aphro went on. "Give the money, let them verify it, and once they are satisfied with the cash, back out and move off slowly. Do not run or make rapid movements." Man! A starring role! Greatness thrust upon me! I've always felt heroism is a lucky path off the road to foolish ends, and I was no fool.

The bag was heavy, tipping me as the Chief looped the straps over my shoulder. At my weight, you don't tip easily. This was a literal bundle of cash. He held his phone to his ear, speaking Greek. He nodded to me. He touched me briefly on the shoulder with his burly arm, and I had a flashback to my dad pushing me forward to stand up to some bullies on the block. The first of many disasters in my life. I looked at Aphro, who narrowed her eyes and gave a stiff smile. Just because I said to Sophie that everything would be okay, they figured I meant it! I was just bullshitting to reassure her, for heaven's sake. Why do people never listen to me when they should, and always listen when they shouldn't?

I walked forward, not wanting to look back at Sophie. I felt I hadn't consulted with her adequately before embarking on this path to an uncertain fate. I wanted desperately to see Elena safe. That would be half the show, something I hoped I could accomplish. It always helps to break down impossible problems into workable parts, like synthesizing taxol or chlorophyll.

Keep your cool, stick with it. One step at a time till the end is in sight, then run like hell home.

I took one slow step at a time across the pier toward the gangplank. When I reached it, I stepped onto it, the point of no return. I waited. And waited. Finally, the door of the cabin opened and Elena's head with wisps of black hair floating about it appeared as she emerged into the morning air. She wore a maroon terrycloth bathrobe over a nightgown, tied with a sash. She moved steadily, anxiously, turning in my direction and stepping tentatively onto the deck. I noticed her feet were bare. She moved toward the gunwale and started slowly down the gangplank. I started upward to meet her.

I found in my heart the will to look upward and smile at Elena. Seeing her gave me confidence, deserved or not, that I had achieved something. She hardly looked at me as she kept walking down with a haunted look, her uncombed hair blowing in the breeze. Her elbows were tight by her side, her forearms crossed over her chest. We approached each other, one step at a time. We passed one another midway, and as we did so, she finally looked at me. She began to cry.

"Go on, Elena, go on," I said softly. When I reached the gunwale, I stopped and turned around, looking at her. She had reached the lower end of the gangplank and now walked rapidly across the pier without turning. Elena reached the Chief and Aphro, and would have fallen had Sophie not stepped over to catch her. I turned and stepped from the gunwale onto the deck. Step two.

The door of the cabin opened slowly. I have rarely—never, in point of fact—had guns trained on me. Not since I was eleven, during my last watergun fight with my brother Harry. There in the cabin stood my buddy Zacharias Stephanopoulos with a handgun, and—wouldn't you know it—old Silverhair himself, wearing a yachting cap and pointing an automatic rifle at me. As I stepped into the cabin, I instinctively raised my hands a little—a reflex learned in a lifetime of watching bad movies. Zorba One might be a petty thief, but Silverhair was a certified killer.

I could hear another person climbing the steps from the hatch below, and within a minute a dapper looking Onarchos entered the cabin. Panic does not mess with this man's wardrobe. You could have cut a dinner roll with the creases in his pants. His beige silk shirt glistened in the light. His disposition seemed as unruffled as his impeccable clothes. He nodded to Zorba, who approached me slowly, gun still leveled, and put a firm grip on the strap on my shoulder. Once he began hefting the bag, Zorba had to put the gun in his pocket to free a second hand. He then kindly relieved me of two million euros. It was a burden I was happy to relinquish. I could now envisage steps three, four, and a Zeno's paradox of smaller and smaller advances to my goal of getting out alive. If they bring me to Sophie again, I promised to go back to Laguna Beach and vegetate there for the rest of my life.

"Well Mr. Redfield," Onarchos said with a thin, oily smile. "How kind of you to accept our invitation. Mrs. Mylonas was especially pleased. I'm afraid you will have to wait for a few minutes." He picked up a cell phone and spoke in Greek to shore. He then put it down and opened the satchel.

Inside were bundles and bundles of cash. Packets of crisp new bills held together by wrappers. Crinkly, used bills held together by rubber bands. I tried to count the number of zeros after the one, but could only glimpse them. Possibly three. 1,000 notes. I tend to sing or do stupid counting or calculation games before inevitable, serious consequences flow from an indiscretion. Let's see, two million is 2×10^6, and a thou is 1×10^3 and that means we have 2000 of these nifty papers in the bag. Now, going on, in wads of 50, no, 100, that would amount to 20 wads. God, it felt good to be a scientist again. And nice to have been that rich, if briefly. I just kept looking at Onarchos as he went systematically through all the wads, putting them back in a bag of his own and finally returning to me the one I had brought. Did he think it was booby-trapped? Or did he think he had enough money now to buy a nice new one in Egypt or Libya?

He startled me by looking up at me. His eyes were no longer the coldly gracious ones he had at his compound but had a little glint of triumph in them. "You'll be pleased to hear that the money is in order. We will leave here in a few minutes. We prefer a smooth exit—smooth sailing, as you might call it—with no injury to the good people on the pier."

Sounded good to me. Step three—or was it four?—had arrived. To myself, I posed the important question. Is there anything else on your mind, Mr. Onarchos, or can I just get the hell outta here? I also wanted to know when I would have a quiet opportunity to pee in my pants, preferably in privacy. Was the head unoccupied? I did not ask.

"Redfield." Onarchos paused. The show, it seemed, was not yet over. "Please remember what I now tell you. The Onarchos Reproductions buildings have been mined with dynamite. Somewhat in haste, but effectively. The buildings sit over one of the minor sites of the Gournia palace. We have found eight more sites worth excavating. Three of these have also been mined."

He paused to let this sink in, but I had no idea what the hell this had to do with me. I must have looked stupid because he felt obliged to explain. "We encountered the sites by chance and have enjoyed their yield for three years. Our find may equal or surpass Knossos in significance and condition. You have been to Knossos?"

I nodded. 'Our find'—what a creep! Takes a national treasure and parcels it up like Costco merchandise.

But he didn't stop there. "Consider how tragic it will be if the four sites we have mined were to be lost to the world. But they will be gone—poof! (Here he made a gesture with both hands of something going up in the air)—if we detonate the charges." He produced a sardonic little smirk. "I think the government might value the sites more than they value you." This was deeply unwelcome, not to say hurtful, especially in view of its correctness.

He continued his smooth delivery. "We expect safe passage out of the harbor, without being followed. We will phone again when we have reached another country—one lacking extradition conventions with Greece." The sonofabitch thought of everything. "At that time, Inspector Kensington will be told the location of our sites." He raised a sleek eyebrow and smirked again. "She should tell her crew to be careful when they dismantle our devices." I remember the guy who defused mines in *The English Patient*—scary stuff.

Something was missing. I didn't have to wait long for it. "Incidentally, as we travel in the open Mediterranean, we expect to see no vessel, helicopter, plane, or radar signals tracking us. If we do, I will instruct my friend in Crete by radio to detonate the mines by cell phone, one at a time. The same, if there is any attempt to inactivate the charges prematurely."

He again paused to let this penetrate my increasingly crowded brain, but my expression must have told him that I'd gotten it.

Then his face softened and he inexplicably added something. "No one appreciates the treasures of my country more than I do. I have never destroyed an artifact from antiquity. I have carefully unearthed them, cleaned them, copied them, and sent them into the world where lovers of ancient culture may cherish and admire them. I would do nothing willfully to cause their destruction."

What a prince, that Onarchos. Sophisticated and cultivated. Probably doesn't dine with his goons. I felt it a compliment that he would unburden himself so eloquently to an overweight rube like me. However, the pressure in my bladder was becoming intolerable and I wished he would speed it up.

"I'll d-do my best," I said. And to myself: Can I go now? In both senses of the word?

"You may go now, before you forget what I have told you. Turn, walk out to the deck and leave the ship. Move slowly, don't trip. We dislike sudden moves and strange noises."

I slowly lowered my hand to pick up the now empty satchel I had brought, and when I turned, saw Silverhair's steely eyes in his tanned face under the yachting cap facing me. His hand, just below the mermaid snaking down his arm and around his wrist still held the bulky rifle, not a cigarette—which I would have welcomed like a junkie out of rehab. I went through the door and slowly out onto the deck, with the sound of Gryoka moving right behind me.

As I emerged into the sunlight on the deck, there was Zorba looking over the gunwale at the prow, yelling in Greek and beckoning. Quickly Gryoka passed me, turning to keep his rifle trained on me, and backed toward Zorba. My knees were weak and shaking. In a flash it hit me: Zorba had seen the box one of the cops had planted on the bow. Gryoka must have seen it too because he barked something toward the cabin, and in another second Onarchos rushed onto the deck and began shouting in Greek at the police contingent below. Gryoka took a step toward me with a look of cold menace and jabbed the rifle against my heaving chest. There it went—a stream of pee—gushing out front to soak my pants and sideways down the inside of my pant legs. Produced by pure terror. Onarchos kept shouting and Silverhair kept poking, almost in time to the shouts, until I saw a cop below approach the boat with his hands in the air and then slowly raise them and pry something off the side. It clattered once on the boards before falling into the water with a soft plop.

After what seemed like an eternity, a gruff bark signaled that I could start walking again. It felt like the longest walk of my life although it was probably less than a minute before I reached the pier. I looked behind me and saw only Onarchos on deck, still shouting at the group below, which dispersed in response. As the yacht powered up, I reached Aphro and the Chief, spreading my arms out to make an important announcement. "Guys, I need clean pants." Not heroic oratory, but this is the part they never show you in gangster films. It was my second pair of pants sacrificed to bodily fluids on this vacation.

The next few minutes were a blur, but soon all was still. The deck of the yacht was empty, as was the pier, since the police, along with Sophie, had retreated. The Chief, much more considerate to me than he had been to Madame, had the presence of mind to point me to a men's room door in a shack in back of the wharf. Even if it was too late, never did the little man icon look so good. After mopping up as best I could, I emerged from the shack and saw Onarchos's yacht draw away and heading into the bay. Scores of little sailboats and motorboats and launches floated on the sunlit water as in a dream. They were unaware that if they were to follow our now rich friends, bad things would happen—if not to them, then to their cultural patrimony near Gaitani.

I now reached Sophie, who opened her arms. I thought she would start to cry, but instead it was me who started to cry. Hey, I'd had a hell of a rough week.

A few minutes later we were in the police car moving out of the waterfront area, and Aphro asked the exhausted Stavros to go by Elena's shop, less than a block away. Another police car with another officer stood by in the street nearby. We left the car and knocked on the locked door. A policewoman came from inside and let us in. She led us out back to the sunny courtyard, where we found a shaken Elena, exhausted by her ordeal, trying to recover. Wrapped in a blanket, she was sipping hot tea and turning her face toward the morning sun as if in gratitude for being alive. She was clearly in the care of the nice policewoman, probably a traffic cop, who sat next to her with a soothing arm around her shoulder.

"Mrs. Mylonas," Aphro said, "Mr. Redfield played his part splendidly. You are both safe."

Elena could hardly speak, but she rose and gave me a hug. "*Efkharistó, efkharistó,*" she whispered into my ear, and I knew she meant it.

Aphro's phone rang. She answered and gasped. She closed it, put it away, and said she had to go. The other car, she said, would give us a ride home.

"What happened?" Sophie asked.

"Onarchos's compound has blown up and has been all but destroyed. One of our men is injured."

Chapter 31
The Frawley Chronicles

We needed sleep, peace, calm. It was only early afternoon, but we had lived a lifetime on this morning. A wake-up call from the police, a bold kidnapping, a ransom delivery at gunpoint, a moment of pee-your-pants panic, and the fiery destruction of an antiquities site—a crowded few hours by any standard. When the policeman dropped us off at our hotel, we went right to our room, tidied up in our absence. I made straight for the bathroom and a long, hot shower. I heard a bit of commotion in the course of it, and when I emerged, my hair wet but luckily wearing a tee shirt and shorts, I was startled to see Gwendolyn Frawley in the room.

It was a different Gwen. Her reddish hair was down, making her look younger and, frankly, more appealing than she did with her customary bun and snoods. But otherwise she looked in bad shape. Her face was flushed and her eyes behind her steelrims were red and sunken. She had no make-up on and she wore informal khaki slacks and flat sandals instead of her signature high heels. She looked—well—human, more like a real woman than the brittle stork we had come to know.

"I apologize for intruding." She was dabbing at her eyes under her spectacles with a white embroidered handkerchief. Who uses a handkerchief in the age of Kleenex? "I fear I'm in terrible trouble and need to talk to someone before I go to the police." Go to the police? Why the hell wasn't she in custody already? Her role in this whole cabal was pretty clear after last night. But I guess Aphro, Stavros, Costa, and the Chief did have a collectively busy night and morning, when you thought about it. Ms. Authenticator here seems to have fallen through the cracks.

But even as I pictured the Frawley in handcuffs and orange jumpsuit, Sophie guided her over to the bench by the terrace and had her sit down.

"I hardly know where to begin." Gwen dabbed an eye with the hankie. "We feared last night that Danielle and Lyle would be apprehended. Kensington plainly knew more than we expected."

We? I couldn't believe she'd admit her collusion like that.

"I've known the Tanners for four years, through my work as an authenticator. We are involved in—in a kind of antiquities matter." Gwen looked at us with a wince from under her steelrims. "Not perfectly legal, you see."

"Gwen," I said, "the Tanners have already been arrested. They tried to leave Crete by boat in the wee hours of the morning but they didn't get off the island."

To our surprise, she didn't act surprised. She had arranged with the Tanners to stay behind in case they needed help. "Flight in the middle of the night is—well, you know—not my style."

"How could you help them, Gwen?" Sophie asked. "You must know that the Tanners could be charged not only with antiquities fraud, but with murder too."

This time Gwen gasped. "How can they do that? Lyle and Danielle have an alibi."

I took the bull by the horns, as they say in Crete. "Look, Gwen, here's the story. Inspector Kensington told us this morning that the man who piloted the boat the Tanners took to that leper island on the day of the murder is an ex-con who's beaten two murder raps on the mainland. He works with Onarchos, and he was seen at Astron Bay around noon on the day Nikos was murdered. The Tanner's alibi is a phony ploy."

"Who saw him here? Can they be sure?"

"I have no idea," I said, lying through my teeth, "but it's pretty sure he was here." I took a smug sip of coffee from a mug Sophie had handed me while we were talking.

"Gwen, dear," said Sophie, "you *are* in terrible trouble. Is there anything you'd like to tell us?

Gwen, *dear*? Sophie sure knows how to soften up a perp. They ought to hire her to be a "good cop" for the L.A.P.D.

Gwen's brow furrowed deeply and she seemed about to cry. "I *never* thought they would kill Gavras—at least at first—just threaten him to negotiate a secure arrangement! He was blackmailing them, the Tanners and

Onarchos—threatening to go to the police about the looting if they didn't bring him into the scheme. They thought all we needed was to persuade Gavras to come in with us. But his price was too high and he was volatile and unpredictable. That changed everything."

"How did you get in so deep with all this?" I asked. "You could have blown the whistle on the whole thing before Nikos was killed." Easy for me to say, since I seem to have no trouble ratting out my acquaintances.

"*Of course* I should have done so. I was simply too blind to see where this was headed. I was under pressure to cooperate because I could easily be incriminated for collaborating in selling the antiquities." She wiped her spectacles with her handkerchief. "And they promised me a seaside cottage in Sitia in return for my help. That may be why I didn't see the plan for what it really was." She sounded genuinely rueful.

"And what was the plan, as you call it?" I took another sip of my coffee. No wonder my bladder felt like a balloon all day.

Gwen's story just confirmed what we already pretty much knew. Gwen's room was chosen for the showdown with Gavras because she had no connection to the dude, and she agreed, believing he would merely be roughed up to make him back off the blackmail. Her only demand was an airtight alibi.

"How did you manage to arrange that museum business?" I was curious since we got to have a starring role in it.

"It was Lyle who contrived the scene with Zacharias. The Tanners met him through his brother. Zacharias took the animal figures from the case earlier that day and put them in his locker. He rearranged the case so no gaps showed later when we all came through. After we passed through the room he simply opened the case, and made the blank areas obvious again. It was very simple."

"And how did they get into Hegel's jacket." Leave it to Sophie to remember the little punk.

"Zacharias wouldn't keep the things after the murder, so Lyle asked me to dispose of them. I didn't want them in my purse or my room, and I knew I couldn't safely take them out of the country. At the same time I couldn't bear to destroy them."

I was touched by her tender care for clay animals—though less so by her not so tender care for old Nikos.

Gwen went on. "Once Latif began airing news about the discovery of the new palace site, the threat to the operation was compounded, and a new plan suggested itself. By then Lyle was improvising. He wanted to scare Latif off and simultaneously cast suspicion on him. After all, Gabor was as close to those artifacts as we were."

Zorba II then apparently bribed Hegel to get him into the Bohnen-Essen compound, which made all that sabotage possible. As a further reward, Lyle planted the critters in Hegel's jacket the day he left it in the dining room and then tipped off the cops.

"The boy had been to the museum with his mother, and we thought this might disturb his father sufficiently to leave the island."

"Why the hell did you bring us into it? We had nothing to do with any of you. Why drag us into all this crap?" Their whole stupid plot was like a cancer, like leprosy off-shore spreading all over Astron Bay, contaminating family and guests.

Gwen's shame made her face redden. "The feud over the memoir made Spiro Santas a perfect—fall guy." American slang doesn't come easily to Brits. "The Tanners worked hard to rile Santas up at Gavras, and he complied by blustering about it—to you, among others. A forged letter had been sent, and Madame's little dog was kidnapped to make Nikos look vengeful—a plan you spoiled when you found the animal on the road the day you were cheated by Gavras. But that turn of events provided a splendid opportunity. After hearing your story of Nikos and the silver bowls, the Tanners planned to slaughter the poodle and fill your bowls with its blood. Nikos would be suspected and Santas's rage would be boundless. The police would look no further than Santas once Nikos was murdered at Astron Bay."

She had just blown her Miss Innocent act about thinking they would only rough Nikos up a bit in her room. Sophie meanwhile looked as though she would throw up. "*Slaughter Basket!* What kind of monsters are these people?" She had clearly forgotten that the cabal didn't hesitate to slaughter a two-legged being—well, maybe not quite as innocent as the pup. Remembering my freak-out over the single bowl with red glop, it was stunning to think of Sophie finding a butchered Basket in our room. It turned out it was only Zoë's vigilance over Basket after the dognapping that foiled the plot. Lyle had to content himself with bribing a maid to get into our room, and had to make do with envelopes of ketchup and soy.

"How did you ever get started in all this?" I really couldn't fathom it.

"Authenticators do important work for a pittance. The museum declared me redundant in the last government cost-cutting. After that, I had to free-lance for collectors and galleries. My income became sporadic and uncertain, and I had no secure pension. I am unmarried and not young anymore." She looked at Sophie for understanding and sympathy, but Sophie wasn't offering.

"I have always been ethical," Gwen went on. "I do fine work. Mister Dalrymple enabled me to buy a comfortable flat in Oxford and best of all, to furnish it with some lovely pieces of Minoan art. I felt I owed him cooperation in the authentications he needed. I didn't ask about provenance."

"You lectured us about the importance of provenance in one of our discussions," Sophie reminded her, but Gwen waved the question away.

"I did it as much for the art as for the money. All I had to do was authenticate pieces that later found wonderful homes in mansions and museums where they were admired and appreciated. Does that seem so terrible?" Oily Onarchos had used the same defense on the boat, if I remembered it correctly. I wasn't buying it here either.

"Some slopes are slipperier than others, Gwen," I said. This wasn't a time for aphorisms, but she *did* ask.

"Gwen," Sophie said, "This scheme ended up with people getting killed. None of this was worth a man's *life*! What could you have been thinking?"

Gwen looked genuinely stricken. "Oh, Sophie, I wasn't thinking! At the beginning, I thought it wouldn't be worse than all those looters in Greece and Italy selling artifacts to rich people who trade them amongst themselves and sell them to museums." Her face was red with a mixture of anger and contrition. We must have looked a little skeptical, because she glanced pointedly first at Sophie then at me and said, "Surely you've read about the difficulties at your own Getty Museum in California."

Good point. She had us there. "Dozens of world famous museums, galleries, and collectors have been turning around looted goods for years. I saw intimately how much these distinguished people profited! With utter impunity! And here I was, stupid, innocent old me. I was good at authentication, I had a solid reputation. I love Minoan art, and here I was, poor as a *churchmouse* and headed for the dole."

I looked steadily at her. "If you love your trade so much, why did you let Onarchos rig mechanisms for dynamiting a bunch of valuable sites?"

Gwen blinked theatrically, and stood up. "How do you know *that*?"

"A long story, Gwen, but that's the threat he's made if he isn't allowed to get away. He's on the open ocean with your pal Zacharias, with his finger on the button."

Still looking out to sea she said, "It's a ruse, Red. He can't destroy the sites! He can't bargain with that. They didn't have time to mine them."

I stepped toward her so I could look at her squarely. "He can, and he did! The Pottery Shack—I mean Onarchos Reproductions—is no more."

Gwen now spoke with intense composure. "If what you say is true, I'm surprised he and his men even had time to mine their compound. But Lyle told me clearly before he left that they couldn't get to any of the major sites in the time they had."

I was surprised how excited and relieved this information made me. Hanging around Wally and Gabor must have rubbed some of their affection for Minoan stuff off on me. We had to tell Aphro, and when I looked back I saw Sophie already at the phone. "Gwen," she said as she waited to connect, "we can't go on with this. I am contacting Inspector Kensington. She needs to know these things."

It was only three minutes after Sophie hung up that the police were at the door. They'd continued to stake out the hotel, we realized. I was thankful we didn't have to drive Gwen to the Agnik police station. But as she was taken off, I felt no satisfaction. Gwendolyn Frawley was both a villain and a victim, and yet I felt supremely and illogically bad for her.

The next day was the first day of the rest of my life, as they like to say. Unlike the day before, that might have been my last. We woke up to the knowledge that the mystery—indeed, the multiple, layered *mysteries* that had plagued us since our first days at Astron Bay—were resolved. My nemesis, Lyle, and his snake of a wife were now in custody, as was Gwen. Aphro was grateful for Gwen's information that no other antiquities sites were mined, and she and the Chief would close out the matter without further help from us. We had our passports and were free to go home.

While we were still in bed, Sophie asked, "Red, do you know what day this is?" Of course, she didn't expect me to remember. Wives always think they're more romantic than their husbands, some petulant at them for their forgetfulness and others proud of themselves. While Sophie was one of the latter, I would never forget the magical day twenty-five years ago when the radiant, golden-haired, freckled Sophia Whitney became my bride forever.

And so we enjoyed the bountiful Astron Bay breakfast buffet as a well-rested couple that morning. In the room afterwards, we confirmed our return flight to the States next day. After all we'd been through, it was amazing that we were heading home on schedule. "At last!" Sophie said when she hung up the phone, "we're going to see our kids tomorrow night!" She speaks now of Gerty and Ezra this way, and I pictured the mad dachshunds leaping and scratching at the back window of the Subaru station wagon when Meredith, one of our human kids, picked us up at LAX.

We packed our suitcases—including the scarves, slippers, mugs, as well as the worry beads we had bought for Meredith on our first trip to Agnik. And something else: five bowls, one silver, the rest tinfoil.

"Should we take these, Soph?" I asked, holding them up as a cluster.

"Wouldn't part with them for a thousand euros," said Sophie. "Oh, the stories these will tell!"

"Last chance for a swim, Pumpkin." The packing was done and it was the end of our vacation.

"Deal," said Sophie, just as the phone rang. "Oh, Madame Delphinos, good morning," Crap. There goes our last swim.

Ten minutes later we were down at the metal gate of Madame's garden, with the woofing of bouncing Basket to greet us. Zoë, impeccable in her black uniform with its white ruffled apron, led us in and to the white metal patio table, where Madame was already seated and waving her lorgnette at us. She wore a seafoam-colored gown this morning, still beautiful in her coiffed white curls and wrinkled visage. But her face was a bit more shriveled and sunken than just days ago, as though the murder at Astron Bay and its attendant events had taken its toll.

"*Bonjour, bonjour*, my dears," she called. "Do come and join me and my naughty Basket." The table had been set with three placemats, and our ample breakfast notwithstanding, we would be treated to a light lunch with Madame.

"Spiro tells me that Astron Bay has sheltered a trio of...*gangsters!*" Madame whispered the last word should anyone overhear this new scandal in her long and scandalous career.

"Yes, but very cultivated and sophisticated gangsters." Sophie knows how to put an elegant spin on practically anything. We filled Madame in on the events of the last week. Making a coherent narrative out of Wally's fall at Knossos, Gabor's and my bingle off the road from Gaitani, the foiled escape of the Tanners and Gwen's confession—not to mention my harrowing ransom of Elena—would have challenged Martha Grimes. But we did our best, in tandem, while Zoë brought a lovely smoked salmon carpaccio with doughy breadsticks and a light, fresh salad and poured each of us a cool glass of crisp Sauvignon Blanc.

"Ah, puh, Onarchos," Madame scoffed. "His father was my Pierro's bootmaker, you know. An honorable profession but not for his oldest son, who was too good for his Papa's trade." She lowered her voice and shook her head in disapproval. "*Parvenu.*"

"Well, to his credit, he didn't destroy the archeological sites he found," Sophie said, again trying to put the best face on the subject. "A glorious new phase of Greek art and culture may be unearthed, practically next door to you, Madame." Sophie was sipping her wine, and loving this unexpectedly nice way of bidding farewell to her favorite *grande dame*.

"Ah, *chérie*, I will not live to see this, you know. Even Angelina Delphinos is not immortal, like our Greek gods!" I tried to picture which figure of mythology would most resemble this sharp, intrepid old lady. Nothing computed; the gods had made her a true original.

She picked up her wineglass and lifted it in a toast. "My thanks to you, Red Redfield, for saving Elena Mylonas." She lightly clinked her thin glass against mine and then Sophie's, and we saw that her crinkled eyes had moistened.

Sophie broke into a warm smile. "You are no longer angry with her family?"

"Oh no, my dear," she said with feeling. "How can we know so little of what we know so well? And be so foolish when we think we are so wise? Poor Erasmo. If Elena had not told me her family secret, I would have gone to my grave without knowing how he suffered. And my memoir…" Madame could not speak for a moment. "I only hope Elena can forgive me. "

And so we ended our last visit with Madame Delphinos on a note of redemption. As I said, I know squat about spiritual stuff, but I sometimes get more than a glimpse of grace in human interactions.

Madame Delphinos's toast at lunch was not the most memorable of our last day in Crete. That night Sophie and I celebrated our twenty-fifth anniversary at a champagne dinner on Spiro's private balcony under the stars at Astron Bay. Sophie, wearing a lovely silver dress, lifted a sparkling champagne flute in my direction, and said, "To Rowan Redfield—*my* hero!"

The next day we ended our fateful stay in Crete by driving to Heraklion, returning our Renault, and boarding a plane. The flight home to Los Angeles via Athens and Paris was a four-martini affair with Sophie agreeably oiled with free wine. It was spoiled only by the onset of the first of my gruesome flashbacks. Strange how they started when all was well, everyone was safe, and we were on our way home. I saw again the look of torment as Nikos clutched his throat with the blood gushing between his knuckles, and began to tremble uncontrollably. In mystery novels the killings are all *wham, bang, thank you, ma'am,* and it's all over. Not in real life, where murder undermines your world for months and maybe even years to come. I longed for the worry-beads, packed in our suitcase, which Sophie had bought for our daughter.

When we arrived in the airport in Los Angeles, Meredith was there, a huge bouquet of lilies in her arms, as we walked up the ramp at the international arrival terminal pushing a cargo cart piled high with our luggage. She beamed broadly and said, "Happy Anniversary!" as she embraced her Mom and then me. We negotiated our way to the Subaru in the parking structure, and there, to Sophie's tearful delight, Ezra and Gerty almost whipped their little tails off as we opened the hatch to greet them.

Epilogue
Easter in Greece

In February 2006, a large, official envelope from the Cretan police authorities in Heraklion arrived in Laguna Beach, with return receipt requested. I was summoned at last to Crete to testify at hearings in the case of Theo Onarchos and Zacharias Stephanopoulos (Zorba I to us) for kidnapping Elena Mylonas. Thanks to Gwendolyn Frawley's assurance that the larger antiquities sites were not mined, the police were able to track the *Ikaros* on the open sea with helicopters and circle the yacht with cruisers as it passed the tip of Kaparthos on the way to Rhodes. Onarchos and Zorba surrendered after a bit of gunfire, but Silverhair was not on board. According to the apprehended guys, Gryoka had left with his share of the ransom by dinghy some hours before. We wondered if he would spend some of his loot getting that showy tattoo removed. Without Gryoka in custody it was hard to make the murder charge stick. But I was expected to testify not only about the ransom delivery but also about my fateful cigarette with the skipper at the cabaña.

Gwen Frawley, we were happy to hear, was getting off easy since her testimony about the scheme Onarchos and the Tanners had cooked up shed valuable light on this peculiar variant of the international trade in antiquities of doubtful provenance. Her sentence was less than five years, and we had learned earlier from Wally Pinnock that her planned memoir on the underground antiquities trade was sending seismic shivers through European and U.S. museum boards. Sophie and I feel we deserve at least minor roles in the *Frawley Chronicles*, and have already bickered over who should play us when Hollywood buys the film rights. Needless to say, I'm holding out for Robert Redford—even though he's probably too gaunt and too old for the part.

Lyle and Danielle Tanner had become two flies in the ointment of Greek justice. They refused to answer questions about the smuggling operation, claiming that they were simply innocent recipients of goods selected by Danielle from Nikos's inventory or distributed by Dalrymple. *So what* if they acquired windfalls from Gavras and Dalrymple for a pittance that they parlayed into small fortunes in Vegas! It wasn't their fault if they were sold "replicas" that turned out to be the real thing. The Greek justice system wasn't buying this, thank goodness. As the Tanner's tans faded in the Greek jail, their ill-gotten gains were slowly consumed by the billable hours of their overpriced and ineffective American attorneys.

The Cretan authorities were good enough to pay my way back to the scene of the crimes, and I was therefore good enough to spring for a ticket for Sophie so we could enjoy our *déjà vu a deux*. Sophie's not the only one in the family who knows how to *parlay-voo*. We figured a vacation without a labyrinth of murder, looting, and kidnapping would restore our faith in Crete as an island paradise. The journey was also prescribed by the therapist who was treating me for the post-traumatic stress that had gotten worse, not better, over the last six months.

Wally had remained in touch with his friend Aphrodite, and, once he had mastered e-mail, kept us up to date on the various legal affairs. The e-mails failed to convey the full charms of his Aussie accent, but we were relieved to see that he could write standard English. The looting issue had other interesting complications. Further investigation by Aphro revealed that several artifacts on display in the Agnik museum were quite competent replicas, the originals probably part of some rich, private collection on the Continent or the United States. This confirmed my growing sense that nothing was immune from replication any more—nearly turning me into a philosophical cynic like the guy in the movie *Blade Runner*.

In January, Wally conveyed some especially sad news. Shortly after the New Year, Madame Delphinos died peacefully in her sleep. Zoë found her in her canopied bed one morning. Madame had signed a book contract with a distinguished French press just before the holiday. It was dedicated to Elena Mylonas, who had read the proofs and assured the publishers that it did not dishonor her family. We liked to think that Angelina Delphinos, seeing her revised memoir finished and in good hands, achieved the peace of mind and heart to let go of her full life. Sophie's only regret concerned little Basket. She had her heart set on bringing the little mutt to California to join Gerty and Ezra in our home. But Madame had willed the toy poodle to the secret celebrity who had visited Astron Bay with her chihuahua on the day of the murder. Sophie was heartbroken to think of the naughty Basket ending up as an *accessory*.

Once we booked our April trip to Crete, we received a stunning surprise. It came from Wally, not in an e-mail but in a real typed letter brimming with his inimitable spirit.

> *Ágios Nikòlaos, Crete*
> *March 3, 2006*
>
> *Dear Red and Sophie,*
> *It was a secret I could hardly keep, but I send you now our happy news.*
> *I'm a lonely man no more. Daft as a brush I may be, but my lovely Elena has accepted my wish she be my BRIDE! She made herself a mate of mine tending me after my wingless Icarus flight at Knossos. I'm aloft again in love, and needn't even stand on a chair to kiss her! I owe her my future, and she's gladly submitted hers to me. Easter is a-comin'—a time of rebirth and new beginnings. We're soon to be joined in MATRIMONY, with both of you part of the rite!*
> *You told us the dates you'd be on these shores in spring, and we felt a wee marriage rite would suit you all just fine. So we moved up the date to put a tail on your visit, and none other than the good Astron Bay will host us on Easter Sunday! We've no better friends to bless our bond than both of you as best man and matron of honor! We won't take no for an answer. It's too late for that, and we wouldn't be wed without you. So be prepared, and bring a gay bow tie to go with your fanciest togs.*
> *And more! The shop being hers, Elena already made my wee self her helpmeet and potter, promising to ply his trade in a Pottery Shack of my own. I'm here to stay on the island of my dreams! My arm and collarbone are fit as ever, and I'll throw me my first pots as early as next*

week. Only reproductions, mind you—I've little talent for
replicas, and I'd rather tame a crocodile than dig up used
goods, legal or not, from Crete's garden of sherds. And
before you come, I'll make you a set of five pots to best
those beastly bowls you bought here, mark my words.

Elena joins me in joy, knowing we'll see you here
soon.

For now, ciao.
(signed) Wally

And so we returned to Crete, in the week before Greek Orthodox Easter. And two days after the hearings concluded we became part of the wedding of a widow and a widower, Elena Mylonas and Wallace Pinnock. The wedding was scheduled for four o'clock, but we went down early—me, dressed in a suit that was too tight, and Sophie, in a delicate mint green chiffon dress, bought with care and a lot of money for the occasion. She reminded me of spring, even with her tinge of middle-age.

The wedding area was roped off and the guests had begun to gather on the lawn by the beach with the canopies and tables. A group of five children, ranging from about three to ten years, ran around twirling crepe streamers and shouting in Greek. All were brightly dressed and their diminutive patent leather shoes reminded me of ones I wore to my hateful dancing lessons when I was a kid. And we know what little good those lessons did. A woman in a yellow flowered dress approached us and introduced herself as Elena's younger sister from Athens. "These are my children," she said, pointing to them. "I have heard so much about you from Elena. 'Red and Sophie,' Elena says, 'saved my life and gave me my Wallace.'" I had to smile at the thought of old Wally stuck with that formal name.

A short, craggy old man in an ill-fitting tan suit came up to us. "Ye be Red 'n' Sophie, am I right now?"

"That's right, sir," I said, "and who might you be?"

"Look close, now," he said, squinching one eye shut shrewdly, "ye know me if you know me Wallyboy, and I know ye do." His eyes opened and twinkled as he smiled. His grey, bushy eyebrows matched the hair growing out of his ears. "Ye both done a fine thing fer me boy, ye did, mark me words." He was about to go on and on when he saw someone beckoning him to come get his boutonniere. "'Scuse me but I'd best get me posy," he said.

"I'll go with you—Da," Sophie said, taking his arm. " And as they walked off I heard her say "Wally quotes you all the time…""

As I turned away, I saw none other than Inspector Aphrodite Kensington, dressed in a simple clinging dress that revealed her wonderful full body. Her hair was swept up to the back of her head, with tendrils of curls on her forehead and around her ears and neck. She wore earrings and a pendant of small gold bees—an antique motif we had seen at the Agnik museum many months ago. She flashed her eyes and a bright smile at me as she approached, followed by a tall, distinguished gentleman in a handsome dark blue blazer with gold buttons. Whoa, Aphro with a date—who would've thunk it. She was always so professional that it never occurred to me that she had a social life, let alone any romance.

"Red! How good to see you outside a court room," she said as she shook my hand warmly. She turned to the tall gentleman and said, "This is my husband, Noel Kensington." Married! Aphro has a husband! Noel Kensington had thinning hair, an almost white, neatly trimmed beard and moustache, with a kind, scholarly look behind his rimless spectacles. I had to admit he seemed like a nice old man.

Sophie returned without Da, but with a white boutonniere for me and a small bouquet of lilies for herself. I introduced her to Noel Kensington. He took her free hand and said in a plummy Rex Harrison accent, "Ditty tells me you're responsible for much of the joy of this occasion. Saving lives, playing matchmaker, that sort of thing. Jolly nice to meet you both." He flashed a snaggle-toothed smile. Ditty? Aphroditty. Aphro. That woman had more names than anyone I'd ever met.

Sophie tugged my sleeve, pointing toward the hotel. Gabor and Samira were coming down the path from the hotel, straight toward us. We greeted each other with broad smiles as the Kensingtons moved off.

"How are things with you?" Sophie asked, "are you still in Crete?"

"We now live in a bungalow near thick sand of Pachia Ammos," Gabor replied, "My firm very busy with airport. It goes very well. And Gournia palace ruins come to light more and more now. They excavate beautiful new rhyton last week." I realized I still didn't know my rhyton from my kylix.

"Is Hegel here?" Sophie asked Samira, who looked different. I suspected she'd had her eyebrows waxed and shaped, and her hair had a more modern cut. She might also have lost a little weight and was dressed in a blue color rather than her perennial black.

Samira pointed to a young couple a few yards from us. Hearing his name, Hegel turned around. He looked like a dude from *People* magazine. His hair was slicked up into a cap of short pointy spikes, and he wore a tan suit with a huge, shiny white tie and a jacket with suede lapels. Good thing his old man is in the chips, I thought. As he turned to come toward us, I noticed he was holding hands with his companion, an exquisite young Asian woman in a slinky black knit dress slit almost to the waist on one side. They came up to us and he greeted us amiably for a change.

"This is Moon Cho," Hegel said. Moon smiled demurely and shook our hands.

"Well!" said Sophie, "where did you two meet?"

"In La Jolla," Hegel said. "We're in the same classes."

"Well isn't that wonderful!" Sophie gushed with delight. "You know, you're just down the road from us! Why don't you come up to Laguna and visit us and our doxies sometime? We'd love to see you." Hegel looked as though he'd rather do time for antiquities theft, and I noticed Samira whispering something to Moon.

"Keanu," Moon said, "your mom says you should comb your hair down."

"We'll have to break up now," I said, looking over to the site of the wedding under a special white canopy. "Curtain time draws near, my friends." And off we went to take our seats and our places in the ceremony.

The ceremony began, with the people seated in rows of chairs protected from the sun. Two witnesses—one of them Spiro Santas—and a civil official from Agnik stood before the crowd under the canopy. I stood with Wally in his suit and black bow tie to one side in front. The official nodded and the music from a small string quartet began. Then we saw Da leading Elena down the short aisle in the midst of the guests. She was dressed in a long ivory gown with a short veil over her face, joined to her black hair by a cluster of small pale roses. As she approached me, I saw her again on that gangplank in her robe and bare feet, and felt a stab of pain for all she had gone through.

The ceremony concluded after the witnesses declared to the group that the wedding had taken place. The entire rite took all of ten minutes. Champagne, poured at a nearby table was served on trays by waiters, together with seafood appetizers. A three-tiered cake stood near the champagne table on a little stand. Other staff appeared and prepared the buffet in the rear against the hill. In honor of Easter, the menu was spit-roasted lamb. The aroma reminded us of that fateful first barbecue, where we had caught our first glimpse of the skipper with the Tanners. But this was no time for thoughts of the past, echoing with old anxieties. And, as it turned out, this was not the last time old Silverhair turned up in our lives. But that's another story.